Flamewalker's Oath

Sadie Bennett

Published by Sadie Bennett, 2024.

This is a work of fiction. Similarities to real people, places, or events are entirely coincidental.

FLAMEWALKER'S OATH

First edition. October 6, 2024.

Copyright © 2024 Sadie Bennett.

ISBN: 979-8227463395

Written by Sadie Bennett.

Chapter 1: The Sun's Embrace

The air was thick with the acrid scent of smoke, curling around me like a serpentine dancer. The sun, a relentless overseer, cast a blinding light that reflected off the ash-strewn streets, creating a mirage of shimmering heat waves that played tricks on my weary eyes. I squinted against the brightness, recalling tales of a time when laughter echoed in these alleyways, and the aroma of street vendors mingled with the sweet melodies of laughter. Now, all that remained were the skeletal outlines of buildings, their charred remains standing as silent witnesses to a civilization that once flourished.

I stepped cautiously over a cracked slab of concrete, my bare feet skimming the rough surface, mindful of the splintered wood and twisted metal that jutted out like the teeth of some long-forgotten beast. Each careful movement was punctuated by the soft crunch of ash beneath my weight—a sound I had grown accustomed to, one that felt almost like a grim lullaby in this desolate world. In the distance, the horizon flickered with the muted glow of a dying sun, bleeding shades of orange and crimson into the remnants of the sky, as if the heavens themselves mourned for the lost souls of this city.

Being a Flamewalker was both a blessing and a burden. I could feel the warmth of the sun pooling within me, a potent energy that coursed through my veins like liquid fire. It was exhilarating and terrifying all at once. Some days, I could harness that energy to ignite flames at my fingertips, illuminating the shadows that had crept into my heart. Other days, it threatened to consume me whole, whispering dark temptations to unleash chaos upon the remnants of civilization. My breath quickened as I thought of the Emberstone, the legendary artifact said to amplify a Flamewalker's power tenfold. If I could find it, perhaps I could not only control the flames that flickered within but also kindle hope for my people.

With each step, I ventured further into the Inferno Plains, an expanse of scorched earth that had once been a lush landscape dotted with wildflowers and towering trees. Now, it was a desolate wasteland, a testament to the elemental fury unleashed upon us. The ground beneath my feet was cracked and uneven, like a giant had stomped through the landscape, leaving deep fissures in its wake. I could feel the heat rising from the ground, a visceral reminder of the flames that had ravaged our land. The air shimmered, creating a distortion of reality that made the horizon seem fluid, ever-shifting, teasing me with promises of discovery and peril.

As I trekked further, the familiar weight of dread settled over me like a heavy cloak. The other Flamewalkers had warned me of the dangers that lurked in these desolate lands—beasts twisted by the fire's embrace, scavengers eager to seize whatever flickered with life. But I was resolute, a flicker of determination igniting in my chest. My fingers tingled with energy, and I instinctively held them out before me, feeling the warmth radiate from my palms like a distant sun. If I could wield this power wisely, I could navigate through the Inferno Plains and uncover the truth behind the Emberstone.

With a steady breath, I let my mind wander back to my childhood, when the city was alive with color and light. I remembered the stories my grandmother used to tell, her voice rich with the cadence of a forgotten time. She would sit by the flickering fire, her eyes glinting with mischief as she wove tales of brave Flamewalkers who had saved our world. Her words filled me with wonder, and in those moments, I felt like a part of something grander than myself. I longed to be a heroine, to be remembered as one of the greats.

But reality often felt like a slap in the face. I was no warrior, just a girl bearing the weight of expectations and a lingering fear that one misstep could plunge me into darkness. As the sun began to dip below the horizon, casting long shadows across the barren landscape,

I came upon a clearing. The remnants of a long-abandoned village lay sprawled before me, its homes crumbling and skeletal. The wind carried the whispers of lost laughter and forgotten dreams, making me ache for the lives once lived here.

There, in the center of the clearing, stood a stone pedestal, weathered and worn, yet defiant against the encroaching chaos. My heart raced as I approached, drawn by an unseen force that urged me forward. The pedestal was engraved with ancient runes, their meanings long lost to the ages, but the energy pulsing around it felt electric. This was it—the pulse of the land, the echo of power waiting to be awakened.

As I reached out, my fingers brushing against the cool surface, a surge of warmth flowed through me, igniting my senses. The flames within stirred, answering the call of the ancient stone. My pulse quickened, an exhilarating dance of energy that felt both familiar and alien. I closed my eyes, surrendering to the moment, letting the world around me fade into a blur of sensations. The warmth of the sun and the coolness of the stone melded into an intoxicating embrace, and for the first time, I felt a glimmer of possibility. The Emberstone was closer than I had ever imagined, its whisper beckoning me deeper into the heart of the Inferno Plains, promising both peril and salvation in equal measure.

The warmth from the pedestal pulsed against my skin, each thrum resonating deep within my bones. I was acutely aware of the significance of this moment, standing on the precipice of something vast and unknown. The air shimmered, teasing at the edges of reality as my surroundings grew eerily silent, as if the very world held its breath, anticipating my next move. With trembling hands, I traced the intricate carvings etched into the stone, feeling the grooves beneath my fingertips, ancient and forgotten.

The village around me was a haunting reminder of what once was—a place where families had laughed, where children had chased fireflies at dusk, and where love had flourished even amidst the chaos. Now, it stood desolate, a husk of memories suspended in time. I could almost hear the ghostly echoes of their lives swirling around me, intertwining with the shadows, whispering secrets of resilience and courage. I breathed deeply, drawing in the heavy scent of ash and earth, each inhalation fueling the flames within.

Just as I leaned in closer, determined to unravel the mysteries held by the pedestal, a gust of wind whipped through the clearing, scattering dry leaves like whispers of long-forgotten promises. My hair danced wildly around my face, and a shiver raced down my spine. It felt as though the very essence of the plains had awakened, urging me to move forward, to dive deeper into the unknown. I stepped back, suddenly aware of the gravity of my mission.

"Stay focused, Kira," I muttered to myself, squaring my shoulders against the weight of anticipation. The stories of the Emberstone had often been laced with warnings; many had sought it, only to lose their way in the fire's embrace. I couldn't let that be my fate. The Flamewalkers had already suffered too many losses, and it was my turn to change the tide. With resolve steeling my heart, I turned away from the pedestal, ready to embrace the treacherous journey ahead.

Navigating through the ruins of the village felt like walking through a tapestry of sorrow and faded dreams. Each step was a reminder of the lives disrupted, yet I carried with me the flicker of hope that the Emberstone could reignite the world. The sun dipped lower, casting long shadows that twisted and danced like phantoms eager to join my quest. I moved quickly, my senses heightened, the air buzzing with a frenetic energy that sent goosebumps skittering across my skin. I could feel the heat radiating from the ground, promising both destruction and transformation.

Ahead, the landscape shifted, revealing a vast expanse of cracked earth stretching toward a jagged horizon. The Inferno Plains were notorious for their treachery, a labyrinth of fire and ash that had claimed many a soul. Yet, within that chaos lay the potential for rebirth. The whisper of the Emberstone echoed in my mind, guiding me like a lighthouse through a stormy sea.

The sky above deepened into a rich, molten orange, streaked with hints of violet as the sun made its slow descent. I caught a glimpse of the first stars flickering timidly against the encroaching darkness. It felt like a blessing from the heavens, a reminder that even in this desolation, light could still break through. My heart raced with anticipation as I forged ahead, eager to uncover the truths hidden within the fiery depths.

I reached a particularly desolate stretch, the ground resembling a patchwork quilt of jagged rocks and hardened clay. The air shimmered with heat, distorting my surroundings as if reality itself had twisted under the pressure of unyielding flames. I paused, wiping a bead of sweat from my brow, and surveyed the area, my senses on high alert.

Suddenly, a low growl echoed through the stillness, sending shivers skittering down my spine. I turned slowly, my heart thudding wildly as a creature emerged from the shadows. It was a beast shaped by fire itself, its body a riot of flames and ash, molten eyes gleaming with hunger. Fear clamped down on me, but I refused to falter. The creature, a hulking mass of chaos, prowled closer, its claws scraping against the hardened ground, leaving trails of smoldering embers in its wake.

I gathered my courage, calling upon the fire that flowed within me. "Back off!" I shouted, my voice firm yet quivering with an edge of uncertainty. With a flick of my wrist, a flame sparked to life at my fingertips, illuminating the encroaching darkness. The creature paused, its molten gaze fixating on the flickering flame, confusion evident in its predatory posture.

I took a deep breath, allowing the warmth of the fire to settle within me. "I don't want to hurt you, but I won't let you stop me,"

I declared, channeling my energy into the flame, making it dance higher. The creature hesitated, caught between the instinct to attack and the strange allure of the fire. In that moment, I recognized a kinship—the creature, like me, was a reflection of the world's fury, a being shaped by flames, lost and searching for purpose.

As the beast regarded me with cautious curiosity, I took a step closer, lowering my flame as an offering rather than a weapon. "We're both products of this world," I murmured, trying to reach the glimmer of understanding that lay beneath its fierce exterior. "I'm on a quest to find the Emberstone. It could help us both."

The creature's growl softened into a low rumble, its fiery form wavering. I could sense the tension melting away, replaced by an unexpected connection—a shared understanding of our struggles. I smiled, the warmth in my chest blooming as I realized that even in the heart of chaos, companionship could flicker to life.

With a sudden movement, the creature stepped back, its molten body shimmering like a mirage in the heat. In that instant, I knew it would not hinder my journey. I watched as it turned away, melting back into the shadows, leaving me alone once more. As silence enveloped the clearing, I felt a new determination rise within me. The path ahead would be fraught with challenges, but I was no longer a solitary Flamewalker. I was part of something greater, a flicker of hope amidst the ashes. And as I continued my journey deeper into the Inferno Plains, I carried the knowledge that even in the darkest of times, unexpected allies could ignite the spark of resilience.

The air crackled with the residue of fear and adrenaline as I resumed my journey, the shadows of the past fading into the distance. Each step felt charged with purpose, a pulse that echoed through the charred earth beneath me. The landscape shifted from the remnants of the village to a more rugged terrain, where jagged rocks jutted out like the teeth of some ancient, slumbering creature.

The horizon stretched endlessly, and I was but a tiny flame flickering against the vastness of this desolate realm.

The Inferno Plains had a reputation for testing the resolve of even the most seasoned Flamewalkers. I had heard the stories whispered around the last embers of our dwindling fires—tales of those who ventured into the heart of the plains and never returned, swallowed by the flames that shaped the very landscape. Yet, with the Emberstone as my guiding star, I pressed on, the promise of a brighter future igniting my determination.

With the sun dipping lower in the sky, the air turned cooler, but I could feel the tension in the atmosphere rising. The winds began to pick up, swirling dust and ash around me in a wild dance, and the distant roar of flames echoed in the background, sending shivers down my spine. Was it my imagination, or did the ground tremble beneath my feet? I couldn't shake the feeling that I was being watched, that something primal and ancient was aware of my presence.

Suddenly, the horizon flickered with a strange light, pulsing like a heartbeat. I halted, squinting against the glare. As I stepped closer, a shimmering veil of heat began to form, revealing a strange structure rising from the earth—a monument of obsidian that reflected the fiery hues of the sky. The closer I approached, the more I realized it was a relic of the old world, a shrine to the elements built long before the fires had consumed our lands. The surface was etched with intricate carvings that glimmered under the dying sun, their meanings lost but their beauty undeniable.

As I reached out to touch the obsidian surface, a low hum resonated through the ground, vibrating in my bones. I jerked my hand back, heart racing, half-expecting the stone to erupt into flames. Instead, the ground around me seemed to pulse with energy, drawing me closer, urging me to uncover its secrets. I took a deep breath and stepped forward, letting my fingers brush against the cool surface once more.

In an instant, the shrine came alive, swirling tendrils of light emanating from the carvings, wrapping around me in a warm embrace. Images flickered before my eyes—visions of flame-wielding warriors, their forms dancing with the fire as they battled grotesque creatures born from the ashes. I felt the surge of power flowing through me, a connection to those who had come before, warriors who had faced the very chaos I now navigated. Their courage became mine, and I could almost hear their voices whispering encouragement in the wind.

But just as quickly as it had begun, the vision faded, leaving me breathless and disoriented. I staggered back, blinking against the disorientation. The shrine now stood silently, its carvings dull and lifeless. I couldn't shake the feeling that it had been a test, a rite of passage that demanded acknowledgment and respect. Whatever was buried beneath the ash was not just a memory; it was a legacy.

"Focus, Kira," I whispered to myself, grounding myself in the present. I had a mission, and while the allure of the shrine was potent, the Emberstone awaited further into the plains. With renewed determination, I pressed on, navigating the rocky terrain. The sun sank further, painting the sky in shades of deep violet and fiery red. My stomach rumbled, reminding me of the need for sustenance, but the hunger for the Emberstone overshadowed everything else.

As I ventured deeper, the wind howled like a pack of lost souls, swirling dust devils around me that felt both playful and menacing. The ground beneath my feet began to shift, the terrain becoming less predictable with each step. It was as if the plains were alive, testing my will, probing my resolve. The sun finally dipped below the horizon, cloaking the world in darkness, and I pulled my cloak tighter around my shoulders, letting the fabric absorb the heat radiating from my skin.

In the depths of night, I felt the pulse of the earth beneath me—a rhythmic heartbeat that resonated with the flames in my soul. I closed my eyes, listening, letting the whispers of the night guide me. As I moved forward, I began to see faint glimmers in the darkness, fireflies dancing in the night, drawing me toward an unseen destination.

Then, suddenly, a low growl echoed from the shadows, freezing me in my tracks. My heart raced, and I could feel the heat pooling in my palms, ready to be unleashed. The darkness thickened, and from the shadows emerged a creature cloaked in flames, its eyes glowing like molten metal. My instincts screamed for me to flee, but something deeper held me rooted to the spot.

"Do you seek the Emberstone?" the creature rumbled, its voice like the crackling of firewood. Its presence was imposing, and I could feel the weight of its gaze upon me, assessing, probing. I forced myself to meet its eyes, the warmth radiating from it both terrifying and oddly comforting.

"Yes," I replied, my voice steadier than I felt. "I need it to save my people."

The creature tilted its head, curiosity igniting the flames that danced across its form. "Many have come seeking the Emberstone, but few understand its true nature. It is not just a source of power; it is a mirror reflecting the heart of the seeker."

I took a step closer, emboldened by the intensity of its gaze. "Then let it reflect strength and hope. I won't let it consume me; I seek to wield it for good."

The creature seemed to consider my words, its fiery form flickering as if caught between realms. "Then you must prove your resolve. The path ahead is perilous, filled with trials that will test not only your strength but your heart. Should you falter, the flames will consume you, leaving nothing but ash."

"Then I will not falter," I declared, the fire within me roaring to life. "I will not let fear control me."

With a deep rumble, the creature stepped aside, revealing a narrow passage obscured by tendrils of flame and shadow. "Then go forth, Flamewalker. The Emberstone lies ahead. Remember, the true strength of a Flamewalker is not in their power but in their ability to embrace both the light and the darkness within."

I nodded, determination coursing through me. The passage felt like a gateway, a threshold to the unknown, and I stepped into the blaze, my heart pounding in sync with the rhythm of the earth. The trials awaited, but for the first time, I felt more than just a flickering flame; I felt like a beacon of hope ready to ignite the world once more. As the warmth enveloped me, I embraced the fire, welcoming the challenges ahead, knowing that with each step, I was reclaiming not just the Emberstone but my place in the world.

Chapter 2: Shadows of the Past

The air grew thick with the acrid scent of sulfur as I approached the Inferno Plains, a realm where molten rivers twisted like serpents through a scorched earth littered with shards of obsidian. The sun, a feeble disk in the sky, cast a dim orange glow over the horizon, its light battling against the oppressive haze. Each footfall echoed in the stillness, the heat radiating from the ground a constant reminder of the power and peril that lay ahead. My heart raced as I crossed the threshold from the familiar echoes of my city to the treacherous embrace of the flames.

My fingers grazed the scorched earth, the remnants of ash swirling like ghosts around me. The fiery glow illuminated memories I had tried to bury: laughter around the dinner table, lessons learned under the flickering light of candle flames, and the stories of heroism my parents had shared. They had been legends among Flamewalkers, fearless and unwavering, yet I was left with a legacy that felt heavy upon my shoulders, like the oppressive heat of the Inferno itself. The tales of their last expedition haunted me, their faces flickering in my mind like the tongues of fire that danced before me.

As I drew closer to the molten river, I could hear the simmering of the lava, a heartbeat pulsing beneath the earth. The landscape shifted, jagged rocks jutting out like teeth from a maw that threatened to swallow me whole. Shadows flitted at the edges of my vision, dark and serpentine, whispers of the past entwining with the tangible present. I took a deep breath, filling my lungs with the warmth that felt both comforting and terrifying, a reminder that flame could both protect and destroy.

It was then that I spotted it—a glimmering fragment of my parents' flame. An ember, small yet fierce, nestled within the twisted roots of a gnarled tree. The tree itself was a rarity here, its bark blackened yet resilient, clawing towards the sky as if defying the very elements that sought to consume it. I knelt beside it, entranced by the flickering glow, and reached out, feeling the warmth radiate against my skin. This was a piece of them, a spark of their legacy that remained, and in that moment, I understood: I was not alone.

The shadows that once instilled fear began to morph, taking on familiar shapes. I could almost see my mother's fiery red hair, dancing like the flames she commanded, her laughter echoing in my ears. My father's deep voice resonated in the air, reminding me of the courage that coursed through my veins. "You are stronger than the fire, my child," he had often said, "but you must learn to wield it wisely."

With renewed determination, I stood, brushing the ash from my knees, and turned my gaze toward the river of lava. It twisted and churned, a vibrant orange glow against the darkness surrounding me. Here, at the edge of the Inferno Plains, I could feel the pull of the flames, a call to embrace my heritage. I could either be consumed by fear or rise like a phoenix from the ashes of my past.

But as I stepped closer, I was reminded of the sacrifices my parents had made. Their disappearance had been a cautionary tale shared among Flamewalkers, a whispered warning about the dangers that lurked within the fiery depths. Their lessons haunted me, but I couldn't shake the feeling that their fate was not mine to inherit. I would carve my own path, and I would not allow their shadows to stifle my flame.

The heat intensified as I crouched near the river, the heat wrapping around me like an old friend. I extended my hand, letting the warmth seep into my skin, embracing the power that surged within. A surge of energy coursed through me, the flames whispering ancient secrets, their cadence a song of hope and danger. I could almost hear their laughter mingling with the crackle of the fire, urging me to let go of the past and dance with the flames.

"Embrace me, child of fire," they seemed to say, and I felt my resolve strengthen. I wasn't here to become a shadow of my parents; I was here to illuminate my own destiny.

Yet, just as the flames licked at my fingertips, a chilling breeze swept through the Inferno Plains, snuffing out the warmth like a candle extinguished in the dark. The shadows morphed, twisting into forms that no longer resembled my parents but rather grotesque figures lurking just beyond the periphery of my vision. I recoiled, instinctively retreating as my heart raced, fear clawing at my throat.

"Who dares to disturb the flames?" a voice boomed from the darkness, low and gravelly, sending chills down my spine. I turned, eyes wide, scanning the area for the source. The shadows coalesced into a towering figure, its outline shimmering with the flicker of heat. The entity was adorned with armor forged from molten rock, the eyes burning like two coals set alight.

"I do," I declared, my voice steadier than I felt. "I am the daughter of Flamewalkers, and I will not be silenced by your shadows."

The figure loomed larger, its presence overwhelming, but I squared my shoulders, letting the warmth of the river wash over me, rekindling my courage. The shadows danced around me, but now I could see them not as harbingers of doom but as reflections of the power that lay within.

"Your lineage speaks volumes, yet can you withstand the fire that seeks to consume you?" the shadow challenged, a smirk curling its ethereal lips.

"Not if I choose to dance instead," I replied, the words surprising even myself. With a flick of my wrist, I summoned the flames, letting them surge through me, a vivid tapestry of orange and red weaving around my limbs.

The river erupted in a cacophony of hissing and bubbling, and for a moment, I was lost in the chaos, the energy pulsating with life.

This was my moment—a dance with destiny amidst the shadows of my past.

The shadows coiled around me, whispering threats and memories, each flicker of light competing with the darkness for dominance. My heart thundered in my chest as I steadied my breath, drawing strength from the flames that flickered within me. This was not merely a battle of fire and shadow; it was a test of will, a rite of passage. The figure's burning gaze bore into me, its fiery intensity a challenge I could not ignore.

"Do you truly believe you can wield the flames without consequence?" the shadow rumbled, the ground trembling with its voice. It stepped forward, each movement fluid and menacing, like molten rock sliding down a mountainside. I felt the heat radiate from it, a physical manifestation of the power I had only begun to understand.

"I'm not afraid of the fire," I replied, surprising myself with the steadiness of my voice. "It's the darkness that scares me. The unknown."

A low chuckle reverberated through the air, almost mocking. "Darkness is merely the absence of light. But light can blind as much as it can guide. Tell me, little Flamewalker, what is it you seek?"

With the molten river behind me, the glow of my own flame flickering in my palm, I realized that the answer bubbled just beneath the surface of my consciousness. "I seek the truth," I said, my voice unwavering now. "The truth about my parents. About why they vanished into this inferno."

The shadow's smirk faded, replaced by a look that hinted at deeper knowledge, secrets woven into the very fabric of the flames. "Truth is a fickle mistress, my dear. What you seek may very well consume you."

As the words hung in the air, a sudden tremor rumbled beneath my feet, reverberating through the earth like a drumbeat of impending danger. The molten river roared, and for a fleeting moment, I felt the ground beneath me shift, as if the very world was warning me against venturing deeper into the flames.

"I'll take that risk," I declared, defiance burning bright within me. The river seemed to echo my resolve, its bubbling cauldron of lava mirroring the tumult of emotions within. "I refuse to let fear dictate my life. Not anymore."

"Bold, but foolish," the shadow replied, its eyes glinting with interest. It stepped closer, a tempest of heat swirling around us. "Very well. If you wish to tread this dangerous path, you must understand the consequences. The flames can reveal much, but they also demand a price."

I nodded, steeling myself against the flickering uncertainty that gnawed at my gut. I had already lost so much—fear was no longer an option. With one determined motion, I thrust my hand toward the river, igniting the air around me with vibrant flames. They leaped and danced, a mesmerizing ballet of heat and light.

"Show me," I urged, and the world around me shifted, the shadows trembling at my command. The flames flared higher, illuminating the landscape with a fierce glow, revealing hidden paths veiled by darkness. The shadow figure regarded me with a newfound respect, and for the first time, I saw a glimmer of something akin to admiration in its molten eyes.

"Very well, brave Flamewalker. Allow the flames to guide you. But be warned: the truth may not be what you expect."

As the last word left its lips, the ground beneath us rippled, the fiery landscape swirling into a tapestry of memories and visions. I felt myself being pulled into the vortex of light, my surroundings morphing into a vivid tableau. Scenes flickered to life around me, each flame a doorway to the past, and I was swept into their fervent embrace.

I stood before a younger version of my parents, their faces alight with passion and purpose. My mother's hair billowed around her like a fiery halo, her laughter ringing out as she conjured flames that danced to life at her fingertips. My father, stoic yet warm, watched with pride, his voice deep and reassuring as he spoke of their adventures among the Flamewalkers.

"We must protect the balance," my mother declared, her eyes bright with determination. "The Inferno is both our greatest ally and our fiercest enemy. We can't let our power consume us."

The words echoed through me, stirring a profound sense of loss and longing. I took a step forward, wanting to reach out and join them in that radiant moment, to feel the warmth of their flames surrounding me once more.

But just as quickly, the scene shifted. Darkness crept in, shadows twisting into forms of despair and chaos. I saw my parents standing at the edge of a rift, the ground beneath them crumbling into the abyss. They fought valiantly against the flames that lashed out, but the inferno was insatiable, a beast that demanded tribute.

"No! Not like this!" I cried out, but my voice was swallowed by the roar of the flames, lost to the chaos that enveloped them.

Suddenly, I was thrown back, landing on the scorched ground, breathless and shaken. The shadow loomed above me, its expression inscrutable. "You have seen the truth, yet it is only a fraction of the whole."

"What do you mean?" I gasped, my heart racing as I struggled to comprehend the visions that had enveloped me.

"The flames do not simply reveal; they can also obscure. Your parents sought to protect the Inferno Plains, but in doing so, they may have uncovered something that was never meant to be awakened."

The weight of the revelation pressed down on me like the heat from the molten river, but curiosity mingled with fear, urging me to push further. "What did they find? What did they awaken?"

The shadow stepped back, the flames dancing around us in a chaotic waltz. "The answers you seek are locked within the heart of the Inferno. It will not yield to just anyone. You must prove your worth."

A sense of purpose ignited within me, fueling the flames that flickered in my palm. "Then let's begin."

With that, I moved forward, my heart a blazing inferno of determination, ready to unravel the secrets hidden within the fiery depths. The shadows shifted and twirled around me, not as obstacles but as guides, leading me toward my destiny. I had taken my first step into the inferno, and I would not turn back. The flames were my legacy, and I was ready to embrace the truth, no matter the cost.

The moment I crossed the threshold into the Inferno Plains, the atmosphere shifted. A cacophony of sounds enveloped me, a symphony of crackles and pops that played like a haunting melody across the undulating landscape. The ground was a patchwork quilt of earth, scorched and cracked, with the occasional burst of flame that flickered like laughter at the chaos surrounding it. My senses were heightened, each breath tasting of smoke and sulfur, yet under it all, a metallic tang hinted at the danger lurking just out of sight.

The shadows that had taunted me now danced like puppets on strings, shifting and morphing in response to my every movement. The once-ominous presence felt less threatening, as if they were nudging me toward some undiscovered truth, urging me to step further into the fire. My fingers tingled with energy, the flames swirling in my palm a vibrant reminder of the power within me.

With each step deeper into the plains, I felt the earth thrum beneath my feet, a heartbeat echoing with the stories of those who had walked this path before. I scanned the horizon, the lava river flowing like a fiery serpent, illuminating the landscape with a glow that was both mesmerizing and foreboding. Each undulation of the molten mass was alive, its surface bubbling as if it were reacting to my presence. The air grew hotter, the heat wrapping around me like a second skin, and I welcomed it, letting it fuel my resolve.

Ahead, a rocky outcrop jutted into the air, its surface coated in a shiny obsidian sheen that reflected the glow of the river. I approached cautiously, drawn by an instinctive pull, the warmth of my own flames mingling with the heat radiating from the rocks. As I touched the surface, the texture felt smooth and cool against my fingertips, and a shiver of energy shot through me.

The moment my skin connected with the stone, images flooded my mind—a vivid tapestry of emotions, struggles, and triumphs. I saw my parents again, standing in front of a council of Flamewalkers, their expressions tense yet resolute. The echoes of their voices rang in my ears, words of caution woven with threads of hope. "We cannot let fear dictate our actions," my mother insisted, her voice fierce as flames danced around her. "We must confront the darkness head-on."

"Remember what lies at stake," my father added, his deep voice steady, cutting through the murmur of dissent. "The Inferno is not merely a source of power; it is a living entity. We cannot allow our hubris to awaken what sleeps beneath."

I pulled my hand away from the stone, the visions fading, leaving only a lingering warmth and the weight of their words. It was clear now that my journey was not just about uncovering my parents' fate but also about confronting the very essence of the Inferno itself.

As I gazed out at the river, I noticed something stirring within its depths—a flicker of light, almost too bright to behold. Curiosity sparked within me, propelling me forward. I climbed over the rocks, navigating the treacherous terrain with a grace I didn't know I possessed, the flames in my palm illuminating my path. Each movement felt instinctive, a dance honed through generations of Flamewalkers before me.

When I finally reached the river's edge, the light pulsed rhythmically, drawing me closer. It felt almost sentient, a heartbeat echoing through the air, compelling me to understand its source. With a steadying breath, I reached out my hand, feeling the warmth of the molten rock beneath me. The energy radiating from the river surged upward, enveloping my fingers in a warm embrace.

"Show me," I whispered, my voice barely audible above the roar of the lava. In response, the light flared, illuminating the landscape around me, revealing a hidden world of brilliant colors and textures. The air shimmered, the atmosphere thick with the scent of earth and fire, merging into a heady concoction that made my heart race.

Suddenly, the light coalesced into a figure, a shimmering silhouette that rose from the molten river. My breath caught in my throat as I recognized the form: it was my mother, or rather, her spirit, radiant and fierce, framed by the golden glow of the Inferno.

"Child of my heart," her voice echoed like a distant flame, both soothing and sharp, "you have come to seek the truth, yet you must understand the power of what you seek."

"Mom!" I exclaimed, my heart swelling with emotion. "I need to know what happened to you and Dad. I have to understand why you disappeared into this place."

Her ethereal form shimmered, flickering like a flame caught in a breeze. "We sought to protect the balance, to ensure the flames did not consume the innocent. But the Inferno is a fickle mistress, and we were drawn into a perilous dance with shadows far darker than we anticipated."

"What shadows?" I pressed, stepping closer, desperate for answers. "What did you awaken?"

The light dimmed slightly, as if she were struggling to maintain her form. "A force lies dormant beneath the surface, an ancient power tied to the Inferno. When we ventured too close, we disturbed it. It demanded tribute, and in our fight to quell its rage, we were consumed."

"No!" I shouted, panic rising within me. "You can't be gone! I won't let the flames take you!"

Her form flickered, the flames surrounding her intensifying, creating an aura that was both beautiful and terrifying. "You must understand, my child. The Inferno is part of you, as it is part of us. You carry our legacy, but it is your choice to forge your own path. Beware the shadows that linger; they feed on fear and uncertainty."

"Then how do I stop it?" I asked, urgency seeping into my voice. "How do I protect myself and those I love?"

"Embrace the fire within you," she advised, her voice steady despite the flickering chaos. "Let it illuminate the darkness and fuel your courage. But remember, with great power comes an even greater responsibility. You must find the balance."

With those final words, her form shimmered and began to dissipate, the light flickering like a dying ember. "Mom, wait!" I cried, reaching out, but she was gone, leaving only the swirling warmth of the molten river in her wake.

A surge of determination coursed through me, igniting the flame within my soul. I would not let fear dictate my path. I would confront whatever shadows lurked in the depths, reclaiming my parents' legacy and illuminating my own destiny.

As I turned back toward the expanse of the Inferno Plains, the shadows morphed into a swirling vortex, beckoning me with whispers of challenge and promise. My heart pounded in my chest, not from fear, but from an unwavering resolve. I would face the darkness, wield the fire, and emerge from the ashes as the Flamewalker I was destined to be.

Chapter 3: The Glimmering Pit

My feet sizzled on the cracked ground as I approached the Glimmering Pit, a perilous chasm that shimmered with a brilliant, fiery glow. The heat radiated from it, warping the air around me like a mirage. Dust motes danced in the golden light, casting eerie shadows that flickered across the rocky outcrops surrounding this forsaken place. This was no ordinary pit; it was a rift in the earth where myths whispered of a creature dwelling within—a Fire Drake named Pyrax, the fierce guardian of the Emberstone, a gem said to contain the heart of a star.

As I peered over the edge, my heart pounded like a drum echoing through a canyon. The ground trembled beneath my feet, a low growl rumbling from the depths below, sending a shiver down my spine. A surge of heat washed over me, more intense than the summer sun at high noon. The air thickened with the scent of sulfur and smoke, swirling around me like an unwanted embrace. I gripped the weathered ledge, my fingers brushing against the rough, sun-baked rock. With every breath, I could taste the ash in the air, gritty and bitter, the bitter remnants of tales spoken in hushed tones around campfires.

And then, through the haze, Pyrax's silhouette emerged from the shadows. His massive wings unfurled like molten gold, glistening under the glow of the chasm, casting a sprawling shadow that seemed to envelop me whole. I had expected something fierce, but there was a strange elegance in his form, the way he moved—fluid and powerful. As he rose, his scales glimmered like liquid metal, each facet catching the light and refracting it into bursts of flame-colored brilliance.

"Who dares to approach?" his voice rumbled, deep and echoing like distant thunder, vibrating through the very earth. I could feel it resonate within my chest, a potent mixture of fear and awe. Despite the coil of dread tightening in my stomach, I swallowed hard, forcing my voice to steady itself, even as my heart raced.

"It's me, Elara," I called out, drawing strength from the name my parents had given me. "I seek the Emberstone." The words hung in the air, charged with a weight that felt almost palpable. The legends had spoken of the stone as a source of immense power, capable of igniting the soul's deepest desires and illuminating the darkest of paths. I had come here not just for myself but for my village, where shadows loomed, and hope flickered like a dying candle.

Pyrax tilted his head, his fiery eyes narrowing, studying me as if I were an oddity—an intruder daring to breach his sanctuary. "Why would I grant you passage, little one? What makes you worthy?"

I could feel the heat radiating from him, like a furnace belching fire, but I stood my ground. "Because I am willing to face whatever trials you have, Pyrax. I am not just a girl seeking treasure; I'm a daughter of the Flameheart Clan. My people are suffering. I've come to bring light back to our darkened skies."

The drake's laughter echoed, a deep rumble that filled the air with a warmth that seemed to chase away the chill of my fears. "Brave words, but bravery is often a foolish mask for naivety. What do you truly know of sacrifice?"

I could feel the weight of his gaze, probing the depths of my soul. What did I know? I thought of the villagers, their faces pale and drawn, the way their eyes glimmered with desperation. I thought of the nights spent listening to my grandmother's stories, the warmth of her voice weaving a tapestry of hope that I now clung to in the face of my uncertainty. "I know enough to understand that true strength comes from sacrifice. I've lost too much already to turn back now."

Pyrax regarded me in silence, the glow of the chasm flickering as if the flames were pondering my words. I couldn't tell if he was intrigued or merely amused by my resolve. Finally, he spoke, his voice softening just enough for me to sense a shift in his demeanor.

"Very well, Elara. If you wish to claim the Emberstone, you must first confront your own darkness. Only then will the light find you worthy."

With that, he beckoned me closer, his wings folding back as he descended into the pit. My heart raced, an exhilarating blend of terror and excitement coursing through me. What awaited me in the depths of the Glimmering Pit? Was it truly the Emberstone I sought, or something far more profound?

I inhaled deeply, the acrid taste of ash mingling with the hope swelling in my chest. The walls of the chasm shimmered like molten glass, beckoning me to descend into the unknown. As I stepped forward, my foot slipped on the edge, and for a fleeting moment, I felt the pull of gravity and fear.

"Don't look down," Pyrax's voice resonated from below, a reminder and a challenge. "Look within."

With renewed resolve, I gripped the jagged edges of the pit, finding my footing. Each step downwards felt like a plunge into another world—a realm where shadows and light danced together, where the echoes of my past mingled with the whispers of possibility. I was not just seeking a gem; I was on a quest to illuminate the darkness that lurked within me and around those I loved. And as the heat embraced me, I felt the fire of my spirit igniting, ready to face whatever lay ahead.

As I descended deeper into the Glimmering Pit, the world above slipped away, the sky replaced by a canopy of shimmering heat waves. The walls of the chasm glistened, like the insides of a vast, luminous geode, as if the earth itself had bled molten gold and left it to solidify in swirling patterns. Each step felt like a plunge into the heart of a volcano, the very air pulsating with warmth, reminding me that I was no longer just a girl; I was a seeker in a realm of fire and shadows.

The path twisted and turned, revealing crevices adorned with glistening minerals that caught the fiery glow. My fingers brushed against the rock face, the surface warm and slightly sticky, as if the earth was alive and breathing. A thousand possibilities danced in my mind—perhaps Pyrax had gathered treasures from across the realms, each glimmer a remnant of forgotten stories.

As I rounded a corner, the narrow passage opened into a vast cavern, and I halted, awestruck. The sight before me was breathtaking, a magnificent underground world filled with glowing crystals and rivers of lava that flowed like liquid gold. The air crackled with energy, and I felt it buzz against my skin, urging me to move forward, to embrace the magic of this place. But it was not just the beauty that captivated me; it was the echo of countless voices trapped in the stone, murmuring secrets from ages past.

In the center of this cavern, Pyrax awaited me, now fully revealed in all his fiery splendor. He perched on a rocky outcrop, his immense wings folded tightly against his sides, resembling molten shields. His golden scales shimmered as he regarded me with a mix of curiosity and something akin to respect. The heat radiating from him shimmered in waves, distorting the air like a mirage, and I could almost see my hopes and fears swirling within those flames.

"You have come far, Elara," he rumbled, his voice echoing off the cavern walls. "But the journey does not end here. To prove your worth, you must face your darkness."

"Face my darkness?" I echoed, feeling the weight of his words settle on my shoulders like a cloak. "What do you mean?"

With a flick of his tail, Pyrax gestured to the far side of the cavern, where shadows pooled like ink. "There lies the Rift of Reflections. Enter it, and you will confront your innermost fears. Only by embracing them can you claim the Emberstone."

I swallowed hard, my pulse quickening. I had heard tales of the Rift, where the mind conjured images of what one feared most, a swirling tempest of insecurities and doubts. But if I wanted to save my village, to restore hope, I had to embrace this challenge.

With a nod, I took a deep breath and stepped toward the shadows. The air grew colder as I crossed the threshold, and the light from the cavern faded, plunging me into a world of darkness. My heart raced as I felt the walls close in, the whispers of the cavern fading to silence. I was enveloped in an all-consuming blackness, and I was not alone.

Figures began to materialize around me—faces I knew and some I did not, their expressions twisted in a silent scream. Each figure mirrored a part of me: the friend I'd lost in the flames of a past fire, the villagers' hollow eyes as they gazed upon their dwindling hope, and worst of all, the reflection of myself—small, fragile, engulfed by self-doubt.

"Why are you here?" the reflection of my younger self asked, her voice echoing like the mournful wind. "You can't save them. You never could."

"No!" I shouted, feeling the heat of my anger rise like a phoenix. "I've come too far to give up now!"

With every word, the shadows flickered, the faces shifting, morphing into new shapes, new fears. I felt them clawing at my resolve, trying to pull me into a spiral of despair. Images of failure flooded my mind—every misstep, every time I had fallen short of expectations. They crashed into me like waves, threatening to drag me under.

But amid the chaos, a flicker of light ignited in my chest. "I may have stumbled," I admitted, my voice steadier now, "but I've learned, and I've grown. Every failure is a stepping stone."

The shadows paused, wavering as my words cut through their hold. My voice grew stronger, fueled by the memories of those I fought for—the villagers who looked to me with trust, my family who believed in my dreams, and the resilience that coursed through my veins.

"I am Elara of the Flameheart Clan!" I proclaimed, the heat of my spirit illuminating the darkness around me. "I am not defined by my fears but by my choices. I will not allow you to consume me!"

With that declaration, the figures began to dissolve, the dark mist retreating as my confidence surged like fire breaking free from its binds. I felt the pull of warmth returning, the shadows replaced by shimmering lights that danced like fireflies in the dusk.

Suddenly, the world around me shifted, and I found myself back in the cavern, panting and exhilarated. Pyrax watched me with a newfound respect, his fiery eyes gleaming. "You have faced your fears and emerged unscathed. Few can claim such courage."

"Does that mean I'm worthy?" I asked, my heart still racing.

Pyrax inclined his massive head, a grin spreading across his draconic face, a flicker of pride in his golden eyes. "You have shown that you can rise from the ashes, Elara. The Emberstone awaits you."

With a sweep of his wing, he revealed a pedestal where the Emberstone rested, glowing with an ethereal light. It pulsed like a heartbeat, radiating warmth and promise. As I stepped forward, I felt its energy drawing me in, a connection sparking between us, igniting the very essence of my being.

This was not just a quest for power but a testament to my journey—my growth, my resilience, and the light that I could bring to others. As I reached for the Emberstone, I knew that I was ready to wield its magic, not just for myself but for the future of my village, the warmth of hope igniting in my chest like a flame reborn.

The moment my fingers brushed the surface of the Emberstone, a jolt of energy coursed through me, igniting every nerve ending in my body. The radiant light enveloped me like a warm embrace, and I could feel the pulse of its magic syncing with the rhythm of my heart. It was as if the stone recognized me, seeing past the doubts and fears I had just conquered. With a deep breath, I wrapped my hands around the cool, smooth surface, and a rush of visions flooded my mind—a kaleidoscope of colors and memories that spun wildly like a whirlwind.

I saw my village, nestled in the valley beneath the shadow of a craggy mountain. A once-vibrant place, now dulled by despair, its people moving like specters through the streets, their eyes hollowed out by hardship. I glimpsed my grandmother, her face lined with worry, her hands shaking as she cradled the last of our family's heirlooms—a delicate fire opal that had once glowed as brightly as the sun. Then came the vision of flames licking at the edges of the forest, devouring everything in their path, as panic spread through the village like wildfire. My heart ached for them, the weight of responsibility settling like a stone in my gut.

But amidst the chaos, I also felt the warmth of hope. I saw laughter echoing through the fields, children playing, the community rallying together, united by resilience and courage. The Emberstone shimmered brighter, weaving these images into a tapestry of possibility, urging me to step beyond my fear and into my power.

As I stood there, lost in the brilliance of the stone, Pyrax approached, his immense figure casting a shadow that darkened the chamber. "The Emberstone will amplify your spirit, Elara, but it demands respect. Its power is a double-edged sword, illuminating both the good and the darkness within."

I nodded, feeling the weight of his words. I knew that wielding such magic meant not just embracing my strength but confronting the scars of my past—the fear of failure, the weight of expectation, the pain of loss. It was more than a quest for the stone; it was a journey toward understanding myself and the legacy I would carry.

"Will it help my village?" I asked, my voice trembling with hope.

"Only if you wield it with intention," Pyrax replied, his voice deep and resonant. "Your heart must guide you. The Emberstone can ignite flames of creation or destruction. Choose wisely."

With resolve hardening within me, I lifted the Emberstone, feeling its warmth surge through my veins like liquid fire. "I will use it to bring back the light to my people. I refuse to let darkness consume us."

Pyrax stepped back, a glint of approval in his eyes. "Very well, brave one. But remember, the path forward will not be easy. Your true test lies ahead, and the Emberstone will illuminate your way, but it cannot shield you from the challenges that await."

He turned, beckoning me to follow. As we ventured deeper into the cavern, the atmosphere shifted, filled with a tangible energy that thrummed in the air. The walls glistened with gemstones that seemed to resonate with my emotions, their hues shifting with each step I took. I felt a connection to this place, as if the very earth beneath us was alive and aware, feeding off my determination and courage.

"Where are we going?" I asked, curiosity bubbling within me.

"To the Heart of Fire," Pyrax said, his wings brushing against the rocky floor, sending a flurry of sparks into the air. "It is where you will learn to harness the Emberstone's power. Only by mastering its energy can you hope to protect your village from the shadows encroaching upon it."

As we entered a vast chamber, I felt a shift in the atmosphere. The room opened up into a colossal expanse filled with roaring flames that danced around a central pit, the Heart of Fire. It was mesmerizing and terrifying, a living entity of molten rock and blazing fire. The heat was overwhelming, but rather than repelling me, it beckoned me forward, calling to the ember within my own soul.

"Now," Pyrax instructed, "place the Emberstone in the Heart of Fire. It will absorb the flames, transforming its energy into a power that is uniquely yours."

I approached the pit, the heat licking at my skin like a playful cat. As I hovered the Emberstone over the swirling flames, I hesitated.

This was it—the moment I had been building toward. With a deep breath, I let the stone slip from my fingers, watching it plunge into the depths of the fire.

The moment it hit the flames, a shockwave of energy rippled through the chamber. The flames roared higher, swirling around the stone, engulfing it in a tempest of light and heat. I could feel the energy reaching out, wrapping around me like a blanket of fire, filling me with a warmth that surged through my body and ignited my spirit.

Suddenly, I was swept into a vision—a cascade of memories and emotions unfurling like a tapestry. I saw myself standing alongside my village, the Emberstone glowing in my hands as it radiated a golden light that chased away shadows. I saw families reunited, laughter echoing in the streets, children playing in fields of wildflowers.

But then, a dark figure emerged, creeping from the edges of my vision, casting an ominous shadow over our happiness. It was a specter of doubt and fear, a manifestation of everything I had fought against. I felt its icy grip trying to pull me down, threatening to extinguish the flame ignited within me.

"No!" I shouted, forcing myself to stand tall against the onslaught. "You will not take my light!"

In that moment, the energy of the Emberstone surged within me, intertwining with my very essence. I felt the flames of the Heart of Fire respond to my call, roaring fiercely as they danced around me. I harnessed that fire, bending it to my will, transforming it into a shield that glowed with a brilliant light.

As the shadow loomed closer, I thrust my hands forward, channeling the power of the Emberstone into a beam of radiant light. The darkness recoiled, unraveling before the brilliance, dissipating into nothingness. I felt the warmth envelop me, the fear melting away, leaving only strength and clarity in its wake.

When the light faded, I found myself back in the chamber, the Heart of Fire pulsing gently. Pyrax stood before me, a proud glimmer in his eyes. "You have harnessed the Emberstone's power, Elara. It is yours to wield."

I held the glowing stone in my palm, its warmth radiating reassurance. The journey had transformed me, igniting a fire within that I knew would guide me through the challenges ahead. With renewed determination, I faced Pyrax, ready to return to my village, armed not just with the Emberstone, but with the understanding that true strength comes from confronting our fears and choosing to light the way for others.

As I stepped back into the world above, I felt the sun warm my face, the sky a brilliant blue overhead. The shadows that had once haunted me seemed less daunting now, as if I had stepped into a new chapter of my life, one filled with purpose and a fire that could not be extinguished. I was ready to fight for my people and reclaim the light that had dimmed in our hearts, for I was Elara of the Flameheart Clan, and this was only the beginning of my journey.

Chapter 4: A Fiery Pact

The air crackled as I fell, a furious blaze of heat and color. It surrounded me like a tempest of flame, enveloping my senses and igniting every nerve ending. My heart thundered in my chest, not solely from fear, but from the exhilarating rush of defiance. I was plunging into the heart of the beast's domain, where legends whispered of ancient powers hidden beneath the surface. Below me, the pit opened wide, a churning cauldron of molten rock and fire, the surface roiling like the belly of a furious dragon.

Each second felt like an eternity as I plummeted toward the incandescent glow, my mind racing with thoughts of what I might face. The shard of Emberstone was a treasure whispered about in hushed tones, said to hold the very essence of fire. And here I was, about to grapple with the living embodiment of that element. Pyrax's roar echoed in my ears, urging me onward, as if mocking my hesitation. The fire could consume me, but it could also forge me anew, transforming fear into purpose.

Finally, I broke through the surface of the molten magma, the heat swarming me like a swarm of angry bees. I gasped, my lungs struggling against the oppressive air thick with sulfur and ash. The world beneath was a surreal landscape, a shifting sea of reds and oranges, punctuated by glowing pockets of molten rock that bubbled like boiling cauldrons. Each pulse sent ripples through the magma, drawing forth a scent that was rich and metallic, tinged with the promise of power.

My fingers tingled as I reached into the heated expanse, the warmth teasing at my skin, almost seductive in its nature. The flames danced around my arms, a living entity that could either save or destroy me. I was aware that every moment spent here would be a gamble, the stakes higher than I had ever imagined. But I couldn't turn back—not now, not when I had a chance to shape my destiny. I closed my eyes, centering my thoughts, letting the fear wash over me like a wave before I dove deeper into the pit.

The first shard of Emberstone caught my eye—a jagged piece glowing like a captured star, nestled between the flowing lava like a secret waiting to be revealed. Its light flickered as if responding to my presence, coaxing me closer. I focused all my energy, a determination surging through me, and lunged toward it, feeling the raw heat envelop my body in a fierce embrace. The magma splashed, a fiery shower cascading around me, and I reached for the shard.

As my fingers closed around the stone, a jolt of energy coursed through me, igniting every nerve and making the hairs on my arms stand on end. It was as if I had pulled lightning from the sky and bound it in my grasp. I felt a connection form, an unbreakable bond as the essence of fire surged within me, roaring in defiance against the depths of my soul. The flames flared higher, illuminating the cavern with a golden glow, illuminating my path as I began my ascent back to the surface.

Every movement was a battle against the sheer force of the pit, the magma hissing and bubbling as if trying to reclaim its prize. I pushed myself, swimming against the current of molten rock, each stroke sending waves of heat crashing over me. The world above felt distant, a mere memory of cool air and freedom, but I could not relent. The promise of guidance from Pyrax burned bright in my mind. I needed this—needed to prove that I was more than just a girl wandering in search of answers.

At last, my fingertips grazed the rim of the pit, a sharp ledge that felt both foreign and familiar. The instant I clambered out, I collapsed onto the rocky ground, the air suddenly cooler against my skin, though still tinged with the heat of my encounter. The shard pulsed in my palm, a heartbeat echoing my own. It was alive, its warmth radiating a soothing energy that countered the ferocity of the flames below.

Pyrax towered above me, his enormous form silhouetted against the fiery backdrop, eyes like molten gold observing my every move. A rumble of satisfaction rolled from his throat, deep and resonant. "You have proven your mettle, little one. You possess the heart of a fireborn," he declared, his voice a sonorous echo that vibrated through the ground beneath me. I felt a swell of pride, warmth blossoming in my chest.

"You're not just a creature of flame," I replied, rising to my feet, the shard clenched tightly in my hand. "You're a guardian of something greater. You've held the essence of fire for eons, and now, so do I."

"Indeed," he rumbled, his voice thick with ancient wisdom. "Together, we can wield that power. The Emberstone will serve as your guide, your ally." His gaze flickered to the shard in my hand. "But with that power comes responsibility. You must learn to control it, or it will consume you as it has many before you."

The weight of his words hung in the air, palpable and daunting. I nodded slowly, absorbing the gravity of what lay ahead. The world stretched before me, vibrant and alive with possibilities. The journey had only just begun, and the path ahead was as unpredictable as the flames themselves. I felt a rush of exhilaration—no longer just a wanderer in a vast, indifferent world, but a force to be reckoned with, a player in a game far grander than I had ever imagined.

As the echoes of the pit faded into the distance, a new flame flickered to life within me, illuminating a path forward.

The moment I clambered to safety, my heart raced with exhilaration, yet I felt like a walking ember, every pulse reverberating with the heat of my recent trial. I glanced at the shard of Emberstone still nestled in my palm, its surface shimmering with a fiery glow that made me feel both powerful and vulnerable. It was a strange dichotomy—this stone was both a blessing and a burden, its warmth whispering promises of strength and adventure, yet cautioning me about the flames that flickered too close.

Pyrax shifted, his enormous frame casting a shadow that felt like a thundercloud overhead. His molten eyes bore into mine, a smirk curling around his lips, which, to my surprise, seemed to crackle with tiny sparks. "You are fortunate to have survived the pit. Many have met their fate in that molten abyss, drawn in by the allure of the Emberstone," he mused, the flames around him licking playfully at the air.

I took a moment to gather my thoughts, still reeling from the rush of fire and fury. "What happens now?" I asked, curiosity mingling with a tinge of trepidation. The promise of guidance was tantalizing, yet the weight of responsibility felt heavier than the stone in my hand.

Pyrax turned, a grand gesture that sent waves of heat radiating from his form, inviting me to follow him. "You must learn to wield that power," he declared, his voice rolling like distant thunder. "The world beyond the pit is riddled with dangers and treachery. You will need to understand the essence of fire and how it intertwines with your own spirit."

As I followed him, the cavern opened up into a vast chamber, walls glimmering with veins of crystal that caught the flickering light of the flames. The colors danced across the rocky surface, casting a kaleidoscope of reds and oranges that seemed to pulse with a life of their own. A river of lava snaked through the chamber, bubbling with a low, ominous hiss. I was in a sanctum of fire, a realm where every crackle echoed tales of ancient power.

"Welcome to the Forge of Ancients," Pyrax announced with a flourish. "Here, you will begin your training." He gestured toward a series of stone platforms that jutted out over the river, each one adorned with symbols that glowed faintly, as if resonating with the energy of the Emberstone.

"What do I have to do?" I stepped onto the first platform, feeling the heat radiate beneath my feet, yet strangely invigorating. My heart thudded in my chest, a steady rhythm urging me on.

Pyrax chuckled, a deep rumble that reverberated through the chamber. "You will learn to harness the flames and bend them to your will. It starts with understanding your own fire." With a dramatic sweep of his clawed hand, he gestured to a pile of smooth, obsidian stones resting on the edge of the platform. "Choose one. This will be your conduit. Your connection to the fire will grow from this simple stone."

I knelt down, studying the glimmering rocks, each one exuding an enigmatic allure. I picked one that shimmered with hints of gold and crimson, its surface cool against my palm yet brimming with potential. "What now?" I asked, holding it tightly.

"Focus," Pyrax instructed, his voice steady as molten rock. "Close your eyes and imagine the fire within you. Feel its warmth, its energy. You must channel that into the stone. Let it guide you."

I closed my eyes, the world around me fading into the background. I envisioned the flames from the pit, the heat that had enveloped me. I recalled the moment I had grasped the Emberstone, the jolt of energy that coursed through me. Slowly, I began to visualize that energy coiling within, building like a flame in a hearth, and directed it toward the obsidian stone.

At first, nothing happened. I felt like a novice magician, attempting to pull a rabbit from a hat, only to be met with silence. My brow furrowed in concentration, and I focused harder, willing the heat within to rise and flow.

Then, a spark ignited, small and flickering at first. I gasped as the stone grew warm, the warmth morphing into a pulse, beating in rhythm with my heart. Encouraged, I pushed harder, envisioning the flame growing within, bursting forth like a wildflower through cracked pavement.

Suddenly, flames erupted from the stone, brilliant and vibrant, illuminating the chamber. I opened my eyes, awestruck, as tendrils of fire danced above my palm. It was beautiful and chaotic, flickering in vibrant colors of orange and gold.

"Excellent!" Pyrax boomed, pride evident in his voice. "But remember, fire is not only a force to command; it is a force to respect. Control is key. Harness the flame without letting it consume you."

As the flames receded, I took a deep breath, exhilaration surging through me. This was a taste of the power that lay ahead, a glimpse into a world where I could wield the fire as an extension of myself.

"What's next?" I asked, the thrill of potential lighting a fire in my own spirit.

"Now, we learn about balance," he replied, stepping closer, his eyes narrowing. "Every flame has its opposite—coolness, calmness, the ebb and flow of air. Without balance, chaos reigns. Let us see how you manage the interplay of elements."

With that, he flicked his wrist, and a rush of cool air enveloped me, mingling with the heat still lingering on my skin. I felt a shiver run down my spine as the temperature shifted dramatically, a gentle breeze brushing against my face like a tender reminder of the world outside.

"Embrace the coolness," Pyrax instructed, his voice steady. "Breathe it in, feel it dance with your flames."

The challenge was set. In that moment, the flames and the cool air swirled around me like a tempest of possibility, and I realized that my journey had only just begun.

The cool breeze wrapped around me, a gentle reminder that I was still tethered to the world outside the flames. I closed my eyes and focused, letting the sensations blend and intertwine, each element an extension of my being. The heat from the stone pulsed in my hand, while the refreshing air swirled around me like a playful companion. Slowly, I began to breathe in harmony, feeling the temperature shifts and currents guiding me, coaxing my body to dance between the fire and the coolness.

As I concentrated, the flames flickered in response, their brightness dancing in rhythm with my heartbeat. I opened my eyes to find Pyrax watching, a blend of curiosity and amusement flickering in his molten gaze. "Now, let's see how you handle this," he declared with a dramatic flair, unleashing a burst of flame that spiraled upward like a fiery serpent.

The air crackled with energy, and I could feel the intensity building as the heat rose. I realized that Pyrax was inviting me to manipulate the flames, to mold them as an artist does clay. The challenge intrigued me. I extended my hand toward the swirling fire, letting my thoughts flow like water around rocks in a stream. I envisioned the flames bending to my will, curving gracefully like vines in the wind.

The air shimmered around me as I channeled my energy, coaxing the flames into a spiral that danced and twirled. It was intoxicating, a rush that filled me with empowerment. Pyrax's eyes widened with delight as I twisted the fire into shapes—a serpentine dragon, a flickering phoenix, all born from my command.

"Impressive!" he roared, laughter rumbling like thunder. "But fire is fickle. Do not let pride blind you." With a swift motion, he sent a gust of wind into the flames, sending them spiraling wildly, throwing me off balance. The fire roared, angry at being disturbed, and I struggled to regain control.

Instinctively, I reached for the coolness, embracing it as it rushed around me. I inhaled deeply, letting the balance of the elements wash over me like a soothing balm. The fiery chaos settled, and I felt the warmth transform into a gentle glow, illuminating the chamber. I looked up at Pyrax, exhilaration coursing through me. "I think I'm getting the hang of it!"

"Indeed, you are," he replied, his tone approving yet cautious. "But there's more to learn. Balance is not merely an act; it is a state of being. You must feel the dance of the elements within you."

He gestured toward the center of the chamber, where an ancient stone altar stood. Its surface was etched with runes, pulsating softly in the dim light, whispering secrets of ages past. "There lies the next step in your training. You must channel your energies into that altar. It will help you solidify your connection to fire and air, allowing you to summon their powers at will."

With my heart racing, I approached the altar, the warm glow of the Emberstone still radiating in my palm. I placed the stone on the altar's surface, feeling its warmth merge with the coolness that surrounded me. A pulse of energy surged through me, wrapping around my bones, igniting every fiber of my being. The runes on the altar began to glow brighter, bathing the chamber in a vibrant light, illuminating the carved figures of ancient guardians who had once wielded the elements.

"Now, channel your focus," Pyrax instructed, his presence looming like a storm. "Let the flame rise and the air swirl. Feel them, understand their essence."

I closed my eyes, letting the sensations overwhelm me once more. The warmth swelled within, and the coolness brushed against my skin, creating a tapestry of elements weaving around me. With each breath, I allowed the fire to rise, pushing it outwards, imagining it spiraling into the runes, merging and glowing like fireflies on a summer night.

Suddenly, the energy shifted. The flames responded, intertwining with the cool air, creating a whirlwind of fire and wind that roared into existence. I opened my eyes, gasping as I beheld the spectacle—a tornado of flame, bright and fierce, swirling above the altar, casting flickering shadows on the cavern walls. The energy thrummed with power, vibrating through my bones, and I felt invincible.

But in that moment of triumph, I felt the rush slip away, and the whirlwind began to falter. The flames flickered uncertainly, and the air grew dense and heavy. Panic surged in my chest as I tried to regain control. "No, no! Come back!"

"Focus!" Pyrax bellowed, his voice cutting through the chaos. "Do not let the fear consume you! Remember, balance is your ally."

Drawing on his words, I fought against the rising tide of anxiety, taking a deep breath. I centered myself once more, feeling the cool air brushing against my skin, melding with the warmth radiating from my core. I visualized the elements as partners in a dance, fluid and harmonious, rather than opponents in a battle.

With a renewed sense of purpose, I directed my energy back into the whirlwind, letting the flames roar higher while the air wrapped around them in a gentle embrace. The fire surged, igniting with fresh vigor, and the tornado swirled faster, higher, until it reached a crescendo that echoed through the chamber.

At that moment, the runes on the altar exploded with light, illuminating the cavern in an ethereal glow, casting brilliant patterns across the walls. I gasped, realizing that I had forged a connection deeper than I could have imagined—a pact not just with the fire, but with the very essence of the elements themselves.

Pyrax watched, his expression a blend of awe and pride. "You have done well, young fireborn," he rumbled. "With practice, you will learn to control not only the flames but also the very air that carries them. Together, you and I will shape the world."

I smiled, exhilaration coursing through me, a blend of joy and determination. This was more than a pact; it was a bond forged in flames, a partnership that would take me beyond the realms of my imagination. With each step I took, I could feel the weight of destiny shifting, the path ahead alive with possibilities.

"Thank you," I said, feeling gratitude swell within me. "For everything."

Pyrax nodded, the flicker of flames dancing in his eyes. "Your journey has only just begun. The world is fraught with challenges, and the darkness stirs. But with the power you now possess, you will be ready."

I nodded, resolute. The thrill of adventure awaited, and I was no longer just a girl adrift in the currents of fate. I was fire, I was air, and together, we would ignite the world.

Chapter 5: The Shard of Destiny

The air around me crackled with anticipation as I stood at the edge of the molten pit, the swirling magma illuminating the cavern in hues of fiery orange and deep crimson. The heat radiated, wrapping around me like a blanket, though I was barely aware of the sweat dripping down my brow. Instead, my focus honed in on the shard of destiny nestled within the inferno, a gem that seemed to pulse with its own heartbeat.

This shard was no ordinary fragment; it shimmered with a kaleidoscope of colors that danced across its surface, like the lights of a carnival flickering against the night sky. I could feel its allure pulling me closer, a siren's call that promised power and understanding, but also danger and responsibility. As I drew nearer, the magma gurgled like a trapped beast, and I wondered for a moment if I was the fool wandering too close to the fire. But the visions that clouded my mind dispelled any lingering doubt. I saw my parents—hardworking, resilient souls with dreams forged in the furnace of hardship. Their faces, weary yet full of hope, flickered through my thoughts, reminding me of the sacrifices they made for a future I had yet to grasp.

With a deep breath, I steeled myself. The shard was within reach, and I could almost feel its energy intertwining with my own, as if it recognized a kindred spirit in me. I extended my hand, fingers trembling with a mix of fear and exhilaration, and brushed the cool surface. The contrast was jarring, a reminder that amid the chaos of the volcanic world, there existed pockets of serenity and power just waiting to be harnessed. As I grasped it, a surge of warmth radiated through my palm, and the cavern erupted with sound—the roar of the magma and the echoes of my ancestors urging me onward.

I staggered back as a flood of visions overwhelmed me. Images raced through my mind: my parents in their youth, standing proud against the backdrop of their hometown, a small yet vibrant place cradled by sprawling oak trees and painted skies. They were warriors of a different kind, battling their own demons, pushing through the constraints of their world to carve out a future for me. The sacrifices they made—the nights spent working, the dreams deferred—were now part of the energy coursing through the shard. It was a legacy of hope and fortitude, intricately woven into the fabric of my being.

Emerging from the pit, my heart thundered in my chest, and I clutched the shard tightly, feeling its energy pulse against my skin, a warm reassurance. Pyrax stood nearby, the fire demon's fiery mane flickering with intrigue, his molten gaze locked onto mine. It was as if he could sense the transformation that had begun within me, the pact we forged sealed by the bond of shared purpose. The flames surrounding him danced higher, illuminating the craggy walls of the cavern and casting playful shadows that leapt and twirled like children at play.

"Well, that was dramatic," he said, his voice rumbling like distant thunder. "You've got guts, kid. But this is just the beginning."

I couldn't help but grin, the thrill of the moment igniting a spark of mischief within me. "If I knew you were going to watch my life flash before my eyes, I would have dressed for the occasion."

Pyrax chuckled, the sound echoing through the cavern like rolling boulders. "You should thank me for the inspiration. Your struggle brought a touch of flair to an otherwise dull afternoon."

As I regained my composure, the shard pulsed once more, an undeniable connection tugging at my core. It felt like an invitation, a call to uncover the secrets of my heritage and the potential that lay dormant within me. I glanced down at the shard, now glowing like the morning sun breaking through storm clouds, and marveled at the destiny it promised. "So, what's next, oh wise and fiery one?"

Pyrax tilted his head, flames flickering thoughtfully. "Now, we train. You have the shard, but it's not just a pretty trinket. It's a conduit of energy, and if you want to wield it, you'll need to learn control. Fire isn't just destruction; it's creation, rebirth. We'll teach you how to bend it to your will."

A shiver of excitement raced down my spine. Training with a fire demon sounded like a wild ride, but I couldn't shake the underlying anxiety. What if I failed? What if the power that surged through me was too much to handle? Those questions echoed in my mind, but the thought of disappointing my parents—of not living up to the legacy they fought so hard to create—stoked the fire of determination within me.

"Let's do this," I declared, the words tasting like a promise on my tongue. "I'm ready to learn."

As the cavern echoed with our resolve, the air shimmered with potential, and I took my first step toward a future I could shape, knowing it wouldn't just be my journey, but a reclamation of everything my parents had sacrificed. The path ahead loomed before me, twisted and daunting, yet glimmering with the promise of adventure. I would rise to the challenge, unearthing the strength that lay dormant within.

The air crackled around us, a tangible tension that felt as if the world itself was holding its breath, waiting for the first spark to ignite. I stood before Pyrax, the fire demon whose smirk could probably melt steel, and felt the weight of the shard pressing against my palm. It was warm, alive, and somehow it seemed to know me better than I knew myself. The flickering flames in the cavern danced to a rhythm that echoed the racing beat of my heart.

"Okay, so where do we start?" I asked, attempting to inject a casual bravado into my voice, though it came out sounding a touch more like a squeak than I intended. Fire manipulation felt like something out of a fantasy novel—exciting yet utterly terrifying.

Pyrax stepped closer, his fiery form radiating a warmth that was both comforting and intimidating. "First, we need to establish your connection with the shard. It's not just a tool; it's a part of you now. The more you understand it, the more you can control it."

"Right, so how do I talk to a glowing rock?" I asked, raising an eyebrow in skepticism.

He let out a laugh that crackled through the air. "Ah, the sass! I like it. But you don't talk to it; you feel it. The shard responds to your emotions. Try closing your eyes."

I hesitated, glancing at the swirling magma, the bright hues of orange and red reminding me that fire was not just pretty light; it was a consuming force. But curiosity outweighed my hesitation, and I squeezed my eyes shut, shutting out the vibrant chaos around me. "Feel. Got it. Easy as pie," I muttered, half-serious, half-mocking the instruction.

As I stood there, the world around me melted away into silence. The first wave of heat enveloped me, a gentle caress that brought forth memories of summer days spent running barefoot through sun-drenched fields, laughter echoing in the wind. I imagined the sun setting over the horizon, casting golden light over my childhood home. I felt the warmth wrap around me, expanding beyond the confines of my skin and merging with the energy of the shard.

In that moment, a vision swept through me—a scene of flames licking the edges of an ancient forest, the crackle of burning leaves punctuating the air. I felt a flicker of fear but also an undeniable sense of power and freedom. The shard vibrated in my hand, and a rush of warmth surged through me, igniting the core of my being. I gasped as the feeling intensified, transforming from a mere spark into a blaze that swirled through my veins.

"Open your eyes!" Pyrax urged, his voice breaking through my reverie.

I did, and the cavern exploded into a riot of color. The shard in my hand glowed brighter than before, its surface shimmering like molten gold under the cavern's flickering lights. The magma bubbled around us, but now, instead of fearing it, I felt a strange kinship with the chaos.

"What just happened?" I asked, bewildered but exhilarated.

"You tapped into the shard's energy," Pyrax explained, pride lacing his voice. "You felt the fire within you. That's the first step to mastering it."

A grin broke across my face, feeling like a child who had just discovered a hidden talent. "Okay, so what's next? Fireball throwing? A grand finale with pyrotechnics?"

"Not quite," Pyrax chuckled, his fiery eyes dancing with amusement. "First, we need to work on control. You don't want to accidentally burn down the world, do you?"

"Not on my to-do list, but thanks for the reminder," I replied, rolling my eyes dramatically.

"Good. Now, let's practice conjuring flames without the shard. Just focus on your emotions. When you can create fire from within, then we'll add the shard back into the mix."

I took a deep breath, summoning the memory of warmth and light—the summer sun breaking through storm clouds, the crackling fireplace during family gatherings. I envisioned those moments, trying to let the warmth fill me, rising from my core like a phoenix from the ashes. The heat was comforting, but I could feel the energy dancing at my fingertips, teasing me like a playful kitten.

"Come on, little fire," I whispered, willing it to ignite. "Let's show this cavern who's boss."

As if in response to my playful challenge, a tiny flame flickered to life at the tips of my fingers, illuminating my face with a soft glow. I gasped, the warmth washing over me like a wave. "Look! I did it!"

"Very good," Pyrax said, his voice booming with enthusiasm. "Now, try to control it. Make it larger."

I focused, channeling my energy, pouring my determination into that tiny flame. It flickered and danced, but as I concentrated, it grew.

The little ember expanded, flickering higher, bathing the cavern walls in a warm glow.

Suddenly, the flame sputtered and threatened to extinguish. Panic shot through me, and I felt the flame begin to falter. "No, no, no! Stay!" I exclaimed, reaching out with my other hand, instinctively trying to coax it back to life.

"Breathe!" Pyrax bellowed, the force of his voice pushing against me like a gust of wind. "Focus on the warmth. Don't let fear extinguish it!"

I inhaled deeply, drawing in the warmth surrounding me, letting it flow through me like a rushing river. I felt the connection—the ember was a part of me. It responded to my emotions, and I needed to embrace the power instead of letting fear claw at it.

With a deep exhale, I visualized the flame roaring back to life. The fire blazed brighter, illuminating the cavern like a torch, and I couldn't help but let out a whoop of triumph.

"Now that's what I'm talking about!" Pyrax cheered, his fiery form flaring up with excitement. "You've got potential! Just remember, power comes with responsibility. Don't lose sight of that."

As I basked in the glow of my creation, a surge of determination swelled within me. I could feel the fires of destiny awakening, promising a future that was both exhilarating and daunting. The cavern was alive with potential, and I was no longer just a girl thrust into this world; I was becoming something more. With every flicker of flame, I could see the path ahead—a journey shaped by the shard, my parents' legacy, and the fire that burned within me.

The cavern buzzed with a newfound energy, the air thick with the scent of sulfur and the heat of the magma creating a stifling blanket that wrapped around me like an unwelcome embrace. I took a moment to bask in my victory, the glow of the flame flickering at my fingertips illuminating the darkened walls. The vibrant colors of the cavern seemed to shimmer with life as if they too were celebrating my small triumph. Pyrax watched with a mix of pride and anticipation, his fiery form pulsating with the rhythm of the magma below.

"Alright, let's take it up a notch," he said, the crackle of his voice resonating through the chamber like a distant thunderclap. "You're ready for the next step."

"What next step? I just figured out how to make a tiny fire. What could possibly follow that?" I asked, half-joking, but the reality of the situation hit me. I was standing on the precipice of something monumental, and my heart raced with both excitement and trepidation.

"More than just flames, young spark," he said, his tone suddenly serious. "Fire is a conduit for emotion and energy. You need to learn how to control that energy and use it for your purpose. It's about intent, not just power."

I nodded, the weight of his words settling into my bones. Intent. Purpose. Those weren't just concepts; they were lifelines. "So, how do I channel my intent? Is there a spell or a mantra I should be reciting? Or do I just shout 'Fire!' really loudly?" I said, trying to lighten the mood, but the gravity of my new role was sinking in deeper.

Pyrax chuckled, the sound rumbling through the cavern like an earthquake. "No need for theatrics, though I appreciate your flair for the dramatic. It's about visualization. Picture what you want to create, not just flames. Envision the form it takes. Fire can be a wall, a weapon, a beacon—it can even be healing."

As he spoke, my mind began to whirl with possibilities. I could see the shapes flickering in my imagination—a protective barrier, a warm light guiding lost souls, or even a fierce flame to defend against adversaries. But then came the wave of doubt. "What if I mess it up?" I asked, my voice barely above a whisper.

"Messing up is part of learning," Pyrax said, his expression softening. "Embrace it. Let the fire teach you. Fear is a dampener. It can smother your flame."

Taking a deep breath, I closed my eyes again. I tried to forget the weight of the shard in my hand and the responsibilities it carried. I envisioned the fire forming into a barrier, an impenetrable wall flickering with intensity, shimmering like the surface of a lake under the moonlight. The thought sent a jolt of energy through me, and I could feel the warmth from the shard merging with my own.

As I exhaled, I opened my eyes and thrust my hands forward, willing the flame to materialize. The cavern erupted in brilliance. A wall of fire sprang forth, brilliant and wild, crackling as it solidified into a radiant barrier that flickered with energy. I gasped, astonished by the sheer force of what I'd conjured. It danced before me, a wall of living flames that felt both exhilarating and terrifying.

"Brilliant!" Pyrax shouted, his voice echoing against the stone walls. "Now, let's see if you can maintain it!"

Panic rushed through me as I felt the barrier wavering under my mental strain. I focused harder, pouring every ounce of determination into it. I thought of my parents' sacrifices, the love they had instilled in me, the fire that had burned within them through every hardship. With each recollection, the flames roared higher, the wall stabilizing into a fierce blaze, illuminating the cavern like a beacon in the night.

"Good! Keep your thoughts aligned," Pyrax encouraged. "Don't let it fade. Visualize it as part of you, something you can mold and reshape."

But even as he spoke, I felt a tremor of doubt creeping in. Would this power consume me? Would I end up like a candle burning too brightly, too quickly? The flames shimmered and flickered, reflecting my uncertainty.

"Focus!" Pyrax commanded, snapping me back to the moment. "This is where the real test begins. Can you use the barrier to protect yourself from an attack?"

"Wait, what?" I stammered, barely registering what he meant. But before I could question him further, he summoned a fireball, a swirling mass of brilliant red and orange, and hurled it toward me.

"Pyrax!" I shouted, panic surging through me as the fireball hurtled closer.

"Defend yourself! Use the barrier!" he barked.

Adrenaline coursed through me, and instinct kicked in. I summoned the wall of flames with a fierce determination, thrusting my hands outward as if I were casting a spell. The fireball collided with the barrier, exploding into a shower of sparks that illuminated the cavern like a constellation of stars. The barrier wavered but held, and I felt a rush of triumph.

"Not bad," Pyrax remarked, eyes glimmering with approval. "But you need to practice using it offensively as well. Try to manipulate the fireball's energy into something more."

My heart raced at the prospect. I felt the shard vibrate in my hand, as if it sensed my ambition. I pictured the fireball, its energy thrumming in the air, and instead of resisting it, I sought to blend with it. I envisioned myself as part of the fire, merging with the swirling energy, and coaxing it to transform.

With a deep breath, I reached out, channeling my will into the fire. I concentrated on creating something new—a blazing phoenix, fierce and free, rising from the ashes. The fireball morphed before my eyes, the energy reshaping itself into the majestic figure of a phoenix. It soared through the air, leaving a trail of sparks in its wake.

"Now that's more like it!" Pyrax roared, a proud grin on his face. "You've begun to understand the dance of fire!"

The phoenix swirled around me, a creature of pure energy, and I felt its warmth wash over me like a comforting embrace. I was no longer just channeling flames; I was becoming them. The boundaries between my spirit and the fire began to blur, and I realized that this was the true power of the shard. It wasn't merely a weapon or a tool; it was a manifestation of everything I was—my fears, my hopes, and the legacy of my parents.

"Now let's see how far you can take it," Pyrax said, excitement sparkling in his eyes. "Try to send your phoenix toward the wall and watch it explode into light!"

With a determined nod, I gestured outward, sending the fiery creature soaring toward the cavern wall. As it collided, the explosion of light illuminated every crevice, the glow cascading like fireworks bursting in a summer sky.

I laughed, the sound echoing in the cavern as the brilliance washed over me. In that moment, I felt invincible. I was a conduit of fire, a bearer of my family's legacy, and a girl with the heart of a phoenix. I had transformed not just the world around me but also myself, emerging from the shadows of doubt and stepping into the blazing light of possibility.

The flames danced around me, a testament to my journey. Together with Pyrax, we would explore the depths of my potential, uncovering the secrets that lay hidden within the shard and the fire. The future was unwritten, but with every flicker and roar, I knew I was ready to embrace whatever came next.

Chapter 6: Flames of Rebellion

The sun hung low on the horizon, casting long shadows that danced across the cracked earth as we ventured deeper into the heart of the desolate landscape. Each step I took echoed in the silence, a rhythmic reminder of the weight of our mission and the urgency that propelled us forward. With Pyrax at my side, his fiery mane flickering like a beacon, the air shimmered around us, crackling with the anticipation of what lay ahead. Emberhold loomed in the distance, a silhouette against the backdrop of an orange sky that hinted at the chaos yet to come.

As we approached, the barren ground gradually gave way to scattered remnants of a forgotten civilization, crumbling stone structures that whispered tales of a once-thriving community. Vines crept over the remnants, a testament to nature's stubborn reclamation. I could almost hear the laughter of children playing among the ruins, a sound long since silenced by the iron grip of the Ashen Council. Memories of my own childhood flickered in my mind, dancing like flames before being snuffed out by the harsh realities of our world.

With every mile, the atmosphere shifted. The stale scent of ash hung in the air, a constant reminder of the oppression we lived under. The Council's influence was pervasive, their eyes everywhere, always watching, always judging. But we were not alone; the rebellion was stirring, a flame flickering to life in the shadows. I felt a flicker of hope ignite within me, spurred by the promise of a collective fight for our freedom.

We rounded a bend, and suddenly, the road opened up to reveal a ragtag encampment nestled among the remnants of a once-bustling town square. Makeshift tents adorned with colorful fabrics swayed in the gentle breeze, and the low hum of conversation filled the air. It was a stark contrast to the bleakness we had traversed, a vibrant testament to resilience. As we stepped into the heart of this gathering, I felt an electric pulse of energy, a sense of belonging that wrapped around me like a warm blanket.

Before we could take in the scene, a figure broke through the throng—a tall, muscular man with a determined glint in his eyes. Jax, they called him, and he carried himself with an air of confidence that immediately drew me in. His hair was a wild tangle of dark curls, and beneath the scars that crisscrossed his sun-kissed skin lay the stories of countless battles fought for a cause larger than himself.

"Welcome, travelers!" Jax boomed, his voice like rolling thunder, reverberating through the square. "You've arrived at just the right time. The Flamewalkers need every spark we can muster against the Council's tyranny." His fierce spirit was contagious, igniting something deep within me. I could see why so many had flocked to him; he radiated strength, embodying the very essence of rebellion.

"Tell me you've come with news of the Emberstone," he pressed, his intense gaze boring into mine, searching for answers.

I exchanged a glance with Pyrax, who flared his nostrils as if sensing the gravity of our words. "We have a plan to retrieve it," I said, my voice steadier than I felt. "But we need your help. The journey won't be easy."

Jax nodded, his expression shifting from urgency to contemplation. "We've faced our share of battles, but the Council's grip tightens by the day. If the Emberstone can turn the tide, then we're all in. But we can't just sit idle while they tighten their hold. We need to strike first."

As he spoke, I felt the weight of my own fear and uncertainty slowly dissipate. This was not just about retrieving an artifact; it was about rekindling the flames of hope in a world dulled by oppression. I had seen too many friends and family suffer under the Council's rule, and the thought of their sacrifices spurred me on.

"Then let's rally the others," I suggested, my heart racing at the thought of uniting these brave souls. "Together, we can inspire more to join our cause."

With a determined nod, Jax whistled sharply, a sound that cut through the chatter like a blade. Almost instantly, a group of warriors emerged from the surrounding tents, their eyes alight with the fire of rebellion. They formed a semicircle around us, a living wall of strength and purpose. Each one bore the marks of their struggles—scars, tattoos, and expressions that spoke of both hope and defiance.

Among them, a woman stepped forward, her presence commanding and fierce. Elara, a healer, stood with an unwavering spirit that seemed to radiate warmth, a stark contrast to the grim surroundings. Her hair flowed like a waterfall of gold, catching the last rays of sunlight, illuminating the determination etched into her features.

"Are you the ones who carry news of the Emberstone?" she asked, her voice soothing yet firm. I could see the strength of her resolve behind her gentle demeanor.

"We are," I replied, feeling the weight of responsibility settle heavily upon my shoulders. "We believe it can be the catalyst we need to bring about change."

Elara's eyes sparkled with the promise of something more. "Then we will fight with you. We've trained, we've strategized, and we've lost too much to let the Ashen Council continue their reign unchallenged."

The atmosphere buzzed with anticipation as plans were set in motion. I felt a part of something greater than myself, a tapestry woven from the threads of each individual's hope and pain. We exchanged stories late into the night, forging bonds of camaraderie that would sustain us through the trials ahead. The flickering firelight danced in our eyes, illuminating the determination that coursed through our veins.

As the stars began to twinkle overhead, I found myself lost in the faces surrounding me. Each one was a warrior in their own right, fighting for a future unshackled from fear. Together, we would rise against the ashes, and I could feel the flame of rebellion begin to roar within my heart, ready to blaze a path toward Emberhold and beyond.

The air crackled with anticipation as Jax called for a meeting, the flames from the central bonfire dancing like fireflies against the twilight sky. I found myself sitting cross-legged on the hard earth, surrounded by an eclectic mix of rebels whose stories intertwined like the branches of ancient trees. Jax took the lead, his commanding presence captivating us all.

"We've heard whispers of a Council convoy carrying supplies and information," he began, his voice steady, drawing our attention like moths to a flame. "If we strike at the heart of their operations, we can disrupt their plans and prove that the Flamewalkers are still a force to be reckoned with."

Elara interjected, her eyes sparkling with enthusiasm. "We can use the cover of darkness. The council soldiers are wary but complacent. They think their power is absolute. We will show them otherwise." Her words stirred something within me, igniting a fire that resonated deeply. I thought of my friends who had suffered under the Council's iron rule, and I could feel their spirits lending me strength.

As the plan began to take shape, each rebel offered their unique skills. A wiry woman named Freya demonstrated her prowess with throwing knives, her hands moving with a grace that made the blades seem like mere extensions of her will. Nearby, a burly man named Thorin fashioned improvised weaponry from the scraps lying around, his booming laughter echoing through the camp. With every shared contribution, the camaraderie grew, a tapestry of determination woven together with threads of defiance.

The hours slipped by as we strategized, the light from the bonfire casting shadows that twisted and turned like the very rebellion we were planning. We laughed, shared stories, and for the first time in a long while, I felt a sense of belonging. These were not just survivors; they were warriors, each carrying the weight of their own stories, each a flicker of hope that could ignite a wildfire against the Council's tyranny.

As night deepened, I found myself alone for a moment, seeking solace by the edge of the encampment. The stars overhead were an ocean of distant lights, twinkling like diamonds scattered across a velvet blanket. I took a deep breath, letting the cool air fill my lungs, reminding myself of why I had embarked on this journey. Pyrax, sensing my turmoil, curled up beside me, his warmth a comforting presence.

"Do you think we can really make a difference?" I whispered, more to myself than to him. The weight of the Emberstone's significance loomed over me, a heavy crown I didn't yet know how to wear. The flame beneath Pyrax's fur flickered slightly, as if in response, igniting a spark of confidence in my heart.

Just then, Elara approached, her soft footsteps barely making a sound. "You've grown quiet," she remarked, her voice gentle but firm. "The road ahead is daunting, but it's filled with purpose. Remember, we fight not just for ourselves but for everyone who has suffered at the hands of the Council."

Her words resonated with me, like the final note of a haunting melody. "I know we need to act, but what if it all goes wrong? What if I fail?" I confessed, vulnerability slipping through my usually confident facade.

Elara smiled, a warm light in the darkness. "Failure is part of the journey. Each step, each struggle, teaches us. The important thing is to keep moving forward, no matter the outcome."

Her unwavering spirit inspired me, and I felt the confidence seep back into my bones. We were all imperfect, each with our scars, but together we formed a force that could rise against the oppressive shadows of the Ashen Council.

When dawn broke, the camp stirred with the energy of a thousand unlit fires. With the sun rising, casting a golden hue over everything, we gathered one last time to finalize our strategy. Jax laid out the details, his enthusiasm infectious. "We'll split into two groups," he explained. "One will create a diversion at the southern gate, while the other sneaks in from the north. Elara will lead the healing squad, ready to patch up anyone who needs it."

As Jax's plan unfolded, I felt a surge of adrenaline pumping through my veins. My heart raced, a drumbeat of rebellion matching the fervor of our cause.

"Where do I fit in?" I asked, a fire igniting in my belly.

"You're with me," Jax declared, a wicked grin splitting his face. "Your flames are the wild card we need. If anything goes awry, we'll need your power to give us an edge."

I could feel the weight of his faith in me, and with it came a fierce determination. I wasn't just a pawn in this game; I was a player, ready to set the board alight.

The sun climbed higher, transforming the landscape around us into a canvas of light and shadow. I could almost taste the anticipation on the air, a mixture of fear and excitement that tingled at the back of my throat. With our plan solidified, we set off, our hearts aligned with the rhythm of rebellion, and I could feel the tides of change beginning to swell around us.

As we moved through the familiar terrain of Emberhold, the tension was palpable. Each rustle of the leaves felt like a call to action, urging us to take that next step, to fight against the suffocating hold of the Council. The silhouettes of our ragtag team loomed larger as we approached the convoy, a testament to our resolve.

The first sign of trouble came when we spotted the guards, their faces blank masks of authority. My pulse quickened as we crouched behind a thicket, adrenaline coursing through me. "This is it," Jax murmured, his voice low. "Time to light the fire."

With my heart in my throat, I nodded, feeling the flames within me roar to life, ready to be unleashed upon those who sought to extinguish the light of rebellion. In that moment, I knew we were no longer just Flamewalkers; we were the torchbearers of a new dawn, poised to ignite a revolution.

As the signal for our strike drew closer, tension clung to the air like morning fog, heavy and charged. The sun, now a blazing orb above us, illuminated the dust swirling in the air, casting everything in hues of gold and shadow. I felt the heat of the moment pressing against my skin, urging me forward, a living reminder of the flames that simmered just beneath the surface.

Jax motioned for us to fall into formation. "Remember, distraction first, then we'll split up. Keep your focus. We're Flamewalkers. We burn brighter when we stand together." His words ignited a spark of confidence within me, emboldening my resolve.

As we crept closer to the convoy, the sound of clattering metal and gruff voices filled the air. A group of Council guards lounged by their supply wagon, their eyes scanning the horizon with the bored vigilance of those who had never experienced real danger. Their arrogance stoked my indignation. Did they really believe themselves untouchable?

"Ready?" Jax whispered, glancing at me. I could see the fire in his eyes—a mixture of defiance and determination. I nodded, feeling the power of Pyrax surging within me, ready to burst forth.

"Now!" Jax shouted.

In a heartbeat, chaos erupted. Jax led the charge, his fierce battle cry cutting through the air like a battle horn. I unleashed a torrent of flames, the fire spiraling from my fingertips like a serpent awakened from slumber. It danced in the air, illuminating the faces of the guards as they scrambled to react.

The flames didn't harm anyone, but the sheer spectacle sent a shockwave through their ranks, leaving them momentarily stunned. Smoke swirled, enveloping the guards, their panicked shouts mingling with the roar of the flames. Elara moved with the precision of a practiced healer, darting between us, her hands glowing with a soft light as she offered encouragement and a touch of warmth to those who faltered.

Freya and Thorin flanked Jax, using their unique skills to keep the guards off-balance. Freya's knives whistled through the air, finding their targets with deadly accuracy, while Thorin wielded a makeshift club, bellowing like a storm as he charged forward. The rebel warriors surged, inspired by the courage of our group.

In the midst of this glorious chaos, I felt my heart race, adrenaline coursing through my veins. With every flicker of flame I conjured, I could feel the collective spirit of our rebellion igniting.

As the guards regrouped, their surprise gave way to anger. "Put them down!" one shouted, his voice cracking with authority. I could see the glint of weapons being drawn, and for a moment, fear tightened around my chest. What if we had miscalculated?

But Jax's voice broke through, sharp and clear. "Flamewalkers, let them know we're not to be trifled with!"

Emboldened, I extended my arms, feeling the heat build at my fingertips, and released a wave of fire that curled into the sky, illuminating the darkening landscape. The flames twisted, forming shapes that danced and weaved, catching the eyes of the Council guards, distracting them long enough for Jax and the others to engage.

The world around me transformed into a frenetic ballet of fire and fury, each movement calculated and fierce. I felt the energy of my comrades wrapping around me like a warm embrace, our spirits intertwined in this fierce battle.

But the guards quickly regained their footing, forming a line of defense with shields raised high. They charged toward us, their faces masks of fury and disbelief, and the moment was upon us. Just as I prepared to launch another burst of flame, Elara darted beside me, her eyes bright with purpose.

"I can create an opening!" she shouted above the chaos. "Cover me!"

Nodding, I summoned my courage and directed a burst of fire toward the advancing guards. The flames spiraled, creating a wall of heat that forced them to hesitate. Elara seized the opportunity, her hands weaving through the air as she murmured an incantation. A shimmering barrier emerged, forming a protective dome around us, warding off the incoming attacks.

"Go!" Jax shouted, his voice filled with urgency. "We need to break through!"

With Elara's barrier shielding us, we charged forward, breaking through the line of guards. I felt like a wildfire unleashed, my flames flickering in tandem with the sparks of rebellion. I glanced back just in time to see Elara's barrier shatter under the onslaught of the guards' fury, but she stood strong, guiding the wounded to safety.

We burst into the heart of the convoy, surrounded by crates labeled with the Council's insignia. Jax and I pushed forward, frantically searching for what could tip the balance in our favor. "The Emberstone!" I shouted, my voice barely rising above the din of chaos. "It has to be here!"

A glint caught my eye—a massive chest, ornate and regal, sitting at the rear of the wagon. "There!" I cried, pointing it out to Jax.

As we rushed toward it, a figure emerged from the shadows, cloaked in dark robes that billowed like smoke. "You won't take it!" they hissed, a voice smooth and chilling. It was a member of the Ashen Council, their presence exuding an aura of power that sent a chill down my spine.

The figure raised a hand, and I felt an oppressive force wash over me, a cold wave threatening to extinguish the fire within. "You think you can challenge the Council? You are merely sparks in the grand scheme."

"Maybe so," I shot back, my voice steady despite the fear gnawing at my resolve. "But sparks can ignite a wildfire."

With that, I summoned the flames once more, pouring every ounce of strength into the fire swirling around me. It flared and surged, breaking through the Council member's dark influence, illuminating the shadows that threatened to consume us.

Jax leapt forward, drawing his weapon with a fierce determination. "We will take back what is ours!"

The confrontation erupted into a whirlwind of action. Jax clashed with the Council member, and I flung flames at their feet, creating a barrier that forced them to backpedal. Each strike reverberated in the air, a clash of ideals—freedom against oppression, hope against despair.

Amidst the chaos, I could hear Elara's voice, clear and melodic, urging the other rebels to press forward, rallying their spirits. "We are stronger together!" she shouted, her power invigorating our fight.

Finally, with one last push, we reached the ornate chest. My fingers brushed against the cool metal, and I could feel a pulsating warmth radiating from within. This was it—the Emberstone, the key to our rebellion, the hope we had fought for.

With a fierce determination, I lifted the lid, and a brilliant light spilled forth, illuminating the battlefield. The Emberstone shimmered with a fiery glow, its power palpable. I could feel it resonating with my own flames, a symphony of energy that surged through me.

The Council member staggered back, their eyes wide with shock. "No! This cannot be!"

"Watch us," I declared, my voice ringing with newfound strength.

I held the Emberstone high, and a wave of light cascaded outward, washing over the guards and dispelling their darkness. The flames danced to my command, swirling around us in a beautiful display of rebellion and courage.

In that moment, I realized we were no longer mere Flamewalkers—we were a wildfire, ready to consume the ashes of oppression and light the way for a new dawn. Together, we would forge our path, igniting hope and turning the tide against the Ashen Council. And as the flames roared and the Emberstone shone brightly, I knew this was only the beginning of our fight.

Chapter 7: Secrets Beneath the Ash

A low rumble echoed through the cavernous halls of the abandoned subway station, the sound of the city above me bustling with life while I stood in the dark, shadowed depths of a forgotten world. It was a realm where the air tasted of iron and soot, where the flickering fluorescent lights struggled against the encroaching darkness, casting erratic shadows that danced like specters on the cracked tiles. I could almost hear the echoes of old trains that had once rattled through these tunnels, their presence lingering like a memory I could almost grasp. The heat from the magma rivers outside hummed through the walls, a constant reminder of the fiery power that could consume everything in an instant, much like the Council itself.

Elara stood beside me, her vibrant auburn hair a fiery beacon against the dimness, framing her freckled face in a halo of warmth. I could feel the weight of her story pressing against my chest, a heavy burden she wore like armor. She had revealed the fate of her brother, taken by the Council during their last raid. Her anguish sparked something fierce within me, igniting a need not just to seek the Emberstone but to challenge the very foundation of the fear that gripped our world.

"Are you sure about this?" I asked, glancing back at the flickering lights overhead, the buzzing sound mingling with the low rumble of the earth beneath our feet. "It's not just a fortress; it's a prison for those they deem unworthy."

"Are you backing out?" Elara shot me a playful grin, her emerald eyes glinting like jewels in the gloom. There was a spark of mischief in her demeanor, an unyielding spirit that I admired. If I were to join this fight, it would take every ounce of that tenacity to succeed.

"Not a chance," I replied, feeling the fierce rush of determination coursing through my veins. "Let's just make sure we don't end up on the wrong side of their fiery moat."

With a shared glance of camaraderie, we stepped deeper into the bowels of the station, the ground shifting beneath our feet as we navigated through the rubble of old ticket counters and tattered advertisements that spoke of a bygone era. It felt oddly comforting, this blend of nostalgia and danger. Each step we took echoed the memories of those who had once traversed this very path, their laughter now swallowed by time and despair. I could almost hear their stories whispering through the air, urging me forward.

As we approached the old maintenance access, the air grew hotter, and the faint glow of lava illuminated the edges of the crumbling walls. I could feel the heat rising like an unseen tide, a reminder that our enemies were never far away. The Council was always vigilant, their eyes watching from the shadows, seeking any sign of rebellion. My heart raced, not only from fear but from the thrill of knowing we were stepping into the lion's den, fueled by a shared purpose and the ghosts of those who had come before us.

"Are you ready?" Elara asked, her voice steady despite the uncertainty swirling around us. The flickering lights above cast a soft glow on her face, highlighting the determination etched in her features.

"Ready as I'll ever be," I replied, my voice steady despite the tremor of anticipation in my stomach.

We crossed the threshold into the access tunnel, the air thick with dust and an unsettling silence that wrapped around us like a shroud. With each step, the world above faded into obscurity, replaced by the deep, throaty growl of the lava rivers outside. It was a reminder of the council's might, an ever-present force that sought to maintain order through fear and intimidation.

Elara's hand brushed against mine, and a spark of connection jolted through me. In that moment, the weight of her brother's absence and the burden of our mission crystallized into a single truth: we were not just searching for the Emberstone; we were embarking on a journey to reclaim hope. The bond between us strengthened as we moved forward, fueled by the knowledge that each step could bring us closer to both liberation and danger.

We reached the entrance to the Council's fortress, a monolith of obsidian stone that loomed above us, dark and foreboding against the backdrop of the molten rivers. The towering walls twisted and curled, much like the fear that consumed those within. I felt the presence of countless souls who had walked these paths, their hopes dashed against the cold stone.

"Look," Elara whispered, pointing toward the shimmering barriers that surrounded the fortress. The energy crackled in the air, a warning that felt palpable. "We need to find a way to neutralize those barriers."

"Is that even possible?" I asked, my voice barely a murmur, but inside, I was grappling with the enormity of what lay ahead.

"Anything is possible if you believe," she replied, her tone firm yet hopeful.

In that moment, I realized that belief wasn't just a fleeting thought; it was an ember of courage we could ignite together.

With determination sparking in my heart, I surveyed the fortress. "Let's find our way in and rescue your brother," I said, conviction sharpening my voice. Elara nodded, her eyes alight with the fervor of our shared mission.

The air buzzed with the electric energy of our purpose as we prepared to challenge the darkness that lay ahead. Together, we would navigate this treacherous labyrinth, fueled by hope and defiance, ready to confront whatever awaited us within those imposing walls.

The silence of the fortress was almost deafening as we slipped through the creaking door, its rusted hinges complaining like an old man disturbed from a long nap. Inside, the air was heavy with the scent of burnt earth and molten rock, an aroma that clung to my skin as if it were trying to pull me back into the shadows. Dimly lit corridors stretched out before us, their walls adorned with dark tapestries depicting the Council's triumphs, each thread woven with the whispers of the oppressed.

Elara moved with a quiet confidence, her nimble feet gliding over the cracked tiles as if she were familiar with the dance of danger. I followed closely, heart pounding a wild rhythm in my chest, a beat that seemed to resonate with the very stones around us. Every footfall echoed in the silence, a reminder that we were intruders in a world where trust was a luxury no one could afford.

"Stay close," she murmured, her voice barely above a whisper, yet it cut through the stillness like a dagger. Her eyes darted around, vigilant, and I could sense her anxiety wrapped tightly around her, a second skin that could easily be shed but wasn't.

As we crept deeper, the walls began to pulse with a strange energy, a dim glow that illuminated the shadows and played tricks on my mind. My thoughts danced back to the lives claimed by the Council, the innocent voices silenced beneath their iron grip. Each memory fueled my resolve, transforming my fear into a potent cocktail of anger and hope.

Suddenly, the ground trembled beneath us, a tremor that rattled the very bones of the fortress. I exchanged a quick glance with Elara, her expression a mixture of concern and fierce determination. "That's just the magma," she said, trying to mask her own apprehension with a brave smile, but I could see the tension in her shoulders.

"Right," I replied, a grin slipping onto my face. "Just a casual reminder that we're walking on a literal sea of lava. Nothing to worry about." It was meant to lighten the mood, to lift the weight pressing down on us, yet as I spoke, the gravity of our situation loomed ever larger.

We pressed on until we reached a narrow corridor where the flickering lights cast ominous shadows against the walls. I noticed faint markings etched into the stone, symbols that seemed to pulse with a life of their own. "What do you think these mean?" I asked, running my fingers over the strange grooves.

Elara studied them, her brow furrowing in thought. "They look like ancient runes. Maybe they're protective wards or a map of some kind?" Her voice was laced with curiosity, and I admired her ability to find intrigue in the danger surrounding us.

"Or a way to summon eldritch horrors," I added, my tone playfully ominous. "You know, the usual."

She rolled her eyes but couldn't suppress a smile. "Just focus on the mission, will you? We need to find your brother and the Emberstone before we wake anything up."

We continued down the corridor, the atmosphere thickening with every step we took, tension crackling in the air like static electricity. Just as I began to wonder how deep into the belly of the beast we could possibly go, a loud clang echoed behind us, sending both of us into an adrenaline-fueled frenzy.

"Elara!" I hissed, grabbing her arm and pulling her into a dark alcove just as heavy footsteps reverberated through the corridor. We pressed our backs against the cold stone wall, hearts racing like wild animals in the thicket.

Through the dim light, I could see figures approaching—Council guards clad in black armor, their faces obscured by menacing helmets that gleamed in the low light. They moved in perfect formation, their boots thudding in unison, creating a rhythm that matched the anxiety thumping in my chest. I could almost hear the collective heartbeat of the fortress as it thrummed around us.

"Are they looking for us?" Elara whispered, her breath hot against my ear.

"Probably," I replied, eyeing the guards with a mix of fear and fascination. "But let's hope they don't decide to check every dark corner."

We held our breath, adrenaline coursing through our veins, as the guards passed mere feet from our hiding spot. The air grew colder, heavy with unspoken threats and unyielding power. It felt like a game of cat and mouse, and the stakes couldn't have been higher.

Once the guards were a safe distance away, we emerged from our hiding place, adrenaline still buzzing in our veins. "That was too close," I muttered, rubbing my arms as if I could erase the lingering chill of fear.

"Closer than I'd like," Elara admitted, her expression darkening. "We can't afford to be caught. If they find us, they'll—"

"Let's not go there," I interjected, not wanting to entertain the grim possibilities. "We need to find a way to shut down those barriers first."

We pressed on, our hearts synchronized in their desperate rhythm, navigating a labyrinth of corridors that twisted and turned like the inner workings of a clock. The faint glow of the lava outside seeped through cracks in the walls, casting a warm light that felt almost inviting amid the oppressive atmosphere.

As we approached a large chamber, the glow intensified, illuminating an enormous stone pedestal at its center. On it lay a brilliant gemstone, radiant and pulsating with energy. It was the Emberstone, the very heart of the Council's power, surrounded by a shimmering barrier that hummed ominously.

"There it is," Elara breathed, her eyes wide with awe and fear. "But how do we get past that?"

Before I could respond, the ground shook violently, sending us staggering against the chamber's walls. Dust rained down from above, and the air thickened with an impending sense of doom. We needed to act, and we needed to act fast. With my heart pounding, I grabbed Elara's hand, determination hardening within me.

"We'll figure it out," I said, more to reassure myself than anything. "Together."

With our fears momentarily quelled by a shared sense of purpose, we stepped into the light, ready to confront whatever the Council had in store for us. The fortress might be a prison for many, but today, we would become the keys to unlock its chains, starting with the Emberstone glowing with promise before us.

The Emberstone radiated a mesmerizing glow, illuminating the chamber with an ethereal light that pulsed like a heartbeat, beckoning us closer. It sat atop the pedestal, ensconced in a web of shimmering energy that twisted and flickered like the flames of a dying fire. My gaze lingered on its surface, which shimmered in hues of crimson and gold, each reflection whispering tales of power and potential. But the vibrant allure masked the danger lurking beneath; that flickering barrier was not just a protective ward; it was a warning.

"Elara, do you see that?" I gestured toward the barrier, its shimmering surface undulating like the surface of a pond disturbed by a stone. "It looks like it's reacting to us."

"I think you're right," she said, stepping cautiously forward. "But if we get too close, we could set off alarms. We need to think this through."

Her brow furrowed in concentration, and I admired how her mind raced through possibilities, the wheels of logic turning beneath the surface of her resolve. If we had any hope of breaching this magical fortress, we needed a plan that was more nuanced than simply running up and hoping for the best.

I leaned against the cool stone wall, letting the chill seep into my bones as I observed the chamber. The intricate carvings on the walls depicted ancient battles, each warrior wielding weapons that crackled with energy similar to that of the Emberstone. It was as if the stories were alive, watching us with wary eyes, urging us to be cautious in our approach.

"What if we need to disable that barrier first?" I mused aloud. "There's bound to be a control panel or something nearby. This fortress can't run entirely on magic."

Elara nodded, her expression shifting from uncertainty to fierce determination. "You might be onto something. If we can find a control mechanism, we could disrupt the barrier long enough to grab the Emberstone."

The plan unfolded in my mind like a map leading us through an intricate maze, and with renewed purpose, we began to search the chamber. I moved to the far wall, tracing my fingers along the runes that flickered in the ambient light. The symbols seemed to breathe under my touch, warm and electric, as if sharing their secrets with me.

"Over here!" Elara called, her voice a mix of excitement and urgency. She pointed toward a hidden alcove behind the pedestal, where a series of levers and knobs glinted under the pulsating light.

I rushed to her side, peering into the dim recess. "Well, that looks promising," I said, feeling a thrill race through my veins. "Let's see if we can get it to work."

As we examined the controls, a series of diagrams etched into the wall caught my eye. They depicted a sequence of movements, a sort of dance that would bring the barrier down. "We need to pull these levers in a specific order," I deciphered, my fingers brushing against the engraved lines. "If we mess it up, who knows what could happen?"

"Let's hope it doesn't involve fiery death," Elara replied dryly, the ghost of a smile on her lips. "I'd prefer to escape this place with our skins intact."

Taking a deep breath to steady my racing heart, I nodded. "Okay, you take the left lever; I'll handle the right."

With a synchronized motion, we grasped the levers, bracing ourselves for the impact of whatever ancient magic we might unleash. "On three," I said, counting down in my head. "One... two... three!"

We pulled down hard, and the levers clicked into place, sending a surge of energy coursing through the room. The barrier flickered violently, illuminating the chamber with bursts of light, each pulse synchronized with our racing hearts. A low hum filled the air, vibrating through the ground beneath us, like the throaty growl of a slumbering beast.

"Elara, now!" I shouted, my voice barely cutting through the cacophony of sound. We dashed forward as the barrier sputtered, its flickering becoming more erratic, the vibrant glow fading to a dim shimmer.

With a final burst, the barrier collapsed, dissolving into a cascade of sparkles that danced like fireflies before disappearing into the air. The Emberstone pulsed brighter than ever, its light enveloping us in a warm embrace. I could feel the power radiating from it, a connection that thrummed in my veins, promising both salvation and chaos.

"Did we really just do that?" Elara whispered, awe mixing with disbelief in her voice.

"We did," I breathed, stepping closer to the pedestal, my heart racing with anticipation and fear. "Now all we need to do is grab it and get out before they realize we're here."

Elara edged forward, her fingers outstretched, but I hesitated, a sudden weight settling on my chest. "Wait! What if it's protected? We don't know the full extent of its power."

"Better safe than sorry," Elara agreed, looking at the stone with equal parts reverence and caution. "Let's be smart about this."

We scanned the chamber for any signs of traps or hidden dangers. Elara's eyes sparkled with determination as she grabbed a nearby cloth, laying it over the surface of the Emberstone to shield it from our touch. With a careful hand, she lifted it, the glow pulsating softly beneath the fabric, casting a warm light that felt like a heartbeat.

In that moment, everything seemed to slow down. The world around us faded, leaving only the stone and the shared understanding that we had to protect it at all costs. Just as she secured the stone in her grasp, the ground beneath us shook once more, sending vibrations racing through the chamber like the warning call of a predator.

"Elara, we need to move!" I shouted, grabbing her arm and pulling her toward the exit. The walls trembled, dust raining down like confetti in a twisted celebration of impending doom.

As we raced back through the corridor, our hearts thrumming in synchrony, I couldn't help but glance back at the Emberstone, now cradled safely in Elara's arms. We had achieved the impossible, but the path ahead was still fraught with peril. The guards would soon realize the stone was missing, and the fortress would come alive with chaos.

Bursting through the door, we plunged back into the bowels of the abandoned subway, the heat of the magma rivers embracing us like a furnace. The world outside felt like a strange, surreal dream—lava glistening in the dim light, the air thick with tension and possibility.

"Elara, do you know where we're going?" I panted, glancing around, the landscape a blur of shadows and heat.

"Follow me!" she yelled, her voice fierce and unwavering. "We can't let them corner us!"

We maneuvered through the tunnels, dodging debris and navigating treacherous paths, adrenaline coursing through our veins like fire. The echoes of our footsteps mingled with the distant roars of the lava, a symphony of survival that urged us onward.

With every twist and turn, the weight of the Emberstone seemed to grow heavier in Elara's arms, and I could sense the growing urgency in her movements. "I can feel it calling to me," she admitted, her voice barely a whisper, vulnerability peeking through her fierce exterior. "We need to understand its power; it's not just a weapon; it's a beacon of hope."

"Then let's make sure we protect it," I replied, gripping her shoulder as we paused for a moment, allowing ourselves to breathe. "We'll figure it out together."

As we continued our escape, the darkness felt less oppressive, and the fear that had once gnawed at the edges of my resolve now fueled my determination. We were not just survivors in this brutal world; we were warriors fighting for something greater than ourselves, carrying the flickering light of hope within us. And with every step, the fire of rebellion ignited in our hearts, ready to face whatever the Council would unleash upon us.

Chapter 8: Into the Lion's Den

The night was cloaked in darkness as we approached the Council's stronghold, flames illuminating the way like beacons. The flickering light danced on the ancient stone walls, casting elongated shadows that seemed to creep and slither, mirroring the trepidation in my heart. Each step I took felt heavier than the last, the weight of the shard nestled in my pocket—a small, pulsing ember of power—threatening to ignite at any moment. Its warmth seeped into my skin, a reminder of the stakes at hand, a heartbeat that synchronized with my own.

Ahead of me, the massive iron gates loomed, a forbidding visage etched with symbols of authority and dread. The air crackled with tension, and I could almost hear the echoes of the Council's whispered commands, chilling as they floated through the night. Each corner we turned brought with it the sense of being watched, an instinct honed through years of dodging danger. My heart raced, not solely from fear but from the thrill of rebellion coursing through my veins.

"Stick close," Eli murmured, his voice low and urgent as we navigated the labyrinthine streets of New York City, where the neon glow of nearby billboards clashed with the historical gravitas of our mission. The cacophony of honking cars and distant laughter painted a surreal contrast to our solemn endeavor. But there was no turning back now. I had joined the ranks of the desperate, my soul intertwined with those of the downtrodden, all united against the Council that had wielded power for too long.

Just as we reached the gates, an alarm blared—an earsplitting siren that ripped through the night like a jagged knife. Panic surged through our ranks, causing shadows to scatter like startled birds. The moment felt suspended in time, my mind racing as adrenaline coursed through me. "Go, go!" Eli shouted, urging us to move as the heavy clang of metal echoed ominously behind us.

We bolted toward the gates, the sound of boots pounding against the cobblestones filling the air. I could feel the heat of breath against my neck as I sprinted alongside Eli, my senses heightened, every detail sharper in this moment of chaos. The aroma of smoke and burnt wood filled the air, a pungent reminder of the fires that had been ignited by the Council's enforcers—fires meant to instill fear, to ward off those who dared to challenge their rule.

"Left!" Eli called, veering down an alleyway, the shadows swallowing us whole. We ducked behind an old, weather-beaten dumpster, the stench of refuse invading my senses. I pressed my back against the cold metal, my heart pounding in my ears. Eli's breath came in quick gasps beside me, the worry etched into his features contrasting sharply with the determination blazing in his eyes.

"They're onto us," I whispered, my voice barely audible over the alarm's persistent wail. "We have to move before they trap us."

"We're not going anywhere until we find a way inside," he replied, scanning the alley's mouth, where the orange glow of the flames flickered menacingly. "We need to get that shard to the Council's main chamber. It's the only way to bring them down."

I nodded, my mind racing. The shard was more than just a weapon; it was a key—a key that could unlock the chains binding our people. But the path to the Council's inner sanctum was fraught with danger. It felt like stepping into the lion's den, knowing that behind those walls lay the very beasts we sought to overthrow.

After a moment, Eli led the way, creeping along the damp bricks, each step deliberate. The world outside faded into a murmur as we focused on our next move. Shadows loomed large and threatening, the weight of every decision pressing upon us. I glanced down at the shard, its glow pulsing softly, a warm beacon against the darkness. It felt alive, thrumming with the energy of the past and the promise of a better future.

As we rounded a corner, a flicker of movement caught my eye—a figure emerging from the shadows. My heart leaped into my throat, a mix of fear and curiosity twisting inside me. The figure was cloaked, the fabric swallowing all light, leaving only the glimmer of piercing blue eyes visible. It was unlike anything I had seen, an ethereal presence that commanded respect.

"Are you here to join us or to betray?" the figure whispered, their voice a silken thread woven through the chaos.

"Join us," Eli replied, stepping forward. "We're taking down the Council."

The figure's eyes narrowed, assessing us. I held my breath, hoping our resolve was enough to convince them. "Then you will need this," they said, producing a small, intricately carved stone. "It will guide you to the heart of their power."

I reached for the stone, feeling its smooth surface, a cool touch against my palm. The warmth of the shard intensified, as if sensing a kindred spirit.

"Go quickly," the figure urged, their voice now urgent. "Time is not on your side."

As we slipped back into the shadows, the weight of destiny pressed down on us. The path ahead twisted with uncertainty, but one thing was clear: we were not alone. With each step, I felt the fire of rebellion reignite within me, forging a bond with those who dared to dream of a world unshackled from tyranny.

The shadows seemed to pulse around us as we sprinted deeper into the maze of the Council's stronghold. With each hurried step, I could feel the pulse of the shard in my pocket, a steady thrum echoing the rapid beat of my heart. The heavy iron gates loomed behind us, now a barrier separating us from our last moments of safety. I glanced over my shoulder, half-expecting to see the Council's enforcers barreling after us, their faces twisted with determination and malice.

Eli grabbed my arm, pulling me into a narrow alleyway lined with crumbling brick walls. The air was damp, the scent of moss and old secrets hanging thick like a fog. "We have to find a way inside," he urged, his breath coming out in quick, anxious bursts. "The longer we wait, the more likely they'll regroup."

"Right," I managed, my mind racing. "We need a distraction."

Without thinking, I pulled the shard from my pocket. Its glow brightened in the murky darkness, illuminating the graffiti-covered walls and the cracked pavement beneath our feet. Eli's eyes widened, a mix of awe and terror flickering across his face. "Are you out of your mind? You want to draw every enforcer in the city to us?"

"No," I replied, holding the shard up like a torch. "But this might be our best shot. If we can channel its energy just right, it could create a diversion. We need to buy some time."

"Alright," he said reluctantly, but there was a spark of excitement igniting in his eyes. "Just be careful."

Focusing on the shard, I felt its warmth spread through my fingers, a surge of energy flowing into my arms. The world around us faded, and I concentrated on drawing the power from within it. The air thickened, and a strange vibration reverberated through me, sending shivers down my spine. I visualized a wave of light bursting forth, a beacon that would draw attention away from our path.

With a flick of my wrist, I released the energy, watching as it exploded in a dazzling array of colors that lit up the night sky. The brilliance danced like fireworks, reflecting off the stone walls and setting the alley ablaze with luminescence. For a moment, it felt as if the entire city held its breath, captivated by the spectacle. Eli grasped my shoulder, his grip a mix of reassurance and urgency as the sound of distant shouts erupted, followed by the unmistakable thud of boots hitting the pavement.

"Let's move!" he shouted, pulling me further into the alley. We rushed forward, the glow of the shard still flickering behind us, drawing the attention of anyone who dared to chase. The sounds of confusion and panic echoed, punctuated by the rhythmic pulse of my heart, urging me onward.

We emerged onto a wider street, the sights and sounds of New York shifting around us. Bright lights flickered from nearby cafés, and the laughter of revelers spilled out onto the sidewalks, oblivious to the chaos unfolding just a few blocks away. The juxtaposition of joy against our desperate mission was surreal, like a film reel showing two entirely different worlds colliding.

"Over there," Eli pointed to a seemingly abandoned storefront, its windows darkened and boarded up. We slipped inside, the musty scent of dust and decay enveloping us like an old blanket. "This should give us a moment to catch our breath."

Inside, the silence was thick, broken only by the faint sound of our breathing. I leaned against the wall, sliding down to sit on the floor, my heart still racing from the thrill of our close call. Eli crouched beside me, his brow furrowed as he peered through a crack in the boarded-up window.

"What do you think they'll do?" I asked, feeling the shard's heat still radiating against my thigh, its power not yet spent.

"They'll send out search parties, maybe even check for any sign of us here," he replied, his voice steady despite the adrenaline coursing through him. "But we can't stay too long. We need to find a way into the Council's inner sanctum before they regroup."

I nodded, my mind racing with possibilities. "Do you think we could use the tunnels? I heard rumors they run underneath the city, connecting different districts. If we can find an entrance, we might be able to bypass the main gates altogether."

"That's a solid idea," Eli agreed, his eyes brightening. "But we have to be careful. Those tunnels are as dangerous as the Council itself. Who knows what kind of traps or patrols they have down there?"

"True," I said, my mind shifting to strategies. "But they also won't expect us to come from below. We need to be stealthy."

With our plan taking shape, I stood and moved to the back of the store, where a broken door led to a dimly lit corridor. The musty air grew colder as I stepped into the shadows, glancing back at Eli, who followed closely behind. We navigated through a maze of passageways, the distant echoes of the city above becoming muffled whispers.

Suddenly, we stumbled upon a rusted iron grate partially hidden behind a pile of discarded crates. Eli's eyes lit up. "This has to be it. If we can pry it open, it'll lead us to the tunnels."

I knelt, examining the rusted hinges, feeling the chill of the metal seep into my fingers. With a firm push, the grate groaned in protest, but slowly, it began to budge. With one final heave, it swung open, revealing a dark, gaping maw that seemed to beckon us forward.

"After you," Eli said, his voice dripping with mock formality.

"Charming," I retorted, feeling a thrill of anticipation as I glanced into the inky darkness. "But I think I'd prefer to be the first one in."

Taking a deep breath, I stepped into the tunnel, the cool air brushing against my skin like a ghostly caress. Eli followed, the grate clanging shut behind us with an ominous finality. As we moved deeper into the abyss, the walls seemed to close in, each step echoing into the void, a reminder of the danger we were courting in our quest to reclaim our freedom.

The tunnel was a world unto itself, each step echoing off the damp stone walls as we ventured further into the unknown. The air grew cooler, thick with the scent of earth and decay, as if we were stepping back in time to an age when secrets were buried and legends whispered through the darkness. Eli kept close, his hand brushing against the wall for balance, while I moved ahead, the shard nestled securely in my pocket, pulsing like a second heartbeat.

"What do you think these tunnels were used for?" I asked, my voice barely above a whisper as we rounded a corner. The dim light from the entryway faded, leaving us surrounded by shadows. "Smuggling? Hiding? Or maybe just a way for Council members to escape when things get dicey?"

Eli chuckled softly, the sound both reassuring and unnerving in the oppressive silence. "Given their taste for theatrics, I wouldn't be surprised if they staged grand exits through here, capes billowing behind them. You know, the usual villainous flair."

I smiled at the image, trying to lighten the heavy air. "Right, because what's a Council meeting without a bit of dramatic flair? 'Oh no, the rebels! Quick, to the secret escape hatch!'"

"Exactly!" Eli's eyes sparkled with mischief. "Perhaps we should try that tactic ourselves. A dramatic exit, cape optional."

But as we pressed on, the lightness faded, swallowed by the gloom. The corridor narrowed, forcing us into single file, and the walls began to glisten with moisture, almost as if they were weeping from the burden of the secrets they held. Each step echoed a question, a challenge: Were we truly ready for what lay ahead?

Suddenly, the path opened into a wider chamber, its ceiling lost in the darkness above. My breath caught as I took in the sight before us. Graffiti from long-forgotten movements decorated the walls, symbols of hope scrawled alongside the remnants of past failures. A mural of a lion, fierce and majestic, roared silently from one corner, its mane flowing like flames, a testament to the strength of those who had fought before us.

"This is incredible," I breathed, moving closer to study the artwork. "It's like a hidden history book."

Eli approached, peering over my shoulder. "Looks like we're not the first to use these tunnels for something other than running away."

He pointed to a small figure painted at the base of the lion—a young girl, eyes bright with determination. "This must have been a rallying point for rebels, a place to remember what they were fighting for."

A pang of recognition struck me. The girl's expression mirrored my own resolve, igniting a fire within me that I had almost forgotten in the shadows of our escape. "We're part of that legacy now," I said quietly, the weight of responsibility settling on my shoulders. "We have to honor them by finishing what they started."

Eli nodded, the playfulness replaced by sincerity. "Together, we will."

As we explored the chamber, a faint glimmer caught my eye. In the corner, partially obscured by a pile of debris, lay a trapdoor. I approached it, heart racing with anticipation. "Do you think this leads to the Council's main chamber?"

"Could be," Eli replied, brushing away the dust. "Only one way to find out."

With a heave, we managed to pry it open, revealing a narrow staircase that descended into deeper darkness. The air grew even colder, a shiver racing up my spine. The anticipation was electric, like standing on the precipice of a storm.

"Ready?" I asked, glancing back at Eli, whose expression was a mixture of excitement and fear.

"Always," he replied, and together we ventured down the staircase, the air growing thicker with each step. The darkness wrapped around us, a heavy cloak that obscured our surroundings. I could barely make out the steps beneath my feet, relying on instinct and the faintest hints of light filtering through the cracks.

At the bottom, the staircase opened into a long, dimly lit corridor, flickering torches illuminating ancient stone walls. The atmosphere crackled with tension, the very air seeming to vibrate with the weight of unspoken histories. I paused, listening intently, straining to catch any sounds that might betray our presence.

"Do you hear that?" I whispered, the hairs on my arms standing on end.

Eli nodded, his expression serious. "Voices. We're close."

We crept forward, staying low and pressed against the wall. As we approached a large archway, the voices grew clearer, echoing through the corridor. I could hear snippets of conversation—urgent, tense, each word dripping with authority and menace.

"—prepare the enforcers. They'll come for the shard, and we cannot let them through—"

"—the council will not stand for rebellion. We must eliminate them—"

My stomach twisted at the implications. They were planning a crackdown, a purge of anyone who dared challenge their authority. A flash of anger ignited within me, fueling my determination to end their reign of terror.

"What's the plan?" Eli asked quietly, his eyes scanning the room beyond the archway.

"First, we find a way to get the shard to the heart of their power," I said, already mapping out the possible paths in my mind. "Then we expose their lies."

"Do you think we can make it past the guards?" he asked, concern threading through his tone.

I smirked, feeling the warmth of the shard's energy thrumming in my pocket. "Oh, I have a few tricks up my sleeve."

With a deep breath, I pushed my way through the archway, peeking into the chamber beyond. The scene that unfolded before us was one of chaos dressed in elegance: Council members gathered around a large stone table, their faces illuminated by the flickering torches. Maps and documents littered the surface, a tapestry of plots woven into the very fabric of their power.

"Now!" I whispered, heart pounding as I gestured for Eli to follow. We darted inside, slipping behind a cluster of ornate pillars that framed the room like sentinels, our presence unnoticed amid the Council's fervor.

The air hummed with tension, each word a thread weaving the fabric of their machinations. I felt the shard's heat against my thigh, urging me forward as I listened to their schemes, plotting the downfall of those who dared to dream of freedom.

"We'll deploy the enforcers at dawn," one of the Council members proclaimed, his voice booming with authority. "Those rebels think they can hide in the shadows, but we will bring them into the light—into the lion's den."

The phrase sent a shiver through me, igniting a fierce resolve. They saw us as prey, mere obstacles in their grand narrative. But we were more than that. We were the spark that would ignite a revolution, the echo of those who had come before, and I could feel the weight of their hopes resting on my shoulders.

As the meeting unfolded, I exchanged a glance with Eli, who nodded imperceptibly, understanding my unspoken plan. I could feel the shard's energy coursing through me, a rising tide of power that surged as I prepared to act. We were not just rebels; we were the storm on the horizon, ready to break through the Council's façade and expose their true nature.

And with a deep breath, I stepped out from the shadows, ready to unleash the power within me, determined to turn the tide of this battle once and for all.

Chapter 9: The Inferno Unleashed

The world shimmered in the blazing heat of the chaos, a backdrop of swirling reds and oranges as the very air crackled with energy. I could feel the pulse of the shard nestled deep within me, a wild heartbeat that syncopated with my own, as though it had come alive in response to my fear and desperation. The inferno danced at my fingertips, flames licking the air, shimmering like molten gold against the darkened sky. Each flicker of light cast long shadows, revealing the jagged edges of debris strewn about like forgotten relics of a once-peaceful square.

The streets of New Orleans, once alive with the music of jazz and laughter, now echoed with the cacophony of clashing bodies and desperate shouts. I could taste the coppery tang of adrenaline mixed with the unmistakable scent of smoke and singed fabric. A Council enforcer, broad-shouldered and fierce, loomed over Jax, who was crouched defensively against the rough brick wall of a crumbling building, his wide eyes reflecting both fear and determination. My heart raced as I pushed through the throng of bodies, the flickering shadows forming a protective cocoon around me.

"Jax!" My voice sliced through the chaos, sharp and urgent. I barely recognized it as my own, the sound barely masking the dread bubbling in my chest. I was fueled by an instinctive need to protect him, this boy who had become an unexpected ally amidst the turmoil. Flames leapt to life around me, a halo of crimson and gold that spread like wildflower blooms in a forgotten meadow. The shard thrummed with energy, urging me forward as I approached the enforcer, a giant of a man who looked as if he had stepped straight out of a nightmare.

I concentrated, feeling the fiery tendrils wrapping around my palms. With a flick of my wrist, I sent a burst of flames cascading toward the enforcer, each spark a blazing star born from my will. The fire ignited the air between us, a brilliant display that illuminated the darkening twilight. My emotions flooded the space: rage, fear, the intoxicating thrill of power. The flames collided with the enforcer, enveloping him in a blinding inferno. For a split second, I saw surprise flicker across his features before he staggered back, allowing me the precious moment I needed.

"Come on!" I yelled at Jax, and without waiting for him to respond, I dashed toward him. The heat from the flames tingled against my skin, but the exhilaration coursing through me drowned out any pain or fear. The shard pulsed with delight, harmonizing with the chaos of the moment, as though it thrived on the intensity of the situation. The enforcer, seething with fury, began to recover, his eyes narrowing on me, and in that instant, I knew I had to move faster.

Jax scrambled to his feet, his expression a mix of awe and bewilderment. "What did you just do?" he breathed, eyes wide as he took in the swirling flames. I could see the wonder in his gaze, the realization dawning on him that I was no ordinary girl caught up in this nightmare.

"It's the shard!" I gasped, adrenaline pushing the words out of me in a rush. "It gives me power, and I need to use it to—" My words were cut off as the enforcer lunged forward, anger radiating off him like heat waves on a scorching summer day.

With a sharp intake of breath, I summoned the energy within me, channeling it through my veins like a river bursting its banks. "Not today!" I shouted, raising my hands to direct a torrent of flames toward the enforcer once more. This time, the flames danced with even greater ferocity, illuminating the alleyway like a sun rising in the east, casting a warm glow over the fear that gripped my heart.

The enforcer stumbled back again, swatting at the fire, but I didn't give him a moment to regain his footing. I rushed past Jax, a living beacon of warmth and fury, and I could feel the strength of my emotions coursing through me, shaping the flames into a shield that surged around us. "We need to get out of here!" I urged, my voice urgent as I turned to face Jax. "This way!"

We dashed down the alley, the air thick with smoke and the sounds of conflict fading behind us, replaced by the rhythmic pounding of our footsteps on the cobblestones. My heart hammered in time with the adrenaline flooding my veins, a pulsing reminder of the danger still lurking in the shadows.

The narrow passage opened up into a larger street, where the remnants of a vibrant festival lay scattered—a tapestry of forgotten dreams interwoven with the chaos of the present. Colorful streamers hung limply from the remnants of booths, their bright hues dulled by the ash swirling through the air. I could almost hear the ghostly echoes of laughter and music, a haunting reminder of what had been.

As we skidded to a halt, I glanced back, searching for the enforcer, and my stomach twisted at the thought of what awaited us. A part of me felt invincible, but another was all too aware of the dangers we faced. The ember in my heart flickered, reminding me that while I had power, I was still just a girl thrust into a world far more dangerous than I had ever imagined.

"Do you have a plan?" Jax's voice broke through the haze of my thoughts, grounding me in the moment. His gaze flickered with hope and fear, a mixture that tugged at my heartstrings.

I took a deep breath, feeling the warmth of the shard seep into my bones, and I nodded. "We just need to keep moving. I can create a diversion."

With a determined smile, I stepped forward, ready to unleash the fire within me once more, the flicker of the ember guiding my every move as we prepared to dive deeper into the inferno that awaited us.

The street stretched out before us, a labyrinth of shadows and flickering lights that teased the edges of safety. My heart raced, a persistent drumbeat matching the pulse of the shard nestled within my core. Flames still danced at my fingertips, but I could feel the weight of exhaustion beginning to settle in. A glance at Jax revealed that he was no stranger to fear; the intensity in his eyes mirrored my own, filled with determination and just a hint of wonder as we maneuvered through the wreckage of the festival.

"Do you know where we're headed?" he asked, casting furtive glances over his shoulder, as if expecting the enforcer to burst from the shadows at any moment. I couldn't blame him; the city had a way of morphing into a living entity, one that thrived on secrets and shadows, and right now, it felt alive with danger.

I shook my head, my mind racing to conjure up a plan. "We need to find a place to regroup, somewhere we can catch our breath and think." A flash of inspiration struck, and I nodded toward the vibrant remnants of the festival. "The old community center should be just down this street. They'll have something we can use—supplies, maybe even an exit."

"Sounds good to me." Jax nodded, determination etching deeper lines into his youthful face. Together, we hurried down the street, the distant sounds of chaos still echoing behind us, a reminder of the precarious nature of our situation.

The community center loomed ahead, a charming old building with ivy creeping up its weathered facade, its bright blue paint peeling like sunburnt skin. It had been a place of laughter and connection once, a heartbeat of the neighborhood, but now it stood as a sanctuary amid the turmoil. I could only hope it still held the warmth of community within its walls.

As we approached, I could see that the doors were ajar, a silent invitation that felt both comforting and ominous. "Ready?" I whispered, feeling the warmth of the shard flare to life within me. Jax met my gaze, a fire ignited in his eyes, and we pushed through the doors together.

The interior was a whirlwind of faded murals and forgotten memories. Old photographs lined the walls, depicting the bustling community that had once thrived here. Now, the air was thick with dust and the musty scent of neglect, the only sound our soft footsteps echoing off the linoleum floor. It was a stark contrast to the chaos outside, but the stillness was a welcome respite.

"Okay, we need to find supplies," I said, my voice barely above a whisper. "First aid, food, anything we can use." Jax nodded, scanning the room as we moved further in.

There was a kitchenette in the back, its countertops littered with remnants of community potlucks, now abandoned and forgotten. My heart sank a little at the sight of the empty coffee pot and the scattered plates. I reached for a cupboard, yanking it open to find it filled with mismatched plastic cutlery and paper napkins. Useful, but hardly the armory we needed.

"Over here!" Jax called from across the room, his voice breaking through the silence like a beacon. I turned to find him rummaging through a large storage bin labeled "Emergency Supplies." My heart soared as I joined him, our fingers dancing over the assortment of items. We pulled out flashlights, first-aid kits, and even a few granola bars that had miraculously survived the test of time.

"Looks like we hit the jackpot," Jax said, his smile infectious as he held up a half-eaten granola bar. I couldn't help but laugh, the tension momentarily lifting as I snatched it from his hands.

"Hey, finders keepers!" I grinned, tearing open the wrapper and taking a bite. The sweet, nutty flavor was a small slice of normalcy amidst the chaos, a reminder that even in the darkest moments, there could be light.

Just then, a low rumble shook the building, sending vibrations through the floor. I felt my heart plummet as the sound grew louder, a reminder that our time was limited. "We need to hurry," I said, hastily stowing the supplies into a backpack. "Let's find a way out."

Jax nodded, and together we navigated the labyrinth of forgotten corners and dusty rooms. We ducked through doorways and around stacks of old chairs, every creak of the floorboards echoing our urgency. The thrill of survival sharpened my senses, the danger pressing against us like the hot breath of a beast lurking just out of sight.

Finally, we found a back exit, a narrow door leading out to an alleyway. I paused for a moment, glancing back at the remnants of the community center—the laughter that had once echoed here, the joy that had filled the air. But there was no time for sentiment. I pushed the door open and stepped into the alley, Jax close behind me.

The alley was cloaked in shadows, but it was a path toward freedom. My instincts kicked in, and I led the way, my senses honed to pick up every sound, every flicker of movement. The air felt electric, charged with the remnants of my flames and the fear still hanging thick in the atmosphere.

As we emerged onto a busier street, the world opened up, revealing a mosaic of life unfolding around us. Vendors called out to passersby, their voices bright against the backdrop of the distant chaos. The air was fragrant with the scent of beignets and fresh coffee, the sounds of laughter and music swirling around us like a warm embrace.

But that warmth was deceptive. I could see the fear flickering behind the eyes of the crowd, the way they moved with urgency, as if they sensed the storm gathering just beyond the horizon. I felt it too, a storm of our own making, ready to break loose and consume everything in its path.

"Where do we go now?" Jax asked, his voice cutting through the fog of my thoughts.

I glanced at him, taking in the determination etched into his features. "We need to regroup with the others. We can't face the Council alone."

The shards of the emberstone within me flickered, a reminder that my strength was intertwined with those I fought beside. It was time to rally our allies and prepare for the battles to come. I took a deep breath, drawing on the warmth of the flame inside me as I scanned the street for signs of our friends.

"Let's find them," I said, my voice steady as I led the way into the fray, the emberstone burning bright with the promise of hope and rebellion against the encroaching darkness.

The vibrant chaos of the street enveloped us as we plunged deeper into the thrumming heart of the city, the air electric with urgency and the aroma of beignets lingering like a promise. People moved past us, their expressions flickering between excitement and alarm, the joyous shouts of vendors blending with the distant thrum of a jazz band. It was as if the city itself was caught in a surreal dance, one foot in celebration, the other teetering precariously on the edge of panic.

"Where do we even start looking?" Jax asked, glancing around as we pressed forward. The street was alive with life, but our focus was razor-sharp, a counterpoint to the carnival atmosphere that surrounded us. My eyes swept the crowd, searching for familiar faces—those who had stood beside us in this fight against the Council.

"There!" I pointed toward a nearby courtyard, where a small group huddled beneath the shade of a sprawling oak tree, its leaves shimmering like emeralds against the warm, golden sun. I recognized them instantly: Zoe, with her fierce green eyes and a wild mane of curly hair, was gesturing animatedly, while Oliver leaned against a weathered wall, his brow furrowed in concern.

As we rushed toward them, my heart pounded with relief and urgency. They turned to us, expressions shifting from worry to hope as we approached. "You made it!" Zoe exclaimed, her voice breaking through the noise. "We were starting to think—"

"No time for that now!" I interrupted, my adrenaline still coursing. "The Council is on our heels. We need to strategize and move."

Oliver nodded, his face serious. "We've been trying to figure out our next steps. The Council is tightening its grip on the city. We need to get to the underground meeting place before they seal it off."

"Underground?" Jax echoed, eyebrows raised in curiosity.

"Yeah," Zoe explained, her voice lowering conspiratorially. "There's a network of tunnels beneath the city—old catacombs from before the city was built up. Some of us have been using them to avoid detection."

"Why don't we just fight them?" I asked, the fiery essence of the shard buzzing within me, yearning for action. The thought of standing idle while the Council prowled felt unbearable.

"Because it's not just about fighting; it's about surviving this," Oliver replied, his tone firm yet understanding. "We need a plan that allows us to regroup and gather more allies. A head-on confrontation would be suicide."

The weight of his words settled over us like a heavy fog, the reality of our predicament crystallizing in the afternoon light. I took a breath, feeling the flames simmering just beneath my skin, a reminder that while I craved the fight, strategy was paramount.

"Okay," I relented, glancing at Jax, who nodded, understanding the unspoken agreement between us. "Let's head to the tunnels, then."

Zoe led the way through a narrow passage that seemed to swallow us whole, the comforting cacophony of the street fading as we delved deeper into the shadows. The air turned cooler, tinged with the earthy scent of damp stone and old memories, and I felt a thrill at the thought of stepping into the forgotten underbelly of the city.

The tunnel opened up into a dimly lit chamber, its walls rough-hewn and ancient. Flickering candles cast dancing shadows, revealing a ragtag assembly of our fellow rebels gathered around a makeshift table. Maps were spread out like spider webs, and the low murmur of conversation hummed in the air, punctuated by the occasional clatter of someone shifting in their seat.

"Look who's back!" called out Marcus, his voice laced with relief as he spotted us. "You two are like cockroaches—impossible to squash!"

Jax chuckled, the tension in his shoulders easing. "Just call us resilient."

I felt a rush of gratitude for this motley crew, a group bound together not just by a common enemy but by the shared conviction that they would fight for a better world. As we settled in, I realized how vital these connections were; they were the true essence of my power, more significant than any flame I could conjure.

"We need to discuss the next steps," Marcus said, spreading a map across the table. "The Council is moving quickly, and we need to outsmart them. We have allies on the other side of the river who can help us."

I leaned in, tracing the paths with my finger, already formulating strategies. "What about a diversion? If we could create enough chaos at the main Council building, we could draw their forces away while we make our move."

"Creating chaos isn't the problem; it's controlling it," Zoe countered, her brow furrowed as she considered the implications. "If we set off any more flames like last time, we might draw even more attention to ourselves."

"We have to make it worthwhile," I replied, my determination flaring to life. "We need something big, something that'll get the Council's full attention."

Oliver nodded slowly, a thoughtful expression crossing his face. "What if we staged a false attack? Something small enough to seem legitimate but grand enough to distract them from our actual mission?"

"Like a phantom threat," Jax said, enthusiasm creeping into his voice. "We could use fireworks, maybe set off some smoke bombs. They wouldn't know what hit them."

The excitement in the room grew palpable, an electric current surging through our group as ideas began to flow. I could feel the emberstone inside me responding, the flame of creativity igniting, swirling with the potential of what we could accomplish together.

"Let's set a timeline," Marcus declared, his voice cutting through the buzz of excitement. "If we can coordinate our efforts, we'll have the Council chasing shadows while we make our escape."

We quickly organized ourselves, assigning roles and responsibilities, the atmosphere alive with urgency and camaraderie. I felt a swell of pride and purpose as I worked alongside my friends, plotting our course and finding strength in our unity.

As the final details fell into place, I glanced around at their determined faces, their trust in me palpable. This wasn't just a fight for survival; it was a fight for our very existence, for the freedom we so desperately sought. And the emberstone within me flickered in rhythm with the fire of our resolve, promising that we would not go quietly into the night.

"Alright, everyone," I said, my voice steady. "Let's show them what we're made of."

With a collective nod, we set our plan into motion, hearts and minds united in a shared purpose. The flames of rebellion burned brightly within us, a beacon of hope that would light the way through the encroaching darkness. As we prepared to unleash our fury upon the Council, I could feel the strength of our bonds surging alongside the shard's power, a testament to the resilience and courage that lay within us all.

Chapter 10: The Flamekeeper's Legacy

The vibrant chaos of the street enveloped us as we plunged deeper into the thrumming heart of the city, the air electric with urgency and the aroma of beignets lingering like a promise. People moved past us, their expressions flickering between excitement and alarm, the joyous shouts of vendors blending with the distant thrum of a jazz band. It was as if the city itself was caught in a surreal dance, one foot in celebration, the other teetering precariously on the edge of panic.

"Where do we even start looking?" Jax asked, glancing around as we pressed forward. The street was alive with life, but our focus was razor-sharp, a counterpoint to the carnival atmosphere that surrounded us. My eyes swept the crowd, searching for familiar faces—those who had stood beside us in this fight against the Council.

"There!" I pointed toward a nearby courtyard, where a small group huddled beneath the shade of a sprawling oak tree, its leaves shimmering like emeralds against the warm, golden sun. I recognized them instantly: Zoe, with her fierce green eyes and a wild mane of curly hair, was gesturing animatedly, while Oliver leaned against a weathered wall, his brow furrowed in concern.

As we rushed toward them, my heart pounded with relief and urgency. They turned to us, expressions shifting from worry to hope as we approached. "You made it!" Zoe exclaimed, her voice breaking through the noise. "We were starting to think—"

"No time for that now!" I interrupted, my adrenaline still coursing. "The Council is on our heels. We need to strategize and move."

Oliver nodded, his face serious. "We've been trying to figure out our next steps. The Council is tightening its grip on the city. We need to get to the underground meeting place before they seal it off."

"Underground?" Jax echoed, eyebrows raised in curiosity.

"Yeah," Zoe explained, her voice lowering conspiratorially. "There's a network of tunnels beneath the city—old catacombs from before the city was built up. Some of us have been using them to avoid detection."

"Why don't we just fight them?" I asked, the fiery essence of the shard buzzing within me, yearning for action. The thought of standing idle while the Council prowled felt unbearable.

"Because it's not just about fighting; it's about surviving this," Oliver replied, his tone firm yet understanding. "We need a plan that allows us to regroup and gather more allies. A head-on confrontation would be suicide."

The weight of his words settled over us like a heavy fog, the reality of our predicament crystallizing in the afternoon light. I took a breath, feeling the flames simmering just beneath my skin, a reminder that while I craved the fight, strategy was paramount.

"Okay," I relented, glancing at Jax, who nodded, understanding the unspoken agreement between us. "Let's head to the tunnels, then."

Zoe led the way through a narrow passage that seemed to swallow us whole, the comforting cacophony of the street fading as we delved deeper into the shadows. The air turned cooler, tinged with the earthy scent of damp stone and old memories, and I felt a thrill at the thought of stepping into the forgotten underbelly of the city.

The tunnel opened up into a dimly lit chamber, its walls rough-hewn and ancient. Flickering candles cast dancing shadows, revealing a ragtag assembly of our fellow rebels gathered around a makeshift table. Maps were spread out like spider webs, and the low murmur of conversation hummed in the air, punctuated by the occasional clatter of someone shifting in their seat.

"Look who's back!" called out Marcus, his voice laced with relief as he spotted us. "You two are like cockroaches—impossible to squash!"

Jax chuckled, the tension in his shoulders easing. "Just call us resilient."

I felt a rush of gratitude for this motley crew, a group bound together not just by a common enemy but by the shared conviction that they would fight for a better world. As we settled in, I realized how vital these connections were; they were the true essence of my power, more significant than any flame I could conjure.

"We need to discuss the next steps," Marcus said, spreading a map across the table. "The Council is moving quickly, and we need to outsmart them. We have allies on the other side of the river who can help us."

I leaned in, tracing the paths with my finger, already formulating strategies. "What about a diversion? If we could create enough chaos at the main Council building, we could draw their forces away while we make our move."

"Creating chaos isn't the problem; it's controlling it," Zoe countered, her brow furrowed as she considered the implications. "If we set off any more flames like last time, we might draw even more attention to ourselves."

"We have to make it worthwhile," I replied, my determination flaring to life. "We need something big, something that'll get the Council's full attention."

Oliver nodded slowly, a thoughtful expression crossing his face. "What if we staged a false attack? Something small enough to seem legitimate but grand enough to distract them from our actual mission?"

"Like a phantom threat," Jax said, enthusiasm creeping into his voice. "We could use fireworks, maybe set off some smoke bombs. They wouldn't know what hit them."

The excitement in the room grew palpable, an electric current surging through our group as ideas began to flow. I could feel the emberstone inside me responding, the flame of creativity igniting, swirling with the potential of what we could accomplish together.

"Let's set a timeline," Marcus declared, his voice cutting through the buzz of excitement. "If we can coordinate our efforts, we'll have the Council chasing shadows while we make our escape."

We quickly organized ourselves, assigning roles and responsibilities, the atmosphere alive with urgency and camaraderie. I felt a swell of pride and purpose as I worked alongside my friends, plotting our course and finding strength in our unity.

As the final details fell into place, I glanced around at their determined faces, their trust in me palpable. This wasn't just a fight for survival; it was a fight for our very existence, for the freedom we so desperately sought. And the emberstone within me flickered in rhythm with the fire of our resolve, promising that we would not go quietly into the night.

"Alright, everyone," I said, my voice steady. "Let's show them what we're made of."

With a collective nod, we set our plan into motion, hearts and minds united in a shared purpose. The flames of rebellion burned brightly within us, a beacon of hope that would light the way through the encroaching darkness. As we prepared to unleash our fury upon the Council, I could feel the strength of our bonds surging alongside the shard's power, a testament to the resilience and courage that lay within us all.

The distant sound of sirens wailed like a banshee on the wind, urging us to move faster. Jax, still catching his breath, glanced at me, his expression a mix of awe and determination. "What was that back there?" he asked, his voice low, almost reverent. I shrugged, though inside, a tempest of thoughts swirled. I had never meant to unleash whatever that was, that surge of fire and fury that had leapt from my fingertips, a flame born from something deeper than mere instinct.

The Emberstone pulsed against my skin, a steady thrum that felt like the heartbeat of the city itself. I could almost hear the whispers of those who had wielded its power before me, brave souls who had battled shadows lurking in the corners of forgotten alleys. The weight of their legacy pressed upon my shoulders, both a gift and a burden. It was a reminder that with great power came the responsibility to protect—not just ourselves, but all those unaware of the darkness creeping closer.

We rounded a corner, slipping into the shelter of a narrow street where the flickering light of a neon sign cast eerie shadows against the cracked pavement. I glanced back, half-expecting to see pursuers with flames in their eyes, hungry for vengeance. Instead, the street lay silent, save for the distant hum of the city. "Do you think they'll follow?" Jax murmured, scanning the darkness like a hawk searching for prey.

"Let them try," I replied, feeling a spark of defiance flare up within me. "I've got something to fight for now." The truth was, I didn't just want to survive; I wanted to uncover the truth of my lineage and protect those who could not protect themselves. As the weight of my newfound resolve settled within me, I knew there was no turning back.

We continued down the street, our feet quickening with each passing moment. I felt the Emberstone in my pocket vibrating with urgency, almost as if it sensed the unfolding destiny that awaited us. But the shadows weren't just remnants of the night; they felt alive, shifting and writhing, as if eager to swallow us whole.

Jax glanced sideways at me, his brow furrowed. "What's the plan, then?" he asked. It was a fair question, and I found myself searching for an answer as we stepped into the dim light of a nearby café. The warm glow of the interior was inviting, a sharp contrast to the chill outside.

"First, we need information. We can't fight what we don't understand," I replied, scanning the café for familiar faces. I spotted Cassie, the local barista, wiping down the counter with a distracted air. She was no ordinary barista; her blue-streaked hair and the tattoo of a phoenix on her wrist hinted at secrets beneath her friendly smile. I knew she had connections—people who were as much a part of the city's fabric as the brick and mortar that surrounded us.

"Let's talk to Cassie," I said, leading Jax toward the counter. She looked up as we approached, her eyes widening momentarily before narrowing with concern. "You two look like you've just run from a fire," she remarked, her voice light but laced with genuine worry.

"Something like that," I replied, leaning in closer, my voice low. "We need your help. It's important." I could see the wheels turning in her mind as she weighed our words.

Cassie hesitated, then nodded, leading us to a small booth in the back, away from prying eyes. "Okay, spill. What happened?"

I recounted the events with breathless urgency—the explosion, the fire, the awakening of my powers. Jax chimed in, adding his perspective, and soon the café felt alive with our shared energy. Cassie listened intently, her expression shifting from surprise to understanding, a flicker of recognition sparking in her eyes.

"Have you ever heard of the Flamekeepers?" she asked, her voice barely above a whisper.

"Only in stories," I admitted, feeling a surge of excitement as the name resonated within me. "What do you know?"

"They were protectors, guardians of the Emberstone, passed down through generations. They fought to keep the balance between light and dark." Cassie leaned back, crossing her arms. "But their numbers dwindled, and the Emberstone was lost for a time. You've awakened something, haven't you? It's no coincidence."

The weight of her words hung heavy in the air. I glanced at Jax, whose eyes mirrored my own uncertainty. "So what does that mean for us?" he asked.

"It means you're not just fighting for yourselves. You're stepping into a legacy," Cassie explained, her gaze intense. "And with that comes the responsibility to gather others, to unite the Flamekeepers once more. The darkness is awakening, and it's looking for its own champions."

A chill ran down my spine at her words. The thought of rallying others—of becoming part of something larger than myself—filled me with both dread and exhilaration. "But how do we find them?" I asked, my voice barely above a whisper.

Cassie smiled, a flicker of mischief in her eyes. "You start by looking for the sparks. The ones who feel different, who sense something in the air. They might not even know what they are yet."

We left the café with a sense of purpose ignited within us, the Emberstone humming in resonance with our resolve. It was time to embrace the flamekeeper's legacy, to seek out those who would stand with us against the coming storm. The night was far from over, and our journey had just begun.

As we stepped into the cool night air, Jax turned to me, his expression fierce. "Let's find our team, then," he said, determination etched on his face. "I'm ready to light the way."

I nodded, a grin breaking through the tension. Together, we stepped into the shadows, not as victims of fate, but as warriors ready to reclaim the light. Each step echoed the promise of a legacy waiting to be ignited, a fire that would burn bright against the encroaching darkness. The city whispered its secrets, and we would uncover them, one flame at a time.

The city felt alive with possibilities, each flicker of streetlights casting shadows that danced like phantoms against the weathered brick walls. As Jax and I traversed its maze-like streets, the weight of our mission hung heavy in the air, a promise entwined with the lingering scent of smoke and ash. Every step took us deeper into the heart of the urban sprawl, a realm where the mundane met the extraordinary, and we would soon discover just how thin the veil separating the two truly was.

The night had a peculiar energy, as if the cosmos themselves were nudging us toward our destiny. I could almost hear the whispers of the Emberstone urging me forward, an unseen force guiding our path. Jax walked beside me, a steady presence, his focus unwavering. "What's our first move?" he asked, glancing around as if expecting to see the other Flamekeepers lurking in the shadows.

"First, we find Cassie's leads," I replied, determination threading my voice. "We need to pinpoint the sparks she mentioned. If we can locate those who resonate with the Emberstone, we can forge a new alliance."

With a nod of agreement, we set our sights on the old district—once a bustling hub of culture, now a shadow of its former self. Crumbling theaters and shuttered shops lined the streets, their facades telling tales of glory long past. But I sensed something deeper beneath the surface, a current of magic that still flowed through the veins of the city. It whispered secrets of those who had come before us, urging us to uncover their hidden legacies.

As we approached a dilapidated bookstore, its neon sign flickering like a heartbeat, Jax paused, a glimmer of recognition sparking in his eyes. "The Book Nook! I used to come here as a kid. The owner, Ms. Lawson, knows everything about the old legends."

"Then that's where we need to go," I declared, my heart quickening at the thought of unlocking more of the Emberstone's mysteries. We stepped inside, the scent of aged paper and ink enveloping us like a warm embrace. Shelves groaned under the weight of countless tomes, their spines cracked and faded—a treasure trove of knowledge waiting to be discovered.

Ms. Lawson appeared from behind a towering stack of books, her silver hair pulled into a loose bun and her round glasses perched precariously on her nose. "Well, well, if it isn't my favorite troublemakers," she said, a smile breaking across her weathered face. "What brings you two back to my little corner of the world?"

"Ms. Lawson, we need your help," I said, urgency threading my tone. "We're on a mission to find others like us—people connected to the Emberstone and the Flamekeepers. Have you heard anything?"

Her expression shifted from playful to serious as she nodded. "The city has been restless of late. Whispers of flame and shadows. I've felt it in the air. There are those who sense the call of the Emberstone, but they need a catalyst—a spark to ignite their potential."

"Do you know where we can find them?" Jax interjected, his voice steady despite the tension that crackled between us.

"Follow the heat," she replied cryptically, her eyes sparkling with wisdom. "The gatherings at the old amphitheater are a good place to start. It's where the flamekeepers would once convene, and where the lost sparks may gather."

With a grateful nod, we exchanged hurried goodbyes, Ms. Lawson's words echoing in my mind as we stepped back into the night. "The amphitheater, huh? Sounds like a place where legends are born," Jax quipped, a grin forming on his lips despite the weight of our task.

As we hurried toward the outskirts of the district, the moon hung low in the sky, a silver sentinel watching over us. The amphitheater loomed ahead, its ancient stones etched with the memories of countless gatherings, a hallowed ground where flames of inspiration once danced freely. I could feel the pulsing energy emanating from within, beckoning us closer.

Pushing through the weathered archway, we stepped into the main arena. The place was surprisingly alive; small groups of people mingled, their voices a low hum that melded with the soft rustle of the leaves overhead. My heart raced, not only from the excitement of being here but from the energy that crackled in the air, electric and intoxicating.

Jax and I moved cautiously among the clusters of people, trying to discern who among them might feel the resonance of the Emberstone. It was a mixed crowd—some dressed in worn jeans and hoodies, others cloaked in vibrant garments that shimmered under the moonlight. I could see a few faces illuminated by flickering flames, their expressions revealing a spectrum of emotions ranging from hope to apprehension.

As we made our way deeper into the throng, a figure caught my eye. A girl with fiery red hair stood near a makeshift bonfire, her laughter ringing out like a melody that drew us in. She radiated warmth, a vibrant aura that felt like a beacon in the night. "You two look like you've seen a ghost," she said, her eyes sparkling with mischief. "Or maybe you just found a little fire in your lives?"

"We're looking for allies," I said, meeting her gaze. "We're trying to gather those connected to the Emberstone and the Flamekeepers."

Her smile faded, replaced by a contemplative expression. "Ah, the Flamekeepers. You're either brave or foolish to tread down that path. But I can help," she replied, her tone shifting to something more serious. "My name's Aria, and I've felt the call. There are others here, too, who are ready to join you. We can't fight this darkness alone."

A wave of relief washed over me. "You have no idea how much that means," I replied, a smile breaking across my face. The flicker of hope ignited within me, fueled by the connection we were forging.

Aria motioned for us to follow her deeper into the gathering. As she introduced us to others, each person brought their own stories, their unique ties to the Emberstone, and a resolve to stand against the encroaching darkness. We shared our experiences, weaving a tapestry of determination that intertwined our fates.

As the night unfolded, I felt the Emberstone in my pocket vibrating with newfound energy. It was as if the shards of our stories were stitching together, forming a cohesive narrative that could stand strong against the storm approaching on the horizon. We had gathered a small band of brave souls, ready to embrace the legacy of the Flamekeepers.

In that moment, under the vast expanse of stars, surrounded by the warmth of camaraderie and the promise of what lay ahead, I knew we were not just fighting for ourselves. We were part of something greater, a legacy that burned brightly within each of us. Together, we would kindle the flames of hope and illuminate the shadows lurking just beyond our grasp. The night was just beginning, and we were ready to face whatever challenges awaited, hand in hand, fueled by the fires of our resolve.

Chapter 11: Revelations of the Council

The air hummed with a restless energy at Emberhold, a sprawling fortress perched on the edge of a cliff, overlooking the churning ocean below. The sky was an angry canvas, painted with deep purples and bruised grays, hinting at the storm that rumbled like a growling beast just beyond the horizon. Flickering flames danced in the hearth, casting flickering shadows that wove like phantoms around us. The rebels gathered, their faces a motley palette of determination and weariness, as they leaned over worn maps strewn across the massive oak table. Each line on the parchment was etched with the sweat and blood of our struggles, a testament to our relentless fight against the Ashen Council.

My heart raced as I addressed my comrades, my voice trembling with a mix of conviction and uncertainty. "The Emberstone," I began, drawing in a deep breath, "is more than just a gem; it's a beacon of our collective power. It binds us together, channeling our abilities into something greater than ourselves." As I spoke, I could feel the pulse of the stone resonating within me, a heartbeat of hope that refused to fade, even as the Council's cruel tactics haunted my thoughts like ghosts in the night.

Jax, my unwavering ally with tousled hair and a steadfast gaze, leaned in closer, his blue eyes glinting with determination. He was a force of nature, always the first to charge into the fray, and yet, he had a tenderness that made him seem more human amidst the chaos. "If we harness its energy, we can turn the tide. We've been on the defensive for too long. It's time we strike back," he urged, his voice a low rumble that felt like thunder rolling through my veins.

I glanced around the table, taking in the faces of our allies—warriors and scholars, healers and dreamers, each with their own burdens etched into their skin. Elara, our fierce strategist with a wild mane of hair that seemed to mirror her untamed spirit, furrowed her brow in thought. "But how do we reach it? The Council has their eyes everywhere. We can't just waltz into their territory and hope for the best."

Her words hung heavy in the air, and I felt the weight of doubt settle over us like a thick fog. The Council was notorious for their surveillance, a web of spies woven into the very fabric of our lives. Each rumor whispered behind closed doors could turn deadly with just a flick of their fingers. They had a way of snuffing out the light, extinguishing the embers of hope with ruthless precision.

"We'll need a diversion," Jax suggested, his fingers drumming against the table, sparking an idea in the electric atmosphere. "Something bold enough to draw their attention away from the Emberstone's location. While they're busy chasing shadows, we can slip in and retrieve it."

The flickering flames cast an orange glow on his determined expression, igniting a flicker of inspiration in my own heart. The very thought of a daring mission sent adrenaline coursing through my veins. "What if we stage a distraction at the Council's gala?" I proposed, a plan weaving itself together in my mind like a tapestry of defiance. "It's a night of celebration for them, a chance to flaunt their power. If we can create chaos there, we might just have a chance to sneak past their guards and retrieve the stone."

Elara's eyebrows shot up in surprise, but then a sly smile crept onto her lips. "I like where your head's at. They'll be too busy to notice anything amiss." The others murmured in agreement, the flicker of hope growing brighter as we began to brainstorm our audacious plan.

We spent hours poring over details, plotting each move with the precision of chess pieces on a board. As we shared laughter and stories amidst the tension, I could feel a bond forming, a sense of family woven through our shared struggles. The flickering firelight illuminated our resolve, casting long shadows that danced with our dreams of freedom.

As the night wore on, the distant rumble of thunder echoed like a heartbeat, reminding us of the storm approaching. The winds howled outside, whipping against the fortress walls as if to challenge our resolve. I felt a tightening in my chest, a reminder that every spark of hope came with its own set of risks.

"Remember," I said, my voice steady despite the tempest raging outside, "this isn't just about us. It's about everyone who's suffered under the Council's tyranny. We owe it to them to fight with everything we have."

The rebels nodded, their expressions fierce and resolute, and I felt a surge of warmth spread through me. It was a feeling that transcended fear—a sense of purpose that ignited the very core of my being. Each one of us was a thread in the tapestry of rebellion, and together we were crafting something beautiful and unstoppable.

As we finalized our plans, I caught a glimpse of the horizon through the fortress windows. Lightning cracked, illuminating the dark sky for a fleeting moment, revealing the turbulent sea below. It mirrored the chaos within me, but alongside it flickered the promise of hope. Our mission was fraught with danger, yet we were ready to embrace it.

Tomorrow would bring a storm of its own—one that we hoped would shift the tides in our favor. And as I looked around at the faces of my allies, I realized that we were not merely fighting for ourselves; we were fighting for a future where the ashes of despair could give way to the flames of renewal. In that moment, I felt an unwavering determination swell within me, stronger than any storm. It was a promise to myself and to those who dared to dream of a brighter tomorrow.

The next morning dawned with a muted grayness, the sky draped in heavy clouds that threatened rain like a shroud over our spirits.

As the sun attempted to break through the gloom, its feeble rays filtered through the fortress windows, casting ghostly silhouettes of our plans on the walls. I stood by the narrow window, my breath fogging the glass as I peered into the misty expanse. The ocean below roared, waves crashing against the cliffs, echoing the turmoil inside my heart. A storm was brewing, both outside and within me, and I wondered if we were prepared for the tempest that lay ahead.

With the rebels still asleep, I took a moment to gather my thoughts. The Emberstone pulsed gently in my pocket, its warmth a comforting reminder of what was at stake. I could almost hear its whisper, urging me to trust in our mission. Yet doubt lingered like a shadow, gnawing at the edges of my confidence. What if we failed? What if the Ashen Council crushed our hopes like so many brittle bones? I shook my head, banishing the thoughts as I prepared for the day. There was no time for uncertainty.

As the sun climbed higher, a chorus of voices erupted in the hallways, bringing the fortress to life. My comrades began filtering into the common room, their faces lined with determination, but there was a flicker of uncertainty in their eyes that mirrored my own. Jax was the first to catch my gaze, his trademark grin plastered across his face as he bounded towards me. "Ready for the grand performance?" he teased, his playful tone a welcome distraction.

"About as ready as a cat in a dog show," I replied, forcing a smile despite the weight pressing down on my chest. "Let's hope the Council doesn't sniff us out before we can pull off our little magic trick."

We gathered around the table once more, the air thick with the scent of fresh bread and spiced stew as our resident cook, a burly man named Thorne, prepared a hearty breakfast. The food was a feast fit for heroes—baked pastries, roasted meats, and fruit, all served on wooden platters. As we ate, the atmosphere lightened, laughter mingling with the aroma of cooking, and for a fleeting moment, I felt the tendrils of hope curling around my heart.

"We need to finalize our roles," Elara said, her eyes sparkling with mischief as she licked the crumbs from her fingers. "I vote Jax gets to lead the distraction. Nothing says chaos like a wild man swinging a flaming sword."

"Hey now," Jax protested, mock indignation flaring in his voice. "I prefer to think of it as a charismatic dance of destruction."

With laughter echoing around the table, we began to solidify our plan. Each of us would take on a specific role to ensure the Council's attention was drawn away from the Emberstone. I would be among those tasked with infiltrating the gala, blending in as a guest while Jax led the diversion outside. His flair for theatrics would hopefully keep the Council's guards occupied long enough for us to slip past their defenses.

After the meal, the mood shifted as we gathered our gear. The camaraderie that had formed during our planning felt like a protective shield around us, bolstering our spirits against the looming unknown. I strapped on my leather armor, the material soft from wear yet sturdy enough to withstand a skirmish. Each buckle clicked into place, a tangible reminder that I was preparing for battle—not just for myself, but for everyone who had ever suffered at the hands of the Council.

As we donned our disguises and packed our weapons, the fortress buzzed with an electric anticipation. I caught glimpses of my comrades—Elara adjusting her cloak with a determined flick of her wrist, Jax playfully twirling a dagger that gleamed ominously in the light, and Thorne sharpening a massive blade with a concentration that bordered on reverence. Each person was a vital thread in the tapestry we were weaving, and together we were a force that could not be ignored.

With our plans set, we made our way to the edge of the fortress, where a narrow path wound down the cliffside to the valley below. The wind howled around us, whipping through our hair like an untamed spirit. I took a moment to breathe in the salty air, the scent of the sea mingling with the earthy tones of damp moss and wildflowers growing among the rocks. It was a reminder that even in the midst of chaos, there was beauty to be found.

As we reached the base of the cliffs, the distant sound of revelry floated toward us—a blend of laughter, music, and the clinking of glasses, signifying that the Council's gala was in full swing. The grand estate loomed ahead, its opulent facade shimmering with golden lights. It looked like a palace plucked from a fairytale, and yet I knew better. Beneath the surface lay a den of vipers, their fangs bared and ready to strike at anyone foolish enough to challenge them.

"Are we ready?" Jax asked, his voice low as he scanned the horizon, a mix of eagerness and trepidation coloring his tone.

I nodded, swallowing the lump of anxiety lodged in my throat. "As ready as we'll ever be."

With one last glance at my companions, I felt the pulse of the Emberstone in my pocket, a silent promise of strength. We took our positions, hearts pounding as we prepared to weave our way into the belly of the beast. Jax's laughter faded into the distance as he ventured toward the crowd, ready to set the stage ablaze with chaos. I slipped into the shadows, my senses heightened, every sound amplified in the stillness.

As I approached the estate, the sound of music wrapped around me like a warm embrace, luring me into the depths of the celebration. I could see the Council members mingling, their attire extravagant and opulent, each one adorned with jewels that glittered like stars in the night sky. The atmosphere crackled with energy, but beneath the surface, I could sense the undercurrents of power, manipulation, and deception. The gala was more than just a celebration; it was a masquerade, each face hiding secrets that could alter the fate of our rebellion.

With my heart pounding, I stepped into the fray, my thoughts consumed by the gravity of what lay ahead. I was no longer just a girl with dreams of freedom; I was a soldier in a war against tyranny. The stakes were higher than I had ever imagined, but I knew one thing for certain: I would not walk away from this fight without giving it everything I had.

As I slipped into the gala, the opulent ballroom enveloped me like a plush cloak, thick with the sweet scent of candied fruits and the sharp tang of spiced wines. Crystal chandeliers hung from the ceiling like stars that had fallen to grace the earth, their light refracting off the polished marble floors, creating a mesmerizing dance of illumination. Guests twirled and mingled in extravagant attire, their laughter ringing like the chime of silver bells—a stark contrast to the dark undertones that festered just beneath the surface. Each smile masked a potential enemy; every handshake held the weight of betrayal.

I moved with the crowd, my heart thumping a chaotic rhythm that rivaled the music wafting through the air. The strings of the orchestra played a lively melody, a deceptive cheeriness that belied the tension swirling among the elite. The Ashen Council members glided through the room, their cold, calculating gazes sweeping over the revelers, dismissing them as mere pawns in their grand game. I felt like an interloper, a whisper of wind slipping through the cracks of their fortress, unnoticed but not without purpose.

I spotted the Council's leader, a formidable woman named Lady Vesper, whose presence commanded the room. Dressed in a gown of deep crimson, she seemed to draw every eye, her porcelain skin contrasting sharply with her raven-black hair. The way she spoke—smooth, deliberate—made it clear she was accustomed to wielding power like a weapon. I shivered, reminded of the fear she instilled in the hearts of the oppressed. Her laughter was musical, but I could sense the poison behind it, a reminder that beneath the beauty of this setting lay danger lurking like a predator in the shadows.

I needed to keep my wits about me, so I carefully navigated through the throng, my senses heightened. The pulse of the Emberstone within my pocket felt like a silent drumbeat, urging me onward as I searched for a way to blend in while keeping an eye on the Council members. I had no intention of being caught off guard; I was here to disrupt their plans, not to be caught in their web.

As I maneuvered through the crowd, I overheard snippets of conversation—fragments that felt like shards of ice. They discussed alliances and betrayals with an ease that turned my stomach. "The rebels are becoming more brazen," one noble sneered, swirling his drink as if it were a harmless toy. "It's only a matter of time before they slip up and expose themselves. Their little spark of hope will be extinguished soon enough."

The words ignited a fire in my chest, propelling me to act. I ducked behind a column, my pulse quickening as I scanned the room for any signs of my friends. The plan hinged on Jax causing enough of a distraction to draw the Council's attention away from the Emberstone's location, but I needed to be prepared for anything. I spotted him across the room, dressed in dark attire that clung to him like a second skin. He was already charming a group of nobles with exaggerated tales of daring escapes and fantastical creatures. His grin was infectious, and despite the gravity of our situation, I couldn't help but smile.

Just as I was about to join him, a commotion erupted near the grand staircase. A ripple of excitement spread through the crowd, and I instinctively turned to see what was happening. A figure emerged from the shadows, a cloaked individual with a hood obscuring their features, raising a hand to silence the room. The atmosphere shifted, charged with uncertainty.

"Attention, esteemed members of the Council," the figure declared, their voice echoing with a chilling resonance. "Tonight, the scales of justice will be weighed."

Gasps echoed around the ballroom, and I felt the air grow thick with tension. Lady Vesper stepped forward, her expression unreadable, masking whatever emotions roiled beneath the surface. "And who might you be?" she asked, her voice smooth yet edged with menace.

The figure lowered their hood, revealing a familiar face—Kira, one of our most skilled spies, known for her cunning and agility. Her eyes sparkled with defiance, and I felt a rush of pride surge within me. She was a force of nature, and in that moment, she was standing against the very embodiment of the Council's tyranny.

"Just a messenger," Kira replied, her voice steady. "I bring news that you've been too blinded by power to see."

With a flourish, she produced a small vial filled with shimmering liquid. The crowd gasped, a mix of intrigue and fear rippling through them. "This is the key to unlocking the Emberstone's true potential," she declared, holding it aloft as if it were a sacred relic. "It belongs to the people, not to you."

The reaction was immediate. Council members scrambled to form a protective circle around Lady Vesper, their faces a mixture of outrage and alarm. I felt adrenaline spike through my veins, the moment ripe with opportunity. This was the chaos we needed.

I made my way through the throng, my heart racing as I approached Jax, who had paused mid-tale, his jaw dropped in shock. "Kira's gone rogue!" he exclaimed, his eyes wide. "This is brilliant!"

"Brilliantly dangerous," I muttered, scanning the room for any sign of our escape route. The Council guards were already moving, their polished armor glinting under the chandelier's light as they began to converge on Kira.

"Let's create our own distraction," Jax said, his smile returning as he pulled out his dagger. "Follow my lead."

With a nod, I drew my own weapon, the cool metal familiar in my hand. The revelry had morphed into a frenzy, and I could feel the panic swelling like a tidal wave. We dashed toward the nearest exit, the sounds of shouting and clinking glasses fading into a chaotic symphony behind us.

As we burst into the courtyard, the night air hit me like a slap, invigorating and cold. The stars twinkled overhead, an unyielding reminder of the hope we fought for. Jax and I ran toward the stables, where we could hear the whinnying of horses. They would be our escape.

But before we could reach them, a line of guards emerged from the shadows, blocking our path. "Halt!" one shouted, drawing his sword. "You won't escape tonight."

"Can't say I was planning to," I quipped, adrenaline surging as I faced the guards. "But if you insist, I'd rather not go quietly."

With a swift motion, I lunged forward, ducking under the guard's outstretched arm, my dagger flashing as I struck at his midsection. He stumbled back, momentarily dazed, allowing Jax to sweep in and take down another guard with a deft kick that sent him crashing into a nearby cart.

We fought our way through the chaos, every movement instinctual and fluid, a dance choreographed by desperation. The night was alive with the sounds of clashing metal and shouts of defiance. I could feel the Emberstone thrumming in my pocket, urging me onward, fueling my resolve.

Just as we broke free from the clutches of the guards, a distant explosion shook the ground, followed by a cacophony of voices echoing from the estate. Kira's gamble had ignited a spark, and the flames of rebellion were spreading.

We reached the stables, the scent of hay and sweat filling the air, and without a moment's hesitation, we mounted two sturdy horses, our hearts racing in tandem with the thundering hooves. As we galloped into the night, I glanced back at the chaos erupting behind us, the once-grand estate now engulfed in turmoil.

This was our moment. The Emberstone's true potential lay ahead, a beacon of hope we could seize if we were brave enough to chase it. The wind whipped through my hair, carrying with it the promise of a new dawn, and I knew—no matter what awaited us—we would rise to meet it, together.

Chapter 12: The Heart of the Inferno

The ground beneath us pulsed with a rhythmic thrum, a heartbeat echoing the wrath of the Earth itself. Each tremor sent a shiver through my bones, a reminder that we were mere mortals stepping into the domain of titans. The landscape morphed into a surreal tapestry of ochre and char, a painter's palette splashed wildly by some deranged artist. Jagged rocks twisted upwards like claws, grasping at a sky smeared with smoky oranges and fiery reds. It felt as though we were intruders in a realm far beyond human comprehension, where the very air shimmered with the heat of a million suns.

Pyrax, with his fiery mane and smoldering gaze, led the way. His presence felt both comforting and unsettling, a dichotomy that lingered as he navigated through the jagged terrain. I had grown to trust him, yet there was an unspoken tension in his shoulders, as if he bore a weight that pressed down harder than the molten rock surrounding us. Every so often, he would glance back at me, his expression flickering between determination and concern, and I felt the unshakeable urge to reassure him that I could handle whatever lay ahead.

As we pressed deeper into the inferno's embrace, the atmosphere thickened, laden with the tang of sulfur and the sharp bite of ash. Each inhalation ignited my lungs, a reminder of the elemental force we were trespassing upon. I could feel the heat radiating from the gaping maw of the volcano, a breath of warmth that tingled against my skin like a thousand tiny sparks. I glanced around, taking in the sight of my companions, their faces reflecting the same fierce determination that coursed through my veins. We were united, a ragtag band of warriors standing against the unknown.

The path twisted and turned, revealing small geysers that erupted sporadically, showering us with droplets of superheated steam. I couldn't help but laugh nervously, the sound bubbling up as we dodged another plume of vapor. Pyrax shot me a quick grin, a flash of fiery determination lighting up his face. In moments like this, I felt the bond we had forged during our tumultuous journey. Each laugh, each glance exchanged in the midst of perilous danger, solidified our camaraderie, reminding me that I was not alone in this hellish landscape.

As we neared the volcano's base, the ground became a patchwork of dark obsidian and molten rock, glimmering like scattered jewels in the dim light. The heat intensified, wrapping around us like a heavy blanket, stifling yet invigorating. It was then that I heard it—a low rumble that resonated through the ground, vibrating through my bones. I stopped, my heart racing, as I turned to Pyrax. "Did you hear that?" My voice felt fragile against the backdrop of the impending eruption.

"Stay close," he commanded, his tone firm but edged with urgency.

With every step forward, the rumble grew louder, a warning that this journey was not just a quest for power but a race against the very forces of nature. I could see it now, the volcano rising like a titan from the ground, its peak wreathed in smoke and fire. The heart of the inferno was alive, breathing, and pulsating with energy that was as mesmerizing as it was terrifying.

We climbed a steep ridge, the ground shifting beneath us like an angry serpent. I dug my fingers into the rock, feeling the warmth seep into my palms. The air was electric, crackling with the promise of danger. My heart beat in sync with the volcano, a drumroll heralding the cataclysm that could befall us at any moment. I took a deep breath, steeling myself for what lay ahead. This was the moment we had been preparing for, the moment that would either crown us with glory or plunge us into oblivion.

As we reached the summit, the view before me was breathtaking—a swirling maelstrom of fire and fury. The caldera gaped like a great mouth, ready to swallow the world whole. Streams of lava flowed like molten rivers, illuminating the darkened sky with a sickly orange glow. I felt a swell of exhilaration and fear, an intoxicating blend that coursed through my veins like wildfire. This was it. This was the heart of the inferno.

"Are you ready?" Pyrax's voice broke through my reverie, grounding me back in reality. His eyes shone with an intensity that mirrored the inferno before us, and I nodded, my resolve hardening like the obsidian beneath our feet.

With each step toward the edge, I felt the heat embrace me, whispering secrets of ancient powers and forgotten legends. The ground trembled beneath us, a warning that echoed in my mind. "Remember," Pyrax said, his voice low and steady. "The heart gives power, but it also takes. We must tread carefully."

As we peered into the depths, a strange pull tugged at my soul, an undeniable calling that resonated deep within. It was as if the volcano recognized me, as if it saw the ember of potential flickering in my chest. I reached out, feeling the warmth radiating from the bubbling lava below. This was not just a volcano; it was a living entity, one that had witnessed the rise and fall of civilizations, a keeper of secrets that demanded respect.

I turned to my companions, their expressions a blend of fear and determination. Each one of us had come here bearing our own burdens, our own reasons for seeking the heart of the inferno. As I looked into their eyes, I knew this was not just a quest for power; it was a journey of self-discovery, a trial that would reveal who we truly were beneath the surface.

And as we stood at the brink of the abyss, I couldn't help but feel that whatever awaited us within that fiery maw would change us forever.

The air around us was thick with an ominous energy, as though the volcano itself had a consciousness, watching, waiting. I could feel the heat rising off the surface, distorting the air in a way that made everything seem like a mirage. The fiery rivers flowed sluggishly below us, occasionally belching forth bursts of flame that sent showers of sparks spiraling into the dusky sky. I couldn't help but wonder what kind of stories this ancient giant could tell if only it had a voice. Would it boast of its fiery births and devastating eruptions, or would it whisper secrets of the Flamewalkers—those mythical beings said to harness its very essence?

Pyrax stepped closer to the edge, his silhouette framed against the glow of the molten river. "It's breathtaking, isn't it?" he said, his voice tinged with awe. "But beauty here is often deceptive."

"Reminds me of my last date," I joked, trying to lighten the tension that had coiled around us like a noose. Pyrax shot me a sidelong glance, a flicker of amusement breaking through his intense demeanor.

Before he could respond, a deep rumble reverberated through the ground, causing us both to stumble slightly. The volcano was alive, and it didn't appreciate our lingering. I steadied myself and took a breath, grounding my swirling thoughts. With my pulse echoing in my ears, I stepped closer to the lava's edge, the heat hitting me like a wave crashing against a rocky shore. The flames licked up towards the sky, swirling like dancers caught in an eternal performance, a hypnotic reminder of the raw power we sought to command.

"Focus," Pyrax said, his tone shifting from jest to seriousness. "We need to find the entrance. The Heart lies deep within this mountain, where the flame is hottest." He scanned the jagged cliffs, his keen eyes searching for something hidden among the chaos. I followed his gaze, taking in the harsh lines of the volcano, its surface pocked with craters and fissures.

"Right, the entrance," I echoed, though I couldn't shake the feeling that it was more of a challenge than it sounded. If I had learned anything from our journey so far, it was that the Heart wasn't going to hand itself over on a silver platter. With our previous encounters fresh in my mind, I knew we were bound to face trials that would test our resolve and ingenuity.

As we ventured further along the ridge, the heat grew more oppressive, and the air became thick with the scent of burnt minerals. I wiped a bead of sweat from my brow, watching as it shimmered in the ambient glow. "So, what are we actually looking for?" I asked, trying to keep the conversation light despite the gravity of our situation. "A giant flaming heart? A door marked with a big 'Keep Out' sign?"

"Something like that," Pyrax replied, his voice serious but with a hint of a smile. "The entrance should be marked by a formation called the Pillars of Flame. They're—"

Suddenly, the ground shuddered violently, and I had to brace myself against the scorching rock to avoid toppling over. We both looked around, hearts racing as the tremors intensified. The volcano was a restless beast, and its irritation was becoming palpable. Just as I feared that we might need to make a hasty retreat, a sharp outcrop caught my eye—columns of stone rising from the landscape like the jagged teeth of some slumbering creature.

"There!" I pointed, adrenaline surging through me. "Are those the Pillars of Flame?"

Pyrax nodded, his eyes lighting up with determination. "Exactly! If we can reach them, we might find the entrance to the Heart."

We moved swiftly, weaving through the treacherous terrain, my heart pounding not just from the exertion but from the thrill of the chase. Each step felt like a dance with danger, the molten rock shifting beneath us as we navigated the ever-changing landscape.

As we approached the pillars, I marveled at their beauty, a striking contrast to the chaos surrounding us. Each column was a testament to the raw power of nature, glowing with a brilliant light that seemed to pulse in sync with the tremors of the volcano. Intricate patterns carved into the stone shimmered like stars, telling tales of ancient flamewalkers who had once roamed these very paths.

Pyrax reached the base of the tallest pillar first, his hands brushing over the warm stone as if seeking answers from the past. "This is it," he murmured, a sense of reverence in his voice. I joined him, feeling a magnetic pull towards the center of the formation, an inexplicable connection that sent a thrill down my spine.

Suddenly, the ground shook again, more violently this time. I clutched at the pillar, my heart racing as the sound of cracking stone echoed through the air. A fissure opened at our feet, a hungry maw that threatened to swallow us whole. "We need to hurry!" I shouted, adrenaline fueling my movements as I searched for any sign of an entrance.

Pyrax was already ahead of me, scanning the base of the pillars with urgency. "There! Look!" He pointed toward a narrow crevice, partially hidden behind the largest column. A flickering light emanated from within, beckoning us closer.

"Great, let's just crawl through the mouth of a volcano. What could possibly go wrong?" I quipped, trying to maintain my composure despite the escalating danger.

"Better than being trapped out here," Pyrax replied, already stepping toward the crevice. "Trust me, this is our best shot."

With a nod, I followed him into the narrow opening. The air grew cooler, a stark contrast to the blistering heat just outside. As we squeezed through the tight passage, I felt a mixture of anxiety and exhilaration. What lay ahead was unknown territory, but I had never been one to shy away from a challenge.

The light grew brighter as we crawled deeper into the heart of the mountain. The walls glimmered with a faint luminescence, pulsating gently as if alive. With each movement, the warmth of the lava outside faded into a distant memory, replaced by an electric energy that tingled against my skin. This was it—the Heart of the Inferno awaited us, a treasure both dangerous and magnificent, promising power and peril in equal measure.

And as I glanced at Pyrax, determination etched across his features, I realized that whatever awaited us, we would face it together. This journey had forged bonds that no volcano could break, and in this moment, I felt ready to confront whatever challenges lay ahead.

The narrow passage opened into a cavern that felt both alive and ancient, the walls shimmering like molten glass. Each surface reflected a warm glow, illuminating the chamber with a gentle flicker that seemed to dance along the edges of our shadows. The air was thick with an otherworldly heat, not oppressive like outside but warm and inviting, wrapping around us like a cozy blanket—if blankets were made of fire, that is. I took a deep breath, inhaling the scent of sulfur and something floral, which felt wildly out of place here.

As I stepped further into the cavern, I noticed intricate carvings etched into the walls—runes that seemed to pulse with energy, telling the story of the Flamewalkers who had once thrived in this hidden realm. Figures, their bodies entwined with flames, danced across the rock, immortalizing their connection to the volcano. I could almost hear whispers emanating from the stone, fragments of incantations and promises forged in the heat of the Earth.

Pyrax stood in the center of the chamber, his fiery hair casting flickering shadows that danced around us. "This is incredible," he breathed, his gaze sweeping over the artwork. "It's like we've stumbled into a shrine dedicated to the Flamewalkers. This is where their legacy was born."

"What do you think it all means?" I asked, my curiosity piqued. I stepped closer to the wall, tracing my fingers over the cool stone, feeling the grooves beneath my fingertips.

"The runes are a mix of elemental magic and history," Pyrax replied, a hint of excitement coloring his voice. "Each symbol likely represents a key to controlling the flames, a way to channel their power. If we can decipher them, we might unlock the secrets of the Heart itself."

I nodded, trying to process the enormity of what he was suggesting. If this place was indeed a repository of Flamewalker knowledge, then the possibilities were endless. But that same excitement bubbled into apprehension—what if we weren't ready to wield such power?

Before I could voice my concerns, a sudden rumble erupted from the depths of the volcano, shaking the very ground beneath our feet. Dust cascaded from the ceiling, and I instinctively grabbed Pyrax's arm, steadying myself against the violent tremors. The runes flickered ominously, a warning that the Heart was restless, and we were treading a thin line between discovery and destruction.

"We need to hurry," I said, urgency spiking in my chest. "Whatever is causing that rumble can't be good."

Pyrax nodded, and together we moved towards a circular pedestal in the center of the chamber, its surface adorned with the same glowing runes. It was slightly raised, the rock smoothed by time and perhaps the touch of countless seekers who had come before us. The symbols spiraled outward like flames, radiating a warmth that beckoned us closer.

"What if this is a key?" Pyrax wondered aloud, excitement igniting in his eyes. "Maybe if we activate it, it will reveal the Heart or grant us the power we seek!"

"Or it could blow us to smithereens," I replied, trying to rein in his enthusiasm. The last thing I needed was for him to leap into danger without fully considering the consequences.

But Pyrax was already studying the pedestal, tracing the runes with a reverence that was both exhilarating and alarming. "Help me decipher these," he urged, his fingers flying over the symbols. "If we can combine our energies, perhaps we can awaken whatever power lies within."

I stepped beside him, my heart racing as I examined the inscriptions. They resembled an ancient language—each curve and angle a puzzle waiting to be unlocked. As I joined him, I felt a rush of warmth spread through my fingertips, a pulse of energy that aligned with the rhythm of the volcano.

Together, we chanted the runes aloud, our voices intertwining, creating a harmonious echo that resonated through the chamber. The air thickened, crackling with energy, and I could feel the ground vibrate beneath me, as if the volcano were responding to our call.

The moment we spoke the final word, a blinding flash of light engulfed the pedestal, illuminating the chamber in a brilliant golden hue. The light pulsed with our heartbeat, and I squeezed my eyes shut against the brilliance, my mind racing with exhilaration and fear. When the light finally faded, I opened my eyes to find a swirling vortex of flames rising from the pedestal, spiraling upward and coalescing into a figure.

A figure draped in robes woven from pure fire emerged, their features obscured but their presence palpable—a guardian of the Heart. Its voice resonated like rolling thunder, sending shivers down my spine. "Who dares awaken the Heart of the Inferno?"

I swallowed hard, stepping forward instinctively. "We seek the power of the Flamewalkers. We wish to understand how to control it, to protect it from those who would misuse it."

The guardian regarded us, flames dancing in its eyes, flickering with an intensity that made my heart race. "Many have come before you, seeking the power to bend the flames to their will. But few have succeeded without paying a price."

"Price?" Pyrax echoed, his voice firm despite the uncertainty that danced in his eyes. "What kind of price?"

"The flames demand respect, balance," the guardian intoned. "To command them, you must first understand the balance between creation and destruction. You seek power, but know that it can consume you if you are not prepared."

I exchanged a glance with Pyrax, both of us grappling with the weight of the guardian's words. The power we sought was not merely a tool; it was a living force that required responsibility and sacrifice. I felt a sense of trepidation wash over me, but alongside it was a glimmer of hope—maybe this was the moment we had been waiting for, the chance to step into our destinies.

"Then teach us," I implored, my voice steady despite the rising flames around us. "Show us how to wield this power, not just for ourselves, but for the world."

The guardian paused, its fiery form shimmering with what could only be described as contemplation. "Very well. To wield the flames, you must undergo a trial. You will face the essence of fire itself—your fears, your desires, and the choices that define you."

Before I could respond, the flames surged, engulfing us in a fiery whirlwind. I felt the heat wrap around me like a lover's embrace, and for a fleeting moment, it felt exhilarating. But then, the fire swirled tighter, pulling me into a maelstrom of memories and emotions, each flicker of flame representing a choice I had made, a fear I had hidden, a desire I had nurtured.

I was spiraling through visions—my past, my hopes, my doubts colliding in a chaotic dance of fire and fury. I saw moments of triumph, laughter shared with friends, and the warmth of community. But they were interspersed with images of loss and fear, the shadows of my choices looming large. The heat pressed against me, urging me to confront the very essence of who I was and what I sought to become.

And at the center of this inferno of emotion, I found Pyrax, his eyes blazing with determination, urging me forward. "Together, we can face this," he shouted over the roar of the flames.

With every ounce of strength, I reached for him, feeling the warmth of our connection in the face of uncertainty. The flames crackled around us, but I felt a surge of confidence igniting within me, a realization that our destinies were intertwined, that together we could harness the power of the Heart.

The fire roared, rising higher as the trials began, but I knew that with every challenge, every flame we faced, we were forging our path, destined to emerge stronger and united, ready to confront whatever awaited us in the depths of the Heart of the Inferno.

Chapter 13: Trials of Fire

The air shimmered with heat as I stood at the precipice of the volcano, its mouth yawning like a monstrous creature ready to devour the unwary. Thick plumes of smoke coiled upward, twisting through the air like a serpent ready to strike. Beneath my feet, the ground trembled slightly, a low rumble that resonated deep within my bones, whispering of the power contained within this fiery beast. Jagged rocks jutted from the earth, their surfaces slick with steam, and I could almost hear the volcano's pulse—steady, relentless, and ominously inviting.

Beside me, Jax's expression mirrored my own—a mixture of trepidation and fierce resolve. We exchanged a glance, the unspoken camaraderie between us thickening the air. Our hands brushed together briefly, a silent promise that whatever lay ahead, we would face it together. I felt a surge of gratitude toward him; his presence was a beacon of light in this molten landscape, grounding me amidst the chaos.

The first trial unfurled before us: a path lined with obsidian stones that led straight into a labyrinth of fiery rivers. The molten rock glistened under the relentless sun, undulating with a life of its own, reminding me of blood pulsing through veins. Each step forward was treacherous, the heat clawing at my skin, a constant reminder of the dangers lurking beneath the surface. The very earth beneath my feet felt like a living, breathing entity, eager to swallow us whole.

We edged forward cautiously, every footfall calculated, testing the strength of the path. I could hear the hiss of steam escaping from the cracks in the ground, a siren song promising both destruction and rebirth. Each breath felt like a challenge, the thick, sulfurous air stinging my nostrils, wrapping around me like a heavy shroud. I took a moment to steady myself, focusing on the rhythm of my heartbeat, the way it thudded in my chest like a drum, urging me onward.

Jax moved with a grace that belied the danger surrounding us, navigating the sharp rocks with an ease that made me envious. I admired the way his dark hair clung to his forehead, slick with sweat, the determined set of his jaw contrasting with the playful glimmer in his eyes. As he gestured for me to follow, I felt a rush of warmth flood my heart. He was more than just a companion on this journey; he was a piece of my own spirit reflected back at me, daring me to push past my limits.

The path twisted ahead, revealing a particularly treacherous section where a narrow ledge dangled perilously above a river of molten rock. A surge of fear gripped me as I looked down into the bubbling depths, the crimson liquid glinting malevolently. Memories surged like the molten flow below—visions of my parents, their faces etched with worry, urging me to play it safe, to tread carefully. But safety felt like a gilded cage; I yearned for freedom, for the chance to forge my own path.

"Hey, you can do this," Jax's voice broke through my reverie, firm and reassuring. "Just focus on me. One step at a time." His words wrapped around me like a lifeline, pulling me back from the edge of my spiraling thoughts.

I nodded, summoning every ounce of courage I possessed. With each careful step onto the narrow ledge, the weight of my fears pressed down on me. Doubts whispered in my ear, taunting me with the specters of failure. The memories of my parents' sacrifices loomed large in my mind—images of their smiles, their laughter, all shattered by the specter of tragedy. I had vowed to honor them, to let their legacy fuel my determination. I couldn't falter now.

As I reached the halfway point, a sudden tremor shook the ground beneath me. The rocks shifted, and I stumbled, heart racing as I fought for balance. Jax's hand shot out, grabbing my wrist, anchoring me in place. The warmth of his grip coursed through me, igniting a spark of defiance. With a quick nod, I pushed past the fear that threatened to consume me.

With renewed determination, I leaped forward, landing solidly on the other side. Relief flooded through me, mingling with the adrenaline still coursing in my veins. Jax followed closely, his grin infectious as he joined me on stable ground once more.

"We did it," I breathed, marveling at how our bond had strengthened with every obstacle we faced. Each trial was a crucible, forging us into something stronger, more resilient. We pressed on, deeper into the labyrinth of challenges awaiting us.

The next trial revealed itself like an unwelcome specter, emerging from the shadows of the volcano's heart. The heat intensified, swirling around us like a malevolent entity, pushing us to confront the very essence of our fears. Visions flickered before my eyes—my parents, their faces distorted by sorrow and regret. I could hear their voices, soft and pleading, urging me to turn back, to abandon this reckless quest.

But I steeled myself against the tide of doubt, refusing to yield to the weight of despair. With each breath, I summoned the anger bubbling beneath my skin—the anger that had ignited this journey in the first place. I would not allow their sacrifices to be in vain. I would forge ahead, fueled by the fire of my own resolve, and emerge from this trial not just as a survivor but as a warrior, ready to claim my destiny.

The oppressive heat became a tangible force, pressing down on us as we continued our perilous journey. With every step deeper into the volcano's core, the atmosphere shifted from intimidating to almost claustrophobic. The walls of jagged rock loomed closer, closing in as though the mountain itself was alive and breathing, exhaling its molten breath onto the land. It was as if the earth itself was scrutinizing us, weighing our worth against the trials it set before us. I could feel its ancient power pulsing in time with my heartbeat, a reminder that we were intruders in its sacred domain.

Jax and I forged ahead, navigating a series of tunnels where shadows danced like specters, flickering just out of reach. The air grew thick with sulfur, burning my throat and stinging my eyes, each breath a challenge as I fought to keep panic at bay. The flickering light from the streams of magma cast eerie shapes against the walls, morphing into faces that seemed to whisper forgotten secrets. I turned to Jax, and he flashed a grin that was both encouraging and mischievous, his energy a stark contrast to the oppressive environment.

"This place is like a sauna gone rogue," he joked, wiping sweat from his brow. "Who knew that a fiery death would come with such great humidity?"

I couldn't help but chuckle, the sound echoing off the walls and momentarily dispelling the gloom that threatened to envelop us. Laughter had a way of lightening the darkest situations, and Jax's humor served as a reminder that even in the direst of circumstances, we could find joy. The heat may have been overwhelming, but so was our determination, and together, we were a force to be reckoned with.

As we ventured further, the walls of the tunnels began to shift, and the ground beneath us trembled once more, this time with greater urgency. I felt it deep within my bones, a warning that something formidable lay ahead. Then, suddenly, the tunnel opened into a vast chamber, the heart of the volcano, where a glowing pool of molten rock bubbled and churned. The sight was both mesmerizing and terrifying—a swirling vortex of red and orange that seemed to pulsate like a beating heart.

In the center of the chamber, a massive stone pedestal rose from the lava, adorned with ancient runes that glimmered with an ethereal light. A pedestal that beckoned us forward, daring us to reach out and claim whatever lay atop it. I exchanged a wary glance with Jax, both of us feeling the weight of the moment. "This must be the next trial," I murmured, my voice barely above a whisper.

As if sensing our presence, the molten pool surged violently, sending fiery tendrils licking towards the edges of the chamber. An echoing voice filled the air, deep and resonant, seeming to rise from the very core of the volcano. "Only those pure of heart may pass. Face your greatest fear, and prove your worth."

My heart raced, the words cutting through the haze of heat and tension. The room shifted around me, the glow of the lava casting flickering shadows that morphed into the faces of my past—the faces of my parents, their expressions caught between pride and disappointment. They stood before me, not as mere phantoms but as solid as the stones that surrounded us, their voices intertwining in a haunting chorus. "You cannot escape your destiny," they warned. "You are not enough."

I felt my chest tighten, the familiar weight of doubt pressing down. "I'm trying," I gasped, grappling with the flood of emotions. The fear of inadequacy surged like a tidal wave, threatening to drown me. I thought back to my childhood, to the endless hours spent studying, to the moments when I felt invisible. Each taunt of "not good enough" echoed in my mind, and I felt the heat of shame rise within me.

But then I heard Jax's voice, cutting through the haze like a lifeline. "You are enough," he shouted, his words a beacon in the tempest. "You've faced so much already. Don't let them win!" His conviction steadied me, anchoring my resolve. I turned back to the phantoms, locking eyes with my parents. "I am not afraid," I declared, each word punctuated by the rising tide of defiance swelling within me.

The shadows flickered and distorted, the faces of my past twisting as though caught in a storm. "Prove it!" the voice boomed, the ground shaking beneath my feet.

Before I could think, a wave of heat surged from the molten pool, engulfing the chamber in a blinding flash. I felt myself pulled into the depths of the lava, the heat wrapping around me like a cloak. My instincts kicked in, and I summoned every ounce of strength I had, fighting against the scorching embrace. Images flashed before me, moments of weakness and fear that had haunted me for years. I had to confront them, face the reality of my fears head-on.

The landscape morphed, and I found myself in a familiar place: my childhood home, vibrant and full of life. My parents were there, their laughter ringing through the air. But the scene quickly darkened as shadows loomed overhead, memories of heartache creeping in—the day we lost everything, the day my dreams felt out of reach.

I stood in the center of it all, my heart pounding, but a new flame ignited within me. "You don't define me," I shouted into the darkness. "I will not let my past determine my future!" With those words, I felt a surge of energy course through me, a heat that rivaled the molten rock surrounding us. The shadows recoiled, dissipating like mist under the sun.

Suddenly, I was back in the chamber, breathless and resolute. The molten pool had calmed, the glowing surface now reflecting my defiance. Jax stood beside me, his eyes bright with pride. The ancient voice echoed once more, softer this time. "You have faced your fear and proven your worth. Claim your reward."

The pedestal before us shimmered, revealing a radiant orb pulsating with energy, an emblem of our triumph. I reached out, fingers brushing against its warm surface, and felt an overwhelming sense of connection—a bond forged through trials, strength drawn from both my past and the promise of the future. In that moment,

I understood that the journey was not just about overcoming fear; it was about embracing who I had become. Together, Jax and I had ignited a flame within ourselves, a fire that would not easily be extinguished.

The moment my fingers made contact with the orb, a wave of energy coursed through me, igniting every cell in my body. The radiant light enveloped us, wrapping around Jax and me like a warm blanket. In that instant, I felt a profound connection—not just to the orb but to everything that had led us to this moment. I was no longer merely a girl haunted by fear; I was a force, a culmination of every trial I had faced, every doubt I had battled, and every piece of my past that I had learned to embrace.

The chamber quaked in response, the molten pool bubbling violently as if excited by our victory. Jax grinned at me, the light reflecting in his eyes, turning them into twin stars. "I'd say we've officially graduated from the School of Fire and Fury," he quipped, his playful tone a welcome distraction from the gravity of our surroundings.

As I laughed, the orb pulsed again, and its glow intensified, illuminating the chamber with a golden light that chased away the shadows. It felt like a promise—a beacon of hope amidst chaos. But as the illumination grew, so did the sound, a low rumble that reverberated through the rock walls. Suddenly, the ground beneath us shifted, cracking like the surface of a fragile egg, and a fissure opened wide, swallowing the pedestal and the orb into the depths of the volcano.

"No, no, no!" I shouted, lunging toward the edge of the chasm that had formed. My heart raced as I watched the radiant light disappear, but before I could fully comprehend the loss, the chamber trembled violently. With a roar that echoed through the volcanic heart, the lava surged, forming fiery geysers that erupted from the ground, showering the chamber with sparks. We were not finished yet; the trials were far from over.

"Looks like we've got a party crasher," Jax yelled over the din, his expression a mix of excitement and dread. I could only nod, adrenaline propelling me forward as we sprinted across the chamber, dodging sprays of lava that threatened to engulf us.

We dashed through the tunnels, our footsteps pounding against the stone floor as we followed the labyrinthine passages that twisted and turned. The air grew hotter, thick with steam that swirled around us, wrapping us in a damp embrace. I focused on the flickering shadows ahead, wondering if we were even going in the right direction or if the volcano was leading us into its fiery maw.

Each turn felt like a gamble, every heartbeat echoing in my ears as we navigated the maze. The walls began to close in, the rock a sinister reminder of the dangers lurking beyond. Just when I thought we might be trapped, we stumbled into another chamber—this one alive with a chaotic dance of flames.

Flames twisted in the air, rising like ethereal serpents, their fiery tongues licking at the stone walls. In the center, a massive bonfire blazed, illuminating the chamber in hues of orange and red. The flames flickered as if alive, shifting to form images that danced before our eyes—visions of past heroes, warriors who had braved their own trials and emerged triumphant. They were etched in fire, their stories woven into the very fabric of this molten world.

A voice boomed from the inferno, deep and resonant. "To continue, you must answer the flames' riddle. Speak your truth, or be consumed by the fire!"

Jax and I exchanged glances, the realization sinking in that we needed to face yet another challenge. The flames swirled, forming a circle around us, an audience eager for our response. I took a step forward, heart pounding in my chest. "What is the riddle?" I called out, trying to keep my voice steady.

"Who are you when the world turns its back?" the flames echoed, their tones rising and falling like a haunting melody.

I closed my eyes, feeling the weight of the question settle over me. "I am the daughter of those who fought for their dreams," I declared, feeling a surge of warmth ignite within me. "I am a seeker of truth, a warrior molded by trials and tempered by fire."

The flames writhed in response, their dance growing more frenetic as they absorbed my words. I could feel the energy shifting, the air around me crackling with power. Jax stepped forward, emboldened by my response. "I am Jax, a friend to the brave, a steadfast ally who refuses to stand by when the world needs defending," he proclaimed, his voice unwavering.

The fire swirled around us, gathering in strength as the chamber trembled. "You speak with conviction, but conviction alone will not suffice. Speak your greatest fear and rise above it, or be swallowed by the flames of doubt!"

My throat tightened, and I hesitated for a moment, the specter of my insecurities creeping back in. "I fear... I fear I will not live up to their legacy," I admitted, my voice trembling. "That my parents' sacrifices will mean nothing if I fail."

As the words slipped from my lips, the flames surged higher, their heat wrapping around me like a fiery embrace. But I refused to be consumed. "Yet I know that I am not defined by my fears. I am here, and I will forge my own path!"

The flames flickered, swirling faster until they exploded outward in a brilliant cascade of light. The heat pulsed around us, but rather than burning, it invigorated me, flooding my veins with energy. I felt lighter, as though the weight of my fears had been lifted, replaced by a fierce sense of purpose.

The flames danced joyfully, and I realized I had faced my truth—not just the fear of failure but the understanding that my journey was uniquely mine. The bonfire flared brighter, illuminating the path before us. The exit appeared, a tunnel that opened like a welcoming embrace, drawing us toward the next challenge.

As we stepped into the light, the air cooled, and the fiery sounds of the chamber faded behind us. Together, we emerged into a sprawling landscape dotted with obsidian formations, glimmering under the distant sun. The ground was charred but dotted with resilient patches of green, nature's defiance against the destruction of fire.

"Look at this place," Jax breathed, taking in the surreal beauty around us. "It's like the aftermath of a dream."

I nodded, feeling a newfound sense of strength. "This is just the beginning. We've proven ourselves in the fire, and whatever comes next, we'll face it together."

The horizon stretched before us, a breathtaking expanse that promised both danger and discovery. Each step felt like an affirmation of who we were becoming, and as I glanced at Jax, I knew we were ready for whatever challenges awaited us. Together, we would continue to navigate this extraordinary world, unafraid of the trials still to come. The fire within us had been ignited, and it would guide our path forward.

Chapter 14: The Elemental Conclave

The moment I stepped into the Elemental Conclave, the air thickened with anticipation, a vibrant energy that crackled and hummed like the flame of a well-tended hearth. Towering stone formations, reminiscent of jagged mountain peaks, loomed around us, their surfaces etched with ancient runes that glowed faintly in the dusky light. Each rune pulsed with a rhythm that matched my heartbeat, a steady thrum that whispered of ages past, of flame and ash, of power both wondrous and terrifying.

My companions stood beside me, equally awed and bewildered. Shae, her hair a wild tangle of fire-kissed curls, reached for my hand, her touch grounding me in the moment. "Can you believe this place?" she breathed, eyes wide as she took in the sprawling expanse of the conclave. Her excitement was infectious, igniting a spark of hope within me. It was easy to forget the weight of the trials we had faced when confronted with such beauty.

The grand gathering was suffused with a warm glow, the colors of the setting sun filtering through the cracks in the rocks above, painting the ground in shades of amber and gold. Yet, even amidst this splendor, an undercurrent of urgency pulsed in the air. The Flamewalkers—beings of both myth and reality—floated before us like phantoms, their forms shimmering in and out of focus, as if they were made from the very flames they commanded. They embodied an ancient grace, their movements fluid, each gesture echoing centuries of knowledge and power.

As they began to speak, their voices harmonized like a choir, resonating deep within my core. Each word wrapped around me, weaving a tapestry of history that engulfed my senses. They shared tales of the Emberstone, a relic of unimaginable power, forged in the heart of a star, imbued with the essence of creation itself. "It holds the balance," one of the Flamewalkers declared, their eyes glowing like coals. "Without it, the line between destruction and creation blurs, leading to chaos."

A ripple of unease stirred in my chest. I had felt that chaos, had witnessed the consequences of imbalance. It wasn't just a distant threat; it was a reality I had faced time and again. A shiver coursed down my spine as they turned their gazes upon me, their intensity palpable. "You are destined to wield this power," they intoned, and the echo of their voices swirled around me, wrapping me in its weight.

"What do you mean?" I asked, my voice trembling slightly as I stepped forward, caught in their ethereal glow. The moment hung heavy in the air, each breath laden with expectation. I had always felt a connection to the flames, an instinctive understanding of their dance, but this? This was something far greater.

The Flamewalkers nodded, their expressions inscrutable yet filled with a deep-seated wisdom. "A prophecy has been foretold," another Flamewalker continued, their form flickering like a candle in the wind. "A new Flamekeeper will rise, one who will unite the elemental forces and restore balance to our world."

As their words washed over me, I felt a swell of pride mixed with a twinge of fear. Was I truly meant to be the Flamekeeper? The responsibility felt monumental, like a mountain I had to climb with no gear, no map. Could I rise to the occasion? The weight of their expectations settled upon my shoulders, heavy yet oddly exhilarating.

Then, as if sensing my turmoil, Shae squeezed my hand tighter. "You've faced down fire and ice, earth and air. You've fought for what you believe in," she whispered, her voice steady. "You can do this." I wanted to believe her, but the shadow of self-doubt loomed large.

The Flamewalkers continued, their voices weaving intricate stories of my ancestors, of those who had come before me. Each tale was a flickering flame, igniting a fire within me. I could almost see their faces—determined, fierce, and unapologetically brave. I closed my eyes for a moment, allowing their energy to flow through me. I could feel the heat of their courage, the passion that had driven them to harness the flames. They had fought battles and forged alliances, and now their spirits were entrusting me with this legacy.

When I opened my eyes, I noticed a flicker of flame dance in the palm of my hand, a small ember glowing with potential. I stared at it, mesmerized. The Flamewalkers were right; I was part of this lineage, bound by fire and flame. My ancestors' wisdom coursed through me like molten lava, urging me to embrace my destiny. "What must I do?" I asked, my voice stronger now, fueled by the fire within.

The Flamewalkers exchanged glances, a silent conversation flowing between them. "To wield the Emberstone, you must first understand the delicate balance of the elements. You will embark on a journey, one that will challenge you in ways you cannot yet comprehend," one of them said, their voice rich and soothing like the soft crackle of a warm fire. "You will learn not only to control the flames but also to respect the forces of nature that swirl around you."

My heart raced with a mix of excitement and trepidation. "Where will this journey take me?" I pressed, my mind racing with possibilities. I was ready, or at least as ready as I could be.

"To the four corners of the earth," they replied, the air shimmering with anticipation. "Each element will reveal itself to you, testing your resolve and teaching you its secrets. Only then will you be ready to wield the true power of the Emberstone."

I felt a fire igniting within me, a sense of purpose blooming like the first flowers of spring. I was not just a bystander in this unfolding tale; I was a part of it, a pivotal thread woven into the tapestry of our world.

As the last echoes of their voices faded, the Flamewalkers turned away, merging into the swirling embers of the conclave. I stood at the center of it all, a spark of determination blazing brightly within my heart. I was ready to embrace my destiny, to learn from the elements, and to become the Flamekeeper this world so desperately needed.

A shimmer of hope ignited within me, mingling with the weight of the Flamewalkers' prophecy. I could feel the heat of their expectations wrapped around me like a cloak, both comforting and suffocating. As the last echoes of their wisdom faded into the fiery ether, the conclave transformed. The vibrant colors of the stones morphed into a deep crimson, glowing with an intensity that mirrored the pulse of my racing heart. I could almost taste the anticipation in the air, thick like the first hint of smoke before a fire breaks out.

"Okay, what now?" I whispered to Shae, who was standing beside me, her eyes still wide, sparkling like two suns caught in a tempest. She glanced at me, her expression a mixture of admiration and disbelief. I could see her struggling to comprehend the weight of what had just been laid at our feet. The journey before us was not merely a matter of personal growth; it was a monumental task of untangling the threads of destiny woven into the fabric of our world.

Before she could respond, the ground trembled beneath our feet, a low rumble that reverberated through the stone. The Flamewalkers began to dissipate, their fiery forms merging with the very air, leaving behind flickers of light that danced like fireflies. Just as I felt the last of their warmth ebb away, a crack split the air, loud and commanding.

From the heart of the conclave, a figure emerged, stepping through a swirling vortex of flame and smoke. This new arrival was unlike the ethereal Flamewalkers; she was solid, her form brimming with a fierce energy that demanded attention. Long, fiery tendrils cascaded down her back, framing a face carved with the elegance of time itself. Her eyes glowed with an inner light, a mix of fiery orange and smoldering ember that drew me in.

"I am Eldara," she declared, her voice resonant and powerful. "Keeper of the Emberstone." Each word rolled off her tongue like molten gold, warm and enticing. "And you, young Flamekeeper, have a path laid before you. But first, you must understand the journey's cost."

I could feel the weight of her gaze, an unyielding scrutiny that stripped away my bravado. "Cost?" I repeated, my heart dropping. There was always a cost. I had learned that lesson well through every trial and challenge I had faced.

"The journey to unite the elements will demand sacrifices," Eldara continued, her voice steady like a flame flickering in the wind. "Every element has its own temperament, its own secrets and desires. To understand them, you must immerse yourself fully, embracing both the joy and the pain they bring."

The air around us grew heavier, charged with an electricity that crackled at my fingertips. I thought of the elements I had encountered before—the fierce tempest of water, the relentless winds, the stubborn earth. Each had tested my resolve, had demanded something of me.

"But what sacrifices?" I asked, struggling to keep my voice steady. Shae leaned closer, her breath warm against my ear, a reminder that I wasn't alone in this whirlwind of uncertainty.

"Time, comfort, perhaps even relationships," Eldara replied, her expression solemn. "The more you learn, the more you will need to let go. It is a burden borne by all Flamekeepers before you."

A lump formed in my throat as I considered the friends and family I had fought to protect. Could I really put distance between us for the sake of a prophecy? The idea felt like a fierce gust of wind, threatening to blow me off balance.

"Your friends are brave," Eldara continued, sensing my turmoil. "But they will not walk this path with you. It is one you must tread alone, at least for a time."

The air crackled with the tension of unsaid words, the energy swirling around us, a force both thrilling and terrifying. "What if I fail?" I managed, each syllable laced with doubt. "What if I can't bring balance to the elements?"

Eldara smiled, a flicker of warmth that seemed to illuminate the shadows around us. "Then you will learn from your failures, as all Flamekeepers do. It is through those failures that wisdom is forged."

Taking a deep breath, I felt the flame within me flicker, growing brighter with resolve. If my ancestors had persevered, if they had faced their trials head-on, then I could too. This was my legacy, my calling. I was destined to unite the elements and restore balance, even if the path was fraught with uncertainty.

"I'll do it," I said, surprising even myself with the conviction in my voice. "I'll embrace the challenges and learn from them."

Eldara's eyes sparkled with approval, and the flames around her intensified, bathing us in an orange glow. "Then it begins. Your first trial awaits you."

With a wave of her hand, the ground before us transformed, revealing a swirling portal of fire and light. I took a step forward, feeling Shae's grip tighten on my hand. "Are you sure about this?" she asked, her voice barely above a whisper, tinged with worry.

I nodded, forcing a smile to mask my uncertainty. "It's what I'm meant to do. We're Flamekeepers, right?"

She gave me a brave smile in return, though I could see the fear lurking behind it. "Together, then."

As we stepped toward the portal, the world around us blurred, the colors swirling together like a painter's palette gone awry. In that moment, I felt the bond between us solidify, our shared resolve a steady flame amidst the chaos. We might be on separate paths, but our spirits would remain intertwined, guiding each other through the darkness.

With a final glance back at Eldara, I felt the warmth of her approval washing over me. Then, without hesitation, I stepped into the unknown, the flames swirling around us as the portal closed behind us with a final crackle.

The air shifted, and we landed in a new realm—a breathtaking landscape bursting with color. Vibrant flowers burst from the ground like fireworks, and towering trees reached toward the sky, their leaves shimmering with an iridescent glow. The scent of blooming jasmine filled the air, intoxicating and sweet. Yet, beneath this vibrant surface lay an undercurrent of unease, a reminder that even beauty could hide danger.

The world around me pulsed with life, each breath of wind whispering secrets. I was no longer just an observer; I was a participant in a grand tapestry woven from the elements, each thread a testament to the journey I had embarked upon.

As I took my first step into this new chapter, I felt a flicker of excitement mixed with trepidation. I was ready to learn, to grow, and to embrace whatever came next. After all, every flame must be fed, and I was just beginning to discover the kind of Flamekeeper I could be.

As I stepped into this new realm, the brilliance of the landscape engulfed me. Each hue seemed to dance with a vibrancy that tugged at the corners of my mind, urging me to explore. Lush greens swirled into deep violets, while crystalline streams twisted through the terrain, their waters shimmering like liquid glass. The sun hung low in the sky, casting a warm golden light that accentuated the world's beauty and hinted at the mysteries hidden within it.

The sound of laughter echoed through the air, bright and effervescent, as though the very elements were celebrating our arrival. Shae nudged me with a grin, her curiosity piqued. "What do you think this place is?" she asked, her voice tinged with awe.

"I'm guessing a little slice of paradise mixed with chaos," I replied, peering closer at a nearby flower, its petals unfurling like flames licking the air. "Or maybe it's just the first stop on our cosmic road trip."

Our banter hung lightly in the air, a shield against the weight of uncertainty we had just left behind. As we ventured further, the landscape shifted, revealing a massive tree with a trunk wider than any I had seen, its branches extending high above, intertwining like the fingers of a giant reaching for the heavens. This tree pulsed with life, its bark etched with symbols that glowed softly, echoing the runes of the Flamewalkers.

"Look at that," Shae breathed, pointing toward the base of the tree where a small opening beckoned us. "Should we?"

"What's the worst that could happen?" I said, though I wasn't entirely sure I believed my own words.

We approached cautiously, and as we entered the hollow, the air grew cooler, infused with the scent of rich earth and ancient wisdom. The interior was adorned with bioluminescent fungi, casting a soothing blue light over the walls. Sitting cross-legged at the center was a figure draped in flowing robes that shimmered like starlight, their head bowed in meditation.

"Welcome, seekers," the figure said, lifting their gaze to meet ours. Their eyes sparkled like the night sky, swirling with galaxies and secrets untold. "I am Sylphina, Guardian of the Elements."

I exchanged a glance with Shae, who appeared equally entranced. "What do we seek?" I asked, my voice barely above a whisper, as if I might disturb the delicate balance of this ethereal space.

"To know the essence of your powers," Sylphina replied, their voice a melody that resonated deep within me. "You will face trials unique to each element, but fear not, for I will guide you."

"What kind of trials?" Shae interjected, her tone half-excited, half-terrified.

"Each trial will challenge your understanding of balance. Fire, water, earth, and air must all be honored and respected. Only by embracing their truths can you hope to wield the Emberstone and fulfill the prophecy."

A flicker of determination ignited within me. "I'm ready," I said, the conviction in my voice surprising even myself.

"Then let us begin," Sylphina said, gesturing toward a swirling portal that appeared behind them, shimmering with the colors of the elements.

Without hesitation, I stepped forward, pulling Shae along with me. As we entered the portal, I felt the world tilt, a kaleidoscope of colors rushing past until we emerged into a vast, open expanse—a desolate landscape where the earth cracked underfoot, and flames danced hungrily in the distance.

Before us, a wall of fire surged upward, roaring like a beast awakened from slumber. My instincts flared to life, and I took a step back, heart pounding. "This is the fire trial?" I stammered, feeling a mix of excitement and dread.

"The flames are alive," Shae observed, her voice steady. "They're not just a wall; they're a challenge."

"Exactly," I said, feeling the heat radiating toward us. "We need to communicate with them, to understand what they want."

As if responding to my thoughts, the flames flickered and twisted, forming shapes that danced in the air. Shadows emerged, images of ancient warriors, their expressions fierce and defiant. I could feel their power vibrating through the air, a challenge that hung between us like a taut wire ready to snap.

"Embrace the fire!" Shae shouted, her voice bold, and I mirrored her energy, channeling my own resolve.

Drawing on everything I had learned from the Flamewalkers, I stepped forward, focusing on the warmth, the energy of the flames.

"We honor you!" I shouted, hoping the sentiment would breach the barrier. "Show us your truth!"

The fire roared in response, and a wave of heat washed over me, enveloping me in its embrace. I felt my heart race, the pulse of the flames syncing with my own. I closed my eyes and surrendered to the sensation, letting the warmth seep into my bones. Images flooded my mind—scenes of destruction, of rebirth. I saw forests engulfed in flames, only to rise again, stronger and more vibrant. I grasped the duality of fire, its destructive beauty, and its ability to renew.

The flames swirled around me, forming a crown of fire that circled my head like a halo. I opened my eyes to see Shae standing beside me, her own connection to the fire glowing brightly. "This is what they want!" she exclaimed, her laughter mingling with the crackle of flames.

As we stood united, the fire transformed, shifting from a wall of wrath to a swirling vortex that drew us in. We were not fighting against it; we were becoming part of it. The flames whispered their secrets, each flicker revealing a new truth, a lesson etched in fire.

In that moment of connection, I understood. I could be both creator and destroyer. The flame within me mirrored the flame around me—a reflection of the world's complexity. It was exhilarating, liberating, and terrifying all at once.

The trial concluded as swiftly as it began. The flames receded, revealing a new landscape—a verdant oasis brimming with life, where a crystalline river wound its way through the greenery. The air was rich with the scent of flowers and the promise of rain.

"Water," I said, turning to Shae. "This must be the next trial."

The river bubbled invitingly, its surface glimmering like jewels in the sunlight. I approached the water's edge, kneeling to touch its cool surface. "What do you want from us?" I called out, my voice steady.

The river responded, the water swirling into intricate shapes, rising higher and higher until it formed a towering wave. "You seek to understand the flow," a voice echoed, sounding like the laughter of countless streams. "But know this: water can be gentle or fierce. It reflects your inner turmoil."

I straightened, feeling the weight of its challenge. I had to find my balance amidst the chaos. "What do I need to learn?"

"Control is only one part," the river answered, undulating softly. "You must learn to adapt, to flow like the current. To embrace change, even when it feels like drowning."

With a deep breath, I stepped forward, allowing the water to envelop me. It rushed around me, its embrace cold and invigorating. I felt the pull of the current, the strength of the river's movement. It was exhilarating, yet terrifying—an embodiment of the unpredictability of life.

I closed my eyes, allowing the water to guide me. Images flooded my mind—memories of chaos, of loss, of moments when I had felt submerged by the weight of expectation. I had resisted change in those times, fought against the current. But now, as the water cradled me, I understood that true strength lay in adaptability.

"I can do this," I murmured, letting the current carry me.

Emerging from the river's embrace, I felt renewed, buoyed by the lesson. The landscape transformed once more, and before us loomed the majestic mountains, their peaks shrouded in mist. The trials continued, each one weaving a complex tapestry of knowledge and experience.

We climbed the slopes together, laughter and determination guiding our steps. Each trial was a piece of a larger puzzle, a roadmap leading me toward my destiny. I was learning not just to wield the elements but to embrace the inherent duality within them.

As we ascended, the wind picked up, swirling around us with a fierce intensity. I could feel its playful energy, teasing at my clothes, wrapping around me like a familiar friend. "What's next?" I called out to the sky, a grin spreading across my face.

"Air," came the response, a whisper carried by the wind, playful and wild. "To conquer the air is to understand freedom."

The trial lay ahead, waiting to test us once again. But as I looked at Shae, her spirit unyielding and bright, I knew we would face whatever challenges came our way. Together, we would weave our own destiny, embracing the fire, water, and air with every breath we took.

I felt a surge of confidence as we approached the precipice. The world before us stretched endlessly, a breathtaking panorama of elements harmonizing in a vivid display. I was no longer just a seeker; I was becoming the Flamekeeper, ready to embrace the trials ahead and discover the depths of my own power. The journey had only just begun, and I was ready to face it all.

Chapter 15: A Spark of Doubt

The air outside the Conclave crackled with an electricity that hinted at the storm brewing overhead. I could feel it, a palpable tension that matched the uncertainty swirling in my chest. We stepped into the open expanse of the great plaza, where cobblestone streets wound their way like ancient rivers, bordered by timeworn brick buildings that leaned in, as if straining to hear the whispered secrets of the world. The sun, a waning orb hanging low in the hazy sky, cast long shadows that danced across the ground, echoing the flicker of doubt flickering in my mind.

Jax walked beside me, his tall frame casting a comforting shadow over my own. He had this way of being both imposing and gentle, a stark contrast that made me feel simultaneously safe and utterly small. His dark hair tousled in the warm breeze, and his deep-set eyes glinted with the kind of earnestness that made you want to confide your deepest fears. It was a quality I found both comforting and disconcerting. I took a breath, the sweet scent of blooming magnolias mixing with the musty aroma of the earth, grounding me just a little.

"Something's eating at you," he said, his voice low and steady, cutting through the soft murmur of the bustling marketplace nearby. A few vendors hawked their wares, vibrant fabrics fluttering in the breeze and the enticing aroma of spiced meats sizzling on open flames wafting through the air. The sights and sounds, normally so vibrant, felt muted, overshadowed by the weight of the revelation we had just unearthed.

I hesitated, my heart thudding in my chest like the distant rumble of thunder. "It's the prophecy," I finally admitted, the words tasting bitter on my tongue. "What if I'm not meant to lead this rebellion? What if I fail everyone?" My eyes searched the ground, tracing the intricate patterns in the cobblestones, as if they might hold the answer.

Jax stopped, turning to face me fully, his expression earnest and unwavering. "You're not alone in this, you know." His words hung in the air, enveloping me in a cocoon of warmth. "You have the support of everyone who believes in you."

But did I believe in myself? The question loomed like a dark cloud, casting a shadow over my heart. I wanted to believe I could be the one, the person the prophecy spoke of. But with each moment that passed, my confidence shrank like a wilting flower in the sun. "What if I'm just a girl playing at being a hero?" I scoffed, trying to inject a note of humor into my doubt, but the wry twist of my lips felt hollow.

"You're not just a girl," Jax said, his voice firm, the weight of his words anchoring me. "You're a force to be reckoned with. You've already shown more courage than most." He stepped closer, his warmth seeping into my skin. "This is about more than you. It's about all of us. You're meant to lead, and we all see that."

A flicker of hope ignited within me at his words, but it was a fragile flame, easily snuffed out by my insecurities. "But what if I let everyone down?" I challenged, the question lingering in the air like the sweet scent of the magnolias.

"Then we pick you up and keep moving forward," he replied without missing a beat. "That's what a team does."

His unwavering confidence tugged at the corners of my heart, weaving a thread of camaraderie that had been growing between us. In that moment, the chaos around us faded into the background, and I could almost hear the soft, steady rhythm of our heartbeats, aligning in perfect harmony. The promise of shared burdens and mutual support shimmered in the air, a tangible bond that wrapped around us.

I raised my gaze, searching his face for any hint of doubt, but found none. "You really believe I can do this?" I asked, my voice barely a whisper, vulnerable yet earnest.

"I don't just believe it. I know it," he stated, the intensity of his stare steadying me. "You're more capable than you realize. This isn't just about the prophecy; it's about your heart and your strength. And you have both in spades."

With each word, a flicker of doubt within me began to dim, replaced by a burgeoning sense of determination. Perhaps I wasn't just playing at heroism; perhaps I was destined to lead this charge, to rally the people who depended on me. The vibrant marketplace around us began to brighten, colors springing to life in sharp contrast against the backdrop of my worries.

"What about you?" I asked, breaking our intense gaze to look around. "What part do you play in all of this?"

He chuckled, a warm, rich sound that seemed to melt away the last remnants of my doubt. "I'm your backup, of course," he said with a teasing grin, his playful demeanor returning. "Everyone needs a sidekick, right?"

I couldn't help but laugh, the sound bubbling up like a fresh spring. "So, you're saying I'm the hero and you're just the comic relief?"

"Hey, every hero needs a good punchline," he replied, smirking as he nudged me lightly with his elbow.

In that moment, surrounded by the buzz of life and the flickering shadows of uncertainty, I felt lighter, as if a weight had been lifted from my shoulders. The warmth of his presence settled over me, igniting a spark of hope that blossomed in the pit of my stomach. Together, we could face whatever storms awaited us, and for the first time in a long while, I believed I could be the hero of my own story.

The sun sank lower in the sky, spilling its warm gold onto the bustling marketplace, transforming the cobblestones into a mosaic of light and shadow. As the vibrant colors of the stalls blended together, I felt the echoes of laughter and the gentle hum of conversation swirling around me, weaving a tapestry of normalcy that contrasted starkly with the tumultuous thoughts racing through my mind. With every step, the weight of expectation clung to me like an unwelcome shadow, trailing closely behind.

Jax fell into step beside me, a steadfast presence amidst the thrumming energy of the crowd. We navigated through the throngs of people, the lively chatter of vendors hawking their wares punctuating the air with laughter and bargaining. The scents of sweet candied fruits mingled with the rich aroma of roasting meats, teasing my senses and tugging at the edges of my awareness. Despite the lively scene, my heart raced with uncertainty.

"What are you thinking about?" Jax asked, glancing at me with a mixture of curiosity and concern. His eyes sparkled, reflecting the fiery hues of the sunset, and for a moment, I lost myself in the depths of their warmth.

"I'm just... feeling the pressure," I admitted, rubbing the back of my neck, where tension had begun to build like a tightly wound coil. "It's one thing to hear about destiny and prophecies, but it's another to actually shoulder that kind of responsibility."

His expression shifted, and a flicker of understanding passed through his gaze. "You know, the more I learn about you, the more I realize you're the kind of person who embraces challenges. You thrive under pressure, even if you don't see it yet."

I snorted softly, the laugh escaping me despite the seriousness of the conversation. "Thrive? More like I trip and tumble, praying I don't faceplant on the way."

"Faceplants can be hilarious," he said, a teasing glint in his eyes. "Just look at me. I've mastered the art of dramatic falls. I might as well have a fan club."

"Your adoring fans must be a real riot," I replied, rolling my eyes playfully.

Jax shrugged with mock seriousness. "You have no idea. My mother keeps a scrapbook."

The light banter brought a smile to my face, and for a fleeting moment, the storm clouds in my mind dissipated, allowing a sliver of joy to seep through. It was strange how easily laughter could soften the edges of doubt, even if just for a moment.

As we wandered deeper into the market, a colorful mural caught my eye, the vibrant depiction of a phoenix rising from the ashes sprawling across the wall of an old building. The artist had captured its majestic wings unfurling, colors swirling with fierce determination. It was a reminder of resilience, of overcoming obstacles, a visual representation of the very journey I now faced.

"Look at that," I said, pointing to the mural, my voice filled with newfound excitement. "Isn't it beautiful?"

Jax stepped closer, examining the artwork. "It is. It reminds me of our situation, doesn't it? Rising from the ashes and all that."

I nodded, the metaphor settling into my mind like a well-placed puzzle piece. "Yeah, but what if I'm just a pile of ashes? What if I can't rise at all?"

He turned to me, his expression serious, the teasing glimmer replaced by genuine concern. "You won't be just ashes. You're more than that. And besides, every phoenix has to go through its own fire first. You have to believe in yourself."

The warmth of his words wrapped around me like a cozy blanket, but the doubt still lingered, a pesky little fly buzzing in the back of my mind. "Belief is easier said than done."

"True," he acknowledged. "But think about everything you've already accomplished. You're a fighter, and fighters adapt. We'll find a way, together."

"Together," I echoed, letting the word linger, tasting its sweetness. The notion of partnership resonated deep within me, and as we continued to meander through the vibrant market, I felt a flicker of something akin to hope begin to kindle.

Suddenly, a commotion erupted nearby, drawing our attention. A crowd had gathered around a street performer, a juggler whose colorful scarves danced through the air like butterflies. He was skillfully flipping a series of flaming torches, each blaze reflecting the gathering dusk. The cheers of the crowd rose, a cacophony of excitement that seemed to lift the very air.

"Now that's some real magic," Jax said, nodding toward the performer, his earlier seriousness momentarily forgotten.

I watched, captivated, as the juggler spun and twirled, his movements fluid and graceful. Each toss of the torch felt like a risk, a dance with danger that left the audience breathless. My heart raced with excitement, and for a brief moment, my worries melted away, replaced by awe and wonder.

As the final torch was caught and the performer took a bow, the crowd erupted in applause. I found myself clapping too, swept up in the collective joy that surrounded us. "See?" Jax leaned closer, a mischievous smile creeping onto his face. "Even the juggling guy stumbles sometimes, but that just makes the successful catches all the more impressive."

"You make it sound so easy," I retorted playfully, though his words resonated with me. "I just need to practice juggling my doubts, it seems."

"Exactly," he said, his tone lightening. "And remember, I'm here to help you juggle."

With his support, the burdens on my shoulders felt a little lighter, as if the weight of the world had been reduced to mere feathers. As we continued to walk through the market, a sense of determination began to blossom within me, fueled by the shared laughter and camaraderie.

There was magic in the air, woven into the fabric of this bustling place, and I could feel it calling to me, urging me to embrace the adventure ahead. The promise of rising, of overcoming the doubts and fears, felt closer than ever. With Jax by my side, I realized that maybe—just maybe—this journey would lead to a transformation far beyond anything I could have imagined.

The chatter of the marketplace ebbed and flowed around us, punctuated by the laughter of children darting between stalls, their giggles intermingling with the melodic notes of a nearby street musician plucking a weathered guitar. As we strolled, the sun continued its descent, casting an amber glow that draped the world in a golden veil, softening the edges of reality and lacing everything with warmth. The air buzzed with life, and yet, in the pit of my stomach, a small storm raged, reminding me that the outside world could be deceptive.

"Can you imagine what it would be like to live in a world where everything is always perfect?" Jax mused, glancing around at the vibrant scene unfolding before us. His tone was playful, but I could see a flicker of seriousness hidden behind his charming smile. "Where the sun always shines, and everyone is endlessly happy?"

I chuckled, shaking my head. "That sounds like a nightmare. Where's the fun in that? Besides, who would ever learn anything? It's the messiness of life that teaches us what we need to know."

"Touché," he conceded, nodding thoughtfully. "And here I thought you were going to say something deep about how we grow from our struggles."

I feigned offense, pressing a hand to my chest. "I'm always deep, Jax. I'm practically an ocean of profundity."

His laughter rolled like distant thunder, infectious and brightening the corners of my heart. "If you're an ocean, then I'm merely a puddle, happy to bask in your depth."

We shared another laugh, and I found myself grateful for these moments of levity, each one a small reminder that life still held pockets of joy, even amidst the chaos. Yet, as the sun dipped lower, the shadows began to stretch, creeping like uninvited thoughts into the recesses of my mind.

As we neared the plaza's edge, a flickering light drew my attention. I turned to see a small group gathered around an old woman who had set up a makeshift fortune-telling booth. Draped in flowing fabrics of deep purple and gold, she sat behind a table adorned with crystals that sparkled in the waning light. The aroma of incense wafted through the air, mingling with the sweetness of the nearby fruit stands.

"Let's check it out," Jax said, his eyes gleaming with curiosity.

"Are you serious?" I raised an eyebrow, skepticism painting my features. "You think she can really see the future?"

"Why not? It could be fun!" He nudged me forward, a playful grin tugging at his lips.

I rolled my eyes but felt a tug of intrigue pulling me closer. As we approached, the fortune-teller looked up, her eyes twinkling with a mix of mischief and wisdom, as if she held the secrets of the universe in her frail hands.

"Ah, seekers of truth!" she crooned, her voice like the rustling of dried leaves. "Come closer, and let me peer into your destinies."

Jax stepped up, practically bouncing with excitement. "What do you see for me?"

The old woman squinted, her gnarled fingers hovering over a deck of cards. "You have the spirit of a wanderer, young man. Adventure lies ahead, but beware of shadows that linger."

Jax's eyes sparkled with wonder. "Shadows, huh? Sounds ominous."

"Shadows are merely reminders that light exists," she replied cryptically, shifting her gaze to me. "And you, dear child, what burdens do you carry?"

My stomach twisted, the weight of my worries crashing over me like a wave. "I'm... not sure I want to know," I admitted, the truth hanging in the air.

"Fear not," she said, her voice soothing yet firm. "The future is not written in stone. You have the power to shape your own path."

Her words resonated within me, and for a fleeting moment, I felt a surge of possibility. But just as quickly, doubt wormed its way back into my thoughts. "What if I can't?" I murmured, the vulnerability creeping in.

"Then you must find strength in the company you keep," she said, her gaze piercing yet warm. "The bonds you forge will guide you through the darkest nights."

As I stepped back, Jax shot me an encouraging smile, and in that moment, I realized the truth in her words. Together, we had already faced so much, and together we would navigate whatever lay ahead.

We moved on, the fortune-teller's cryptic wisdom echoing in my mind. The sun dipped below the horizon, casting a vibrant orange glow that bled into shades of deep purple and navy, the stars beginning to twinkle like scattered diamonds against the canvas of the night.

"This place is beautiful," I said, taking a deep breath. "It feels alive."

"It is," Jax replied, his gaze distant as if he were soaking in the essence of the moment. "And it will only get better. We'll find a way to make a difference."

With each step, the promise of possibility intertwined with my thoughts, weaving a tapestry of hope. Yet, even as I felt that spark reignite within me, I knew that the path ahead would not be easy. The prophecy loomed like a thundercloud, dark and heavy, but I refused to let it dictate my fate.

As we strolled along, I caught sight of a large fountain at the center of the plaza, its waters cascading in a graceful dance, illuminated by the soft glow of lanterns strung overhead. I approached it, captivated by the way the water sparkled under the night sky, each droplet catching the light and sending it dancing in myriad directions.

"Let's make a wish," I suggested, the playful notion seeping into my heart.

Jax grinned, leaning against the fountain's edge. "Alright, but only if it's a good one."

I closed my eyes, letting the sounds of the fountain wash over me. "I wish for strength," I whispered, the words barely audible above the rush of water. "And clarity... and maybe a little bit of courage."

Jax chuckled. "If I wished for courage, I'd be wishing for a miracle."

I opened my eyes, laughter spilling out as I nudged him with my elbow. "You're braver than you think."

He tilted his head, a playful challenge in his eyes. "Alright, I'll take that as a compliment. And I wish for an endless supply of snacks on this journey."

I shook my head, unable to suppress my grin. "Only you would wish for food."

"Hey, snacks are essential for energy," he declared, puffing out his chest as if he were a warrior proclaiming his battle strategy. "And they make every adventure better."

I couldn't argue with that logic. "Okay, fine. Snacks it is!"

As laughter echoed between us, I felt a warmth bloom in my chest, the sense of camaraderie growing stronger, bolstered by the uncertainty that lay ahead. I took a deep breath, the air thick with possibility, and in that moment, I knew that no matter how daunting the path might become, I would face it head-on. I would rise to meet my destiny, flanked by the unwavering strength of friendship and the flickering spark of hope, illuminating the shadows that threatened to consume me.

Chapter 16: The Council Strikes Back

The air in Emberhold was thick with a suffocating blend of smoke and despair, a grim reminder of the Council's reach. Ash floated through the twilight like a dark confetti, settling on everything with a melancholy grace, draping the vibrant colors of our camp in muted shades of gray. I stood at the edge of our makeshift encampment, my heart pounding in rhythm with the distant echoes of chaos. The flickering flames illuminated the horizon, painting a hellish portrait that made my blood boil. How dare they unleash such devastation upon us?

Our rebellion had been ignited by whispers of freedom, and now it felt as though the Council had thrown a bucket of cold water on that flame, snuffing out any flicker of hope. I clenched my fists, feeling the reassuring warmth of the Emberstone against my skin. It pulsed in time with my heartbeat, a rhythmic reminder that power thrummed through me, waiting to be unleashed. I had to rally our forces. We had to rise from the ashes, both literally and figuratively, and I would not let fear chain us down.

"Gather around!" I called, my voice cutting through the murmurs of confusion and despair. Faces turned towards me—some weary, others fierce, all marked by the smoke that clung to their skin and the shadows that danced in their eyes. There was Samira, her wild curls framing a face that had seen far too much for her tender age. I could feel the warmth of her spirit even from a distance, a flame that burned bright and undeterred. Beside her stood Jace, his sharp jaw set in defiance, his hands clenching and unclenching like he was already preparing for battle.

They all looked to me, and I could see the flicker of hope struggling against the tide of fear. I drew a deep breath, letting the scent of charred wood and embers fill my lungs, focusing on the power of the Emberstone coursing through me. "This isn't just our fight anymore," I began, my voice gaining strength as I spoke. "What we've witnessed today is not just a strike against our camp; it's a declaration of war against our very existence. But we are not powerless. We are the children of the flame, and we will rise up!"

As I spoke, I could feel their spirits begin to lift, the embers of courage stoked into a growing blaze. My words wove tales of our ancestors—warriors who had once fought against the Council's tyranny, who had sacrificed everything for the freedom we dared to claim. I told stories of the fires they had kindled, of the bravery that had lit their paths, illuminating the darkness that threatened to consume them. With each tale, I could see the tension easing from their shoulders, the determination sparking in their eyes.

"We stand on the brink of something monumental!" I continued, feeling the Emberstone's heat rise as my passion surged. "The Council thinks they can intimidate us into submission, that their flames can silence our voices. But look around you! Each of us carries the flame within! We are not just numbers in their game; we are a force, a wildfire that cannot be contained!"

Samira stepped forward, her fiery spirit mirrored in the vibrant red fabric of her cloak, a flag of defiance against the ash-choked sky. "And what do we do, Ember?" she asked, her voice steady and bold, emboldened by my own resolve. "We can't just stand here and let them burn us to the ground!"

I nodded, knowing the fierce heart of a true warrior when I saw one. "We will gather what remains of our strength. We will forge alliances with those who have also suffered under the Council's hand. We will rally the people in the neighboring towns and ignite the flames of rebellion in their hearts. We will strike back—together."

The energy in the crowd shifted, morphing from despair into something tangible, a determination that rippled through the air like a sudden gust of wind. Faces that had been shadowed by defeat brightened, the flicker of hope growing into a roaring blaze. I felt that energy wrap around me, an invisible bond that tied us together in our shared mission.

"Tonight, we prepare!" I shouted, my heart racing as adrenaline surged through me. "We will gather supplies, rally our friends, and prepare our strategy. We will not let the Council define our fate! Let them see that we will not back down!"

In the moments that followed, a flurry of movement ignited our camp. The once-dim atmosphere sparked with activity. People rushed to gather weapons, provisions, and anything that could aid in our fight. I felt the rhythm of determination thrumming through the ground beneath my feet, mingling with the vibrations of the Emberstone, a tangible promise of what lay ahead.

As night fell, the stars flickered like distant campfires in the vast expanse of the sky, a reminder of our ancestors watching over us. I moved through the camp, offering words of encouragement and drawing strength from the tenacity in every determined gaze. Each face, marked by soot and resolve, was a reminder that we were not alone in this fight. Together, we would become the storm the Council never saw coming, the fire that would scorch their tyranny from our land.

And as I prepared to lead my people into the heart of battle, I could feel the weight of destiny pressing upon me, guiding me toward a reckoning that was long overdue. The Council had underestimated us, thinking they could extinguish our flames. Little did they know, we were the very embodiment of fire—unpredictable, unyielding, and ready to reclaim what was rightfully ours.

The air in Emberhold was thick with a suffocating blend of smoke and despair, a grim reminder of the Council's reach. Ash floated through the twilight like a dark confetti, settling on everything with a melancholy grace, draping the vibrant colors of our camp in muted shades of gray. I stood at the edge of our makeshift encampment, my heart pounding in rhythm with the distant echoes of chaos. The flickering flames illuminated the horizon, painting a hellish portrait that made my blood boil. How dare they unleash such devastation upon us?

Our rebellion had been ignited by whispers of freedom, and now it felt as though the Council had thrown a bucket of cold water on that flame, snuffing out any flicker of hope. I clenched my fists, feeling the reassuring warmth of the Emberstone against my skin. It pulsed in time with my heartbeat, a rhythmic reminder that power thrummed through me, waiting to be unleashed. I had to rally our forces. We had to rise from the ashes, both literally and figuratively, and I would not let fear chain us down.

"Gather around!" I called, my voice cutting through the murmurs of confusion and despair. Faces turned towards me—some weary, others fierce, all marked by the smoke that clung to their skin and the shadows that danced in their eyes. There was Samira, her wild curls framing a face that had seen far too much for her tender age. I could feel the warmth of her spirit even from a distance, a flame that burned bright and undeterred. Beside her stood Jace, his sharp jaw set in defiance, his hands clenching and unclenching like he was already preparing for battle.

They all looked to me, and I could see the flicker of hope struggling against the tide of fear. I drew a deep breath, letting the scent of charred wood and embers fill my lungs, focusing on the power of the Emberstone coursing through me. "This isn't just our fight anymore," I began, my voice gaining strength as I spoke. "What we've witnessed today is not just a strike against our camp; it's a declaration of war against our very existence. But we are not powerless. We are the children of the flame, and we will rise up!"

As I spoke, I could feel their spirits begin to lift, the embers of courage stoked into a growing blaze. My words wove tales of our ancestors—warriors who had once fought against the Council's tyranny, who had sacrificed everything for the freedom we dared to claim. I told stories of the fires they had kindled, of the bravery that had lit their paths, illuminating the darkness that threatened to consume them. With each tale, I could see the tension easing from their shoulders, the determination sparking in their eyes.

"We stand on the brink of something monumental!" I continued, feeling the Emberstone's heat rise as my passion surged. "The Council thinks they can intimidate us into submission, that their flames can silence our voices. But look around you! Each of us carries the flame within! We are not just numbers in their game; we are a force, a wildfire that cannot be contained!"

Samira stepped forward, her fiery spirit mirrored in the vibrant red fabric of her cloak, a flag of defiance against the ash-choked sky. "And what do we do, Ember?" she asked, her voice steady and bold, emboldened by my own resolve. "We can't just stand here and let them burn us to the ground!"

I nodded, knowing the fierce heart of a true warrior when I saw one. "We will gather what remains of our strength. We will forge alliances with those who have also suffered under the Council's hand. We will rally the people in the neighboring towns and ignite the flames of rebellion in their hearts. We will strike back—together."

The energy in the crowd shifted, morphing from despair into something tangible, a determination that rippled through the air like a sudden gust of wind. Faces that had been shadowed by defeat brightened, the flicker of hope growing into a roaring blaze. I felt that energy wrap around me, an invisible bond that tied us together in our shared mission.

"Tonight, we prepare!" I shouted, my heart racing as adrenaline surged through me. "We will gather supplies, rally our friends, and prepare our strategy. We will not let the Council define our fate! Let them see that we will not back down!"

In the moments that followed, a flurry of movement ignited our camp. The once-dim atmosphere sparked with activity. People rushed to gather weapons, provisions, and anything that could aid in our fight. I felt the rhythm of determination thrumming through the ground beneath my feet, mingling with the vibrations of the Emberstone, a tangible promise of what lay ahead.

As night fell, the stars flickered like distant campfires in the vast expanse of the sky, a reminder of our ancestors watching over us. I moved through the camp, offering words of encouragement and drawing strength from the tenacity in every determined gaze. Each face, marked by soot and resolve, was a reminder that we were not alone in this fight. Together, we would become the storm the Council never saw coming, the fire that would scorch their tyranny from our land.

And as I prepared to lead my people into the heart of battle, I could feel the weight of destiny pressing upon me, guiding me toward a reckoning that was long overdue. The Council had underestimated us, thinking they could extinguish our flames. Little did they know, we were the very embodiment of fire—unpredictable, unyielding, and ready to reclaim what was rightfully ours.

The fire crackled around us as we gathered, the warmth contrasting sharply with the chill that settled in my bones from the sights beyond our encampment. Shadows danced in the flickering light, twisting and turning like the hopes and fears that swirled among my comrades. I could see their faces illuminated, the sharp angles of determination carved deep, resolute even as despair hung heavy in the air. I had ignited their spirits, but the embers of courage needed stoking; they craved a plan.

With urgency weaving its way through my veins, I called for our strategists. Finn, a wiry young man with an eye for detail sharper than any sword, stepped forward. His sandy hair fell in wild curls, framing a face that held a mix of anxiety and eagerness. Beside him stood Lyra, her fierce emerald eyes sparkling with intensity. She was a natural leader, the kind of person who could rally a crowd simply by walking into a room, her presence commanding attention. Together, they formed a duo that complemented my fiery resolve with their steady focus.

"We need to gather intelligence on the Council's next move," I instructed, my voice steady. "If they've retaliated this fiercely, they must be planning something bigger." Finn nodded, jotting down notes with quick strokes on a battered piece of parchment.

Lyra spoke up, her voice calm yet urgent. "And we need to secure the support of the towns beyond our borders. If we can convince them of our cause, we'll have allies who can help us launch a counteroffensive."

"Agreed," I replied, feeling the embers of hope spark brighter within me. "Let's divide our efforts. Finn, I want you to scout the Council's movements. Use whatever stealth you can muster. Lyra, you and I will travel to Greystead. They've always been sympathetic to our cause; we just need to remind them of the stakes."

As they began to disperse, I felt a surge of responsibility wash over me, coupled with an undeniable thrill. The journey ahead would be fraught with dangers, but I felt invigorated, like a spark eager to leap into flame. I turned to face the encampment, my heart swelling with purpose as I addressed the group again. "Tonight, we prepare for what lies ahead. We will not merely endure; we will rise, ready to reclaim our freedom!"

The night unfolded into a tapestry of plans and preparations. As I walked through the encampment, I could hear the conversations buzzing like the crackling fire, warriors forging bonds, sharing memories, their laughter momentarily banishing the shadows. Each face I saw reminded me of why we fought—their hopes and dreams were wrapped up in this rebellion, just as mine was.

Once the plans were set, I slipped away to a quiet corner, the pulse of the Emberstone grounding me amidst the chaos. I needed clarity. I reached out to touch its surface, feeling the warmth radiate through me. In that moment, I closed my eyes and focused, letting the power flow through my fingertips, visualizing the paths we needed to take, the alliances we would forge.

In the early hours before dawn, I gathered my supplies—a few essential provisions, a map of the surrounding territories, and a small dagger tucked into my belt, its blade glinting with the promise of protection. I made my way toward Lyra, who was already preparing for our departure.

"Ready?" she asked, her expression resolute.

"Always," I replied, a smirk playing on my lips. Together, we set off into the shadows, our silhouettes swallowed by the dense forest surrounding Emberhold. The trees loomed above us like ancient sentinels, their leaves whispering secrets in the breeze, reminding me of the countless stories hidden in their bark.

The path was fraught with the tension of the night, the air electric with anticipation. As we walked, the sounds of the forest enveloped us—a rustle of leaves, the distant call of a night owl, and the soft crunch of twigs beneath our feet. Each step was a reminder of the battle ahead and the resolve needed to face it.

As dawn broke, streaks of gold and pink sliced through the horizon, casting a warm glow over the landscape. It was a beautiful sight, yet it felt bittersweet, a stark contrast to the destruction left behind. We pressed on, crossing the threshold into Greystead, a town draped in early morning mist that clung to the ground like a shroud.

The streets were eerily quiet, a stark reminder of the Council's grip on the region. Yet I sensed the spirit of the people lurking beneath the surface, a silent cry for change just waiting to be heard. We approached the town square, where the old stone fountain still gurgled softly, an echo of life that had once thrived here.

Lyra and I exchanged glances, an unspoken agreement passing between us. We needed to gather our allies, ignite the fire of rebellion among the townsfolk, and show them the path forward. As we approached the tavern, its weathered sign creaking in the gentle breeze, the scent of fresh bread wafted through the air, a tantalizing reminder of simpler times.

Inside, the atmosphere was thick with the chatter of morning patrons, their voices mingling with the clinking of mugs. The innkeeper, a stout woman with a warm smile that belied the hard life she led, greeted us. "What brings you two to Greystead? Not often we see outsiders here."

"Change," I replied, my voice steady, drawing the attention of nearby tables. "We seek to rally the people against the Council. They've struck at our home, and it's time to rise up together."

Gasps rippled through the crowd, a mixture of fear and curiosity igniting the air. Whispers spread like wildfire, and I could see the flickers of recognition and longing in their eyes—the same desires that had once lit our own flames of rebellion.

Lyra stepped forward, her voice confident. "We are not alone in this fight. We need your strength, your voices to join ours. Together, we can turn the tide against the Council and reclaim our freedom!"

A murmur swept through the crowd, uncertainty and courage warring within them. But just as I felt the spark of hope begin to catch, the door swung open violently, and a figure clad in dark robes strode in, the emblem of the Council emblazoned across his chest. A chill swept through the tavern as silence fell like a guillotine blade.

The Council had found us.

Chapter 17: The Scorched Siege

The sun dipped below the horizon, casting an amber glow across the scorched landscape. I stood at the edge of the battlefield, the scent of charred earth and singed grass thick in the air. It was a smell that clung to my senses like an unwelcome reminder of our last skirmish, the memory of defeat hanging over me like a dark cloud. Each breath felt heavy with the weight of anticipation, a prelude to the chaos that would soon unfold.

Around me, my comrades prepared for what felt like the inevitable clash. We were an eclectic group, united not just by our purpose but by the trials that had shaped us. Talia, with her fierce red hair pulled back into a taut braid, paced anxiously beside me. Her emerald eyes sparked with defiance, catching the last light of day as she gripped her sword with a white-knuckled determination. I admired her resolve; she was like a thunderstorm contained within a fragile body, ready to burst forth with ferocity.

In contrast, Lyle lounged against a gnarled tree, his signature smirk plastered on his face, as though he were watching a comedy rather than preparing for battle. "You know, if I had a nickel for every time we've faced down the Council, I'd have enough to buy a small island," he quipped, twirling a dagger in his fingers, the light catching its blade and reflecting a multitude of tiny, shimmering stars.

I couldn't help but smile despite the tension. "An island? Sounds nice. Just you, me, and a bottomless supply of coconut water," I replied, trying to lighten the atmosphere. "I'd trade all of this for a little bit of peace and quiet."

"Coconut water? Please, I'd want something stronger," he retorted with a playful wink, but his eyes held a glimmer of seriousness beneath the jovial facade. He understood, as we all did, that tonight's battle was more than just another confrontation; it was a fight for our future.

Above us, the skies darkened, and the rumble of distant thunder reverberated ominously. Pyrax, our formidable dragon ally, soared against the backdrop of the encroaching night, his scales glistening like molten metal. I glanced up, momentarily awed by his majestic form. Each powerful flap of his wings sent gusts of wind cascading down, ruffling my hair and drawing a few strands across my face. His roars were both terrifying and exhilarating, a primal anthem of our shared defiance.

"Time to get moving," I declared, feeling the Emberstone at my chest pulse with warmth. It was an extension of my spirit, a reminder of my own fire, my own strength. As I wrapped my fingers around its smooth surface, a surge of energy coursed through me, igniting the resolve within my heart.

We advanced through the charred remnants of what had once been a thriving forest, the trunks blackened and twisted, reaching towards the sky like skeletal hands pleading for salvation. The ground was uneven, littered with debris from previous battles, the remnants of our fight against the Council's oppressive grip. I could almost hear the whispers of the fallen, the echoes of their courage urging me onward. Each step was a reminder of what was at stake—not just for us but for everyone who had been silenced by the Council's iron fist.

As we neared the stronghold, the air thickened, electric with tension. The Council's fortress loomed ahead, a foreboding edifice of stone and shadow, its towers piercing the sky like fangs ready to devour the brave. Flashes of light erupted from within, a violent dance of power that signaled our enemies were aware of our approach. The time for hesitation was long gone; our resolve steeled against the impending storm.

I felt the heat radiating from Pyrax as he landed with a thundering crash, his presence casting an awe-inspiring shadow over us. "Let's show them what we're made of," I shouted, my voice rising above the din of battle preparations. My heart raced, fueled by the adrenaline surging through my veins.

The command rang out, and we surged forward, a tide of fury and hope. As we charged, flames erupted overhead, igniting the night sky. Pyrax unleashed a torrent of fire upon the Council's guards, the inferno illuminating our path and casting eerie shadows that danced like spirits across the ground. The air crackled with energy as I felt the Emberstone's warmth intensify, synchronizing with the chaos that unfolded around us.

I dodged a swing from a guard's sword, the blade whistling through the air just inches from my face. Adrenaline propelled me forward, my own weapon glinting in the firelight as I swung with precision, the blade connecting with the guard's armor and sending him staggering back. Each clash of steel resonated like music—a cacophony of defiance, a symphony of our resistance.

The chaos of the battlefield was intoxicating; it was a blend of screams, shouts, and the crackling of flames. I fought with a singular focus, my movements fluid and instinctive, each strike a testament to the training and sacrifice that had brought me here. The Emberstone pulsed in rhythm with my heartbeat, each thrum empowering me further, reminding me of my purpose, of the fire within that refused to be extinguished.

As I fought side by side with Talia and Lyle, I felt an unbreakable bond form between us, forged in the crucible of battle. Together, we were unstoppable—a trio of fire and fury, united against the darkness that sought to engulf us. The world around me faded into a blur, the battlefield becoming an extension of my very being, every breath a call to arms, every heartbeat a reminder that we were not alone.

In the eye of the storm, amidst the chaos and the heat, I found my resolve. With the Emberstone guiding me, I could feel the tides shifting, the possibility of victory igniting a fire in my heart that was as fierce as the flames Pyrax unleashed. The Council would know our names by the end of this night, and with every strike, we carved our legacy into the very fabric of our world.

Flames flickered wildly, casting a warm glow over the battlefield, and I lost myself in the rhythm of the fight. The Emberstone, warm against my chest, pulsed in time with my heart, resonating with the power coursing through me. Each enemy I faced was another puzzle piece in the chaotic mosaic of battle, and with every twist and turn, I felt more alive than I had in years. I ducked beneath a swinging blade, the steel glimmering in the firelight, then retaliated with a swift thrust that sent my opponent reeling.

To my left, Talia was a whirlwind of fury, her sword slicing through the air with a precision that seemed almost dance-like. She was the embodiment of passion and fire, her every move a testament to her training and resolve. The once-bright red of her hair now seemed to shimmer with the flames around us, a fiery halo framing her fierce expression. "Stay close!" she shouted, her voice a rallying cry amid the din of battle. I felt an odd sense of comfort knowing she was there, battling by my side, her unwavering spirit igniting my own.

Lyle, ever the trickster, was weaving through the chaos like a shadow, using his speed to disarm opponents before they even realized what had happened. His laughter rang out, echoing like a battle horn, each burst of humor a sharp contrast to the grim reality surrounding us. "Hey, don't fall too far behind!" he called, a devil-may-care grin plastered across his face. "I'd hate to have to rescue you, and you know how I feel about getting my boots dirty!"

The thought of Lyle's boots—always perfectly polished, despite the chaos—almost made me laugh. Almost. Instead, I focused on the oncoming wave of guards, their armor glinting ominously in the firelight. They were a sea of menace, but we were a tempest ready to collide with them head-on.

As I pushed forward, I felt the Emberstone's energy heighten, a beacon of warmth that wrapped around me like a comforting embrace. With each thrust of my weapon, I called upon its power, summoning flickers of flame that leapt from my blade, engulfing my enemies in a bright inferno. It was exhilarating and terrifying, the very essence of fire embodying my will to fight, to protect those I loved. I fought not just for survival but for a future where laughter could exist freely, untainted by the Council's iron grip.

The ground beneath my feet was a patchwork of scorched earth and crumbled stone, remnants of past battles etched into the landscape like scars. I could feel the spirits of those who had fought before us lingering, their courage infusing the air with an unyielding strength. It was a reminder that we were not alone, that we carried their hopes and dreams as we charged forward.

In the midst of the chaos, I caught sight of Pyrax swooping low, his massive form creating a gust of wind that knocked several guards off their feet. He was a creature of pure majesty, a living embodiment of the fury we fought with. I had always admired him, but watching him unleash his fury felt like witnessing a storm—a beautiful, terrible force that could level everything in its path. As flames poured from his mouth, I couldn't help but feel a surge of gratitude for having him as our ally.

The tide of battle shifted; our forces began to gain ground. With every fallen guard, the weight on my shoulders lightened, if only just. I fought my way toward the main entrance of the fortress, determined to breach the stronghold. My heart raced as the stone walls loomed closer, a formidable barrier separating us from our goal. I could feel the pulse of the Emberstone in tune with my racing heart, and for a moment, the world around me faded to a dull hum. All that mattered was the fight, the urgency of the moment, and the bond between my comrades and me.

With one final push, I broke through the remaining guards, my sword slicing through the air, leaving a trail of flames in my wake. Talia and Lyle were right beside me, a flanking force that drove us forward. We were unstoppable, a trinity of fire and spirit, united in our quest for freedom.

Inside the fortress, the atmosphere changed drastically. The air was cool and heavy, thick with the scent of damp stone and fear. Flickering torches illuminated dark corners, casting long shadows that seemed to reach for us like grasping hands. My heart thumped loudly in my chest, an echo of the battle outside slowly fading into the distance. We had entered the heart of the beast, and I could feel the weight of anticipation settling over us.

"Stick together," Talia whispered, her voice low but firm. "We don't know what we're up against in here."

I nodded, gripping my sword tighter. The Emberstone's warmth was a comfort, a reminder that I was not alone. I could feel the shared determination radiating from my friends, each of us fueled by the same purpose—to dismantle the Council's reign of terror, to reclaim our lives.

As we stepped further into the stronghold, I sensed a shift in the atmosphere. Shadows moved, darting just beyond the periphery of my vision, teasing my senses. "What's lurking in the dark?" I muttered, half to myself and half to the group.

"Probably something that could eat us for breakfast," Lyle quipped, though his voice held an edge of tension. The dark hallways felt alive, a slumbering beast that would awaken at any moment.

Suddenly, a loud clang echoed down the corridor, a resounding alarm that sent shivers racing up my spine. I felt the energy in the air shift, thickening like a fog. A moment later, figures emerged from the shadows—Council guards, their eyes glinting with malice, weapons drawn, ready to unleash their fury upon us.

"Here we go," I breathed, stepping forward as the guards advanced, their boots pounding against the stone floor. The Emberstone flared with heat, a wild and untamed blaze that mirrored the fire in my heart. This was it—the moment where everything we fought for would be put to the test.

The sun hung low in the sky, casting a reddish hue over the battlefield that mirrored the chaos unfolding below. Shadows of our comrades, hardened by countless trials, flickered like wraiths against the blazing backdrop. With every step we took toward the Council's stronghold, the heat of the flames seemed to reach out, licking at our boots, a fiery reminder of what was at stake. Clutching the Emberstone tightly, I felt its warmth pulse against my palm, syncing with the thundering of my heart, as if the stone itself was a part of me—a living, breathing entity eager to unleash its power.

As we reached the outer defenses, our advance was met with the piercing shrieks of the Council's sentinels—mechanical beasts that towered over us, their metallic forms glinting ominously in the dying light. They moved with an unsettling precision, their gears grinding, a mechanical symphony of war that sent shivers down my spine. With a flick of my wrist, the Emberstone flared, and a wave of fire erupted, engulfing the nearest sentinel. Its shrieks mingled with the roar of the flames, a cacophony of destruction that echoed across the scorched earth.

My comrades rallied around me, emboldened by our collective resolve. Brenna, her emerald eyes gleaming with determination, flanked my right. With a swift movement, she summoned a torrent of wind, channeling it to scatter the ashen remnants of our enemies. "We fight for our home!" she shouted, her voice rising above the clamor, a clarion call that ignited our spirits. Her words wrapped around us like a protective shroud, urging us onward. On my left, Garin charged, brandishing his sword, which shimmered with an ethereal light. He was the embodiment of raw strength, a force of nature bent on crushing the Council's iron grip.

As the battle raged, I found myself reflecting on the intricate web of alliances and betrayals that had brought us here. The Council, once a beacon of hope, had twisted its purpose, turning against those it was meant to protect. Each face of the fallen sentinels reminded me of the sacrifices that had been made—of families torn apart and dreams turned to ash. Yet, within the fire and fury, I sensed something deeper—a flicker of camaraderie igniting among us, weaving a tapestry of resilience that no tyrant could tear asunder.

Above us, Pyrax soared like a blazing comet, a majestic embodiment of fire and fury. His roars filled the air, a sound both terrifying and thrilling, as he dove toward the fray. He exuded an aura of ancient power, his scales shimmering like molten gold, a reminder of the dragons' legacy that coursed through our veins. With a mighty beat of his wings, he unleashed a torrent of flames that swallowed a battalion of the Council's forces whole. For a moment, the world turned to an infernal sunset, a tableau of fiery chaos that danced across the horizon.

But even as we pressed forward, I could feel a sinister undercurrent. The Council had prepared for this, their defenses strengthened by dark magic and cunning. As the last of the sentinels fell, the ground trembled once more, not from the weight of our victory, but from the awakening of something far more formidable. The earth split open with a deafening roar, revealing a hidden abyss—a chasm pulsating with an ominous glow. From its depths emerged the Council's dark champion, a creature forged from nightmares, its form shifting like smoke, eyes like burning coals boring into our souls.

Fear gripped my heart, but the Emberstone flared in response, its power resonating with my determination. "We stand together!" I bellowed, my voice slicing through the air like a sword. "Together, we will conquer this darkness!" My words ignited a fire within my comrades. One by one, they rallied around me, their spirits unyielding even in the face of despair.

Brenna conjured a shield of wind, wrapping it around us, while Garin led the charge, his sword glinting with fierce resolve. The beast loomed before us, a titanic mass of shadow and malice, yet we pressed on, emboldened by our shared purpose. The Emberstone throbbed with energy, urging me forward. I focused on the creature, channeling the ancient magic of the stone. Fire danced at my fingertips as I conjured a blazing projectile, launching it straight toward the dark champion.

As the flames collided with the creature, it roared—a sound that resonated through the air, shaking the very ground beneath us. The beast staggered back, its form shifting and twisting in response to our collective might. It was a moment of unity, a testament to the strength of our bonds. We were more than individuals; we were a force, a living tapestry woven from threads of courage, sacrifice, and defiance.

But the battle was far from over. The creature recovered, its dark energies swirling with a vengeance. It lashed out, tendrils of shadow snaking toward us. I felt the pull, an icy grip around my heart, but the Emberstone flared brighter, pushing back against the darkness. "Hold the line!" I shouted, my voice fierce and unwavering. "We will not falter!"

The ground shook as we faced the creature together, our spirits intertwined like the flames of a firestorm. Each breath was an act of defiance, each heartbeat a reminder that we were alive, that we fought for a future free from tyranny. We were not mere pawns in the Council's game; we were the architects of our destiny.

With renewed fervor, we surged forward. Brenna unleashed a tempest of wind, forcing the creature back, while Garin's blade cut through the air, a shimmering beacon of hope. As I raised the

Emberstone high, it illuminated the battlefield with a fiery glow, an emblem of our struggle against the encroaching shadows. Together, we unleashed a wave of fire, a brilliant explosion of light and heat that engulfed the dark champion, a climax of fury that would resonate through the ages.

In that moment, we became legends—not just of our own making, but as harbingers of change, a collective force that would reshape the future. The Council's stronghold trembled, the very foundations quaking under the weight of our determination. As the smoke cleared, and the echoes of our battle faded into the night, we stood united, ready to forge a new world from the ashes of the old.

Chapter 18: Betrayal in the Flames

Amidst the swirling chaos of the battlefield, the air crackled with an energy that felt alive, a tangible force that thrummed in my veins. Smoke billowed from the charred remnants of what had once been a thriving market square, its vibrant colors now dulled by ash and fire. The scent of singed wood mingled with the acrid tang of sulfur, stinging my nostrils and urging me to fight harder. Jax stood beside me, his dark hair whipping wildly in the heat of the inferno, his eyes blazing with determination as we fended off the onslaught of Council soldiers.

The sun dipped low on the horizon, casting a crimson hue over the devastation, illuminating the shards of glass that lay scattered like fallen stars across the cobblestone. Each clash of metal against metal echoed through the chaos, a discordant symphony that fueled the frenzy of battle. I swung my sword with practiced precision, feeling the weight of it in my hands, the familiar grip comforting even as fear gnawed at the edges of my resolve. My heart raced, not just from the fight but from the sinking sensation that something was profoundly wrong.

Then, in that frantic moment, I caught a glimpse of movement—a shadow slipping through the throng, a figure whose face was obscured beneath a hood. My stomach twisted with unease as I instinctively turned my focus from the soldiers pressing in around us. Who was this interloper, and why did they feel so out of place in this melee? I had fought alongside friends and allies, people whose faces were etched in my memory, but this shadow was different, carrying an air of treachery that sent a chill crawling up my spine.

Jax noticed my distraction, his brow furrowing as he caught my gaze darting toward the cloaked figure. "Focus, Ava!" he shouted, his voice cutting through the clamor. But my instincts were already screaming at me, urging me to investigate. I nodded sharply, trying to shake off the feeling of foreboding, but the urge to uncover the truth tugged at my core, stronger than the need to defend myself in the moment.

With a surge of adrenaline, I maneuvered through the mass of combatants, each step bringing me closer to the elusive shadow. The clashing swords and cries of anger and pain faded into a dull roar, drowned out by the pounding of my heart. The crowd thickened, pushing me forward like a current in a raging river, yet I found myself fueled by a single, burning question: who was betraying us?

As I drew nearer, I felt the tension coiling in my chest, tightening like a vice. The figure glanced over their shoulder, just as I closed the distance, and I caught a fleeting glimpse of familiar features before they vanished again into the throng. A gasp escaped my lips, slicing through the din. No. It couldn't be. My mind raced back to moments shared, laughter echoing through the halls of our makeshift camp. It was a face I had trusted, a companion whose allegiance I had never doubted until now.

The betrayal struck me like a blade, cold and sharp, a feeling so foreign that it left me momentarily paralyzed. I felt anger bubbling up, hot and fierce, but it was quickly quenched by the rising tide of panic. I had to find Jax. Had to warn him.

I spun on my heel, weaving through the chaos, my instincts guiding me back to my partner in arms. When I finally reached him, breathless and wild-eyed, I grabbed his arm. "Jax, we have a traitor among us. It's... it's someone we know!"

His expression shifted from determination to confusion. "What do you mean? Who?"

I shook my head, trying to ground myself in the reality of the battlefield around us. "It was—" I couldn't say the name. I couldn't bear the weight of the truth just yet. But the firelight caught the determination in his gaze, the understanding that my fear was palpable.

Just then, the shadowed figure reappeared, not far from us. My stomach sank as I watched them slip behind a fallen cart, one that was now a makeshift barricade amidst the chaos. My heart pounded like a war drum, each beat echoing my mounting dread. Jax's grip tightened around my arm as he followed my gaze, comprehension dawning in his eyes.

"Stay close," he ordered, and I nodded, a shiver running down my spine as we advanced. Every step was a delicate dance, the ground beneath us littered with remnants of what had been—a child's toy, a ripped tapestry, and now, the vestiges of trust among our group.

The battle raged on, the air thick with the taste of blood and ash, but all I could think about was the betrayal I had witnessed. It wasn't merely a singular act; it felt as though the very fabric of our unity was fraying at the edges, threads unraveling beneath the weight of secrets and lies. I felt the need to confront the traitor, to tear back the veil of deception and expose them for who they truly were.

We maneuvered through the smoke and flames, the shadows dancing eerily, and I could sense the danger lurking just out of sight. Then, as we rounded the cart, I froze. The traitor stood before us, their hood pulled back to reveal the familiar face, the eyes I had once trusted now alight with a sinister glint. Recognition crashed over me like a tidal wave, drowning out everything else as betrayal engulfed me. In that moment, I realized the true battle was not against the Council alone but against the very forces that sought to divide us, tearing apart our shared resolve.

The clash of swords continued around us, but in that instant, I felt suspended in time, the world narrowing to the confrontation before me. The air was thick with tension, and I could hear my own heartbeat, a frantic reminder of what was at stake. My grip tightened on my weapon, and as the flames flickered, casting long shadows across the ground, I braced myself for what was to come. The battle was no longer just for survival; it was a reckoning, a fight for trust in a world quickly becoming unrecognizable.

The clash of steel echoed through the smoke-choked air, a chaotic symphony underscored by the desperate cries of comrades caught in the crossfire. I strained to catch my breath, heart pounding like a war drum in my chest, as the fray around us unfolded like a twisted tapestry of valor and treachery. Jax, a steadfast ally, parried a strike aimed at me, his eyes flashing with determination. But even amidst our struggle, the air crackled with the unsettling tension of betrayal.

Suddenly, a flicker of movement snagged my attention—a silhouette darting through the haze, slinking away as if woven from the very shadows themselves. My instincts screamed; something was dreadfully wrong. Panic surged, hot and suffocating, as I registered the danger lurking just beyond the melee. Who could it be? Who had we let into our ranks, only to find them conspiring against us? The weight of uncertainty was a stone in my gut, but I pushed it down, focusing on the immediate battle.

We fought on, each blow struck with a fervor that spoke of desperation and hope. The Council's forces pressed closer, an unyielding tide seeking to drown us. Each time Jax and I managed to carve a small victory, it was met with a ferocious counter, as if the universe itself conspired to test our resolve. It was a maddening dance of blades and fury, and I could feel the rhythm of chaos wrapping around me, threatening to pull me under.

"Stay sharp!" Jax shouted, sweat mingling with the grime of battle on his brow. His voice cut through the din like a beacon, pulling me back from the precipice of despair. I nodded, resolute, and we moved as one—a seamless flow of strategy honed through countless skirmishes. But even as we struck and defended, I couldn't shake the growing sense of dread. Each swing of my sword felt heavier, each step laden with the ghost of our traitor.

Amidst the din, I spotted a flash of fabric—dark and unmistakable—slipping through the shadows at the edge of the battlefield. My heart sank. There was no mistaking it; the traitor was slipping away, escaping the chaos they had sown. The air thickened with fury, my grip tightening on the hilt of my sword. It was infuriating, to know that we had been so close, and yet so far from the truth. They had played us like puppets, and we had danced to their tune.

"Jax, I'll hold them off!" I shouted, determination fueling my resolve. He met my gaze, his expression a mixture of fear and understanding. The battle was far from won, but the betrayal stoked the fire in my veins. If I could intercept the traitor, perhaps I could uncover their motives and turn this tide back in our favor.

Without waiting for his reply, I plunged into the fray, weaving between fighters and dodging blows as I pursued the elusive figure. Every instinct screamed at me to stop, to regroup, but I couldn't. The shadows seemed to reach for me, clawing at my resolve as I navigated through the chaos, intent on uncovering the truth behind this betrayal.

The battlefield twisted around me, a blur of conflict and desperation. My breath quickened, muscles coiling with anticipation as I closed the distance. But with each step, the shadows grew denser, shrouding the traitor's path. A thrill of danger coiled in my gut, mingling with the pulse of adrenaline as I darted forward. I had to know who had betrayed us, and why.

Just as I neared the edge of the fray, a sudden commotion erupted—cries of confusion punctuated by the clash of weapons. I stumbled slightly, instinctively ducking as a barrage of flames burst forth, illuminating the darkness with an ominous glow. My heart leaped into my throat as the flames flickered dangerously close, illuminating the visage of the traitor—a familiar face twisted with malice.

"Why?" I gasped, the word bursting from my lips like a desperate plea. Recognition washed over me, stark and chilling. The traitor had been one of us, a trusted ally who had fought alongside us through countless battles. The betrayal cut deeper than a sword, a jagged wound that left me reeling.

The traitor smirked, a cold glint in their eyes. "You really thought you could win? This was never about the Council," they hissed, their voice dripping with disdain. "It's about power, and I've chosen my side." With that, they turned on their heel, eyes narrowing as they retreated into the shadows, leaving behind a tempest of uncertainty.

As the flames flickered and died, I felt the weight of their words settle heavily in the air, wrapping around me like a shroud. Jax pushed his way through the chaos, reaching me with a breathless urgency. "What happened? Where did they go?"

I could barely find my voice, my heart still racing with disbelief. "It was... it was someone we trusted. They've betrayed us for power." The words tasted bitter on my tongue, each syllable a reminder of the fracture in our unity.

Jax's expression darkened, realization dawning as the implications sank in. "We need to regroup, figure out our next move. This isn't just about the Council anymore; it's about everything we stand for."

His words rang true, echoing in the hollow space where hope had once resided. We had thought we were fighting for our cause, but now we were grappling with the insidious rot that threatened to consume us from within. The Council may have been our adversary, but the true battle lay in reclaiming our trust, uniting against the forces that sought to divide us.

As we turned to face the ongoing chaos, I felt a flicker of resolve igniting within me. No longer would I let shadows dictate our fate. If betrayal was to be our foe, then I would fight back—every step, every swing, every heartbeat would be a defiance against those who sought to tear us apart. With renewed determination, I stood alongside Jax, ready to confront the storm that was to come, forging ahead into the heart of the flames.

In the aftermath of that harrowing moment, the battlefield morphed into a surreal landscape of shifting allegiances and fractured resolve. The air hung heavy with the acrid scent of smoke, mingling with the metallic tang of spilled blood, a visceral reminder of the conflict that had erupted so suddenly. Each face around me was marked by a tumult of emotions—fear, anger, confusion—as the realization of betrayal seeped like poison through our ranks. The Council's forces were not the only enemies we faced; treachery lurked in the hearts of those we had called allies.

Jax's hand clamped around my shoulder, a steadying presence amid the chaos. "We can't let this break us," he urged, his voice low but firm, cutting through the cacophony. The flickering firelight danced in his determined eyes, casting shadows that seemed to mimic the doubts gnawing at my resolve. "We need to gather the others, fortify our position, and figure out how to counter this."

His words resonated within me, igniting a spark of determination. We were not merely fighting for survival; we were standing on the precipice of something greater. The Council had declared war, and our unity was our greatest weapon. If we faltered now, we would be lost, swallowed whole by the very darkness that threatened to consume us.

Navigating through the remnants of our battle, I caught glimpses of my fellow warriors, each one a tapestry of grit and resilience, stitched together by shared experiences and a common cause. We had weathered storms together, endured trials that would have shattered lesser spirits. Yet, now the fabric of our brotherhood felt threadbare, fraying at the edges, as uncertainty seeped into our hearts.

We regrouped, finding a momentary haven behind the crumbling stone wall of an abandoned structure, its ancient stones imbued with stories long forgotten. The air inside was cooler, the stifling heat of battle giving way to a chill that settled around us like a cloak. Here, we caught our breaths, our faces illuminated by the flickering glow of nearby embers, shadows playing tricks on our minds.

"Everyone," I called out, my voice rising above the murmurs, drawing attention. "We've faced enemies before, but this betrayal is different. We need to confront it head-on." A murmur of agreement rippled through the group, faces tightening with determination. I continued, "The Council is manipulating us, using our fears against us. If we want to win this war, we need to reclaim our trust and stand together. We must expose the traitor."

As I spoke, I noticed the flicker of doubt on some faces, the questions that lingered unspoken in the air. Who could be trusted? Was anyone safe from suspicion? I could feel the atmosphere thickening, the camaraderie fraying like old rope, but I pressed on. "Our strength lies in our unity. We cannot let one deceitful shadow shatter everything we've built."

Jax nodded, stepping forward to bolster my words. "We'll gather information, retrace our steps. There has to be a trail—a sign that can lead us back to the traitor. They can't hide forever." His voice held a fervor that was infectious, rekindling the flame of hope within the group.

The atmosphere shifted, the tension coiling tightly around us as we forged a plan, a network of determination threading its way through our collective consciousness. We would not cower in the dark. Instead, we would hunt the shadows that threatened to consume us.

Under the guise of night, we set out, splitting into small teams to cover more ground. The city around us was a labyrinth of stone and steel, an intricate network that had seen centuries of conflict and revolution. With every alley and corner, the echoes of history resonated, whispering tales of courage and betrayal. I felt a connection to the stories hidden within the stones, a reminder that we were part of a larger narrative, one that spanned beyond our immediate struggle.

Jax and I navigated the narrow, winding streets, eyes scanning for any hint of movement. The shadows seemed to lengthen with every step, warping around us, playing tricks on our minds. Whispers of uncertainty fluttered through my thoughts, a specter of doubt that I desperately tried to push aside. I couldn't afford to lose my focus; not now.

As we ventured deeper into the heart of the city, we encountered a small tavern, its flickering lantern casting warm light against the encroaching darkness. The air outside was thick with laughter and the clinking of glasses, an oasis of normalcy amid the chaos. Jax gestured toward the entrance, and I nodded, sensing that information often dwelled where least expected.

Inside, the atmosphere was a stark contrast to the grim reality outside. Patrons shared stories, laughter ringing like bells, oblivious to the storm brewing just beyond their doors. Jax and I maneuvered through the crowd, our eyes keenly observing the interactions, searching for clues among the revelers.

Seated at the far end of the bar was a figure that drew my attention—Elara, a skilled rogue known for her sharp tongue and sharper instincts. She had a reputation for weaving through the underbelly of society, collecting secrets like other people collected stamps. I approached her cautiously, Jax flanking me, his presence a reassuring anchor.

"Elara," I began, attempting to keep my tone casual despite the urgency pressing at my chest. "We need to talk."

She looked up, amusement dancing in her eyes as she appraised us. "In the middle of a war, and you choose the local pub? Bold move."

"Desperate times call for desperate measures," Jax quipped, leaning against the bar. "We need information about the Council, and we think you might have some insights."

Her expression shifted, curiosity piqued. "Oh, I've got my ears to the ground, but what's it worth to you? Secrets don't come cheap in these parts."

I felt a rush of frustration bubble within me. "Lives are at stake here, Elara. We're fighting for our freedom, and betrayal is creeping through our ranks."

Her smile faded, replaced by a seriousness that sent a chill down my spine. "Then you need to listen closely." Leaning in, she shared what she had uncovered—whispers of dissent among the Council's ranks, of factions splintering and vying for control. It was a labyrinth of power plays, alliances, and betrayals.

"Your traitor is likely a pawn in a much larger game," she warned. "The Council isn't just fighting you; they're fighting each other. If you can exploit that, you might just find the advantage you're looking for."

Her words echoed in my mind as we stepped back into the cool night air. A flicker of hope ignited within me, but it was tempered by the weight of what lay ahead. We had to navigate the treacherous waters of deception, steering clear of the jagged rocks of mistrust.

With renewed determination, Jax and I made our way back to the rendezvous point, hearts racing with a blend of trepidation and anticipation. The battle was far from over, but perhaps, just perhaps, we had a fighting chance to reclaim what was ours and unveil the shadows lurking in the dark. The war was on, and we were ready to face whatever challenges awaited, united against the flames of betrayal that threatened to consume us all.

Chapter 19: Ashes of the Past

The embers glowed with a fierce intensity, crackling as they released spirals of smoke that curled into the night sky. I stood amidst the chaos, surrounded by the remnants of our latest skirmish, the air thick with the smell of charred wood and scorched earth. Each flicker of the flames seemed to dance with the shadows of those we had lost, their faces etched in the glowing embers, a haunting reminder of our fragile existence. My heart felt like a stone lodged in my throat, heavy with the weight of grief and remorse.

The battlefield had become a graveyard, littered with the remnants of our comrades—warriors who had fought valiantly alongside us, their sacrifice now part of the scorched soil beneath my feet. I could almost hear their laughter, echoing in the recesses of my mind, juxtaposed against the stark reality that we would never share another drink or a moment of quiet camaraderie. They had trusted me to lead, and I had failed them. I felt like a ship lost at sea, adrift in a storm of doubt, with no compass to guide me home.

As I stared into the flames, Jax emerged from the chaos, his silhouette framed by the firelight. He was a mountain of a man, with broad shoulders that had carried the weight of our burdens for far too long. His presence, usually a beacon of strength, now seemed to echo my despair. The shadows clung to his face, accentuating the lines of weariness that had etched themselves around his eyes. He approached cautiously, as if afraid to disturb the grief that enveloped me like a shroud.

"Hey," he said softly, his voice barely above a whisper, yet it carried the weight of a thousand unspoken words. "You okay?" The question hung in the air, an offering of solace I didn't know how to accept.

I nodded, though the gesture felt hollow, like the empty shells that lay scattered around us. "Just thinking." The flames crackled again, and I found my gaze locked onto the swirling embers, mesmerized by their chaotic beauty. "About them. About what we could have done differently."

"Don't," he replied, his tone sharp, cutting through the thick fog of guilt that clung to my thoughts. "You can't carry this alone, Ash. We all fought. We all lost something today."

The truth of his words struck me, and I felt a fresh wave of sorrow wash over me. I wasn't alone in this; the pain was a shared burden. Still, I could not shake the feeling that I had let everyone down. The Elemental Conclave had whispered promises of unity and strength, yet here we stood, divided by grief and fear. The weight of their expectations bore down on me like an anvil, and I wondered if I could ever rise to meet them.

As I turned my back on the flames, I caught sight of the remnants of our camp—makeshift tents fluttering weakly in the breeze, their fabric stained with the ashes of our fallen. I could almost see the silhouettes of my friends moving through the camp, their laughter ringing in the air like the sweet notes of a forgotten song. A pang of longing twisted in my chest. Would I ever feel that lightness again?

Jax, sensing my turmoil, stepped closer, the heat from the fire illuminating his features. "We need to honor them, Ash. Not by dwelling on our losses but by ensuring their sacrifices were not in vain."

His words resonated with a flicker of hope, igniting a spark deep within me. I could feel the echoes of the Conclave's teachings, their wisdom wrapping around my heart like a gentle embrace. From ashes, new life would emerge. Perhaps it was time to transform our grief into something powerful—something that could push back against the encroaching darkness.

As I looked around at the faces of my companions, each one a mixture of sorrow and resolve, I felt a renewed determination swell within me. "We will rise," I declared, my voice gaining strength with every word. "We will turn this pain into power. We owe it to them—to honor their memory by continuing the fight."

Jax's eyes sparked with a glimmer of approval, and he placed a reassuring hand on my shoulder. "That's the spirit, Ash. We're a family, and families don't give up on each other."

The warmth of his words wrapped around me like a comforting blanket, and for the first time since the battle, I felt a semblance of peace. The night air, once oppressive, now felt charged with possibility. It was time to take a stand, to transform our losses into a rallying cry.

As the fire crackled, I turned back to it, watching as the flames danced higher, licking at the night sky. Each flicker, each glow seemed to carry the voices of our fallen friends, urging us to move forward, to fight for the future they would never see. My heart swelled with purpose, and I felt the weight of my sorrow shift, replaced by a burgeoning sense of responsibility.

In that moment, I resolved to lead us not just through the trials of battle but toward a future where our sacrifices would light the way. As I breathed in the smoky air, I felt my spirit begin to rise, unfurling like a phoenix from its ashes.

The darkness may have encroached, but we would not be consumed. The flames of our unity would burn brighter, guiding us through the shadows. Together, we would forge a path forward, transforming our pain into strength and rising from the ashes of despair, united against the forces that sought to extinguish our light.

The fire crackled, illuminating our makeshift camp as if it were a beacon amidst the darkness. Shadows flickered along the edges, creating the illusion of movement, and for a moment, I imagined our fallen friends walking among us, whispering words of encouragement. It was a comforting thought, one that allowed me to hold onto the memory of their laughter, even as the chill of loss crept into my bones. I turned to face Jax, his expression a mixture of concern and determination. He had always been my anchor, a steadfast presence amid the tempest of chaos that our lives had become.

"Let's gather everyone," he said, his voice steady and reassuring. "We need to talk about what comes next."

I nodded, appreciating his pragmatic approach. There was no time to wallow in our sorrow. Instead, we needed to channel it into something constructive. I called out to the others, my voice stronger than I felt. Slowly, one by one, they emerged from the shadows, each of them carrying their burdens, yet united in purpose.

The flickering firelight illuminated their weary faces—Mira, with her fierce determination, and Theo, ever the optimist despite the grim circumstances. They formed a circle around the flames, and I felt a rush of gratitude for each of them, for their resilience and unwavering spirit. This was our family, forged in the fires of battle, each scar a testament to our strength.

"Listen up," I began, the words flowing more easily than I anticipated. "We've lost too much, but we can't let that be our legacy. We need to honor them—not with tears, but with action." The group nodded, their eyes glinting with the same determination I felt swelling in my chest. "We've fought against darkness before, and we've survived. Together, we can rise from this."

The fire crackled again, sending a shower of sparks into the night. Mira spoke up, her voice carrying a fiery intensity. "We need to plan. We can't just let the darkness grow while we sit around mourning. What do we know about our enemies? What are they planning?"

Theo, always quick to think, chimed in, "They thrive on fear and division. We need to keep our spirits high and our minds sharp. If we're going to stand against them, we need a strategy."

As they spoke, ideas began to form, threads weaving together in a tapestry of resolve. I could feel the energy shift in the air, the atmosphere thick with determination. We huddled closer to the fire, and I could see the embers reflecting in each of their eyes, a silent promise that we would not falter.

"We should scout the area," I suggested, looking around at my companions. "Gather intelligence on their movements, find out how many are left, and what they're planning next. If we can disrupt their operations, we might just stand a chance."

"Agreed," Jax said, his gaze steady. "But we need to be cautious. The last thing we want is to walk straight into a trap."

Mira smirked, her competitive spirit shining through. "When have we ever done things the easy way? We've faced worse odds before."

Her confidence was infectious, and I felt a renewed sense of purpose. We divided our tasks, each of us taking on a role that played to our strengths. Theo volunteered to lead the scouting mission, his natural curiosity and stealth making him the ideal candidate. Jax and I would work on fortifying our camp and preparing defenses—if the darkness was looking to take us down, we would not go quietly.

As we moved about the camp, gathering supplies and checking our equipment, I couldn't shake the feeling of purpose coursing through me. The weight of grief still lingered, but it was tempered by the hope of what we could accomplish together. Each task felt like a tribute to our fallen comrades, a promise that their sacrifices had not been in vain.

The night wore on, and as we worked, I found myself stealing glances at the fire. The flames flickered and danced, reminding me of the lives that had once burned bright beside me. Each memory was like a thread, woven into the fabric of my being, reminding me that while we had lost much, we still had each other.

With the camp fortified and a plan set in motion, we gathered around the fire once more, the warmth a soothing balm against the chill of the night. I watched as Theo shared a story, his laughter infectious even in the face of our shared sorrow. It felt good to smile, to let the weight of despair lift, even if just for a moment.

"Remember that time we got trapped in that cave?" he began, and soon the air was filled with laughter, the sound a sweet melody against the backdrop of our grief. "I thought we were going to become cave-dwellers forever!"

Mira rolled her eyes playfully. "You were the one who insisted on going down there, remember? We could have just stayed above ground, enjoying the sunshine!"

The banter continued, a welcome distraction from the grim reality that awaited us at dawn. As the fire crackled and the stars twinkled overhead, I felt a warmth spread through me, a sense of belonging that rooted me to the spot.

In that moment, as laughter echoed into the night, I understood the truth of the Conclave's words: from ashes, new life would emerge. We were not just survivors; we were a force to be reckoned with. United, we could rise from the depths of despair and confront the darkness together, our spirits intertwined like the flames that danced before us.

The night may have been shrouded in uncertainty, but as I looked around at my friends—my family—I felt a surge of courage. We would face whatever lay ahead, not as individuals bound by grief, but as a united front, ready to reclaim our destiny. And with that thought nestled deep in my heart, I finally allowed myself to hope for what was to come.

The night deepened around us, wrapping the camp in a cool embrace that whispered secrets among the leaves. As the laughter faded, replaced by the quiet hum of crickets and the rustling of branches, I felt a strange mixture of comfort and urgency. The warmth from the fire danced against my skin, but my thoughts spiraled back to the battle, the stakes now more evident than ever.

The coming dawn would bring new challenges, and I could feel the weight of our impending mission pressing on my shoulders.

"Tomorrow," I said, breaking the silence that had settled among us, "we rise before the sun and scout the enemy's territory. We'll need to be sharp and ready." The others nodded, their expressions shifting from mirth to serious resolve.

Jax stood, brushing the dirt from his hands as if it would somehow shake off the memories of the day. "Let's not wait for the dawn to practice. We can't afford to be complacent. There might be watchers out there, and we need to be stealthy."

With a quick nod, I initiated our training session, setting up a makeshift obstacle course using the remnants of our camp—fallen branches, crates, and whatever we could scavenge. Each task would remind us of the agility we needed to escape detection and the precision required in our movements.

Mira took the lead, darting through the course with a grace that belied her sturdy frame. Her laughter echoed as she leapt over a low branch, a hint of the fiery spirit that had brought our group together. "Come on, slowpokes! You'll need to do better than that if you want to keep up with me!"

Theo was next, bounding through the course with uncharacteristic enthusiasm. He had always been the optimist, but tonight, he exuded a fervor that ignited the spirits of the others. He stumbled over a fallen branch and tumbled, but instead of embarrassment, he laughed heartily, a sound that reminded me why we fought.

As I took my turn, my body moved through the course instinctively, each leap and roll a rehearsal for the battle ahead. I felt the tension in my muscles, the adrenaline coursing through my veins, but even more, I felt a connection with my companions, a shared understanding that we were all in this together.

After several rounds, we collapsed onto the cool earth, panting and grinning at our efforts. The fire crackled nearby, casting flickering shadows that danced playfully across our faces. The stars twinkled overhead, a scattered blanket of light that felt almost impossibly far away.

"Okay," I said, catching my breath. "Tomorrow we'll need to rise before dawn. It's essential we find out how many enemies we face and what their next move might be. Jax, you and I will lead the scouting team. Theo, you take charge of communication. If things go south, we'll need a plan to regroup."

Theo nodded, his excitement bubbling over. "I'll set up a signal. If we see trouble, I'll send a warning with a flare, like the old forest fires. Just hope it doesn't attract more of those things."

Mira leaned back on her elbows, her dark hair framing her face like a crown of shadows. "And what if they catch us? We can't fight them all; there's too many."

"Then we run," Jax said, his voice steady. "We've faced the darkness before, and running is a skill we've all perfected."

With a newfound clarity, we strategized well into the night, our voices blending with the sounds of nature. The fire crackled, sending sparks flying like tiny stars that had fallen from the heavens, each one reminding me that we were still alive.

As the night wore on, sleep tugged at me, yet my mind churned with the realities of our situation. I lay awake, staring at the vastness above, my thoughts wandering. What awaited us in the light of dawn? Would the enemy be waiting? Or would we find a path through the darkness, one illuminated by the light of our resolve?

Morning came too soon, the sun peeking over the horizon like a reluctant traveler. I stirred, feeling the chill of the morning air seep into my bones. The others were already stirring, their faces shadowed by the remnants of sleep but lit by determination. We gathered our supplies and shared a quick breakfast, the atmosphere buzzing with anticipation.

Once we were ready, we slipped into the forest, the trees surrounding us like sentinels. The early light painted the world in soft hues, casting long shadows as we navigated the familiar terrain. Each step felt heavy, as if the very ground we walked on was aware of our fears.

We ventured deeper into enemy territory, our senses heightened. The forest had transformed; it was no longer a sanctuary but a labyrinth filled with unseen dangers. The air felt thick, every rustle and crack echoing ominously, each shadow a potential threat.

As we crested a small hill, we paused, taking in the scene below. A clearing opened before us, the remnants of a makeshift camp sprawling out like a dark stain against the vibrant green. Figures moved among the tents, their postures lazy but their eyes scanning, vigilant.

"Looks like we found their hideout," Jax whispered, his voice barely above a breath.

I squinted, trying to gauge their numbers. "There's at least a dozen of them, maybe more. We need to be careful."

Theo's eyes sparkled with mischief. "What if we create a diversion? Something to draw them away?"

"Like what?" Mira asked, eyebrows raised.

"Fireworks," he grinned, the idea taking shape in his mind. "We could set off a few flares at the edge of the woods, get them to scatter while we sneak around and gather intel."

I glanced back at the camp. The plan had potential but would be risky. "If we do this, we have to be quick and quiet. One mistake, and we're in deep trouble."

With a nod from the group, we set our plan into motion. Theo and I moved toward the edge of the clearing, the adrenaline coursing through me like wildfire. Jax and Mira remained behind, ready to execute the distraction while we slipped into the camp.

As Theo prepared the flares, I surveyed the area, my heart pounding in my chest. We could turn this moment into a victory, but first, we needed to keep our heads cool amidst the chaos.

With a loud whoosh, Theo ignited the flares, the vibrant colors bursting forth like flowers in bloom. The bright light illuminated the trees, casting our shadows long and eerie against the ground.

"Now!" I shouted, and we dashed toward the camp, the sound of shouts and confusion erupting behind us. The enemy was reacting, scattering like startled birds, their chaos our opportunity.

As we slipped into the encampment, I felt a thrill wash over me. This was our moment, our chance to turn the tide. Among the tents, we spotted maps and weapons scattered about, remnants of their planning, and I realized we could gain the upper hand.

With every whispered word and hurried action, we collected what we needed, insights into their plans that would aid us in the battles to come. And as I glanced back at my friends—still a heartbeat away but close enough to feel their resolve—I understood that from the ashes of our past, we were rising again, our spirits intertwined, forging a path through the darkness together.

Chapter 20: The Infernal Showdown

The fortress loomed ahead, an ominous silhouette against the blood-orange sky, its spires clawing at the heavens like the desperate fingers of the damned. Once a sanctuary of learning and creativity, it now stood as a testament to the Ashen Council's twisted grip on our world. The flames, a menacing crimson, danced across the weathered stone, illuminating the grim faces of my comrades as we gathered for what felt like the last stand in this age-old battle of good versus evil. Each flicker of light seemed to whisper the stories of those who had fought before us, their sacrifices echoing in the chambers of my heart.

A soft wind rustled through the ashen trees surrounding the fortress, carrying with it a scent of charred earth and despair. I inhaled deeply, feeling the smoke curl into my lungs like a serpent, reminding me of the stakes at hand. We were not merely warriors; we were the remnants of hope, each one of us a living tribute to the fallen. The weight of that responsibility pressed down on my shoulders, but I straightened my back, channeling that burden into resolve.

I glanced at my closest friends, their faces a collage of determination and grief, each line etched deeper from our battles. Val, her once-vibrant hair now streaked with grey, stood resolute beside me. She had been my mentor, my anchor, and the embodiment of strength through adversity. I saw the flicker of fire in her eyes, a promise that our fight was not in vain. Her sword gleamed with an otherworldly light, infused with the remnants of our fallen allies. "This is for them," she whispered, her voice steady but laced with emotion. I nodded, feeling the warmth of camaraderie enveloping us like a protective shield.

Just beyond Val, Caleb fidgeted with the hilt of his dagger, his boyish features betraying the turmoil inside. He had come so far from the naïve kid who joined us on this journey, now a fierce warrior hardened by loss. I could see his fingers tremble, but I knew it wasn't fear; it was the thrill of battle, the blood singing through his veins as it had for so many of us before. "Remember, we're doing this together," I reassured him, reaching out to squeeze his shoulder. He flashed a nervous smile, but it was a glimmer of hope amid the impending darkness.

The fortress itself felt alive, pulsating with a malevolence that wrapped around us like a fog. Each step we took towards its threshold resonated with the echoes of past confrontations. I closed my eyes for a moment, allowing the memories to wash over me—the laughter, the friendships, the faces of those we had lost. But amid the sorrow, I found the flicker of courage igniting within me, ignited by the Emberstone's warmth resting against my chest, a reminder of the flame we must kindle.

As we reached the grand entrance, the heavy doors groaned in protest, revealing an interior that felt like the bowels of a beast—dark and foreboding. The air was thick with the scent of burnt offerings and despair, the very essence of the Council's power feeding off the fear of those they had conquered. Dimly lit torches flickered along the walls, casting eerie shadows that danced as if mocking our bravery. Each flicker illuminated grotesque statues of past leaders, their faces twisted in expressions of eternal torment. I swallowed hard, pushing back the nausea that threatened to rise. This was the birthplace of our greatest fears, yet we stood united.

We stepped inside, the chill of the stone floor creeping up my spine. Our footsteps echoed in the cavernous hall, the sound swallowed by the oppressive darkness that seemed to leech away our resolve. But I could feel it—the pulse of the Emberstone thrumming in time with my heart, a beacon of hope in this sea of despair. "Stay close," I whispered, my voice barely breaking the suffocating silence.

Suddenly, a voice cut through the gloom like a knife, sharp and mocking. "Ah, the brave little band of rebels. How quaint." The Ashen Council's leader emerged from the shadows, his presence radiating a sinister charisma. Dressed in robes of shadow, his eyes glinted like shards of ice, betraying nothing of the fear he inspired. "You dare to challenge us? You, who have already tasted defeat?"

I squared my shoulders, the weight of the Emberstone growing heavier against my chest. "We've tasted loss, yes, but we've also tasted vengeance. We will not allow you to continue your tyranny." Each word felt like a spark igniting the fuel of my resolve. I could sense the fire building within my comrades, their wills merging with mine as we prepared to unleash our collective fury.

He laughed, a chilling sound that reverberated through the chamber. "Foolish girl. Do you think you can stand against the power of despair? You are nothing but embers before a raging inferno."

With a flick of his wrist, shadows coiled around him, shifting and writhing as if alive. The darkness thickened, creeping towards us like an army of tendrils, each one eager to snuff out our light. Panic surged through me, but I pushed it down, focusing on the warm glow of the Emberstone. I could feel its energy pulsing through my veins, resonating with the truth that we were not alone.

"Now!" I shouted, unleashing the power of the Emberstone. A burst of light erupted from my hands, a radiant explosion that illuminated the darkness, driving back the tendrils that sought to ensnare us. The glow surged through the room, momentarily blinding everyone within its reach. I could see the surprise flash across the Council's faces, a brief crack in their armor of arrogance.

The flames danced to my will, swirling in vibrant hues of orange and gold, a manifestation of our collective strength and sacrifice. We were not mere embers; we were a wildfire, ready to consume everything in our path.

The flames surged forth, bright and defiant, casting away the shadows that had clung to the fortress's walls for far too long. The light illuminated my comrades, their faces transformed from masks of fear into expressions of fierce determination. Val raised her sword, its blade gleaming in the fiery glow, her battle cry echoing through the hall like a battle hymn, calling forth courage from the very depths of our souls. Caleb stood beside her, his youthful face hardened with resolve as he brandished his dagger, its edges glinting like stars against the night sky.

The Council's leader staggered back, his previously confident smirk replaced by disbelief. "You think your flickering flames can withstand the shadows?" he snarled, rallying his own dark energy. He thrust his hands forward, and a wave of darkness surged towards us, threatening to extinguish our light before it could truly ignite.

But with a surge of will, I drew deeper from the Emberstone, feeling its warmth spread through me like liquid sunlight. "Together!" I shouted, and my friends responded with a roar that shook the very foundations of the fortress. As if responding to our collective strength, the flames expanded, bursting forth in a torrent of vibrant light that surged towards the shadows, colliding with them in an explosive cacophony.

The clash sent ripples of heat coursing through the air, and I could almost taste the ash that hung thick around us, mingling with the crackling energy that surged through my veins. In that moment, it felt like the world had narrowed down to a single point: the flickering dance of fire against darkness, the visceral pulse of our shared defiance against despair.

The shadows writhed and recoiled, hissing as they attempted to snuff out our light, but I pressed on, channeling my energy through the Emberstone, feeling it resonate with my determination. "Now!" I urged, my voice carrying the weight of our shared hopes and dreams. In a synchronized movement, we unleashed our powers, a whirlwind of fire and light that crashed into the encroaching darkness, illuminating the hall in an explosion of brilliance.

With a sharp inhale, I summoned my courage and leaped into the fray, weaving through the tumult of swirling flames. Val and Caleb flanked me, their movements a well-rehearsed dance of survival, expertly navigating the chaos. The shadows screeched, an unsettling sound that clawed at my ears, but I pressed forward, unwilling to falter.

In the heart of the chaos, I spotted a figure moving through the darkened corners of the hall, weaving in and out like a wraith. The second member of the Council emerged, his eyes a blazing ember, contrasting sharply with the abyss that surrounded him. "You dare to challenge us?" he spat, the sneer curling his lips, as if we were little more than flies buzzing against an impenetrable wall.

"Dare? No, we've come to ignite!" I retorted, the words spilling from my lips as if they had been waiting for this very moment. I felt the Emberstone pulse in time with my heart, urging me on. "You've feasted on fear for far too long. Your reign ends here!"

As I spoke, the air thickened with tension, crackling with the energy of our confrontation. I could feel the emotions of my comrades wrapping around me—an electric blend of fear, rage, and unyielding hope. We were not alone. The spirits of those we had lost surged beside us, their whispers urging us forward.

With that surge of motivation, I summoned a wall of flames, a protective barrier against the Council's onslaught. The air shimmered with heat, bending light as the fire roared like a beast, hungry and alive. The figure before us faltered, the confidence draining from his face as my flames danced hungrily toward him, flickering like the hopes we carried in our hearts.

But he quickly regained his composure, and with a sharp gesture, sent a wave of shadows crashing towards us, dark and forbidding. "You think your pathetic flames can stand against the void?" he bellowed, a chilling laugh escaping his lips as the darkness began to envelop the fire. I felt the panic claw at my throat, but I refused to surrender. Instead, I held my ground, the warmth of the Emberstone a constant reminder of my purpose.

"Together!" Val shouted, raising her sword high, its gleaming edge catching the light as she drew forth her own energy. "Channel your pain, your loss—make it fuel!"

Caleb mirrored her movement, his young face lit with fierce determination. "We've fought too hard to let it end like this!" His voice was raw, carrying the weight of all the sacrifices we had endured. With that, the three of us unleashed a torrent of flame, swirling together like a storm—a unified front against the darkness.

The collision was cataclysmic. Flames met shadows in a brilliant explosion, sending shockwaves through the hall. The brightness swallowed the darkness for a heartbeat, illuminating the faces of my friends, their eyes alight with fierce resolve. But the Council would not go quietly. As the shadows recoiled, they hissed, swirling back to reform into a looming figure, undeterred and menacing.

"We are eternal!" the leader of the Ashen Council screamed, his voice a thunderclap. "You are but fleeting sparks in the grand design of despair!"

"We are sparks that can ignite a fire!" I countered, my heart racing as the Emberstone blazed with newfound vigor. "And fires can consume everything in their path!"

With every ounce of strength and love coursing through me, I pushed forward, the flames at my command roaring higher, fueled by the memories of our fallen friends and allies. Each flicker of fire was a testament to their sacrifice, and each beat of my heart echoed their names in a fierce declaration of resistance.

The darkness shrieked as our flames surged, a cacophony of sound and light that became a symphony of rebellion. I felt the heat wash over me, invigorating my spirit and knitting together our resolve. With a final rallying cry, we surged as one, breaking through the remnants of the Council's dark power, determined to emerge victorious from this infernal showdown.

The battle raged on, each clash of light and shadow a symphony of defiance echoing through the hall. I could feel the heat of our combined fury warming the air, igniting my spirit like a wildfire fueled by a thousand memories of hope. Val fought with the grace of a dancer, her sword slicing through the darkness with each precise movement, illuminating our path with a brilliance that seemed to defy the very laws of despair. Caleb mirrored her with a fervor born from youthful zeal, darting in and out, a whirlwind of determination.

I took a moment to survey our surroundings, the ornate carvings in the fortress walls now hidden beneath layers of ash and soot, once-glorious figures twisted into grotesque visages of fear and malice. The flickering torches cast erratic shadows, as if the very stones were trying to escape the weight of despair that had settled like a shroud over this place. With every strike against the darkness, I could feel the oppressive air beginning to lift, a sense of freedom slowly permeating the suffocating gloom.

"Push forward!" I shouted, the words rising above the din of battle. "We cannot let fear claim this ground!" My voice was a rallying cry, a lifeline thrown into the tumultuous sea of chaos. The Emberstone pulsed with energy against my chest, a heartbeat that synchronized with my own, urging me onward.

As we pressed deeper into the fortress, the Council's defenses crumbled like stale bread beneath the might of our resolve. The shadows screeched in agony, their forms dissipating in the brilliance of our flames, though I could feel their leader rallying for one final stand. The tension in the air thickened, each breath a mixture of smoke and adrenaline. I could sense it—a powerful surge gathering on the edges of the hall, a maelstrom of dark energy that promised devastation if left unchecked.

"Val! Caleb!" I yelled, catching their attention. "We need to disrupt their concentration. If we can take out their focus, we can turn the tide!" My heart raced as I pointed toward the leader of the Ashen Council, still reeling from our initial assault but regaining composure as he prepared to unleash his final gambit.

Val nodded, determination blazing in her eyes, while Caleb clenched his fists, energy crackling around him. "Let's do this!" he shouted, his voice ringing with an infectious enthusiasm that spurred us on.

We charged as one, weaving through the remnants of darkness that still clawed at our heels. The flames surged around us, dancing and spiraling like a living thing, eager to consume anything that dared to stand in our way. The leader met our advance with a fierce glare, shadows swirling protectively around him, the dark energy coalescing into tendrils that lashed out like serpents seeking their prey.

"Fools!" he bellowed, his voice reverberating through the hall. "You will learn that hope is a fragile candle against the storm of despair!" With a swift gesture, the shadows launched toward us, dark tendrils snaking through the air, aiming to ensnare us in their clutches.

"Now!" I shouted, channeling every ounce of strength I had left into the Emberstone. A brilliant flash erupted from my hands, an inferno of light that cut through the encroaching darkness, illuminating the chamber as if the sun had decided to take its place among the stars. The force of the light collided with the shadows, creating a shockwave that reverberated through the walls, sending tremors through the very ground beneath us.

Val and Caleb, seeing the opportunity, surged forward, their weapons gleaming as they struck at the heart of the dark tendrils, their combined strength a force of nature. The shadows writhed and shrieked, but the fire held strong, consuming the darkness until only the leader remained, standing amidst the ashes of his defeated comrades.

"You think you can extinguish me?" he spat, fury burning in his ember-like eyes. "I am despair incarnate! You cannot kill what has always existed!"

"Watch us," I replied, my voice steady despite the maelstrom of emotions swirling inside me. "We'll not only extinguish you; we'll light the way for others to rise." The power of the Emberstone thrummed through me, an affirmation of everything we fought for—the love, the laughter, the lives we'd saved and lost.

In a final burst of energy, I surged forward, channeling the Emberstone's brilliance through my palm. The energy coalesced into a blinding spear of fire, bright enough to banish shadows. "For everyone you've hurt!" I shouted, releasing the energy with all the strength I could muster.

The spear of light shot forward, piercing through the shroud of darkness. The Council leader's eyes widened in horror as the light engulfed him, flames licking at his form, consuming the despair he had clung to so tightly. "No!" he howled, the sound reverberating through the hall, a mix of rage and disbelief as he was pulled into the inferno, the darkness unraveling in his wake.

With a final, deafening roar, he was extinguished, leaving behind nothing but a faint whisper of shadows that slowly dissipated into the air. The hall, once heavy with the weight of despair, felt lighter, as if the fortress itself were taking a deep breath after centuries of oppression.

A moment of stunned silence filled the chamber as we stood there, breathless and wide-eyed, gazing at the remnants of what had been our greatest foe. Then the reality of our victory washed over us, breaking the tension like the dawn after a long night. Val fell to her knees, laughter erupting from her lips, a sound that rang with pure relief and joy.

"We did it!" Caleb exclaimed, his voice high and bright, a beacon of innocence in the aftermath of our battle. "We really did it!"

I sank to the ground beside Val, the adrenaline slowly ebbing away, replaced by an overwhelming sense of gratitude. "We fought together," I breathed, looking at my friends, their faces flushed with victory and pride. "We honored our fallen, and we carried their spirit with us."

As the remnants of the shadows faded, the glow of the Emberstone pulsed gently, now a warm ember instead of a raging inferno, a reminder of our strength and resilience. I could almost hear the whispers of those we had lost, their voices mingling with the wind, urging us to carry forward—to ignite new fires of hope in a world that had been dark for far too long.

Together, we stood as a testament to the power of love, friendship, and the unyielding spirit of those who dared to dream of a brighter future. The fortress, once a symbol of oppression, now stood as a monument to our victory, a place where hope could flourish anew. And as we stepped out into the light, I knew this was only the beginning.

Chapter 21: The Council's Wrath

The air crackled with tension as we burst into the heart of the stronghold, a labyrinthine fortress carved from the dark rock of the Colorado mountains, nestled beneath a sky bruised by the twilight. Shadows flickered like restless spirits on the walls, and the dim light only heightened the sense of dread that clung to us like a heavy fog. The scent of scorched earth filled my nostrils, mingling with the metallic tang of blood, a reminder that this was no mere fortress but a battleground soaked in the history of countless conflicts.

Jax and I stood shoulder to shoulder, adrenaline thrumming through our veins. He was a wiry figure with sharp cheekbones and hair that gleamed like burnished copper in the dim light. I caught a glimpse of his fierce determination in his green eyes, mirroring my own. Together, we were a force, igniting the air around us with our connection, the Emberstone nestled snugly against my chest pulsing in time with my heart.

The Council's elite enforcers materialized before us, their silhouettes menacing against the flickering torches that lined the stone walls. Clad in obsidian armor that absorbed the light, they advanced with an unsettling grace, their eyes glinting like predatory animals waiting for the right moment to strike. Each step echoed through the corridor, sending tremors of dread rippling through the stone, and I could almost hear the echoes of their past victories whispering from the shadows.

Without a word, the enforcers lunged. I felt a surge of energy coursing through me, the Emberstone responding to my emotions like a living creature. It was a searing flame of power, and in that moment, I was more than just a girl from a small town; I was the embodiment of defiance, the inheritor of a legacy that spanned centuries. As I lifted my blade, its edge shimmering with fiery energy,

I was aware of the responsibility that weighed upon me—this was not just a battle for survival; it was a reckoning.

The first enforcer charged, a hulking figure with muscles rippling beneath their dark armor. I sidestepped, my blade arcing through the air like a comet, and struck at the exposed joint in their armor. The blade connected with a satisfying crunch, and they stumbled back, the dark magic that shrouded them flickering like a dying flame. I could see the glint of surprise in their eyes, a brief moment of vulnerability before rage flooded back in.

Jax was a blur beside me, weaving in and out of their ranks with a dancer's grace. He deflected blows with a finesse that belied his size, his laughter cutting through the tension like a summer breeze. "You'll have to do better than that!" he shouted, his voice ringing with bravado as he dispatched another enforcer with a swift kick, sending them crashing against the stone wall.

Every clash of weapons created a rhythmic symphony—a chaotic harmony of metal against metal, punctuated by the occasional grunt of pain or exhilarated battle cry. I felt the exhilaration coursing through me, a heady mix of fear and excitement, each swing of my blade pushing me deeper into a primal rhythm, a dance of life and death that felt both foreign and familiar.

But then, the Council's leaders unveiled their true magic, a torrent of dark energy swirling through the air like a malevolent tempest. I could feel it approaching, a sinister force that pulled at my very core, attempting to snuff out the light that flickered within me. My skin prickled, and I stumbled backward, trying to center myself as I grappled with the onslaught.

"Focus, Kayla!" Jax's voice cut through the haze, grounding me. "We can't let them get to us!"

He was right; I had to fight back. Drawing on the Emberstone's power, I felt it swell within me, flames licking at my fingertips. I let out a fierce cry, channeling the energy, and thrust my hands forward, unleashing a wave of fire that surged through the hall. The flames danced like living entities, consuming the darkness, illuminating the faces of the enforcers, twisting from confidence to fear as they realized the tides had shifted.

The heat surged around me, enveloping my senses, and I could feel the raw energy coiling like a serpent ready to strike. I embraced it, letting it flow through me, fueling my movements, igniting my spirit. The fire wrapped around my form, and I was no longer just Kayla; I was a phoenix rising from the ashes, a storm ready to unleash its fury upon the world.

But just as victory seemed within reach, a piercing scream echoed through the stronghold. The sound reverberated off the stone walls, a haunting melody of despair that sent chills racing down my spine. I turned, my heart clenching as I saw one of the enforcers—an imposing figure whose dark armor had begun to glow ominously—raising their hands, weaving a spell that drew upon the very darkness we fought against.

"No!" I shouted, dread gnawing at my insides. I had seen this type of magic before, the kind that could consume entire lives in an instant, leaving nothing but echoes in its wake. I had to act, had to protect those around me and the legacy we fought to uphold.

"Together!" Jax called, positioning himself beside me, a resolute expression etched across his face. He lifted his weapon, and I could see the Emberstone's light reflected in his eyes. We were not just two fighters; we were allies bound by purpose, ready to face the oncoming storm.

The energy between us crackled, an electric current that surged through the air as we prepared to confront the darkness head-on. The enforcer's spell was powerful, but we had something they didn't—hope, fire, and the indomitable strength of our spirits. We were going to fight for our future, and I would not let the Council take that away from us.

The enforcer loomed larger as we stood our ground, their malevolent energy swirling like a stormcloud above a calm sea. I could feel the weight of their dark magic pressing down on me, a tangible force that threatened to swallow us whole. But alongside Jax, with his steadfast presence and unyielding spirit, I felt a spark of defiance igniting deep within. We were not merely opposing forces; we were intertwined destinies fighting against the same shadows.

"On three?" Jax's voice was low, teasing a grin at the corners of his mouth, even in the face of impending doom. The banter was a lifeline, a reminder of our shared humanity amidst chaos. I nodded, adrenaline coursing through my veins, feeling the warmth of the Emberstone intensify as if responding to our shared resolve.

"One... two..." I counted down, feeling the familiar rush of energy build between us, a vibrant current like the electric hum of a live wire. The enforcer cast a dark glance, their smirk twisting into something sinister as they gathered their power for another spell, their hands sparking with raw, twisted energy.

"Three!"

We charged together, side by side, and my heart thundered in rhythm with the battle cries erupting around us. I thrust my palm forward, channeling the Emberstone's flames into a concentrated burst that exploded from my fingertips like a comet streaking through the night sky. Jax mirrored my movements, his weapon arcing in a deadly dance as he thrust forward, releasing a gust of wind that amplified my fire, creating a whirlpool of flame and air that surged toward the enforcer.

The impact was explosive, a fiery spectacle that lit up the dim hall and momentarily pushed back the shadows that cloaked the stronghold. The enforcer staggered, eyes wide with shock, but the dark magic roiled around them, coiling like serpents, refusing to yield. They raised their hands, the shadows writhing, twisting together to form a barrier that shimmered ominously.

"Not today!" I shouted, the defiance in my voice cutting through the tension like a blade. This was our moment, the turning tide in a battle that had lasted far too long.

Jax's laughter echoed like a battle cry, fierce and filled with an exuberance that bolstered my courage. "Let's show them what real fire looks like!" He lunged again, his weapon crackling with energy as he advanced, his movements fluid and confident, a predator hunting down its prey.

Fueled by our combined might, I drew upon the Emberstone once more. The familiar heat surged through me, but this time it was accompanied by a newfound clarity. The flames flickered around my body, radiating a golden light that pushed back the encroaching darkness. I could feel the pulse of life and hope thrumming in my veins, a testament to everything we had fought for.

With every ounce of strength, I focused on the enforcer's barrier, weaving my fire into a tapestry of color and light. The air crackled with energy as we charged forward, the collision of our forces producing a shockwave that reverberated through the stone walls.

For a heartbeat, time suspended, and the world narrowed down to that singular moment of collision. Then, the barrier shattered in a burst of smoke and light, the enforcer's sneer morphing into sheer disbelief as they were engulfed in our flames. It was a beautiful, terrible sight, like the first light of dawn breaking over the horizon after a long, dark night.

But there was no time to celebrate. More enforcers flooded into the hall, their numbers a tide that threatened to sweep us away. I turned to Jax, who stood resolute at my side, and we exchanged a glance filled with determination.

"Time to dance," I said, a wicked smile breaking through the tension.

With a nod, we plunged back into the fray, our movements synchronized, an elegant choreography of survival. Jax deflected a blade with a flick of his wrist, sending his opponent staggering back, while I spun low to the ground, my own weapon slicing through the air. The chaos swirled around us, a tempest of clashing steel and roaring flames, and for a moment, we were invincible.

Each enemy fell before us, the tide of battle shifting as we fought our way deeper into the stronghold. But the Council's leaders were not idle; I could sense them, lurking in the shadows, their dark magic rippling through the air like a storm on the horizon. The ominous weight of their power grew heavier, and I knew they were preparing for something catastrophic.

Suddenly, a deafening roar echoed through the halls, shaking the very foundations of the stronghold. I paused mid-strike, heart pounding in my chest as I turned toward the source of the sound. My pulse quickened; this was no ordinary clash of warriors; it felt as if the earth itself was rebelling against the dark forces that sought to control it.

The enforcers hesitated, fear flickering in their eyes as the shadows began to twist and turn, forming into shapes that were at once familiar and terrifying. From the depths of the darkness emerged creatures—monstrous figures wreathed in shadow, their eyes glowing with an unholy light, the embodiment of nightmares given form. They surged forward, intent on joining the fray, and for a fleeting moment, my heart sank.

But then I felt it, the Emberstone pulsing fiercely against my chest, igniting my spirit with its unwavering warmth. I had faced darkness before; I could do it again.

"Together!" I shouted to Jax, raising my weapon high, summoning the flames that surged around me like a beacon of hope. "We fight for our freedom!"

Jax grinned, fierce and bright, his laughter ringing through the air as he mirrored my stance. "Let's show them what we're made of!"

We launched ourselves at the encroaching horde, flames illuminating the shadows around us, a firestorm born from our resolve. I could feel the magic of the Emberstone intertwining with my spirit, transforming fear into power, doubt into determination.

As we fought, the energy between us surged, a living entity that connected our hearts and minds, propelling us forward into the maelstrom. The shadows shrank back, their twisted forms retreating before the onslaught of our flames, and with every step, I felt a fierce clarity of purpose settling within me. This was not merely a fight; it was a declaration of existence, a statement that we would not be silenced, that the Council's wrath would not extinguish the light we held within.

With renewed vigor, we pressed onward, knowing that every blow struck, every enemy felled, brought us closer to reclaiming our world from the grasp of darkness.

The battle raged on, a chaotic ballet of fire and shadow that twisted through the dim corridors of the stronghold. My heart raced as I moved with Jax, his fierce laughter mingling with the sounds of clashing metal and the acrid smell of burnt air. Together, we pushed back against the tide of enforcers, their dark armor now scarred and battered, desperation creeping into their ranks. The Emberstone thrummed against my chest, resonating with the heat of my anger and the brightness of my resolve.

As I fought, the power within me began to transform, spiraling into something larger than mere flames—a tempest of energy that swirled around my fingertips, wrapping me in a cocoon of warmth and light. I could feel every moment of the struggle as though it were a story written in the stars, and for the first time, I embraced the deeper magic that was awakening inside me. It was a primal force, a connection to the world that seemed to shimmer just beyond my reach, and I was determined to unleash it.

An enforcer lunged, their blade slicing through the air with a whistling sound. I ducked and rolled, feeling the rush of air as it passed just above my head. With a fluid motion, I sprang up and retaliated, my blade striking true against the armor, a flash of fire exploding on impact. The enforcer cried out, stumbling back, their confidence crumbling under the force of our determination.

But the tides of battle were fickle. In the midst of our surge, the shadows around us began to writhe more violently, and I could sense the Council's leaders rallying their dark magic, a twisted energy swirling in the air. I turned to Jax, whose face had tightened with determination. "They're gathering strength," I warned, my voice rising above the din.

He nodded, wiping sweat from his brow as he glanced at the growing shadows. "Then let's give them something to remember us by."

With a shared glance of understanding, we dove into the fray, weaving through the chaos with renewed purpose. I focused on the center of the vortex where the Council's dark leaders coiled like smoke, and with every breath, I drew upon the strength of the Emberstone. Flames erupted from my fingertips in wild spirals, illuminating the darkened hall and casting elongated shadows that danced along the stone walls.

But the Council was not without its own defenses. A sudden gust swept through the chamber, followed by a roar that seemed to shake the very foundations of the fortress. From the darkness emerged a creature born of nightmares, a massive figure wreathed in shadows with glowing eyes that pierced the haze. It was an embodiment of the Council's wrath, a sentinel meant to instill fear and quash rebellion.

"Hold steady!" Jax yelled, defiance spilling from his lips. He charged forward, his weapon raised high, a flicker of bravery in the face of dread. The creature lunged, its clawed hand sweeping through the air, but Jax ducked just in time, rolling beneath the blow and regaining his footing with an agile twist.

This was a dance of death, a performance of light and darkness, and I could feel the rhythm of it thrumming through my veins. As the creature turned to face Jax, I took a deep breath, channeling every flicker of warmth that the Emberstone provided. The air shimmered, and with a fierce cry, I thrust my hands forward, summoning a torrent of fire that surged toward the beast.

The flames curled around its form, illuminating the tendrils of shadow that writhed at its edges. It screeched, a sound that echoed off the walls and reverberated deep within my chest, but I pressed forward, focusing my energy. The heat grew more intense, and as the flames engulfed the creature, it staggered, the darkness that shielded it flickering under the blaze.

Jax seized the opportunity, darting forward to strike at its vulnerable underbelly, a flurry of movements fueled by adrenaline and fear. The beast roared again, swiping its claws wildly, but Jax was quick, weaving in and out, as if the chaos was a dance floor and we were the stars.

My heart thundered as I felt the shadows pressing closer, enveloping the room in a thick darkness that threatened to swallow us whole. The Emberstone pulsed once more, and I concentrated on the light within me, the flame of resistance that flickered against despair. I was more than just a fighter; I was a beacon of hope, a torch in the murky depths, and I would not be extinguished.

Drawing the heat into my core, I unleashed it in a brilliant burst, light piercing through the veil of shadows. The creature recoiled, its form shuddering as if the very essence of darkness was repelled by my determination. I advanced, my flames swirling around me like a tempest, my feet firm on the ground as I closed the distance between us.

With every ounce of strength, I struck, the fire meeting flesh with a crackling hiss, searing away the darkness. The creature shrieked, a sound of pain and fury, and in that moment, I felt the tide of battle shift beneath us. Jax's laughter echoed again, a triumphant sound that filled the air like music, pushing me onward.

"Now!" he shouted, and I nodded, drawing on the energy we had cultivated together. We were a force, two flames merging into one, and I felt the Emberstone's brilliance reflected in Jax's eyes as we prepared to deliver the final blow.

As I lunged forward, I felt a sudden pull, a ripple in the fabric of our magic. The Council's leaders were fighting back, drawing on their dark powers to summon even more shadows. But we were not done yet. I planted my feet, refusing to give in, grounding myself in the heat that surged within.

I reached out, feeling the connection between Jax and me, letting our combined energy swirl and ignite around us. "Together!" I cried, and we struck as one, our flames merging into a single wave of radiant fire that surged forward, obliterating the shadows and crashing against the creature with an intensity that sent shockwaves reverberating through the hall.

The creature disintegrated into a shower of sparks and smoke, a brilliant display that illuminated the stronghold with a fierce light. In that moment, I felt a sense of victory unfurling within me, the thrill of defiance against the dark.

But the celebration was short-lived. The Council's leaders were not defeated, merely enraged. The air thickened with their power, the temperature dropping sharply as shadows coalesced into a swirling mass above us. I could feel their magic twisting and tightening like a noose, and dread surged anew within my chest.

"We need to finish this," Jax said, his expression shifting to one of steely resolve. "We have to confront them, head-on."

I nodded, steeling myself for what lay ahead. The darkness pulsed ominously, but the fire within me blazed with a renewed vigor. Together, we would face whatever came next. We would reclaim our freedom and the light, no matter the cost. With a final glance at Jax, I took a step forward, ready to plunge into the heart of darkness, where the Council's wrath awaited us, and where our destinies would be forever altered. The fight was far from over, but I could feel the embers of hope igniting, ready to blaze forth and light the way for those who had fought for so long in the shadows.

The air crackled with tension as our adversary summoned another wave of ash, each particle swirling like an angry storm. It clawed at the edges of my senses, seeking to choke the breath from my lungs and extinguish the fire that burned within me. Jax and I had fought side by side before, but never against something so primal, so relentless. The ash was more than an elemental force; it was a manifestation of despair, a suffocating cloak of finality that threatened to bury us.

But as the ash surged forward, dark and all-consuming, I felt something stir deep inside me, something ancient and unyielding. My flames flickered, sputtered, and then roared back to life with renewed fury. The heat of it coursed through my veins, igniting every nerve, every thought, until all that remained was a single, blazing truth: I was not afraid.

"Don't let it touch you!" Jax's voice cut through the chaos, sharp and commanding, but there was an edge of desperation there too. He knew as well as I did that if the ash enveloped us, we were done. There would be no coming back from that.

I nodded, though I wasn't entirely sure how to prevent the inevitable. The ash was everywhere, creeping closer with every breath, and the Council member who controlled it stood in the distance, watching us with cold, calculating eyes. He moved his hand in a slow, deliberate motion, as if orchestrating the very death we were trying so desperately to avoid.

I could feel the weight of his power pressing down on me, but I didn't falter. Instead, I raised my hands and summoned the flames again, pouring every ounce of my strength into them. The fire leaped from my palms, bright and fierce, meeting the advancing ash head-on. For a moment, the two forces collided, crackling and hissing in a volatile dance of destruction.

I pushed harder, drawing on reserves of energy I hadn't known existed. The flames grew hotter, brighter, until they weren't just pushing the ash back—they were consuming it, turning the blackened particles into nothing more than wisps of smoke. My heart pounded in my chest, but I held steady, refusing to let the ash gain ground.

Beside me, Jax unleashed his own power, a shimmering wave of energy that pulsed outward, creating a barrier between us and the Council's deadly onslaught. His face was a mask of concentration, his jaw clenched in determination. We had been in tough spots before, but this was different. This was a battle for survival, and neither of us could afford to lose.

The Council member scowled, clearly displeased with our defiance. With a flick of his wrist, he sent another wave of ash surging toward us, thicker and more aggressive than the last. But I was ready. I gathered my flames once more, hurling them forward with everything I had. The fire exploded outward in a dazzling display of light and heat, engulfing the ash and reducing it to nothing before it could reach us.

For a heartbeat, there was silence, the air thick with the lingering scent of smoke. The Council member stared at us, his expression unreadable. Then, without a word, he turned on his heel and disappeared into the shadows, leaving us standing alone in the aftermath of the battle.

I let out a breath I hadn't realized I'd been holding, my body sagging with exhaustion. The flames flickered out, leaving only the faint glow of embers in their wake.

"We did it," I whispered, more to myself than to Jax. My voice sounded hollow, even to my own ears. The victory felt fragile, like it could crumble at any moment.

Jax placed a hand on my shoulder, his touch grounding me. "For now," he said quietly. His eyes, normally so full of warmth, were clouded with worry. "But they'll be back."

I nodded, knowing he was right. The Council wouldn't stop until they had what they wanted—control, power, and the destruction of anyone who stood in their way. And right now, that meant us.

But as we stood there, battered and bruised but still standing, I couldn't shake the feeling that something had changed. The fight wasn't over—not by a long shot—but we had faced down the Council and lived to tell the tale. That had to count for something.

"Come on," Jax said, his voice gentle but firm. "We need to get moving before they regroup."

I glanced around at the scorched battlefield, my muscles aching with the effort it had taken to survive. The ash had left its mark, coating everything in a thin layer of soot, but the fire had burned brighter. We had burned brighter.

Without another word, I followed Jax into the shadows, the weight of the battle still heavy on my shoulders. But even as the darkness closed in around us, I held onto that flicker of hope, that spark of defiance that refused to be snuffed out.

We had survived the Council's onslaught, and though the road ahead was uncertain, I knew one thing for sure: the fire inside me wasn't just a weapon. It was a promise. A promise that we would keep fighting, no matter what they threw at us.

Because as long as the flames still burned, we weren't finished yet.

The night stretched on, the air thick with the scent of ash and smoke. But as we made our way through the silent, ruined streets, a new kind of determination settled in my chest. The Council had underestimated us once. They wouldn't make that mistake again.

The ash spiraled around us in relentless waves, dark as night and thick enough to swallow light. It was alive, sentient almost, each particle a twisted reflection of the Council's will. I felt the weight of it pressing down on me, like thousands of tiny hands trying to smother the flames inside. Every breath was a battle. Every movement, a struggle. But Jax stood firm at my side, his eyes locked on our foe, his presence a constant reminder that we weren't alone. His power thrummed through the ground, a steady pulse of energy that kept the ash at bay, for now.

The Council member, draped in robes that seemed to blend with the smoke and shadows, watched us with a cruel smirk. He moved with calculated grace, his hands weaving intricate patterns in the air as he controlled the ash with a mere thought. There was no hesitation in him, no flicker of doubt. To him, we were already defeated. He had seen the fear in a hundred others before us, and he expected it to swallow us whole, just as it had them.

But he didn't know me.

I felt the fire in my chest, a burning core of defiance that had been stoked long before this battle. Fear was familiar, sure, but it had never been my master. The ash might try to bury me, but I had faced worse, and I had learned that the only way out was through. I closed my eyes, drawing in a deep, steadying breath, feeling the flames inside me pulse in rhythm with Jax's power. When I opened them again, the ash didn't seem so heavy. The Council member didn't seem so invincible.

Without a word, I raised my hands, summoning the fire once more. It surged forward, a torrent of bright, hungry flames that roared to life with newfound intensity. The ash recoiled, hissing as it met the heat. For a moment, the battlefield was a chaotic swirl of light and dark, the two elements clashing in a vicious, primal dance. But I didn't stop. I couldn't. I pressed harder, pouring every ounce of my strength into the fire, pushing it toward the Council member with a singular focus.

His smirk faltered.

The flames licked at his robes, casting flickering shadows across his face. He moved to counter, his hands a blur as he summoned more ash, thicker and darker than before. But this time, I was ready. This time, I didn't flinch. The fire surged forward, cutting through the ash like a blade through smoke, and for the first time, I saw uncertainty flicker in his eyes.

"You think this will stop us?" I shouted, my voice barely audible over the roar of the flames and the crackling air. My words were for him, but they were also for me, for Jax, for everything we had fought for up until this moment.

The Council member sneered, but there was no humor in it. "You have no idea what you're up against," he said, his voice low and cold. "The Council's power is absolute."

"Maybe," Jax cut in, his voice steady but laced with defiance, "but you don't control us."

With that, Jax unleashed his own power—a wave of energy that pulsed outward, shaking the ground beneath us. It rippled through the ash, scattering it like dust in the wind. The force of it was enough to send the Council member staggering back, his robes fluttering as if caught in a storm. For a moment, I thought we had him. I thought the battle was finally turning in our favor.

But then, with a snarl, the Council member slammed his hands into the ground, and the very earth beneath us began to shift. The ground cracked and splintered, sending jagged fissures racing toward us. Out of the broken earth rose pillars of ash and stone, towering monoliths that loomed over us, casting long, twisted shadows across the battlefield.

Jax's energy faltered, his brow furrowing as he took a step back. "This is bad," he muttered under his breath, his eyes darting to the rising pillars. "Really bad."

"No kidding," I replied, my voice strained as I struggled to keep the flames alive. The fire was still burning bright, but the ash was relentless, and now with the ground itself turning against us, our chances of survival seemed to be shrinking by the second.

The Council member straightened, his smirk returning as he surveyed his handiwork. "You can't win," he said, his voice dripping with arrogance. "The elements obey me. You're nothing but embers waiting to be snuffed out."

I clenched my fists, feeling the heat of the flames warming my skin, but there was a truth in his words that I couldn't ignore. The elements did obey him. He had control, and he wasn't afraid to use it. But I wasn't ready to give up—not yet. There was something he hadn't accounted for, something he couldn't understand.

We weren't just fighting for survival. We were fighting for each other.

I glanced at Jax, who met my gaze with a nod. He didn't need to say anything. We had fought together long enough to know what needed to be done. We couldn't beat him on his terms. So we would change the game.

"Together?" I asked, my voice barely a whisper over the crackling flames.

"Always," Jax replied, a small smile tugging at the corner of his mouth.

In unison, we shifted our stances, our powers merging in a way we hadn't dared before. The fire in my hands pulsed in time with Jax's energy, the two forces intertwining, growing stronger as they fed off each other. The ground beneath us shuddered, but this time, we didn't waver. This time, we stood firm.

The Council member's eyes widened, a flicker of doubt crossing his face. "What are you—"

But he didn't get to finish.

With a final surge of power, we unleashed everything we had. The flames roared to life, brighter and hotter than before, merging with the raw energy that radiated from Jax. It wasn't just fire anymore—it was something else, something new, something that couldn't be controlled by the Council's twisted manipulation. It burned with purpose, with the strength of our bond, and it swept across the battlefield like a tidal wave, swallowing the ash, the stone pillars, and everything in its path.

The Council member barely had time to react before the fire engulfed him, his screams lost in the inferno.

When the flames finally subsided, the battlefield was silent. The pillars had crumbled to dust, the ash reduced to nothing more than smoldering embers. And in the center of it all, where the Council member had stood, there was only empty space.

I let out a shaky breath, my body trembling with exhaustion. The fire inside me had dimmed, but it was still there, a small, steady glow that refused to go out.

Jax placed a hand on my shoulder, his grip reassuring. "We did it," he said softly, his voice filled with a mix of relief and disbelief.

For a moment, I just stood there, staring at the ruins of the battlefield. We had won. But as the adrenaline began to fade, a new thought crept into my mind—this wasn't the end.

The Council would come for us again. And next time, they wouldn't underestimate us.

The wind howled through the ruins, carrying with it the scent of ash and iron. Jax staggered back, clutching his side, eyes wide with shock and betrayal. I wanted to scream, to rage, but the words caught in my throat, as if they too had been stabbed by the traitor's blade. My pulse quickened, and every fiber of my being demanded vengeance. But there was no time to wallow in fury. The traitor—once a friend, now a venomous shadow—slipped further into the fray, their movements as serpentine as their lies.

I could feel the Emberstone thrumming at my core, its heat seeping through my veins. The power it held had always been a burden, but now it felt like a burning torch lighting the path of my rage. It pulsed with an intensity that blurred the line between my anger and its molten core. Jax stumbled again, groaning through gritted teeth, and the flicker of pain in his eyes snapped me into action. He needed me now. Revenge could wait.

I knelt beside him, pressing my hands against the wound, though my fingers shook with fury. "Hold on," I whispered, though it felt more like a plea to the universe than to him.

"They—" Jax gasped, his voice ragged as he fought to speak through the pain. "They were one of us... Why?"

I didn't have an answer. I wasn't sure if I ever would. Betrayal isn't something that follows reason; it's a knife in the back when you least expect it, a smile that masks a deadly strike. All I knew was that this wound—both literal and metaphorical—would leave scars on all of us. And I wasn't sure if they'd ever heal.

I heard a rustling behind me and whirled around, the Emberstone responding to my agitation, a spark of flame dancing at the edges of my vision. The traitor had doubled back, no doubt thinking we were weakened and ripe for the kill. I stood, muscles taut, every nerve alive with the Emberstone's energy. The air crackled with its heat, and I could feel the power welling up inside me, begging to be unleashed.

"You've already lost," they sneered, eyes glinting with cruel satisfaction. "The Council will hunt down the rest of you. This is just the beginning."

I smiled, but there was no warmth in it. "Maybe," I said softly, the heat building in my chest. "But I'm still standing."

The flames erupted from my palms without warning, a torrent of heat and light that scorched the air between us. The traitor dodged, barely, but the Emberstone's fire didn't stop. It swirled around me, as much a part of me as my own blood, and I directed it with a thought. They darted and weaved, but I could see the fear creeping into their eyes. Good.

I stalked forward, fire snapping and curling around me like a living thing. Each step felt deliberate, heavy with purpose. I wasn't going to let them escape again—not this time. They had chosen their side, and I was done playing nice.

"You don't understand what you're dealing with," they spat, retreating as the flames closed in. "The Council—"

"I don't care about the Council," I interrupted, my voice low and dangerous. "You betrayed us. That's all that matters."

The fire surged forward, engulfing them in a blinding flash of light. For a moment, there was nothing but the roar of flames, and then—silence. I stood there, panting, the Emberstone's heat finally subsiding. The traitor was gone, consumed by the fire and their own treachery.

I turned back to Jax, feeling the adrenaline drain from my body, leaving behind a bone-deep exhaustion. He was watching me, eyes wide with something that looked like awe—or maybe fear.

"Are you okay?" I asked, my voice softer now, the anger ebbing away as quickly as it had come.

He nodded weakly. "I'll live. Thanks to you."

I smiled, but it felt hollow. The fight might've been over, but the war—the real war—was just beginning. And now, with the traitor gone, it felt more personal than ever. They had taken too much from us already. I wouldn't let them take anything else.

As I helped Jax to his feet, I couldn't shake the feeling that something had shifted within me. The Emberstone's power was stronger now, more responsive. It scared me, if I was being honest with myself. I had always struggled to control it, but this... this was something else. The flames had moved with a mind of their own, bending to my will with frightening ease.

Jax must've noticed my unease because he put a hand on my shoulder, his grip surprisingly steady despite his injuries. "We'll figure it out," he said quietly. "Together."

I nodded, though I wasn't sure if I believed him. Still, the weight of his words settled over me like a blanket, comforting in its simplicity. We would figure it out—together. Because we had to. There was no other option.

As we made our way back to the others, I couldn't help but glance over my shoulder at the charred remains of the battlefield. The traitor's betrayal had cut deep, but it had also lit a fire in me—one that wasn't going to be easily extinguished.

For better or worse, the Emberstone and I were bound now, its flames a part of me as much as my own heartbeat. And while that thought terrified me, it also gave me a strange sense of comfort. Because for the first time, I felt like I had the power to protect the people I cared about.

And I was going to need every bit of it for what came next.

The air tasted of iron and smoke, a bitter reminder of what had just transpired. Jax leaned heavily on me as we moved, his breath shallow, but determined. Each step echoed with a shared resolve between us, the silence humming with unspoken understanding. His wound, though deep, was not fatal. But the damage had been done—trust shattered like glass, its edges too sharp to ever fully mend.

Behind us, the remnants of the battlefield lay like a graveyard of misplaced loyalties and broken oaths. The traitor's face still lingered in my mind, their smirk etched into my thoughts. I had seen that smirk before, back when they were one of us, back when we believed in the same fight. How easily they had traded it all for power. The Emberstone stirred within me, as if it, too, was unsettled by the idea that betrayal could come from within.

Jax hissed in pain, bringing me back to the present. I tightened my grip on his arm, guiding him through the uneven terrain as best I could. "We're almost there," I said, more for my own reassurance than his.

"I didn't think you could still lie," he grunted through clenched teeth.

"Guess I've still got a few tricks left," I replied, though my voice was far from light. The truth was, I didn't know where we were going. The safehouse we had once relied on was no longer an option. The Council had eyes everywhere now, and with our traitor in the mix, we couldn't trust anyone. Not even the shadows that stretched long and thin across the ground, hiding who knew what.

But we needed to regroup, find the others, and plan our next move. As much as I wanted to tear through the Council's ranks and burn their strongholds to the ground, I knew we couldn't do it alone. Not with Jax injured and the rest of us scattered like leaves in a storm.

We reached a small grove of trees, the canopy overhead offering a brief respite from the open sky, and I gently lowered Jax against the trunk of a gnarled oak. He winced, his face pale but resolute.

"You don't have to look at me like that," he said, his voice strained but defiant. "I'm not dead yet."

"Could've fooled me," I muttered, but there was no bite in my words. Just a heavy, sinking worry that clung to the air between us. I knelt beside him, rummaging through my pack for the small bundle of supplies we had left. Not much—a few bandages, a flask of water, and some herbs that barely counted as medicine. It would have to do.

As I worked, binding his wound as tightly as I dared, Jax's gaze never left my face. "You're thinking too hard again," he said after a long silence.

"Can't help it," I shot back, though I knew he was right. My mind was racing, trying to piece together what little we had left. The Emberstone, the traitor's warning about the Council, the dwindling number of allies we could still trust. None of it added up in a way that left us standing at the end.

"Then stop," Jax said simply. "At least for a minute. Let the world catch up to you."

I almost laughed at that, the absurdity of it. But there was wisdom in his words. I hadn't stopped since the betrayal, hadn't let myself feel the weight of what had happened. The Emberstone thrummed again, like a heartbeat syncing with my own. It had always been there, a constant reminder of the burden I carried, but now it felt more alive—more present, as if it were waiting for something.

"I'm not sure I know how," I admitted quietly, my hands stilling as I finished wrapping his wound. The bandages were crude, but they'd hold for now. Jax gave a weak smile, but it was enough to spark some small bit of warmth in the pit of my stomach.

"We'll figure it out," he said. "Together, remember?"

Before I could respond, a rustling in the bushes snapped my attention back to the world outside our conversation. I was on my feet in an instant, the Emberstone flaring to life in my chest, its heat spreading through my limbs like wildfire. Whoever—or whatever—was out there was about to learn the hard way that I wasn't in the mood for surprises.

But as the figure stepped into view, the flames licking at the edges of my vision faltered. It wasn't an enemy. It was her.

Elara.

Her cloak was torn, hair matted with dirt and blood, but her eyes burned with the same fierce determination I had always admired. She stopped short when she saw us, her gaze flicking to Jax and then back to me. Relief washed over her features, but there was something else too—something darker, buried beneath the surface.

"I found you," she breathed, but her voice was hollow, the triumph in her words overshadowed by whatever news she carried. "I—there's no time. We have to move."

"Elara—" I began, but she cut me off, her tone sharp and desperate.

"The Council's closing in. They know where we are. We don't have long before they reach this place. We need to get to the others—now."

I clenched my fists, feeling the Emberstone hum with frustration beneath my skin. Of course the Council knew. Of course there was no time to rest, to breathe, to think. That was the way of things now, wasn't it? Always running, always fighting, always one step behind the people trying to kill us.

But Elara was right. There was no point in standing here, waiting for the inevitable. We had to move, and we had to do it fast.

Jax groaned as he pushed himself to his feet, but his eyes were steady. "Lead the way."

Elara nodded, her expression grim. "We've got a lot to catch up on, but I'll explain as we go. Just... be ready for anything."

I didn't like the sound of that, but I didn't argue. There wasn't time. We followed her into the woods, leaving behind the grove that had briefly served as our refuge. The trees seemed to close in around us, the shadows growing longer with every step we took.

I could feel the Emberstone pulsing at my core, its heat a constant reminder of the power I held—and the responsibility that came with it. We were heading toward something—something dangerous, something I wasn't sure we were ready for. But there was no turning back now. We had made our choice. And whatever waited for us on the other side of this forest, we would face it together.

With the Emberstone burning brighter than ever, I was ready to fight. To protect those I still had left. And, if necessary, to avenge the ones I had lost.

Chapter 24: Flames of Redemption

The air tasted of iron and smoke, a bitter reminder of what had just transpired. Jax leaned heavily on me as we moved, his breath shallow, but determined. Each step echoed with a shared resolve between us, the silence humming with unspoken understanding. His wound, though deep, was not fatal. But the damage had been done—trust shattered like glass, its edges too sharp to ever fully mend.

Behind us, the remnants of the battlefield lay like a graveyard of misplaced loyalties and broken oaths. The traitor's face still lingered in my mind, their smirk etched into my thoughts. I had seen that smirk before, back when they were one of us, back when we believed in the same fight. How easily they had traded it all for power. The Emberstone stirred within me, as if it, too, was unsettled by the idea that betrayal could come from within.

Jax hissed in pain, bringing me back to the present. I tightened my grip on his arm, guiding him through the uneven terrain as best I could. "We're almost there," I said, more for my own reassurance than his.

"I didn't think you could still lie," he grunted through clenched teeth.

"Guess I've still got a few tricks left," I replied, though my voice was far from light. The truth was, I didn't know where we were going. The safehouse we had once relied on was no longer an option. The Council had eyes everywhere now, and with our traitor in the mix, we couldn't trust anyone. Not even the shadows that stretched long and thin across the ground, hiding who knew what.

But we needed to regroup, find the others, and plan our next move. As much as I wanted to tear through the Council's ranks and burn their strongholds to the ground, I knew we couldn't do it alone. Not with Jax injured and the rest of us scattered like leaves in a storm.

We reached a small grove of trees, the canopy overhead offering a brief respite from the open sky, and I gently lowered Jax against the trunk of a gnarled oak. He winced, his face pale but resolute.

"You don't have to look at me like that," he said, his voice strained but defiant. "I'm not dead yet."

"Could've fooled me," I muttered, but there was no bite in my words. Just a heavy, sinking worry that clung to the air between us. I knelt beside him, rummaging through my pack for the small bundle of supplies we had left. Not much—a few bandages, a flask of water, and some herbs that barely counted as medicine. It would have to do.

As I worked, binding his wound as tightly as I dared, Jax's gaze never left my face. "You're thinking too hard again," he said after a long silence.

"Can't help it," I shot back, though I knew he was right. My mind was racing, trying to piece together what little we had left. The Emberstone, the traitor's warning about the Council, the dwindling number of allies we could still trust. None of it added up in a way that left us standing at the end.

"Then stop," Jax said simply. "At least for a minute. Let the world catch up to you."

I almost laughed at that, the absurdity of it. But there was wisdom in his words. I hadn't stopped since the betrayal, hadn't let myself feel the weight of what had happened. The Emberstone thrummed again, like a heartbeat syncing with my own. It had always been there, a constant reminder of the burden I carried, but now it felt more alive—more present, as if it were waiting for something.

"I'm not sure I know how," I admitted quietly, my hands stilling as I finished wrapping his wound. The bandages were crude, but they'd hold for now. Jax gave a weak smile, but it was enough to spark some small bit of warmth in the pit of my stomach.

"We'll figure it out," he said. "Together, remember?"

Before I could respond, a rustling in the bushes snapped my attention back to the world outside our conversation. I was on my feet in an instant, the Emberstone flaring to life in my chest, its heat spreading through my limbs like wildfire. Whoever—or whatever—was out there was about to learn the hard way that I wasn't in the mood for surprises.

But as the figure stepped into view, the flames licking at the edges of my vision faltered. It wasn't an enemy. It was her.

Elara.

Her cloak was torn, hair matted with dirt and blood, but her eyes burned with the same fierce determination I had always admired. She stopped short when she saw us, her gaze flicking to Jax and then back to me. Relief washed over her features, but there was something else too—something darker, buried beneath the surface.

"I found you," she breathed, but her voice was hollow, the triumph in her words overshadowed by whatever news she carried. "I—there's no time. We have to move."

"Elara—" I began, but she cut me off, her tone sharp and desperate.

"The Council's closing in. They know where we are. We don't have long before they reach this place. We need to get to the others—now."

I clenched my fists, feeling the Emberstone hum with frustration beneath my skin. Of course the Council knew. Of course there was no time to rest, to breathe, to think. That was the way of things now, wasn't it? Always running, always fighting, always one step behind the people trying to kill us.

But Elara was right. There was no point in standing here, waiting for the inevitable. We had to move, and we had to do it fast.

Jax groaned as he pushed himself to his feet, but his eyes were steady. "Lead the way."

Elara nodded, her expression grim. "We've got a lot to catch up on, but I'll explain as we go. Just... be ready for anything."

I didn't like the sound of that, but I didn't argue. There wasn't time. We followed her into the woods, leaving behind the grove that had briefly served as our refuge. The trees seemed to close in around us, the shadows growing longer with every step we took.

I could feel the Emberstone pulsing at my core, its heat a constant reminder of the power I held—and the responsibility that came with it. We were heading toward something—something dangerous, something I wasn't sure we were ready for. But there was no turning back now. We had made our choice. And whatever waited for us on the other side of this forest, we would face it together.

With the Emberstone burning brighter than ever, I was ready to fight. To protect those I still had left. And, if necessary, to avenge the ones I had lost.

The heat from the Emberstone coursed through my veins, igniting a strange calm amidst the chaos. Flames crackled around me, their ferocity matched only by the steady rhythm of my heartbeat. As I stood there, the weight of Jax's unconscious form slumped against me, it became clear that the stone's fire wasn't meant to burn for the sake of destruction alone—it was alive, a force both wild and purposeful. It had been feared for its volatility, but perhaps its true power had always been overlooked.

I braced myself, the stone glowing with an intensity that mirrored the resolve building within me. The flames surrounding us didn't scorch the earth; they danced, a barrier of heat and light, warding off the darkness that threatened to overwhelm us. My comrades, scattered and wounded, stirred faintly at the warmth that enveloped them. The fire wasn't only protecting them—it was healing. The Emberstone had been misunderstood, its potential twisted by those who sought only to dominate through its might. But now, I saw its true nature: it was an instrument of restoration.

The ground beneath my feet trembled as more of our enemies charged, their eyes gleaming with the madness of desperation. They came in waves, relentless and unyielding, believing that sheer numbers would bring us down. But they underestimated the connection that had formed between me and the Flamekeepers, whose spirits had once safeguarded this very power. I could feel them, their presence a steady flame in my mind, guiding my hands, strengthening my resolve.

Drawing on their collective will, I raised my arm and felt the Emberstone respond, its heat surging through me. Fire leapt from my outstretched hand, spiraling upward in a column of molten energy. The flame stretched high, painting the sky in hues of gold and crimson, a burning beacon that signaled not our defeat, but our defiance. I could see the confusion in the eyes of our attackers as the fire split the battlefield, searing through their ranks, forcing them to retreat. Yet, instead of turning to ashes, the ground beneath their feet pulsed with life—vines and roots pushing through the scorched earth, blooming in the wake of the flames.

This was the Emberstone's gift, one misunderstood for centuries. It didn't consume without purpose. It cleansed. It renewed.

A voice, soft but commanding, echoed in my mind—one of the Flamekeepers, her presence as warm as the fire around me. "Do not fear the fire, child. It is only when we embrace its duality that we find the balance between destruction and creation."

I closed my eyes, letting her words settle over me like the flicker of a candle's flame. There was a rhythm to the energy now, a pulse in the very air, as though the Emberstone and I had finally found harmony. I called out to the spirits again, this time not with desperation but with conviction. They responded, their whispers entwining with mine, amplifying my voice as it resonated through the battlefield.

The remaining enemies faltered, their confidence shattered by the sight of the flames they could neither extinguish nor escape. But this battle was not just about survival anymore. It was about reclaiming something deeper—our connection to the Emberstone and the legacy of the Flamekeepers. It had never been about conquest or power for the sake of power. It was about protecting what was sacred.

Without hesitation, I knelt beside Jax, resting a hand on his chest. The fire that surrounded us softened, its fierce heat now a gentle warmth. The Emberstone pulsed, and I felt its energy flow into him, weaving through his injuries, mending what had been broken. Slowly, his eyes fluttered open, confusion giving way to recognition as he met my gaze.

"Did we... win?" His voice was weak, but there was a hint of that old bravado in his tone.

"Not yet," I replied, helping him to sit up. "But we will."

Jax looked around at the battlefield, his expression hardening as he took in the scene—the enemies retreating, our comrades slowly stirring as the fire healed their wounds. "You did this?"

I shook my head. "We did this."

Before he could respond, a rumble shook the ground beneath us, far more ominous than before. The Emberstone flared in warning, and I turned to see a figure emerging from the shadows at the edge of the battlefield. Tall and cloaked in darkness, his presence radiated malice, a stark contrast to the Emberstone's flame.

The General.

Jax tensed beside me, and I could feel the weariness creeping back into my limbs. We had fought so hard, but this was the true battle—the one we had been building toward from the very beginning. I could feel the Emberstone's heat in my chest, but it was no longer the raw, uncontrolled energy it had once been. Now, it felt steady, its flames tempered by understanding.

The General stepped forward, his voice cold and grating like metal on stone. "You think fire will save you?" he sneered. "The Emberstone is nothing but a tool of destruction, a weapon that has broken kingdoms and shattered lives. And now, it will be the end of you."

His words, dripping with disdain, would have once filled me with doubt. But not anymore.

I stood, meeting his gaze with unflinching determination. "The Emberstone isn't what you think it is. It's not here to destroy. It's here to restore."

He laughed, a harsh, mocking sound that cut through the night. "Restore? You fool. It only knows how to burn."

I smiled, feeling the warmth of the Flamekeepers at my side, their strength bolstering my own. "Maybe you just don't know how to wield it."

With a roar, the General raised his weapon, dark energy crackling along its edge. But this time, I wasn't afraid. I stepped forward, the Emberstone blazing with renewed purpose, ready to face whatever darkness he would throw at us. This was no longer just a fight for survival. It was a fight for redemption, for everything the Emberstone had been meant to protect.

And I was ready to reclaim it.

The heat of battle seemed to slow as the Emberstone's power coursed through me, no longer a wild, untamed force, but something far more refined. The flames that had once threatened to consume everything in their path now wrapped around my comrades like a protective cloak, flickering with purpose. Each burst of fire felt deliberate, a pulse of life instead of destruction. I could feel it, the Emberstone breathing with me, each beat of my heart matched by the rhythm of the flames as they danced around us.

The enemies recoiled, their savage confidence eroded as they watched the fire respond to my call, bending to my will. The air shimmered with heat, and yet, I felt a strange coolness settle over me. The Emberstone's rage had always been terrifying, but now I saw it as something more—something that could heal as much as it could harm. The connection between us was no longer one of domination, but of harmony.

A glint of recognition flickered in the eyes of the enemies before me—fear creeping into their expressions as they realized this was not the same power they had sought to conquer. They'd come expecting chaos, believing the Emberstone to be a weapon of devastation. What they hadn't anticipated was its true nature: redemption. With this new understanding came control, and with control came hope.

I stood tall, my gaze sweeping over the battlefield. Jax, still slumped at my feet, stirred, his breath coming in shallow gasps. The Emberstone flared, responding to my unspoken command, and the flames that had surrounded him softened. They became warm, gentle, and I could feel the energy flowing from the stone into his body, knitting together broken bones, mending torn flesh. He blinked groggily, his eyes finding mine.

"Still alive?" he rasped, his voice a dry whisper of humor. Even on the edge of death, Jax could never resist a quip.

"Barely," I replied, my voice steady despite the chaos around us. "But we've got work to do."

Jax managed a weak grin, though the effort seemed to cost him. I glanced up, seeing the ragged remnants of our enemies still advancing, though their pace had slowed. They were watching now, calculating. The tides had shifted, and they knew it. The Emberstone was no longer just a threat to be neutralized. It was something they couldn't control, and that terrified them.

"Stay down for a bit," I said, helping him to lean against a half-burnt tree. The bark crackled under his weight, but the flames that had scorched it were now gone. "You'll be fine."

Jax opened his mouth to argue, but he must've thought better of it. With a curt nod, he closed his eyes, his breath evening out as the Emberstone continued its quiet work of healing. I rose, the weight of the stone at my chest both familiar and strange—like meeting an old friend who had changed, yet remained the same at their core.

The battlefield lay before me, a sea of ash and ruin, but there was something else too—life. Tiny green shoots pushed through the blackened soil, defying the destruction that had swept through the land. The Emberstone's fire had not only cleared the battlefield; it had paved the way for something new to grow. This, I realized, was its true power. Not just fire for fire's sake, but fire with purpose. A flame that could destroy and create in equal measure.

The General had not yet made his move, but I could feel his presence at the edges of the battlefield, a dark shadow looming just beyond the reach of the Emberstone's light. His forces had been decimated, yet he remained, watching, waiting. He had underestimated us—underestimated me—but he would not make the same mistake twice.

A low rumble spread through the ground, the earth shaking as though waking from a deep slumber. The General was coming, and with him, something darker, something that even the Emberstone's flames might struggle to overcome. I could sense it, a void in the world, a place where light didn't exist, where fire couldn't burn. He would bring the Voidstone, the only thing capable of extinguishing the Emberstone's light.

I clenched my fists, the fire inside me rising in response to the thought. The Voidstone was nothing but absence—a cold, empty nothingness that sucked the life out of anything it touched. It had destroyed entire realms, leaving them barren and lifeless. But this time would be different. I had the Emberstone, and I had something the General would never understand—hope.

The shadows shifted, and he appeared, his figure tall and imposing, cloaked in black, the Voidstone gleaming darkly at his side. His eyes locked on mine, and for a moment, the battlefield was silent. The wind itself seemed to hold its breath, waiting for what would come next.

"You think fire will save you?" His voice was a jagged edge, cutting through the silence. "Fire is nothing but a flicker in the dark. It will burn out, as it always does. And when it does, the Void will claim everything."

I met his gaze, unflinching. "You're wrong. Fire doesn't burn out. It changes. It grows. It spreads."

The General's lip curled in disdain. "Spreads? It consumes. It destroys. That's all it knows how to do."

"Maybe," I said, stepping forward. "But sometimes things need to be destroyed to make room for something new."

He scoffed, his hand resting on the hilt of his blade. "And you think you're something new?"

"No," I said softly, the Emberstone glowing brighter in my chest. "But what comes after me will be."

Without another word, the General unsheathed his blade, the Voidstone crackling with dark energy. The air around it seemed to warp, the very essence of the world bending away from its presence. It was as though the Voidstone was rejecting reality itself, creating a vacuum where nothing could exist.

But the Emberstone flared in response, its flames burning hotter, brighter. The ground beneath me shifted, the earth cracking open as fire erupted from below, meeting the cold darkness of the Voidstone. The clash of the two forces sent shockwaves through the battlefield, and I could feel the strain of it, the Emberstone fighting against the overwhelming pull of the void.

The General advanced, his blade slicing through the air, each stroke leaving a trail of emptiness in its wake. I dodged, barely avoiding the lethal touch of the Voidstone's energy, and retaliated with a blast of fire that scorched the ground around him. But it wasn't enough. The Voidstone absorbed the flames, snuffing them out before they could reach him.

"You can't win," he sneered, his voice thick with arrogance. "The Voidstone devours all."

"Maybe," I replied, my mind racing. "But not this time."

With a final surge of energy, I called on the spirits of the Flamekeepers, their voices rising in unison with mine. The Emberstone blazed brighter than ever before, a beacon of light and life in the face of the encroaching darkness. Flames spiraled around me, coiling like serpents, their heat so intense it made the very air shimmer.

The General paused, his eyes narrowing. He could sense it too—something had changed. The Emberstone was no longer just a tool; it was alive, pulsing with the strength of the Flamekeepers who had guarded it for generations.

And in that moment, I realized something. The Emberstone wasn't just mine to wield. It belonged to all of us—to the Flamekeepers, to my fallen comrades, to everyone who had fought for something better. And together, we would see this through.

The General swung his blade one final time, but it was too late. The Emberstone exploded in a brilliant blaze of light, its fire engulfing the battlefield, not to destroy, but to cleanse.

Chapter 25: The Final Confrontation

The wind had the audacity to be cold. Of all the days it could've chosen to remind me that my jacket was, in fact, a glorified sheet, it picked now. I tugged the collar up, but it didn't do much good. The fabric was threadbare and, frankly, I should've retired it three towns ago, but part of me was superstitious enough to believe that as long as I wore it, I'd stay alive. In retrospect, that was probably stupid.

Jax walked beside me, his boots scuffing the dirt road with that lazy swagger of his. You'd never know he'd taken a beating an hour ago, but that was Jax. The guy could wrestle a tornado and come out the other side, dusting off his jacket and asking if anyone had a light. A small part of me envied his resilience, the way he could just bounce back from anything, while I was perpetually bruised, in body and spirit.

Ahead of us, the fortress loomed like some cruel punchline to a joke no one asked for. It wasn't majestic, not in the way you think fortresses should be. There were no gleaming turrets or shining battlements. No, this one was all sharp angles and dull stone, crouching in the middle of the desert like a giant dead thing left to rot. The sun, barely a suggestion behind the smog, made the walls look like bruised skin.

"This is it?" I said, more to myself than to Jax. Because if I were talking to Jax, I'd have to acknowledge that we were actually going in there.

"Yup," he replied, popping the 'p' as he glanced at me sideways. "You look like you're about to faint. You're not gonna faint, are you?"

"Shut up."

"Real convincing, Lila." His grin was infuriating, as usual. "You sure you're up for this?"

I wasn't, but I wasn't about to say that out loud. Instead, I squared my shoulders, making sure my jacket was still in place. The illusion of invincibility was all I had left. We both knew this wasn't going to be a simple walk in and smash the bad guys operation. There were too many unknowns, and every step closer to that fortress made my stomach twist tighter.

"Let's just get this over with," I muttered, trying not to sound like a walking bundle of nerves. Jax's smirk softened a bit as if he could see right through my tough-girl act, but he didn't push it.

The doors—massive slabs of metal that looked like they'd been welded together by someone with a grudge against aesthetics—were wide open. An invitation, or maybe a trap. Who was I kidding? Definitely a trap. We hesitated at the threshold for just a second, long enough to hear the wind whistle mournfully around us. It sounded like it was trying to say, Don't go in there, you idiots. But of course, we did.

The interior was worse than I expected. I thought it'd be all shadows and gloom, but no. The Council had taste, apparently. The walls were lined with polished obsidian, reflecting everything like distorted funhouse mirrors. And at the far end of the room, they stood waiting for us—six of them, their faces obscured by those ridiculous masks they loved so much. I was pretty sure the masks were a power play, a way to make us feel small, anonymous, like we were nothing in the grand scheme of things. Jokes on them, I always felt like nothing, so their weird psychological warfare didn't exactly faze me.

The air was thick with something I couldn't quite place. Not smoke, not fog, but it made breathing harder, like the very atmosphere was conspiring against us. I could feel the hum of energy, that dark, oppressive kind of magic that sticks to your skin and makes you want to scrub yourself raw.

Jax stood a little closer to me, his body tense in a way that only I could notice. We weren't friends in the traditional sense—we never had heart-to-heart talks or shared secrets over campfires. But we'd saved each other's lives enough times that something deeper had formed, something that didn't need words. Right now, that bond was the only thing keeping me from bolting.

The Council didn't speak, not at first. They just stared at us, or at least I imagined they did behind those masks. I'd gotten used to the weight of their gazes over the past few months, but now it felt different. Heavier. I wasn't sure if it was fear or the suffocating magic in the room, but my chest tightened.

"We've been expecting you," a voice said. It was smooth, like oil on water, and I couldn't tell who it came from. Maybe they all spoke at once. Maybe the sound was just in my head. Either way, it made my skin crawl.

Jax took a step forward, and I could feel the bravado radiating off him. He was always the one to act first, to throw the first punch even when it wasn't wise. I reached out and grabbed his arm, a silent plea for patience. He didn't shake me off, which was a small victory.

"Nice place you got here," he said, flashing that reckless grin. "I mean, a bit much on the creepy décor, but hey, to each their own."

The Council didn't respond, which was probably for the best. Jax's jokes didn't land well with people who had no sense of humor, and I had a feeling these guys weren't the type to laugh at anything, much less at themselves.

I took a breath—steady, calm. Or at least, that's what I tried to tell myself. My heart was racing, and my hands were slick with sweat inside my jacket pockets. I could feel the weight of the little dagger I carried, the one I always kept hidden for moments like these. It wouldn't do much against the Council, but holding it reminded me that I wasn't helpless.

"You have something that belongs to us," the voice said again, this time colder. There was a finality in those words, like they were already writing the ending of our story.

Jax's confidence was maddening, but I guess that's why he was the one with the scars and I was the one with the headaches. He adjusted his stance, all bravado and swagger, like he had the situation under control. Meanwhile, my palms were so sweaty I could barely keep a grip on my dagger. Not that it would do much against magic-wielding Council members who could probably turn me into a puddle of regret with a snap of their fingers. Still, I had to hold onto something, and it was either the blade or my sanity, and we both knew the latter was already on shaky ground.

"We don't have anything that belongs to you," Jax shot back, still grinning like a guy who hadn't just waltzed into a deathtrap. "Unless you count my patience, but that ship sailed about five minutes ago."

The silence that followed was thick, heavy, the kind that presses against your eardrums and makes you second-guess every life choice you've ever made. The Council didn't move, didn't flinch. I couldn't even tell if they were breathing under those masks. For all I knew, they could've been statues. Or worse, puppets.

Then one of them, the one in the middle—probably the leader, because of course they'd stand in the center for dramatic effect—stepped forward. I felt the shift in the air immediately, like a cold draft sneaking under a door, curling around my ankles. The hairs on the back of my neck stood up, and I fought the urge to take a step back. Jax didn't move. Typical.

"You're lying," the leader said, and even though I couldn't see their face, I could practically feel the smugness radiating off them like cheap perfume. "We know what you've taken. And we know why."

"Well," I muttered under my breath, "this escalated quickly."

Jax shot me a sideways glance, a warning, but it wasn't like I could help myself. Sarcasm was my default setting, especially when things were circling the drain. The leader's head snapped in my direction, and though their face was hidden, I felt the weight of their stare, like they were peeling back layers of me, trying to get to something beneath the surface.

"That one is afraid," the leader said, voice smooth and cutting. "She doubts herself."

Jax let out a small chuckle, though there was an edge to it. "You think that's news? We're all afraid. Welcome to being human."

I wanted to slug him, but now wasn't the time. He wasn't wrong, though. Fear was gnawing at my insides like a wild animal, but I couldn't let it win. Not now. Not with so much on the line. I tightened my grip on the dagger, though I knew it wasn't the weapon that would win this fight.

"We know why you've come," the leader said, turning their attention back to Jax. "And we will not let you leave."

There it was. The finality, the inevitability of it all, laid bare in those cold words. My throat tightened, but I forced myself to swallow it down. We didn't come all this way to be snuffed out like candles in a breeze. There had to be a way out. There was always a way out.

Jax took a slow step forward, his posture shifting from cocky to something more calculated. "You've got this all wrong," he said, his voice low and smooth, like he was negotiating a peace treaty instead of standing in front of the people who probably wanted to melt us into a fine paste. "We're not your enemies."

The leader tilted their head slightly, like a curious animal. "No?" The word dripped with skepticism. "Then what are you?"

I had about three dozen snarky responses lined up, but I bit my tongue. Jax was working his angle, and I wasn't about to mess it up by being, well, me.

"We're survivors," Jax said, and for the first time, his voice didn't have that edge of humor. He was serious. "We've fought through hell to get here, not to destroy you, but to end all of this. No more war, no more fighting. Just... an end."

The silence stretched out again, thick and suffocating. The leader didn't respond right away, and I could almost hear the gears turning behind that mask. Jax was giving them something to think about, something to latch onto. And maybe—just maybe—that was enough.

But of course, nothing's ever that easy.

The chamber shifted. I don't know how else to describe it. One second, the floor was solid beneath us, and the next, it was like the whole room was tilting sideways, like gravity had decided to take a lunch break. I staggered, catching myself against the wall just in time to see one of the other Council members raise their hand.

"Enough," they hissed, their voice like nails on glass. "We don't negotiate with thieves."

Jax cursed under his breath. The diplomatic approach had officially failed. I braced myself as the air crackled with energy, dark and sharp, and I knew what was coming. I'd seen this before—magic, raw and dangerous, about to be unleashed.

"Move!" I yelled, shoving Jax just as a bolt of something—not quite lightning, not quite fire—shot toward us. We dove to the side, rolling across the cold stone floor. My heart hammered in my chest, but I didn't stop. I couldn't. Not when the whole room was alive with energy, more attacks coming from every direction.

Jax was up first, already swinging his blade toward one of the Council members. I scrambled to my feet, dodging another blast of whatever dark magic they were hurling at us. My instincts kicked in, and I moved without thinking, ducking and weaving between the flurry of attacks, my mind racing for a plan.

There were six of them, and two of us. Not exactly great odds. But then again, we'd faced worse. I just needed to keep moving, keep dodging, and—oh, there it was.

The glint of the amulet around the leader's neck. The thing we'd come for, the object that held the key to ending this entire nightmare. I hadn't expected it to be right there, out in the open, like they were taunting us with it. But there it was, shimmering in the dim light like a beacon.

"Jax!" I shouted, but he was already on it, his eyes locking onto the prize. We didn't need to exchange words. We'd been in this game long enough to know what needed to be done.

Now we just had to survive long enough to do it.

The room before us felt alive, throbbing with an oppressive atmosphere. Shadows clung to every corner, whispering secrets we couldn't quite hear but could almost feel, like the brush of cold fingers against the back of our necks. The leaders of the Council sat on elevated thrones, arranged in a semi-circle that left no room for escape or retreat. Their gazes were as sharp as daggers, yet none of them moved. They didn't need to. Their mere presence was enough to stall our breaths, to force our bodies to remain still, like prey in the presence of a predator. But fear was a luxury we couldn't afford.

Jax shifted beside me, his hand brushing the hilt of his blade, his knuckles white from the tension. Even after everything we'd been through, he remained a rock—steady, grounded, though the blood on his face told the story of a thousand battles fought. There was an odd comfort in his resolve. If Jax could stand firm in the face of the Council, so could I.

The central figure, cloaked in robes that seemed woven from night itself, leaned forward slightly, his voice a raspy, insidious whisper that reverberated through the chamber. "You think you can defy the inevitable?" His words slithered like snakes, winding themselves into the core of our determination.

"You misunderstand us," I replied, my voice steadier than I felt. "We're not here to defy fate. We're here to rewrite it."

There was a flicker of amusement, a twitch of the Council leader's lips, but it vanished just as quickly. Behind him, the other leaders remained statuesque, unreadable, yet their presence felt like a looming storm. They were waiting for something, for us to make a move, for one wrong step that would seal our fates. But we were no longer playing by their rules.

The tension snapped like a taut wire, and the chamber erupted into chaos. Jax moved first, faster than I could have expected, a blur of motion as he lunged at the nearest Council member, his blade meeting steel in a ringing clash. I felt a surge of power rise within me, a heat that burned through my veins, demanding release. This wasn't just about survival anymore. It was about liberation, about ensuring the Council never had the chance to manipulate anyone else again.

My feet barely touched the ground as I moved, energy coursing through me like a river in flood. The room became a battlefield, blades flashing, shadows dancing, and the sharp tang of metal filling the air. The Council members, for all their power and arrogance, hadn't expected us to fight back with such ferocity. They had ruled for so long, untouchable, that they had forgotten the danger of desperation.

But desperate we were not. We were something far more dangerous—determined.

The Council leader turned his gaze on me, and for a heartbeat, the world slowed. His eyes were pits of endless black, devoid of humanity, filled only with cold calculation. "You are nothing," he hissed, his voice scraping like nails on glass. "A flicker of light in an eternal darkness."

I met his gaze, refusing to flinch. "Maybe. But even a flicker can start a fire."

With a roar, the energy inside me exploded outward, a wave of light and heat that sent the leader staggering. His grip on reality faltered for just a moment, and that was all I needed. I surged forward, my hands crackling with power, and slammed them into his chest. He screamed, a sound of pure rage and disbelief, as the energy consumed him, unraveling the darkness that clung to him like a second skin.

The other Council members faltered, their connection to their leader severed. For the first time, fear flashed in their eyes, and it was intoxicating. But the battle was far from over. Jax fought beside me, his blade a whirlwind of steel, while I wielded the energy within me like a weapon forged from pure will. We were unstoppable, not because we were invincible, but because we refused to yield.

Time blurred, a whirlwind of movement, sound, and fury, until finally, only silence remained. The last of the Council fell, their bodies crumpling like withered leaves, and the oppressive weight in the air lifted. The fortress, once a monument to their power, now felt hollow, empty. It was over.

Jax stood beside me, his chest heaving with exertion, but a triumphant grin spread across his face. "We did it," he said, his voice rough but filled with disbelief.

I nodded, too exhausted to speak, but the weight in my chest lifted. We had done the impossible. We had brought down the Council.

But as the dust settled, a new reality began to creep in. The fortress may have fallen, but the world outside still lay in ruin. The people who had suffered under the Council's reign wouldn't be healed overnight. There was still so much work to be done. And the question that haunted me now was simple: What would fill the void we had created? Power never truly disappeared—it only changed hands. And I wasn't naive enough to believe that our victory meant an end to the fight.

Jax caught my eye, reading the thoughts that must have been clear on my face. "We'll figure it out," he said, more to reassure me than himself.

I offered a weak smile, though I wasn't sure I believed him. But as we turned our backs on the fallen Council and walked toward the crumbling doors of the fortress, a sense of cautious hope flickered in my chest. We had won the battle, and for now, that was enough.

But the war—the war was just beginning.

Chapter 26: Rise of the Flamekeeper

Heat seared the air around me, twisting it into ripples like the surface of a desert road on a scorching summer day. My fingers tightened around the Emberstone, its warmth familiar and yet strange, a pulse of life beating alongside mine. The battle raged on all sides, a chaotic symphony of fire and smoke, but for a moment, I stood still, transfixed by the raw power coursing through me. The Emberstone hummed with purpose, vibrating in tune with the storm of energy swirling around us. It called to something ancient within me, a legacy that had waited too long to be claimed.

I could hear them—the Flamekeepers, voices from another time, whispering their secrets and urging me forward. Their strength filled my veins like molten lava, burning away the fear and uncertainty that had once plagued me. All around, the sounds of clashing metal and shouted commands mingled with the crackle of flames, but they faded to the background as the Emberstone's light grew brighter, bathing the battlefield in a brilliant, fiery glow.

I didn't need to look to know that the others were watching. My comrades, the ones who had fought beside me for what felt like a lifetime, stood on the edge of desperation, waiting for a sign that this wasn't the end. And somehow, it wasn't. Not yet. I had always been reluctant to claim the title, to take on the mantle of Flamekeeper that I hadn't asked for, but now... Now there was no more running.

"Well," I muttered to myself, my voice barely audible above the roar of the inferno, "I guess it's time to embrace the family business."

The Emberstone flared, as if in response to my acceptance, sending a burst of warmth through my entire body. I raised my hand, letting the light guide me. It streamed outward, expanding in a rush of heat that tore through the battlefield like a wildfire. For a brief, surreal moment, everything stilled. The air itself seemed to hold its breath.

And then it exploded.

Flames erupted from the ground, not wild or destructive, but controlled, purposeful. They surged through the ranks of our enemies, driving them back with a precision that was both terrifying and awe-inspiring. I could feel it, the connection between myself and the fire, as if the flames were an extension of my own will. I directed them with a thought, weaving them through the battlefield like a seamstress threading a needle.

"Okay," I whispered, the weight of the moment settling in, "this is new."

But there wasn't time to reflect. The Emberstone demanded more, pulling me deeper into its power. I could feel the Flamekeepers with me, their strength woven into the very fabric of the fire itself, guiding me, lending me their power. The flames swirled in a great arc around me, a living, breathing force that I now commanded.

There was a part of me that marveled at it all—the raw beauty of the fire, the way it moved with grace and fury, its light dancing on the faces of my allies as hope sparked in their eyes. I'd never seen them look at me like that before. Not with fear. Not with doubt. But with belief.

The ground trembled beneath my feet as the last of our enemies staggered back, eyes wide with shock. They had been winning only moments before, the weight of their numbers and the sheer brutality of their attack overwhelming us. But now... now they hesitated, fear flickering in their eyes as they saw the flames rise higher, as they realized they were no longer the predators in this battle.

I allowed myself a small, grim smile. "I'd run if I were you."

They didn't need to be told twice. The retreat was sudden, frantic, as they scrambled to escape the inferno. But even as they fled, I knew this was far from over. The battle may have turned in our favor for now, but the war still loomed on the horizon, vast and unrelenting.

Still, for the first time in a long time, it didn't feel hopeless.

The fires around me began to calm, the Emberstone's glow dimming as the immediate danger passed. I felt drained, my legs shaking beneath me, but the power still lingered, humming quietly in the back of my mind. It was there now, a part of me. I wasn't just wielding the Flamekeepers' power—I was the Flamekeeper. And that was a responsibility I could no longer run from.

"Well," I said, mostly to myself, though I could feel the others approaching, their footsteps cautious as they neared the still-smoldering ground, "that was... something."

"Something?" A familiar voice, laced with exhaustion but undeniably relieved, echoed from behind me. "That was more than something. You just turned the entire battle around, Quinn. If that's 'something,' I'd hate to see what 'everything' looks like."

I turned to find Alex standing there, his armor dented and streaked with soot, but his expression was one of awe and... was that a hint of pride? It was hard to tell with him sometimes.

I shrugged, trying to downplay the monumental shift that had just occurred. "Eh, just a little fire."

Alex snorted. "A little fire? You've got to be kidding me. That was—"

"Quinn!" Another voice, sharper and more urgent, cut through the moment. I turned just in time to see Lila sprinting toward us, her face a mixture of relief and panic. "Are you okay? You looked like you were about to collapse back there. And what was that, anyway? You—"

"I'm fine, Lila," I interrupted, holding up a hand to stop her from spiraling into full-blown worry mode. "Just... give me a minute to catch my breath."

But even as I said it, I knew there was no rest for us. Not now. The enemy had retreated, but they'd be back, stronger and angrier than ever. And when they came, we'd need more than just fire to stop them.

The heat of the battle was almost unbearable, the clash of elemental forces creating a chaotic symphony of crackling flames, howling winds, and the roar of shifting earth. I could feel the Emberstone pulsing against my chest, its energy no longer foreign or distant, but a part of me—alive, aware, and growing stronger by the second. Every spark that flared around me, every gust of scorching air, responded to my thoughts, bending to my will like an extension of my own being. The battlefield was vast, a tapestry of destruction and defiance, and yet, I stood as its center, the eye of the storm.

The enemies pressed closer, their dark forms mere shadows through the heat and ash. They were relentless, driven by a hunger for conquest that mirrored the rage bubbling inside me. For a fleeting moment, I wondered how long it would take them to realize they were fighting a losing battle. The Emberstone flared again, a warm hum beneath my fingertips, and I realized with a sudden clarity that this wasn't just about defeating them. It was about something far bigger. Something ancient.

With a deep breath, I summoned the memories of the Flamekeepers before me, their wisdom like whispers carried on the wind. My ancestors had guarded this power, wielded it to protect, to heal, to defend what was sacred. But it had been so long since anyone had been able to claim the title. The last Flamekeeper had vanished without a trace, leaving behind only the Emberstone and the weight of expectations that had since fallen on me. Now, I understood why. The power wasn't something that could be tamed by just anyone. It needed a bond, a harmony with the fire itself, a recognition of its potential for both creation and destruction.

The ground beneath me trembled as I took a step forward, the wave of heat parting the smoke and revealing the approaching horde. Their eyes gleamed with malice, their jagged weapons gleaming in the fiery light. But I could sense their hesitation now. They could feel the shift, the turning of the tide, and the Emberstone was more than just a trinket in their eyes. It was a symbol of their downfall.

As the first of the enemy soldiers reached me, I raised my hand, fingers curling into a fist. The air around us ignited instantly, a wall of flame rising between us, sending them reeling back in terror. I heard their commander shout orders, rallying his forces, but his voice was drowned out by the roar of the fire, the sheer force of it overwhelming even my own senses for a moment. I wasn't just using the Emberstone's power anymore. I was the power.

A strange calm settled over me as I walked forward through the flames, the inferno parting at my command. The soldiers scrambled away from me, their bravado crumbling as they realized there was no escape from the fire. I was no longer just a participant in this war. I was its master.

I allowed myself a moment to survey the battlefield. The land, once vibrant with life, now lay scorched and blackened. But amidst the destruction, there was still hope. My allies, emboldened by the sudden surge of power, fought back with renewed vigor. I could see them now, their figures outlined by the flickering flames, and for the first time, there was no fear in their eyes. Only determination.

Suddenly, a sharp crack split the air, and I turned to see a figure emerging from the thick smoke. It was him—the one I had been dreading, the one whose power rivaled my own. His presence was cold, a stark contrast to the heat that surrounded me. He strode forward with an arrogance that made my blood boil, his dark armor shimmering with an otherworldly light. I knew, without a doubt, that this was the true test.

He stopped a few paces from me, his eyes narrowing as he took in the sight of the Emberstone. "So," he said, his voice low and menacing, "the new Flamekeeper has finally risen. I had hoped for more."

I met his gaze, feeling the weight of his words but refusing to let them sink in. "You'll find I'm more than enough," I replied, my voice steady, though my heart pounded in my chest. The Emberstone flared in response, a pulse of warmth that reassured me even as I prepared for the inevitable clash.

He didn't waste any more time with words. In a blur of motion, he lunged toward me, his sword gleaming with a cold, silver light. I met his attack with a blast of fire, the heat so intense that the very air around us warped and shimmered. But he was fast, impossibly so, dodging the flames and closing the distance between us in an instant. I barely had time to raise my arm before his sword came crashing down, a strike so powerful that it sent shockwaves through the ground.

I stumbled back, the force of the blow knocking the wind out of me. But the Emberstone burned brighter, feeding off my resolve. I gritted my teeth, pushing myself to my feet as he circled me, his cold gaze unwavering. "You're not the first to wield that stone," he taunted, his voice dripping with disdain. "And you won't be the last."

I smirked, despite the tension coiling in my chest. "Maybe not," I said, lifting my hand to the sky. "But I'll be the last one you face."

With a roar, I called upon the full might of the Emberstone, summoning flames that leapt from the ground like hungry serpents. They coiled around my enemy, wrapping him in a prison of fire that burned hotter and brighter with each passing second. He thrashed and struggled, but there was no escape. This was no ordinary fire. It was the flame of the Flamekeepers, ancient and unyielding.

As I watched him fall, consumed by the flames, I felt a strange sense of peace settle over me. The battle was far from over, but this victory—it was mine. And with the Emberstone pulsing steadily against my chest, I knew that the legacy of the Flamekeepers was safe. For now.

But as the fire died down and the battlefield grew quiet, I couldn't shake the feeling that this was only the beginning. The Emberstone's power was great, yes—but it came with a cost. A responsibility. And I had only just begun to understand what that truly meant.

Chapter 27: The Ashen Fall

The stars had abandoned New Orleans, the thick cloak of smoke and ash blotting out the night sky. Only the weak flicker of streetlights, half-suffocated in the fog of war, gave us any sense of direction as we staggered through what used to be Jackson Square. It had been days—weeks, maybe—since the Council's grasp had been shattered, and the city still wore its scars like a mournful lover clutching mementos of the dead. My boots sloshed in the ankle-deep water that had pooled on the uneven cobblestone, a foul mixture of ash and rain, thick enough to taste the sulfur in the air.

Jax's footsteps were heavy beside me, even for him. Normally, he moved with the grace of a guy who had spent half his life on rooftops or squeezing between alleys, but tonight his shoulders hung low, weighed down by the cost of survival. His machete, chipped and dull from the countless battles we'd fought, clinked against the buckle of his belt as he pulled it free, turning it over in his hands. I couldn't blame him for staring at the blade as if it held answers. Neither of us had asked for this fight, but once the Council set its sights on us, what choice did we have?

Ahead, the husk of St. Louis Cathedral loomed, its once-pristine façade now streaked with black, half the spires crumbled into jagged ruins. It used to be a sanctuary, a place where people came to pray for miracles. Now it was just another graveyard, like so many others scattered across the French Quarter. My fingers twitched, brushing against the cool hilt of the dagger at my side, though I knew no enemies waited for us here tonight. The Council's forces had scattered into the shadows, but those shadows still felt... alive, watching us.

"We should go back," Jax muttered, barely loud enough to hear over the hum of wind and destruction. His voice was as cracked as the city's foundations, the strain of battle still gnawing at him. "Check on the others."

"The others can take care of themselves," I shot back, though my tone lacked the bite I'd intended. It wasn't that I didn't care. It's just that after all the fires we had put out, after all the lives we couldn't save, I wasn't sure if seeing their faces—what was left of them—would do anything but drag us deeper into the pit we'd been clawing out of. "Besides, this is what we agreed to. We scout the perimeter, see if the Council left any surprises behind."

Jax grunted, a sound somewhere between agreement and resignation. We both knew it wasn't that simple. No one came back from a fight like this whole, no matter how hard you tried to convince yourself otherwise. The problem wasn't the physical wounds—those could be bandaged, stitched up, even ignored with enough adrenaline. No, it was the creeping, insidious kind of damage that got you. The kind that set up camp in your skull, replaying the screams of the people you couldn't save. The kind that made the darkness feel just a little too comfortable.

We wove through the remains of the market stalls, overturned and pillaged long ago, their colorful awnings now nothing more than shredded rags flapping helplessly in the wind. The scent of burnt coffee beans and spices still clung to the air, mingling with the stench of rot and decay. I paused for a moment, the memory of pre-war New Orleans flickering in the back of my mind like an old postcard—vibrant, chaotic, full of life. How had it all gone so wrong?

Jax stopped beside me, his brow furrowed in that way that meant he was overthinking again. "You think it's worth it?" he asked, not looking at me. He wasn't talking about tonight's patrol. He meant all of it—the fighting, the sacrifices, the blood that now stained every corner of this city.

I didn't answer right away. It wasn't because I didn't know what to say—I had rehearsed this conversation a thousand times in my head. The truth was simple, really. No, I didn't think it was worth it. Not the way things stood. But what choice did we have? You don't get to hit the reset button just because you don't like the way the game's going.

"We keep fighting," I said, finally, though my voice felt hollow in my own ears. "Because if we don't, then everything that's happened means nothing. And I'm not ready to live with that."

The silence that followed stretched between us, heavy and thick, punctuated only by the faint whistle of wind through the wreckage. Jax shifted on his feet, glancing toward the cathedral again, his jaw set in that determined way of his. He didn't say anything, but the look he gave me said enough. We both knew what came next, even if neither of us wanted to admit it.

We moved toward the ruins of the cathedral, the door hanging crooked on its hinges like a gaping mouth. Inside, the once-grand altar was barely recognizable, reduced to a pile of broken marble and twisted iron. Candles, long since extinguished, lay scattered across the floor like fallen stars. I knelt, running my fingers along the cold stone, feeling the pulse of something ancient, something dark, still lingering in the air.

"They left something behind," I murmured, my breath catching in my throat as the realization hit me. I could feel it, deep in my bones—the Council wasn't done with us yet.

Jax's eyes darted to mine, his hand tightening around the hilt of his machete. "Then we end this," he said, the fire in his voice a stark contrast to the icy dread settling over me.

I nodded, standing slowly as the weight of what was to come pressed down on my shoulders. The Council may have fallen, but their shadow still lingered over us, a ghost we couldn't shake. And if there was one thing I knew for certain, it was that ghosts never stayed buried for long.

The quiet after a battle is a strange thing, like the universe holds its breath waiting for the next shoe to drop. Every small noise feels exaggerated—the rustle of fabric, the scrape of steel against stone, even the distant drip of water leaking through the cracked streets. I could hear Jax breathing, slow and steady, beside me. If I listened hard enough, I thought I might even hear the heartbeats of those we had left behind.

I wanted to savor the victory, to let it settle in my bones and ease the tight knot of tension that had been coiled in my chest for as long as I could remember. But there wasn't time for that. There never was. Freedom always came at a cost, and the receipt was always waiting, impatient and brutal.

Jax, as usual, had already moved on. He wiped the edge of his machete on the hem of his jacket, cleaning off the ash and grit from our fight with the Council's last guard. His jaw clenched and unclenched as though chewing on a thought too bitter to swallow. He looked at me from the corner of his eye, and I knew he could sense my unease. We didn't talk about feelings, not unless we had to, and even then, it was usually through a haze of exhaustion and sarcasm.

"So," he said finally, his voice more gravel than word. "What's next?"

I looked around the wreckage, half-expecting something—or someone—to rise from the shadows again, but nothing stirred. The thick air of New Orleans' late summer clung to me like a second skin, sticky and oppressive. I inhaled deeply, trying to find the remnants of the city I used to know beneath the layers of dust and death. The tang of beignets and coffee? Gone. The lively music that once pulsed through these streets like a heartbeat? Faded into silence.

"We rebuild," I said, the words tasting strange on my tongue. It felt like a lie even as I said it. "If we can."

Jax snorted, a dry, humorless sound. "Rebuild what, exactly? The Cathedral's toast. Half the Quarter's underwater, and the rest..." He didn't have to finish. I knew what the rest was—broken, shattered, more ghosts than people.

"People still live here," I said, though it sounded weaker than I wanted it to. "And they'll need a place to call home. We owe them that."

His eyebrows lifted, the skepticism plain on his face. "You're talking about playing city planner now? I thought you didn't even like people."

"I like people fine," I muttered, though we both knew that wasn't exactly true. I liked a select few people on a good day. The rest? They were tolerable as long as they stayed out of my way. But now, I was starting to wonder if staying out of the way was what had gotten us into this mess in the first place.

Jax shrugged, shifting the weight of his machete onto his shoulder like some kind of grim reaper in street clothes. "Rebuilding's fine and all, but we can't just slap some plaster on the cracks and call it a day. The Council's dead, but the world doesn't go back to the way it was just 'cause we took down the big bad."

"I know." I kicked at a chunk of debris at my feet, sending a small cloud of ash into the air. It swirled for a moment before settling back into the dirt like it had always belonged there. I felt a strange kinship with that ash. No matter how hard you tried to clear it away, it always found a way to cling to you, to remind you of what was burned down.

The truth was, even though we had won, I wasn't sure what we were supposed to do now. Fighting had been easy. It was straightforward. Take out the enemy, survive the day, rinse and repeat. But living—rebuilding—was messy. And messy wasn't something I excelled at.

"Maybe we don't have to rebuild it the way it was," I said quietly, more to myself than to Jax. "Maybe we start over. Do things better this time."

Jax gave me a look that was half amused, half exasperated. "Better? Since when are you a politician?"

"I'm not. I'm just... tired." The confession slipped out before I could stop it, and I felt a weight settle in my chest, heavier than any sword or shield I had ever carried. The kind of tired that didn't go away with a good night's sleep, the kind that lingered deep inside, whispering that maybe, just maybe, you weren't cut out for this.

But Jax didn't laugh at me, didn't make some smartass comment. He just looked at me with those dark eyes of his, seeing too much, as usual. "Yeah," he said, his voice softer than I expected. "I know."

We stood there for a while, side by side, watching the city try to breathe again. It was broken, sure, but not dead. Not yet.

The wind shifted, carrying with it the distant sound of water lapping against stone, and I could've sworn I heard the faintest hint of music—someone's radio still crackling to life in the ruins. Maybe it was my imagination. Or maybe, just maybe, the city wasn't ready to give up either.

"I think I know where we start," I said, finally pulling myself out of my thoughts.

Jax raised an eyebrow, skepticism etched across his face. "Oh yeah? Care to enlighten me, oh wise one?"

I rolled my eyes, but the edge of a smile tugged at the corner of my lips. "It's simple. We find the survivors, we figure out who's left standing, and we get them together. We can't do this alone."

He nodded slowly, considering my words. "Alright," he said. "But you're giving the speeches."

I groaned. "I hate speeches."

"Too bad." His grin widened, the tension finally breaking as he nudged me with his elbow. "You're the one with the grand ideas. That means you get to play the hero now."

"I'd rather fight ten more Council soldiers than give a speech."

"Then it's a good thing I kept a few in my back pocket for you," Jax teased, and I couldn't help but laugh, the sound strange in the stillness of the night. It was probably the first time either of us had laughed in days, and it felt… good. Like maybe we weren't as broken as the city around us. Not yet, anyway.

And so, with our tired bones and ragged spirits, we moved forward, ready to face whatever came next. Together.

The aftermath of battle was always quieter than I imagined it would be. You picture something grand in your head—triumphant horns, maybe some cheering, but the reality was a lot of silence. It felt too loud, like the absence of sound had its own weight, pressing down on my chest. Every step I took seemed to echo through the ruined streets, the crunch of broken stone under my boots the only sound for miles. Even the crows that usually loitered around, picking at the fresh remains of whatever unfortunate soul got left behind, were absent. Maybe they knew better than to hang around when magic still crackled in the air.

Jax didn't speak, and I didn't expect him to. We'd been through enough together to know when words weren't necessary. He just walked beside me, machete still swinging at his side, though I doubted we'd need it again tonight. Not here, anyway. The Council's reign was over. The shadow that had loomed over us for so long had finally lifted, but the darkness it left behind was something else entirely.

There was a bitter taste in my mouth—ash, mixed with the metallic tang of dried blood. I couldn't tell if it was mine or someone else's. Probably both. The edges of my vision were still blurry from the adrenaline, like everything was smeared with the ghost of violence. The fires we had set in the Council's stronghold burned in the distance, sending thick plumes of black smoke spiraling into the sky. But the flames didn't roar with victory; they just sputtered, like they were as tired as the rest of us.

I reached up to wipe the sweat and grime from my forehead, but my hand came back stained red. Not good. The gash on my brow was deeper than I thought. Typical. I'd gotten used to pain, in a way, though not in the noble, stoic sense you hear about in stories. It was more like I'd learned to ignore it, to file it away for later. After a while, everything just became one long, dull throb, like background noise you couldn't turn off.

"Need to patch that up," Jax said finally, his voice cutting through the silence. He didn't look at me, just gestured vaguely toward my head.

"It'll hold," I muttered, which was code for "I don't want to deal with it right now." He knew that as well as I did, but thankfully he didn't push. Instead, he knelt down and rummaged through the debris at our feet, pulling out a dirty piece of cloth and offering it to me.

I took it without a word and pressed it to my forehead. The fabric was rough and reeked of smoke, but it was better than bleeding all over myself. "Thanks," I said grudgingly, earning a faint smirk from Jax.

"You're welcome, oh fearless leader," he said, his voice laced with mockery. "Wouldn't want you keeling over before the party starts."

"Party?" I raised an eyebrow. "We barely survived."

"Exactly. What better time for a party?" His grin was sharp, a flash of the old Jax peeking through the exhaustion. "Celebrate while we still can, before we realize just how deep the mess we've created goes."

I snorted, but didn't argue. He wasn't wrong. Sure, we had toppled the Council, but that didn't mean we'd fixed anything. The rot ran deep, and we were just the ones who had ripped off the bandage. There was still a gaping wound underneath, and no amount of fireworks or drunken revelry would change that.

But Jax was right about one thing—if we didn't take the small victories where we could find them, we'd be swallowed whole by the enormity of what lay ahead. So I humored him. "Fine. After we check on the survivors, we'll throw a parade. Confetti, floats, the whole nine yards."

He laughed, the sound short and sharp like the crack of a whip. "I'll hold you to that."

We turned down a narrow alleyway, navigating through the twisted wreckage of buildings that had once been vibrant and alive. Now, they were nothing but skeletons, their bones jutting into the sky, clawing for something that would never return. It wasn't just the city that had been torn apart—our lives had been, too. The people we were before this fight, before the war, didn't exist anymore. We were fragments now, pieced together by the thinnest of threads.

Ahead, the faint flicker of candlelight caught my eye. Not the dangerous, angry orange of fire, but the soft, steady glow of something... hopeful. I picked up my pace, my heartbeat quickening as I rounded the corner, only to find a handful of survivors huddled around a small fire. They were wrapped in torn blankets, their faces streaked with soot and grime, but they were alive.

One of them—an older woman with silver hair and hollow eyes—looked up at me, her gaze hard and unwavering. "Is it over?" she asked, her voice brittle, like she'd forgotten how to use it.

I nodded. "For now."

She didn't thank me, didn't cry out in relief. She just turned back to the fire, like the weight of the news was too much to process all at once. I understood the feeling.

Jax crouched beside the group, offering them what little food and water we had left. It wasn't much, but it was something. As he worked, I scanned the faces of the survivors, trying to see if there was anyone I recognized. But no. The people I had known, the ones I had fought for, they were gone.

I turned away, staring out into the dark, ash-filled streets. The city felt like a graveyard now, but not the kind where you buried bodies. No, this was where we buried our pasts, our hopes, our futures.

Jax stood, wiping his hands on his already filthy jeans. "So," he said, his voice low, "what do we do now?"

I didn't answer right away. The truth was, I didn't know. We had won, sure, but in a way, that was the easy part. Now came the rebuilding, the cleaning up of all the blood and ash, the finding of something worth fighting for in a world that had forgotten how to be worth it.

"We keep going," I said finally, though my voice lacked the confidence I wished it had. "We help the people who need it. We figure out what's left of this city, and we make it work."

Jax nodded, but I could tell he wasn't entirely convinced. Then again, neither was I.

The stars were still hidden behind the thick veil of smoke, but I could feel them there, waiting, just out of reach. One day, they'd break through again. Maybe tomorrow. Maybe in a year. But for now, the night was ours, and for the first time in what felt like forever, it belonged to us.

We weren't heroes. Not really. We were just survivors, clinging to whatever scraps of hope we could find in the wreckage. And maybe that was enough.

Chapter 28: Rebirth from the Flames

The sun hung low over the battered skyline of Emberhold, casting its golden light over the charred remains of a city that once echoed with chaos. Now, a strange quietness had settled in, as if the very air were trying to decide what to make of this new world we had shaped. I shifted uncomfortably, wiping a smear of ash off my face with the back of my hand, and squinted toward the horizon. There was no use denying it—victory tasted different than I had imagined.

Emberhold was...well, it wasn't pretty, but it was alive. That had to count for something. Every building, every crumbling wall, carried the scorch marks of our battle. The streets, once filled with panic and terror, now seemed almost peaceful in their emptiness, like they were waiting for someone to fill them with purpose again. I could still smell the faint odor of smoke and sulfur, a reminder that no matter how far we'd come, there was no erasing the scars of what had happened here.

Jax was standing a few feet away, his usual cocky grin replaced by something that looked suspiciously like introspection. He was fiddling with a piece of broken metal, turning it over and over in his hands. Probably the remains of one of the streetlamps. His fingers traced the jagged edges as if he could somehow make sense of it. I watched him for a moment, wondering how someone so reckless, so infuriatingly reckless, could be so gentle in these quiet moments.

"We did it," I said, more to myself than to him, as the wind caught in my hair, tugging at the frayed edges of my jacket.

Jax didn't look up. "Yeah," he muttered. "We did."

But there was something in his voice that didn't match the words. Something heavy. I knew he felt it too. The weight of the lives we couldn't save, the friends who wouldn't be standing with us as we rebuilt. Emberhold might have survived, but it had cost us more than we could ever recover.

I found myself absently running my thumb over the Emberstone that hung around my neck. It had grown warm, pulsing softly like a heartbeat, as if it were alive. Maybe it was. After everything we'd been through, I wouldn't be surprised if it started talking to me next.

Jax finally tore his gaze from the twisted scrap metal and looked at me, his blue eyes piercing in that way that always made me feel like he could see through the bravado I wore like armor. "What do we do now, Evie?"

What do we do now? That was the million-dollar question. The thing no one wanted to ask, because none of us had the answer. We had spent so long fighting for this moment, clawing our way through flames and rubble, that we hadn't stopped to think about what came next. We had defeated the tyrants, torn down their walls, but now...we were left standing in the ruins of their empire, holding the pieces in our hands and wondering how to put them back together.

"We build," I said, more confident than I felt. "We build something better."

The words hung in the air between us, a promise I wasn't sure I could keep. But the Emberstone pulsed again, a reminder of the power I carried, the legacy left to me. I didn't ask for this burden, didn't want it. But here I was, with the weight of the future resting on my shoulders. And like it or not, I was the one who had to figure out what that future looked like.

Jax nodded, a small smile tugging at the corners of his mouth. "Better, huh? I like the sound of that."

He turned, his boots crunching against the broken pavement, and started walking toward what used to be the center of town. I hesitated for a moment, looking around at the wreckage, at the hollowed-out shells of buildings that had once stood tall and proud. There was something poetic about the way the sun kissed the tops of the broken structures, as if trying to breathe life back into them. Or maybe that was just wishful thinking.

I followed Jax, my fingers still clutching the Emberstone like a lifeline. We passed a few others as we walked—survivors. Their faces were gaunt, their clothes torn and dirty, but they were alive. That was something. They nodded as we passed, a silent acknowledgment that we were all in this together now. No more factions, no more divisions. Just people, trying to figure out how to live again.

When we reached the square, I couldn't help but let out a low whistle. The once grand statue of some long-forgotten leader lay in pieces on the ground, its head lying several feet away, staring up at the sky as if it were contemplating its own demise. Fitting, really.

"Think we should put it back together?" Jax asked, tilting his head toward the shattered remains.

I snorted. "Nah. Let it stay broken. We'll build something new."

He grinned, that familiar mischievous glint back in his eyes. "Spoken like a true revolutionary."

I rolled my eyes, but there was a small part of me that was proud of that title. Revolutionary. It wasn't something I had ever set out to become, but here I was, standing in the ruins of a city that we had torn down, ready to build it back up again. Maybe this was what rebirth felt like—not some grand, sweeping moment of triumph, but the quiet determination to keep moving forward, to keep fighting, even when the battle was over.

As we stood there, looking out over the broken square, I could almost see it—the future we would build. Not perfect, not without its struggles, but better.

The Emberstone pulsed again, its warmth slipping through the fabric of my shirt, and for a brief moment, I swore I could hear it—like a heartbeat in rhythm with mine. I wasn't sure if that was a comforting thought or a terrifying one. I mean, who in their right mind wanted a sentient rock hanging around their neck? But then again, I wasn't exactly in my right mind most days, was I?

As we moved further into the square, the shadows of the broken buildings stretched longer, giving everything a kind of post-apocalyptic charm. If you squinted hard enough, you could almost convince yourself the place had potential. I'd always been a sucker for underdogs, though—people, cities, you name it. Maybe that's why I didn't bolt when the revolution started, even though every part of me screamed that I should. There was something about fighting for the scrappy, broken things that just felt right.

Ahead, a group of kids darted between piles of debris, playing some version of tag that involved a lot of yelling and jumping over obstacles like they were in some twisted playground. I couldn't help but smile. Leave it to kids to find fun in the middle of a disaster zone. One of them, a boy who couldn't have been more than ten, skidded to a stop when he saw us. His eyes went wide as he recognized Jax, and then, to my utter disbelief, he saluted. Saluted. I bit the inside of my cheek to keep from laughing.

Jax, for his part, handled it like a pro. He gave the kid a mock-serious nod, saluting back with exaggerated precision. The boy beamed, then took off running again, his friends in tow, probably to spread the news that Jax, the hero of Emberhold, was patrolling the streets. I shook my head, half-amused, half-incredulous.

"Hero worship, huh? Didn't peg you for the type," I teased, elbowing Jax in the ribs.

He shot me a sidelong glance, the ghost of a smirk playing on his lips. "Jealous?"

"Please," I scoffed, flipping my hair in mock offense. "I prefer my admirers to be at least...I don't know, old enough to drive."

Jax chuckled, and for a moment, things felt normal—like the world hadn't just been ripped apart and stitched back together with duct tape and stubbornness. But then the smile faded, and the weight of reality settled back over us, heavier than before.

"You really think we can do this?" he asked quietly, his voice losing some of its usual bravado. "Rebuild all this?" He gestured to the ruins around us, his fingers tracing the jagged edges of the world we'd just shattered.

I didn't answer right away. What was I supposed to say? Of course, we could rebuild. Of course, we'd make everything better. But I wasn't in the business of lying to myself, and I wasn't about to start now. So, I shrugged, settling for the only truth I could offer.

"I don't know," I admitted, kicking at a loose stone. "But we'll figure it out."

He gave me a long look, like he was waiting for me to say more, to offer some grand plan or a rousing speech about hope and resilience. But I didn't have any of that. Not today, anyway. All I had was the Emberstone's steady warmth and the faint hope that maybe, just maybe, we weren't as alone in this as we felt.

The sun dipped lower, casting a reddish glow across the sky, and I realized we had been standing in the same spot for far too long. I nudged Jax with my elbow again, this time more gently.

"Come on," I said. "Let's go check on the others."

He nodded, and we started walking again, our footsteps echoing off the empty streets. There weren't many others left in Emberhold—not yet, anyway. Most had fled when the fighting started, seeking refuge in the outskirts or in neighboring cities. But a few had stayed behind, stubborn as weeds, determined to see this through. People like us. And as much as I hated to admit it, I was starting to think we might need those stubborn weeds if we had any hope of turning this place into something worth fighting for.

We rounded a corner, and the makeshift camp came into view. It wasn't much—just a cluster of tents and hastily constructed shelters, built from whatever scrap materials we could scavenge. But it was home, for now. Fires crackled in small pits scattered around the camp, their smoke curling lazily into the evening air. A few figures moved around the camp, tending to the fires, talking quietly among themselves. The sense of camaraderie was palpable, even from a distance. These people—our people—had been through hell and back, but they were still here, still standing. That had to count for something.

As we approached, I caught sight of Nia sitting by one of the fires, her dark hair gleaming in the firelight. She was sharpening a knife, her expression focused, determined. Nia was one of the toughest people I knew, and that was saying something, considering the company I kept. She glanced up as we drew near, her eyes narrowing slightly.

"Back from your romantic stroll, I see," she said, not bothering to hide the smirk that tugged at her lips.

I rolled my eyes. "Please, if I wanted romance, Jax wouldn't be my first pick."

Jax let out an exaggerated gasp, clutching his chest dramatically. "I'm wounded! You wound me, Evie."

"Good," I said, plopping down on the ground beside Nia. "Maybe it'll teach you some humility."

Nia snorted, returning her attention to her knife. "Fat chance. Jax and humility don't belong in the same sentence."

"You're both insufferable," Jax muttered, but there was no bite to his words. He dropped down on the other side of Nia, stretching out his legs and leaning back on his elbows. The three of us sat there in companionable silence for a while, the crackle of the fire and the distant murmur of voices the only sounds.

For the first time in what felt like forever, I allowed myself to relax, just a little. The Emberstone had cooled against my skin, its earlier urgency fading to a gentle hum. I could still feel it there, always present, always waiting. But for now, it was content to let me breathe.

Eventually, Nia spoke, her voice low and thoughtful. "You think we'll make it?"

It was the same question Jax had asked earlier, and once again, I didn't have an answer. But maybe that was okay. Maybe we didn't need answers right now. Maybe it was enough just to keep going, one step at a time.

"We'll figure it out," I said again, and this time, the words didn't feel like a lie.

The fire crackled softly as the night settled in around us, casting flickering shadows that danced across the ragged edges of the camp. I leaned back against a rock, feeling the weight of the day settle in my bones. Emberhold might've been a beacon of hope, but right now, hope felt a lot like exhaustion wrapped in grime. My muscles ached in places I didn't even know existed, and the Emberstone, which had been pulsing with life earlier, now sat cool and quiet against my chest. If it was trying to tell me something, I was too tired to listen.

Nia was still sharpening her knife, the rhythmic scrape of metal on stone oddly soothing. Jax had drifted off into some kind of half-sleep, his head resting on a makeshift pillow he'd fashioned out of an old jacket. He looked younger when he slept, the lines of worry and determination softening into something almost innocent. Almost.

I glanced around the camp, watching the others as they huddled around their fires. It was strange, seeing them like this—laughing, talking, even joking—after everything we'd been through. You'd think that after watching the world burn, people would lose the ability to smile. But here they were, proving me wrong again. Maybe that was what resilience really looked like, the ability to find something to laugh about even when the sky had been falling just days before.

The scent of something cooking drifted through the air, and my stomach growled in response. I hadn't eaten since...well, since before the final battle. Time had blurred together into one long, continuous moment of survival, and I couldn't remember the last time I'd sat down to eat something that wasn't cold or scavenged. The idea of hot food seemed almost too good to be true.

I pushed myself to my feet, wincing as my knees protested. I wasn't that old, but it sure felt like it sometimes. Moving toward the fire, I caught sight of one of the younger kids stirring a pot of something that smelled vaguely like stew. He looked up as I approached, wide-eyed, clearly not expecting anyone to disturb his culinary masterpiece.

"Smells good," I said, trying to sound casual. "Mind if I grab a bowl?"

He blinked, then nodded enthusiastically, scrambling to find something that resembled a bowl. After a few moments of rummaging through a pile of mismatched supplies, he handed me what looked like an old tin cup. Good enough. I held it out, and he ladled a generous portion of the stew into it, the steam rising in little curls that tickled my nose.

"Thanks," I said, flashing him a quick smile before retreating back to my spot by the fire.

The stew wasn't anything fancy—mostly root vegetables and some kind of meat that I didn't want to think too hard about—but it was hot, and that was enough for me. I blew on it to cool it down, then took a careful sip. The warmth spread through me like a sigh of relief, chasing away some of the lingering chill that had settled into my bones.

Jax stirred beside me, his eyes blinking open slowly as if he was surfacing from a deep dream. He glanced at the cup in my hands, his expression a mix of groggy confusion and mild jealousy.

"Where'd you get that?" he muttered, sitting up and rubbing his eyes.

"Kid over there's playing chef," I said, nodding in the direction of the makeshift kitchen. "You should grab some before it's gone."

Jax grunted in acknowledgment and pushed himself to his feet, making his way over to the stew pot with all the grace of someone who hadn't slept properly in days. I watched him go, my gaze lingering on the way he moved—slow, deliberate, like he was carrying the weight of the world on his shoulders. Maybe he was. We all were, in one way or another.

Nia finally sheathed her knife, her work apparently done for the night. She leaned back on her hands, staring up at the sky, which was now dotted with stars. It was strange, seeing the stars so clearly after everything. For a while, it had felt like the sky itself had been swallowed up by smoke and fire, like the stars had abandoned us, too. But here they were, shining as bright as ever, like nothing had changed.

"You think it'll last?" Nia asked suddenly, her voice cutting through the quiet. "This...peace. You think it's real?"

I didn't answer right away. How could I? Peace was such a fragile thing, easily shattered by the wrong word or the wrong move. We had fought for it, bled for it, but that didn't mean it would last. The world had a funny way of pulling the rug out from under you just when you thought you'd found solid ground.

"I think," I said slowly, choosing my words carefully, "that it's real enough for now. And maybe that's all we can ask for."

Nia didn't respond, but I could see the wheels turning in her head. She was always thinking, always planning, always ready for the next fight, even when there wasn't one on the horizon. That was just who she was. She'd probably never be able to fully relax, never be able to let her guard down. I understood that. In a way, I was the same.

Jax returned a few minutes later, his own tin cup filled with stew, and plopped down beside me with a heavy sigh. He took a sip, then made a face.

"This tastes like someone boiled dirt," he said, grimacing.

I shrugged. "Could be worse."

He gave me a skeptical look. "Name one thing."

I opened my mouth to respond, then paused. "Okay, fine. Maybe it's as bad as it gets."

Nia snorted, but didn't say anything, and the three of us fell into a comfortable silence, the crackling of the fire the only sound.

The wind picked up slightly, carrying with it the faint scent of pine and earth. It was the smell of home—what home had been before everything had gone sideways. I closed my eyes for a moment, letting myself imagine what it would be like to go back to those simpler days. But that was a dangerous road to go down. There was no going back. Only forward.

Eventually, the fire began to die down, the flames shrinking into glowing embers. Most of the camp had already turned in for the night, the sounds of laughter and conversation fading into the background. I wasn't quite ready to sleep yet, though. There was something about the night—about the stillness—that made it hard to let go. It was like the world was holding its breath, waiting for something to happen.

Jax leaned back on his elbows, staring up at the stars. "You ever wonder what's next?"

"Every day," I admitted, my voice barely above a whisper.

We didn't have the answers. None of us did. But as I sat there, surrounded by the quiet of the night and the warmth of the dying fire, I realized that maybe we didn't need the answers right now. Maybe it was enough just to be here, together, alive.

Tomorrow would come, and with it, a whole new set of challenges. But for now, we had this moment. And maybe, just maybe, that was enough.

Chapter 29: A New Dawn

The sound of gravel crunching beneath my worn sneakers was the only thing keeping me grounded in that moment. The cool, damp air clung to my skin, mingling with the tangy scent of fresh-cut pine and motor oil. The woods behind my old house always felt like home—well, as much of a home as a girl could have when her actual house was about ten feet away from crumbling into dust. The porch sagged more every year, like the universe had forgotten about it along with everything else in this godforsaken town. But out here, with the trees breathing quietly around me, I could almost pretend that things still made sense.

That morning, though, the woods didn't feel right. The silence wasn't the usual peaceful hush, but something else. Something uneasy. My fingers itched, and I couldn't stop shifting the straps of my backpack. Not that I had much in there—just a flashlight, some matches, and a half-eaten granola bar. Nothing too helpful if things went sideways, but I wasn't planning on anything going sideways. Not today, anyway. Still, I couldn't shake the feeling that I was being watched.

I didn't think anyone had followed me when I left the diner. I'd been careful, or at least I thought I had. Who would even bother? Half the town thought I was crazy, and the other half just didn't care. If anything, they'd probably think it was a mercy if I disappeared into the trees and never came back. I wasn't about to give them that satisfaction.

I shifted my weight and squinted at the clearing ahead. The old gas station crouched there like a forgotten relic from some bygone era, its rusting pumps standing like sentinels guarding nothing but empty air. The sign still hung crookedly from its frame, advertising gas at a price no one had seen in years. It wasn't much to look at, but it was far enough off the main road that most people didn't bother with it anymore. Which was exactly why I was here.

I ducked under a low branch and crept closer, my heart thudding in my chest like it always did when I got too close to a place I shouldn't be. The door was hanging off one hinge, creaking in the wind, like an invitation that no one in their right mind would accept. Perfect.

The inside smelled like mildew and stale coffee, the kind of sour scent that made you want to scrub your skin raw just from standing near it. I kicked aside some empty cans and wrappers, peering into the dimness. No sign of anyone—not yet, anyway.

I wasn't stupid. I knew what I was getting into. I'd overheard enough conversations in the diner to piece together the basics. Something weird was going on, something big. People didn't just up and vanish around here for no reason, and the fact that everyone was pretending they weren't noticing? That was the biggest red flag of all. My gut told me this place—this run-down gas station in the middle of nowhere—was the key to it all.

And if I was wrong? Well, then I'd just wasted a perfectly good Saturday morning poking around in a place that smelled like raccoon pee.

The floorboards groaned as I stepped inside, the sound reverberating off the walls like some kind of warning. My eyes adjusted to the gloom, and I moved farther in, running my hand along the counter as I passed. It was sticky with something that I didn't want to think too hard about. Dust motes danced in the thin beams of sunlight slanting through the broken windows, making everything look even more abandoned than it already was. There was something eerie about it, something that made the hair on the back of my neck stand up.

I headed toward the back, where the storage room was. That's where I'd heard the stories centered—where people said things got strange. I wasn't sure what I expected to find. Ghosts? Hidden doors? Maybe the whole thing would turn out to be just some elaborate prank.

I pushed open the door, the hinges squealing in protest. The air back here was even heavier, thick with the musty smell of old wood and something else I couldn't place. The room itself wasn't much—a couple of shelves lined with dusty cans, an old sink in the corner, and some cardboard boxes stacked haphazardly near the back wall. But it was the floor that caught my eye.

Or, more specifically, what was beneath it.

The boards near the far corner were different, newer. It was subtle, but I'd spent enough time snooping around places like this to know when something was off. I crouched down, running my fingers along the edges, feeling for any kind of catch. My heart was racing now, the quiet ticking of my watch the only sound in the room. For a second, I wondered if maybe I should just leave it alone. Maybe some things were better left hidden.

But then, where's the fun in that?

With a sharp tug, the boards gave way, revealing a narrow staircase descending into the darkness below. My pulse quickened, and I grabbed the flashlight from my bag, flicking it on. The beam cut through the blackness, but it didn't reveal much—just the first few steps, worn smooth from years of use. The rest disappeared into the shadows, like some kind of endless void.

I took a deep breath, swallowing the lump in my throat. There was no turning back now. This was what I came for, wasn't it? Answers. Truth. Or, at the very least, a good story.

With one last glance over my shoulder, I started down the stairs, the soft creak of the wood beneath my feet echoing in the stillness. The air grew colder the deeper I went, and the smell of damp earth filled my nose, making it harder to breathe.

The stairwell seemed to stretch on forever, each step creaking like the floorboards were groaning under the weight of not just me, but every soul that had ever made this same descent. My flashlight flickered once, twice—just enough to make my stomach drop—but stayed lit. Lucky me. The air down here was cooler, damp like I was wading through a basement long forgotten by the sun. The smell, thick and earthy, settled into my lungs, making it harder to breathe the deeper I went. I told myself it was just the musty air, but the truth was, fear was winding its way into my bones, tightening like a snake around my ribs.

I reached the bottom of the stairs, but the room that greeted me wasn't what I expected. No secret lair or underground bunker, no stockpile of weapons or treasure chests filled with stolen goods. Instead, it looked like... well, like someone had decided to set up shop in the ruins of the 1970s and never left. Shag carpeting covered the floor—matted, discolored, and so filthy I almost gagged at the sight of it. A beaten-up old couch slouched in one corner, springs poking through its threadbare cushions. There was a low table cluttered with empty beer cans, cigarette butts, and a collection of objects that looked suspiciously like bones. Great.

I shined the flashlight over the walls, which were plastered with yellowing posters of bands I didn't recognize and spray-painted symbols I definitely didn't want to. There was an unsettling hum in the air, like something was vibrating just below the range of my hearing, and it made my skin crawl. I wasn't alone down here. I knew that without having to see anyone. The weight of eyes on my back was unmistakable, and I'd been around long enough to recognize when someone—or something—was watching.

"Well, well," a voice drawled from the shadows, smooth and slick like oil dripping over rocks. "What have we here?"

I spun around, flashlight beam cutting through the gloom until it landed on the source of the voice. He was leaning against the far wall, arms crossed, a half-smirk on his face. He looked young—late twenties, maybe early thirties—but there was something in his eyes that didn't fit the rest of him, something ancient, as though he'd seen too many sunrises and had forgotten what it was like to feel them anymore.

"You lost, kid?" he asked, his voice slow and lazy, like he had all the time in the world. Which, judging by the way he seemed perfectly at ease in this mess of a place, maybe he did.

"I'm not a kid," I snapped, even though it was probably the least important thing to argue about right now. "And I'm not lost."

He tilted his head, the smirk widening just enough to show a glimpse of teeth. Too sharp, too white.

"Not lost, huh? Then what brings you to my humble abode? Sightseeing?"

I swallowed hard, but my throat felt like it was stuffed with cotton. "Just... looking for answers."

"Answers," he repeated, like the word was a joke. "And what makes you think you'll find them here?"

"I heard people talking. About this place." The words were tumbling out of my mouth now, too fast, too reckless. "About people disappearing, strange things happening. And I want to know why."

He pushed off the wall and started walking toward me, slow and deliberate, like a predator sizing up its prey. My instinct screamed at me to run, but my feet stayed glued to the ground. I wasn't sure if it was fear holding me in place, or something else. Some kind of pull, like gravity, keeping me there despite every part of me screaming to get the hell out.

"Strange things happen everywhere," he said, now just a few feet away. "But not everyone goes looking for trouble like you."

"I'm not looking for trouble," I said, though it sounded weak even to me.

"Sure you aren't," he said, stopping just within arm's reach. His eyes glittered in the dim light, and there was a sharpness to his grin that set my teeth on edge. "But you found it anyway."

There was a long, tense silence between us, the kind that stretches and snaps like an overdrawn bowstring. My heart was thumping in my chest so loudly I was sure he could hear it. Then, just when I thought he was going to make a move, he stepped back, his expression softening just slightly.

"Well," he said, almost casually, "since you're so eager for answers, I suppose I can give you a little something."

I frowned. "Why?"

"Why not?" He shrugged, that grin still lingering like a ghost on his face. "Call it a... professional courtesy."

Before I could respond, he reached into his jacket and pulled out a small, weathered notebook. It looked ancient, the pages yellowed and the leather cover cracked and worn. He tossed it to me, and I fumbled to catch it, my fingers brushing against the cold, rough surface.

"What's this?" I asked, holding it up like it might bite.

"Answers," he said, as though it was the most obvious thing in the world. "You want to know what's been happening around here? Start there."

I glanced down at the notebook, flipping it open to the first page. The handwriting inside was jagged and uneven, like someone had scrawled it in a hurry, but the words sent a shiver down my spine.

They are watching. Always watching.

I looked up, but the man had already turned away, heading back toward the far side of the room. "Wait," I called after him, but he didn't stop.

"You'll figure it out," he said, without looking back. "Just make sure you don't dig too deep. Some things are better left buried."

I stared after him, my heart still racing, the weight of the notebook heavy in my hand. Whatever this was, whatever I'd just stepped into, there was no going back now. The door behind me was still there, but it felt a million miles away.

The Emberstone hummed in my hand, the pulse of it in time with my own heartbeat, as if we were connected in some primal, ancient way. The weight of it was comforting and unsettling all at once, like holding onto a piece of something too powerful for one person to fully comprehend. And yet here I was, standing at the edge of the molten river, the glowing stone resting in my palm like it belonged there all along.

The river flowed sluggishly, thick as tar and glowing with a faint red hue. The heat from it radiated up in waves, searing the air around us, making the hairs on the back of my neck prickle with static energy. The ground trembled beneath my feet, a low, constant rumble that never quite stopped. Everything here was alive in a way that felt both familiar and alien. The world had been forged in fire, and now it seemed like the fire had never really left.

Behind me, I could hear the quiet murmurs of the others, those who had survived the last battle, the ones who still had enough fight left in them to stand by my side. They were waiting for me to say something, to lead them, to tell them everything was going to be fine, that we were going to be okay.

But I wasn't sure I believed that. Not yet.

I closed my fingers around the Emberstone, the rough edges biting into my palm, grounding me in the moment. The flames inside it flickered and danced, reflecting the fire in the sky and the molten river at my feet. It felt like the world was burning down around us, and maybe it was. Maybe this was what it took to start over. To rebuild.

The silence behind me stretched out, taut as a bowstring, and I knew I had to speak. Even if I didn't have all the answers. Especially then.

"We've been through hell," I started, my voice rougher than I intended, but at least it was steady. "And it's not over. Not by a long shot."

I turned to face them, and their eyes—so many eyes—looked back at me, filled with the same exhaustion, the same weariness that had settled deep into my bones. But there was something else, too. Something I hadn't expected to see. Hope. It was small, barely there, like a flicker of a candle in the wind, but it was there.

"We've lost people," I continued, my gaze sweeping over the ragtag group of survivors. "We've lost homes. We've lost everything we thought we couldn't live without."

A pause. The weight of what we'd lost sat heavy in the air, but I wasn't here to let it crush us. I wasn't here to give a eulogy for the world that had been. That world was gone, and the sooner we accepted that, the sooner we could move forward.

"But we're still here," I said, my voice growing stronger. "We're still standing."

The Emberstone pulsed in my hand, as if in agreement, the flames within it flaring brighter for a brief moment. It felt alive, like it was waiting for something—for me.

"And as long as we're still standing," I said, holding the stone up so they could see it, "we can rebuild. We can start again."

Their eyes followed the Emberstone, their expressions a mix of awe and uncertainty. They'd seen what it could do, what it had done to the land around us. They knew its power, but power wasn't the same as leadership. Power didn't guarantee safety or success. And that was what I had to make them believe—that together, we were stronger than this stone, stronger than the fire that had torn everything apart.

"I'm not going to promise you it'll be easy," I said, lowering the stone back to my side. "It won't be. But we've come this far, haven't we?"

There were a few murmurs of agreement, a shift in the crowd that told me they were listening. Really listening. That was a start.

"We'll rebuild," I said, more confidently now. "Not just the land, not just the cities, but everything. Our way of life, our traditions, our future."

I turned back to the molten river, the heat from it licking at my skin, as if the flames themselves were testing me, daring me to follow through on my words. I'd seen what this world had to offer—the beauty and the terror, the creation and the destruction. It was all part of the same cycle, and now it was my job—our job—to make sure that when the fire finally burned itself out, something new could rise from the ashes.

"Together," I said, glancing over my shoulder at the others. "We can build something better. Something stronger. But we have to do it together."

The Emberstone flared in my hand again, a bright, burning light that seemed to chase away the shadows around us, if only for a moment. And in that moment, I knew—knew—that no matter what came next, we could face it. We had to. There was no other choice.

The crowd behind me began to stir, whispers turning into words, words turning into something more. I didn't need to hear what they were saying to know that they were with me. For now, at least, that was enough.

I took one last look at the molten river before turning away from it, walking back toward the group, the Emberstone clutched tightly in my hand. The fire inside it burned bright and steady, a beacon in the darkness, a reminder that we were still here, still fighting.

And as long as we kept that fire alive, there was hope.

Hope for a future that we could build with our own hands. Hope for a world that would rise, stronger and brighter than the one that had fallen. We weren't just survivors anymore.

We were builders, creators, Flamekeepers.

And no matter how many battles we had left to fight, no matter how many losses we had yet to endure, that was the truth I held onto. That was the truth that would carry us through the fire.

I took a deep breath, the air still heavy with smoke and ash, and started walking. The others followed, their footsteps echoing in the quiet, as we moved forward into the unknown.

But we weren't afraid. Not anymore.

We had fire in our hands and hope in our hearts.

And that was enough to start a new dawn.

Milton Keynes UK
Ingram Content Group UK Ltd.
UKHW040257181024
449757UK00001B/87